GALAXY'S EDGE

EDGE

RETRIBUTION

JASON NICK
ANSPACH COLE

Galaxy's Edge: RETRIBUTION
By Jason Anspach & Nick Cole

Edited by David Gatewood
Published by Galaxy's Edge Press

Cover Art: Fabian Saravia
Cover Design: Beaulistic Book Services
Formatting: Kevin G. Summers

For more information:

Website: GalacticOutlaws.com
Facebook: facebook.com/atgalaxysedge
Newsletter: InTheLegion.com

HISTORY OF THE GALAXY

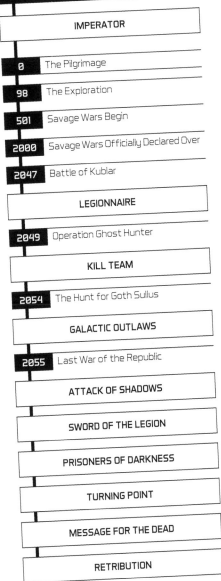

IMPERATOR

0	The Pilgrimage
98	The Exploration
501	Savage Wars Begin
2000	Savage Wars Officially Declared Over
2047	Battle of Kublar

LEGIONNAIRE

| 2049 | Operation Ghost Hunter |

KILL TEAM

| 2054 | The Hunt for Goth Sullus |

GALACTIC OUTLAWS

| 2055 | Last War of the Republic |

ATTACK OF SHADOWS

SWORD OF THE LEGION

PRISONERS OF DARKNESS

TURNING POINT

MESSAGE FOR THE DEAD

RETRIBUTION

01

I'm crouched inside a shipping container marked "Radioactive. Do Not Handle." It wasn't supposed to be in the cargo hold of the Imperial corvette *De Zuan*, but there it is, along with three others.

And yes, I said Imperial.

It's all the rage nowadays. Like it adds legitimacy to the regime that resisted Article Nineteen and put a tyrant at its head. So now we've got an *Imperial* House of Reason and an *Imperial* Senate. See, that's the trick: you don't have to actually make the galaxy better. You just have to declare an empire and expect the rest to fall into place.

Only, Kill Team Victory doesn't play nice with tyrants. No matter how many times the House of Reason and Senate insist Goth Sullus was duly elected as emperor.

An elected emperor.

Only in the Republic.

But no one ever asked Cohen Chhun if the galaxy was headed in the right direction. And they wouldn't like my answer if they did.

"You know, I've been thinking, guys." The voice over my L-comm belongs to Aldon Masters. One of my best men. The earnest—albeit sometimes annoying—heart and soul

1

of this kill team. "What are the odds that the Legion actually bought new labels that said 'radioactive, do not handle,' and put them on these crates? Because we've done this trick a bunch of times, and when I think about it, the stickers have always looked beat-up. But if they were new stickers... they'd look new, right?"

Bear, the only one of us with a crate all to himself, answers. "First of all, shut up. And second, they're *supposed* to look old. It's intentional."

"Possibly, possibly," says Masters, not missing a beat. "*Or* they just grabbed actual crates that were once used to house incredibly volatile radioactive elements, and now we're just sitting in a sort of rad soup."

Bombassa, who's sharing a crate with Masters, says, "Our helmets would warn us of unsafe radiation levels."

"Unless our buckets got fried because there's so much of it, 'Bassa! The next thing you know we're all going to start mutating. Or possibly dying. But probably mutating. Like... Bear will become an actual bear. So a little less hairy and drooly."

"Bombassa, will you please shoot him?" says Bear.

But Masters is on one of his rolls. "We'll all become hybrids of who we normally are. Like, Exo will have like a... skull face. And Chhun will be even more boring. And Bombassa will grow twice as tall. And... worst of all, *I'll* go from being handsome to being radioactive-*super*-handsome."

"A skull face would be pretty badass," says Exo. He and I are sharing a crate. It's nice to have him back on the team. "But Bear is right. Shut up, Masters."

"You know what?" Masters says. "I won't shut up. Because, quite frankly, the galaxy is *not* equipped to handle smoking-hot radioactive Masters."

My legionnaires fill my comm with laughter. And it's all fine and well, but if we keep up with the small talk, there's too much of a chance we'll miss our narrow window to take control of this *Imperial* corvette.

"Let's maintain L-comm discipline," I say.

I bring up the display on my bucket's HUD. It's linked to the hull-tracker that Wraith affixed to the ship while we were sneaking on board at the last port of call. We're still in hyperspace, but not for much longer. Based on the time we've spent cooped up in these possibly radioactive dummy containers, we should be arriving any minute.

"Call it three minutes tops before we dump out of hyperspace," I tell the team. "Everybody be ready to KTF."

"Dude," Exo says to me via our direct comm. "I never stopped being ready."

Ain't that the truth? I've never met a legionnaire who's ever come close to Exo in terms of tenacity and a willingness to fight.

I get a warning indicator that the *De Zuan* has emerged into real space. This is the first stop since the ship made the jump, and according to the data Ravi sent our way, the initial jump coordinates lined up with an Imperial deep-space station.

An isolated space station seems like an odd place for a Republic senator to visit. But then, the galaxy has become an odd place.

"Okay, Victory boys," I say through the L-comm, repeating an old term that Pappy used to call us. "You know the drill. Time to KTF."

"We go fast and we go hard," Bombassa adds.

It's been an interesting dynamic, blending Exo and Bombassa in with the rest of the team. For Exo it was like riding a hoverbike, almost like he'd never left. And while Bombassa wasn't Dark Ops before he left the Legion, he probably should have been. He's become an unquestioned assistant team leader in the months since the Legion fell.

But only assistant. No one doubts that Kill Team Victory is led by Bear.

My role is similar to the one Major Owens placed me in, only now I have the freedom to go out with my kill teams when I say so. And so far, I've always said so.

I have a lot of say now. After I healed up, we found that *Intrepid* was still out there, along with a number of other ships loyal to the Legion. We started consolidating. I started planning operations with Admiral Deynolds to bring about Article Nineteen. The Legion is a shell of its former self, but we're enough of a force to be able to bloody anything else in the galaxy. And we're growing.

"Do it to it," growls Bear, speaking the words with such casual aplomb that you'd think he was just giving the okay to start up a backyard barbecue.

We pull quick-release triggers inside the crates. Immediately the lids pop off and the sides partially collapse so that we're right up in close company among the freight—and crew—of the cargo bay. Two loadmasters are in the hold, right where protocol requires them to be after dropping from hyperspace. Our sensors told us they were out there. No surprise there.

But them? They're just a wee bit surprised.

Both of them jump back in fright at our sudden appearance. The smart one throws up his hands and drops to his knees almost immediately—before Exo even has the chance to shout for him to do so.

The other one—the dumb one—reaches for a small service pistol. The type that has no hope of getting through our armor. Exo drops him without so much as a word, double-tapping his blaster rifle and sinking two bolts into the chest.

"Oba!" cries the surviving loadmaster as he covers his head. He looks panic-stricken at his dead comrade.

"Search 'em and put 'em in the crates for now," Bear orders. "*Separate* crates, Exo."

"Yeah, yeah."

Other than giving updates on what Wraith feeds to me—he and his crew are shadowing our course on board the *Indelible VI*—I do my best to remove myself from the team dynamic, leaving Bear and Bombassa to run the mission. Bear was a promising team leader before everything went to hell, and 'Bassa is a natural.

But I won't clint you. It isn't easy to suppress a desire to run the show after leading Kill Team Victory for years. Still, leadership is now a scarce commodity in what's left of the Legion, and people like Bear—really, *all* of my leejes— need to be able to reach their full potential so they're prepared to step in and fill my shoes should the time come.

Because after us, there's no one else. If we fail, that's it. We're the last line.

"Okay, buddy, in the crate," says Masters, swinging his blaster rifle to show the loadmaster where to go.

"But it says radioactive," the crewman protests.

Masters grabs the man by the back of his jumpsuit and pushes him into one of the crates. "Don't worry, your armor will protect you."

"I don't have any armor..."

"Sucks to be you, then!" Exo slams the lid down and punches in a security key that disables the interior escape latches.

"How we reading?" Bear asks me.

"Holocams are on loop, alarms disabled... standard setup."

Garret, Wraith's skinny code slicer, has made our jobs a whole lot easier. He seems to have a million ways to keep us operating in the shadows, and without him I don't know how we'd have endured the loss of support and resources that came with the majority of the Legion going up in flames over Utopion.

That hardly seems real most days.

But I guess that's the way it goes. You want a final showdown... sometimes you get it.

"Let's go kick some teeth in, nab us a traitor," Bear says.

Other than some new branding—such as a replacement for the flag of the Republic, because *that's* what the galaxy *really* needed—the interiors of these Imperial ships are unchanged. Same polished black decks and white walls. Secure in the knowledge that we're invisible to onboard monitoring holocams and other sensor screens, we move swiftly from the cargo bay and down the access tunnel, our combat boots not making a sound. Sometimes there are guards in these access tunnels, but not today. We move on into the main corridor that runs from the bridge of the ship all the way to the engine rooms at the aft.

And that's where we get our first contact.

Four shock troopers—though they're called legionnaires now. Or actually, *Imperial* legionnaires. As if it could ever make sense to put those two words together. As if the Legion weren't in ruins. Clad in the dark armor of the Black Fleet, these shock troopers are being dispersed throughout the galaxy in lieu of the actual Legion as if that's just how it always was.

They might adopt the name, but when these defending soldiers see a kill team jocked up and moving down the corridor with weapons hot, they don't play the part. They fold immediately. Hands go up and weapons drop. Almost like they were looking for an opportunity to surrender.

"Chain 'em to the deck," Bear orders as he kicks their discarded rifles away.

Bombassa and I take a knee, our weapons aimed farther down the primary corridor for any new arrivals, while Bear watches our backs. Exo has his weapon pointed at the kneeling shock troopers, and Masters ener-chains their hands behind their backs and magnetically locks the restraints to the deck, forcing the captives to lie prone. He then removes their buckets.

We can only hope that their surrender is genuine and they didn't already report us over their comms. But we're ready for the alternative. And anyway, a blaster fight would have notified the ship of our presence no matter what.

"Recognize any of these guys?" Masters asks.

I glance over. "No."

Neither do the rest of the team. Which doesn't mean anything; the Imperial Legion is a big force. But sometimes it has familiar faces. It includes some old legionnaires who were unhappy with the direction of the galaxy—guys like Exo—as well as a bunch of psychotic ex-leejes who never belonged in the Legion in the first place. Plus, according to Exo, plenty of former mercs, muscle, and malcontents who saw a new power structure forming and wanted to get in on the ground floor.

"Okay, we can check 'em out once we have our target," Bear says. "Hood 'em."

"You best hope you check out," Exo says to the captives as he unfolds an isolation hood. "'Cause if you're Nether Ops trying to sneak in our ranks again… you get shot on sight."

Nether Ops went in whole-pigasaur for Goth Sullus. He's all their black little hearts ever wanted. Not surprising, really, that his brutal, ends-justify-the-means philosophy turned out to be popular with people who betrayed their principles ages ago. People who refuse to acknowledge that their manipulations have taken them down the wrong path, and so have no hope of turning themselves around.

Four hoods are draped over the prisoners, and we leave them to the sleeping arms and pins-and-needles that will come along over the next few minutes.

Better than getting shot.

We continue down the main corridor, creeping toward the bridge at the end of the ship. Each door we pass gets locked up with a special slicer package that affixes to the control panel. This is standard Dark Ops tech, but Garret punched it up considerably. The kid could make a fortune doing R&D somewhere if the galaxy weren't on fire. Or if he weren't so enamored with being a part of Wraith's crew.

"I really figured we'd have shot more people by this point," Masters remarks. "I think this might be a setup." There's an edge of concern in his voice—a concern I share. He's just saying what we're all thinking.

Thanks to our man on the inside—Imperial Legion Commander Washam—we've been busting up the plans of every senator and House of Reason delegate stupid enough to leave Utopion. We are the galaxy's outlaws, dedicated to bringing about Article Nineteen, while Admiral Deynolds and the *Intrepid*, leading what little is left of the Legion—the *real* Legion—are working to cut off the corrupt wealth of the House and Senate.

So far, we're making them howl.

Eventually they'd have to set a trap for us, right?

In fact, we've probably already fought our way through more than one. There've been some pretty stiff battles— too stiff—in the tight confines of the corvettes and luxury shuttles popular with delegates desperate enough to leave Utopion to check on their crumbling empires off-planet. We've won every time.

But success is never guaranteed.

"Trap or no," Bombassa says, pausing to seal up another door, "we know the senator is on this ship."

"Worst case, we dust one more scumsack before going out in a blaze of glory," says Exo. "Besides, it can't be any worse than *Pride of Ankalor*."

"Here's the VIP suite," Bombassa says.

We stack up outside the door, not simply sealing this one up. The senator is most likely either here or on the bridge.

I unlock the door with a slicer box and keep to the side as the team storms in under Bear's supervision. By the time I'm up and following them inside, they've already cleared the room. It's spacious but open—a bed, kitchenette, and lounge-like work area.

"Empty," Bear says. "We'll check the bridge next. I hope this doesn't turn into a game of hide-and-seek throughout the ship. Ain't got time for that."

"Ah, that sounds fun," says Masters.

We file out of the room and seal up the suite behind us. Still no one pays us a visit. Something's definitely up. Way too quiet.

When we finally reach the end of the corridor, we stack up outside the blast doors that lead to the bridge. It's funny Exo brought up the *Pride of Ankalor*. We trained for that mission so much that stacking up outside a corvette bridge almost feels nostalgic. I remember how often we got dusted in those simulations. How Twenties and Kags got dusted when it went down for real.

Possessed by a sort of premonition, I say, "Exo, let me go in first."

"Uh... all right."

We switch positions, Exo pulling out his own code-slicer box to get the doors open.

"Ready?" he asks.

"Do it," says Bear.

"Go!"

The doors slide open with a whoosh and I rush inside, the rest of the team behind me. The bridge is devoid of crew, as if run by AI—but standing before the bridge's main holoscreen is our target senator, a slight man who looks ill, like he's taken with a virus. Above him, holocams buzz and hover. The senator is holding a device in his hand. Some kind of activator. He's speaking for the cameras.

"The galaxy will witness the end of—"

I thumb the selector on my rifle to stun, and send a pulse of energy that completely paralyzes the senator. He falls over like a toppled statue.

Masters rushes over and removes the device from the senator's hand as the rest of the team clears the empty bridge. Bombassa works at the command console.

I hear a chime in my bucket announcing the arrival of the *Indelible VI* to sector space. Ravi's reassuring voice comes over the comm.

"Kill Team Victory, we have control of the corvette. It appears to be laden with explosives."

"Yeah," I say, casting a scowl at the senator. "We took out the ignitor."

"These... could be of use against that Imperial platform."

On the main holoscreen is the distant Imperial space station. It's basically just a docking platform with a few defenses, mostly interceptors and heavy blaster cannons. But it's definitely a military target. And we're at war.

"You're thinking we run this ship into the station? Ravi, are we sure there aren't any friendlies on that thing? Leejes have been coming over in droves..."

"I am not sure of that."

And then Wraith's voice comes over the comm. "He doesn't have to be. Chhun, the guy running this place is a point major. You don't have to blow it up, you just have to tell him you will. Trust me."

"That's... that won't work. Will it?"

"Why wouldn't it?" Wraith asks, sounding incredulous that I'd even question the idea.

This entire time my team—Bear's team—has been listening in on our conversation. Masters finally has to butt his way in. "What's the worst that could happen?"

"They evacuate," Exo growls.

"Isn't that what we want?" asks Bombassa.

Exo turns, his ever-present scowl working overtime. "It's not what *I* want. I vote we follow the ghost guy's plan and blow them all up."

"This was not my plan," Ravi interjects.

"Okay, Wraith," I say, motioning for Bombassa to open up a comm channel with the station. "I trust you. Bear, it's your team. You wanna get your face on the news? Whatever we broadcast here is gonna end up replayed on all the holofeeds..."

"Hell no," says Bear. "You can keep on being the public face of this campaign."

"Ooh! Ooh! Can I be on the holos?" Masters is raising his hand like the kid in class with all the answers. "I've got a face for the entertainments. Everyone says so. Especially Bear's mom."

"Not the time, Masters. And I can't trust you not to use the opportunity to try to get yourself some dates."

Masters's eyes go wide. "Sir... that's *brilliant*. Now I *really* want to do it."

"Comm channel is ready for you," Bombassa says.

I remove my bucket and stare into the bridge's forward-facing holocam. "Imperial supply station Kappa-II, this is General Chhun. You have five standard minutes to surrender your facility or you will be classified as treasonous and seditious elements of a rogue government in violation of Article Nineteen and will be subsequently destroyed. There are no other terms. Chhun out."

Wraith was right. The point commander surrenders the station before I've even finished signing off.

02

"You see, Ravi, I told you the point would give it up." Captain Keel laced his fingers behind his head, his boots crossed at the ankles and resting on the console of the *Indelible VI*.

"And you are wanting congratulations?" the navigator asked, his fingers blurring over his controls. He paused to give Keel a thumbs-up. "Good job, Captain Keel!"

Leenah sniggered from her seat behind them.

Keel shot her a scornful look over his shoulder. "Okay, I see how it is."

Caressing his shoulder with a soothing hand, Leenah said, "I'm proud of you, Aeson. The old Wraith would never have even asked before sending that corvette in to blow the whole place up."

"I'm still the old Wraith." Keel swung his feet off the console and sat upright in his pilot's chair. "I just think the Legion could use the corvette intact. Not to mention whatever might be on that station."

The comm flashed blue. "Hey, Wraith." It was the aggressive voice of Exo. "Bear wants to know when you're gonna pick us up. Some of us are a little antsy about hanging out on board a giant space bomb."

Keel looked at his cockpit's chronometer. "Just wanted to stay nimble until the admiral arrives with *Intrepid*."

"Screw that. Get me off of this death trap."

Keel looked over at Ravi and shrugged. The station *had* surrendered. "Okay, if it means that much to you..." He flipped through switches on his console, bringing the heavily modified Naseen freighter around. "Stand by for extraction."

"Hurry, all right?" said Exo.

Keel switched off his comm. "Ravi, drop us down to one-quarter speed. We're hurrying."

The navigator made no attempt to reduce the *Six*'s propulsion. "Actually, Captain, I think it would be wise to reach attack speed."

Keel smiled. "Buzz the tower?"

"No, not buzz the tower!" Ravi said, his voice betraying annoyance. "When the Imperial station surrendered I was able to obtain access to all of its data logs. And while it is true that an appointed officer is running the station's weapon systems and operations, I have discovered an anomaly. There is a wing of Black Fleet—Imperial— tri-fighters taking up residence in most of the station's hangar space. I calculate a seventy-eight point nine percent chance that—"

An urgent warning beeped steadily from the cockpit's instrument panels.

"Incoming fighters!" Leenah shouted. She'd started to really get familiar with the *Indelible VI*. Keel had even let her fly the thing a few times. She wasn't half bad.

"I see 'em," Keel growled, his brows knitted, his day ruined. He flipped open the comm to the captured corvette. "We've got incoming fighters. You'd better get your shields up and see what weapon systems you can bring online. I'll try to hold them off until *Intrepid* arrives."

"Copy that," answered Bombassa.

"They're headed straight for the corvette," Ravi warned.

"Good," said Keel as he looped the *Six* around, orienting it so that he was on a course to intercept the six-ship formation. "That'll make it easier to take 'em all out in one pass."

The *Indelible VI* raced wide of the corvette, streaking through the open space toward the fighter squadron like a galaxy-spanning comet. Two of the rear starfighters peeled off from the formation to deal with the freighter bearing down on them.

Keel ignored those two. He'd deal with them later. "Ravi, arm concussion missiles."

"Already done."

Keel felt a half smile creep across his face. "Watch this."

He flipped open the guard and pressed the launch button. Six streaking missiles with blue ethereal tails shot out toward the starfighters.

Evidently the squadron was not expecting this sort of a payload to be delivered by the freighter. They attempted to break off their attack run, but there wasn't time; the missiles pursued and exploded within fifty meters of the ships. A concussive wave engulfed the four tri-fighters, rattling them apart and setting off secondary explosions inside the ships themselves. The pilots—unless they were equipped with fully armored protective flight suits—were likely turned to jelly.

He turned around and flashed a smile at Leenah. "See? Still the same old Wraith. It's all in the wrist."

"That does not make sense," commented Ravi. "Your wrist was not required to depress the button."

"Nice shooting," said Chhun over comm. "But I thought you said they were going to surrender."

Keel's eyes darted around the cockpit as if looking for an excuse. "Uh... Ravi mis, uh, calculated."

"Well, if you can, hurry up and get us all off of here. Bombassa can't raise the shields, and the weapon systems are not responding."

Keel located the two starfighters that had broken off from the main group. They weren't following him. They had swung around to make an attack run on the unshielded, loaded-with-explosives corvette.

Jerking his flight controls hard, Keel spun the *Six* and got the remaining starfighters in his sights. "Ravi..."

"The guns are ready but we are not yet in range. They will succeed in this attack run."

Keel could only watch as the tri-fighter's blaster cannons raked the unshielded hull of the corvette. Small plumes of electrical sparks and flammable gases quickly erupted before burning out.

"What the hell, man!" Exo shouted.

"Sorry," said Keel. "Sorry. Blame Ravi. I'll get them before they make another pass. Your hull will hold up."

Keel turned to Ravi. "It *will* hold up, right?"

Ravi arched an eyebrow. "In what way is this my fault?"

"Stop thinking so much about yourself," Keel said, swooping the *Six* behind the two tri-fighters as they banked to attempt another attack run.

He flew a perfect line behind the trailing starfighter. Ravi unleashed a salvo from the *Six*'s blaster cannons, sending the ship up in flames.

"That's one," said Keel.

The remaining tri-fighter yawed portside to avoid the blast of its incinerated wingman.

Keel guided the *Six* into an easy barrel roll, lining the starfighter up dead center. He squeezed the manual control to send forth a deadly burst of blaster fire that sheared off the tri-fighter's wings and sent it into an uncontrolled spin before it exploded. "Aaand that's the other!"

He swung himself around to take a good look at his Endurian sweetheart. "See? No problem."

But Leenah's wide eyes and sudden gasp told Keel that there was, in fact, a problem. He turned back around.

Where once there had been only empty space, there was now an Imperial destroyer—painted black, of course. Goth Sullus had painted almost everything black upon rising to power. Evidently redecorating was right at the top of the list of things to do for a new emperor.

Keel flipped open the comm. "Guys, I think we got a problem."

"Oh, you think?" Masters shot back.

"The Imperial destroyer has already launched starfighters," said Ravi. "They are on a course to attack the corvette."

"A trap within a trap," said Leenah. "They must've been standing by in case the senator didn't blow everybody up."

"Yeah," said Keel. "And they probably have a remote det-switch of their own." He activated the ship-wide comm. "Garret! Jam all signals! Shut it all down."

"Okay!"

A moment later everything inside the cockpit went haywire. Screens read gibberish, trackers showed targets so thick as to appear as a solid red mass on the display.

Keel activated the ship-wide comm again. He was greeted with a spectral, avant-garde squeal. "Son of a—" He jumped from his seat. "Leenah—don't get us killed! Ravi—guns!"

Trusting his crew, he sprinted out of the cockpit and down the corridor to find his resident code slicer. Garret was where he always was, in the little nook he had made for himself just outside the lateral repulsor access hatch. The kid was moving a mile a minute, his hands occupying several fixed datapads while he spoke verbal commands to the *Six*'s AI.

Garret handled tech the way Keel handled blasters.

"What did you do?" Keel shouted.

The code slicer turned to face his captain, his ever-present pair of welding goggles dangling from around his neck. "You said jam it all."

"I didn't mean *us*!"

"Oh. Well… this way's faster anyhow. But I'll start bringing our channels and feeds back online one by one. What do you want first?"

"Comms. I need to tell Chhun to jump away."

Garret nodded and turned back to his workstation, swiping, dragging, tapping, and typing. "Okay. Secure comms are back up."

Not wanting to waste the seconds it would take to run back to the cockpit, Keel hailed Chhun through his personal comm. "Chhun, buddy... I think you better make the jump to light speed."

"Tried that. They disabled their hyperdrive after finishing their jump. This is a well-planned trap. Wraith, we're sitting ducks here."

Keel cursed. They'd had a good run, a lot of successful missions. A few close calls here and there, but not like this. Now it seemed like the Imperial Republic really had their number. Still, with the *Six*'s speed and the kill team's efficiency, they still had a small chance of getting out of this.

Keel had no desire to find out from Ravi just how small a chance it was.

"Get everyone to the docking hatch behind the bridge," he told Chhun. "I might be able to get you all off before the fighters reach us."

"Okay, but don't get you and your crew killed for a lost cause."

"Oh, well in that case I'll just set out. Good luck, General."

"You know what I mean."

"Just be ready."

Keel pinged Leenah and Ravi in the cockpit. "Bring us over to the corvette. I'm gonna try to get them out through the access hatch behind the bridge."

"On it," replied Leenah, and the ship banked.

Keel moved to the retractable access tube and grabbed an emergency suit to keep him protected in case of an integrity breach. He'd feel much more comfortable in the Wraith armor, but there wasn't time to put it on now.

"What should I do?" asked Garret.

"Try to keep those Black Fleet ships busy."

"Um... okay. I'll see what I can do."

The access hatch inside *Indelible VI*'s airlock was designed for ship-to-ship transfer when proper docking was impossible—or, as in this case, unwise. While the corvette was more than large enough to fit the *Six* inside its main hangar bay—with room for a small snub fighter like an old Preyhunter left over—Keel doubted there would be time to enter the hangar and wait for the kill team to run the length of the ship and reach them.

Besides, he wasn't eager to fly his ship directly into a death trap. If this all went south... well, at least his crew should make it out.

He checked the monitor showing a live feed directly outside the *Six*. They look to be lined up and on target. He hailed the cockpit. "We good?"

"You may begin emergency docking operations," said Ravi.

Keel went right to work, extending the docking tube until it aligned with the corvette's emergency hatch, where it locked in place with a powerful electromagnetic bond. The *Six*'s shield array would include the tube and the portion of the corvette immediately surrounding its emergency docking hatch. Leenah had gotten them nice and close. She really was becoming a good pilot.

"Okay, I've got a connection. Docking integrity looks good. Right above you, Chhun."

"We're here," answered the legionnaire. "Opening the access hatch on my end."

Keel did the same. He was oriented so that he was looking down, through the tunnel to the corvette. Chhun's helmeted face looked back up at him, no more than thirty meters below.

"Better get a move on," Keel said, even as Chhun stepped out of the way to allow Masters, with a hooded figure—that must be their target—grab hold of the tube's guideline. "Those fighters ought to be here any second."

"I'm ready," called Masters. "Pull us up."

Keel activated a winch attached to the guideline and zipped Masters and the senator inside the *Indelible VI*.

"Airlock's gonna get pretty crowded, kid, so you better hug the walls."

"Nice to see you too, Wraith."

Keel gave a lopsided frown. "How are you doing up there?" he asked the cockpit.

"Black Fleet fighters are closing in fast," answered Leenah, her voice tense. "Ravi thinks he can fend them off, but you'd better hurry!"

Keel look down into the tube. "Let's keep this line moving."

He pulled up Exo next, then Bombassa.

"Sucks to be those security guards," Exo said on arriving.

"Perhaps the general will recover them in time," said Bombassa.

Keel looked at the pair incredulously. "What do you mean, 'recover them'? Isn't Chhun down there waiting his turn up?"

"Nah," said Exo. "Said he was gonna go get 'em in case they really were loyal to the Republic."

Keel screwed up his face. "Why would he do that?"

Exo shrugged. "Beats me. I wanted to dust 'em back when we first found 'em."

"Are you ready to go?" asked Leenah. "Because we need to go right now."

"We *should* be," Keel grumbled into his comm. "But we're gonna need to sit tight a little while longer."

The ship lurched and rocked as blaster fire pounded into its shield array.

"Captain Keel," Ravi said, the sound of the *Indelible VI*'s blaster cannons competing with his voice, "I calculate that our odds of escaping without major damage decrease by three percent for every minute we are docked to this corvette. This is very bad."

"Sorry to disappoint you, Ravi. But it's not like I'm keeping us here just for fun." Keel looked around at the members of the kill team. "Might be a good time for you guys to get on some gun emplacements and help out."

"On it," said Bear as he emerged from the docking tube, leaving only Chhun and whoever he was attempting to bring with him still somewhere on the corvette. "I love using them guns."

The kill team hustled to find quad burst turrets and get into the fight. That should help with keeping Goth Sullus's attack ships at bay. The Black Fleet fighters didn't have a shot at taking down a corvette—he hoped—but they could certainly damage Keel's ship if they punched through his shields. And if they dislodged it while it was docking... well, so much for Chhun getting back on board.

"Not you, Masters," Keel said before the leej could escape with his sickly prisoner. "You get the senator to the med bay and keep an eye on him."

"Fine." Masters grabbed the senator by his shirt collar and pulled him roughly along. "Let's go, kelhorn."

Opening up an L-comm channel, Keel hailed Chhun directly. "Will the general will be joining us in not dying? Or would you prefer to stay aboard the who-knows-how-many-megaton explosive space coffin?"

"Yeah, I'm coming. Thirty seconds."

Keel could tell that Chhun was sprinting, which meant that either he'd convinced those captured security guards that it was in their best interest to also run, or he was coming alone. Keel guessed it was the latter. "Just you? I thought you were playing the hero and attempting to rescue some innocents."

"The guards ended up not being innocent. Same goes for the techs we detained in the cargo hold ."

The ship rocked from another strafing barrage of blaster fire.

"Really difficult to get a clean shot when we have to sit in one place," grumbled Exo over comm.

As soon as Chhun started up the access hatch, Keel turned to leave. "Chhun, I'm leaving you to lock up. It's going to take some fancy flying to get us out of this mess."

"Affirmative."

Keel left the emergency docking hatch and emerged on the main deck. He could hear the guns spitting out blaster fire and could feel the return fire raking his shields. He doubted they would hold up much longer. It would only be a matter of time before—

"Captain," Ravi said, "shield integrity is at ten percent."

"I'm heading your way! Chhun should be on board and all locked up by the time I reach the cockpit."

Keel ran past Garret. The code slicer was busy as ever at his workstation, but whatever he was doing didn't seem to be making a difference. "Tell me you're about to do something amazing, Garret!" Keel shouted as he ran by.

"Yes… I am. I mean, I'm about to. I hope."

The ship shook again and the onboard lights flickered off for a second. The blast sent Keel bouncing shoulder first into one of the padded walls along the corridor leading to the cockpit. He righted himself, found his balance, and burst into the cockpit, a shower of sparks raining down on him.

"What the hell's going on up here?" he asked as Leenah left his seat, allowing him to drop in. "And why is my ship trying to light my hair on fire?"

Leenah strapped herself in behind Keel. "That boom was the shields failing. The sparks are from our hull getting raked. Get us out of here!"

"We have been the stationary ducks," Ravi said, his fingers and hands a blur over his console. "Perhaps now we can leave?"

"We're all set, Wraith," reported Chhun.

"We can leave," a self-assured Captain Keel replied. "I can outrun a squadron of starfighters in my sleep, shields or no—"

He stopped himself as he surveyed the scene. It wasn't just a single squadron of starfighters swarming through the *Six*'s waves of blaster fire. It looked like an entire wing of Imperial tri-fighters.

"What gives?" Keel said, rolling the ship away from the corvette and blasting head-on toward the tri-fighters on an attack run. The pilots of the interceptors had to bank hard in opposite directions to avoid being rammed. "I thought it was just the one squadron."

"They kept coming," said Leenah.

They were in the middle of a Styberian hornets' nest. Even with Keel's piloting skills, it would take a tremendous amount of luck to weave through this many fighters, without shields, and not get dusted.

It looked grim, but he didn't have to hold out forever. Help was on the way. He'd planned to be alone for only a short amount of time. He looked up at the cockpit's timer, counting down to zero.

Legion destroyer *Intrepid*, its noble prow illuminated by the system's nearest star, dropped in from hyperspace between the space station and the corvette. A squadron of Legion Raptors emerged with it and immediately engaged the Imperial tri-fighters.

Detailed planning was often just as good as luck.

Dax Danns, the squadron flight leader, came on over the comms. "We got you, *Six*! Looks like Reaper Squadron arrived just in time!"

03

Legion Raptors piloted by the exceptional featherheads of Reaper Squadron now filled the front canopy of the *Indelible VI*. The versatile starfighters jinked and juked their way through the Black Fleet tri-fighters, who were taken completely off guard. The Imperial pilots had moved in greedily, thinking they were about to feast on two stationary ships, only to discover that they were the main course.

"How do you like our odds now, Ravi?" Keel asked as he swooped around exploding starships to avoid trailing arcs of enemy blaster fire.

"You are still more likely to die than live," the AI replied while monitoring the unfolding battle and making deadly use of the *Six*'s fixed forward cannons. "But this seems not to matter in your case."

"Yeah, I'm pretty amazing, aren't I?"

"I believe the Raptors are perhaps more deserving of the credit, Captain."

The arrival of Reaper Squadron certainly helped; Dax Danns and his pilots were among the best the Republic—or now just the Legion—had to offer. But the chaos brought about by their arrival had brought with it some new difficulties for Keel. With no shields, he had only so much room for error before a catastrophic hold breach, or worse yet, a direct stream of blaster fire to the cockpit, caused irreparable harm.

A Legion Raptor drifted lazily in front of the *Indelible VI*, swerving left and right as a pursuing tri-fighter attempted to shoot it down. Keel recognized the maneuver; the Raptor pilot was baiting his pursuer, drawing him in. And the Imperial pilot bit. With his concentration fixed on the impending kill, he was easy pickings for the Raptor's wingman.

The tri-fighter blew apart, and pieces of the interceptor went flying in all directions, including directly for the *Six*. Keel had barely enough time to nose the ship down, and even so a section of smoldering wing shaved the top of the cockpit as it streaked past. A nanosecond later a boom sounded within the ship, and the *Six* lurched.

Lights flickered and alarms wailed.

"What happened?" Keel shouted.

Ravi was swiping through displays. "We were struck on the overhead quad turret. It is showing disabled and we are slowly venting from a newly formed breach."

"Not good," Keel said. He was in the process of avoiding still more debris, and more tri-fighters were coming in for an attack. "Leenah! See if you can't —"

"She has already left the cockpit to see about restoring shields," said Ravi.

Keel threw everything he had into the engines. The best hope they had right now was flat-out running until they reached the safety of *Intrepid*. "Ravi, who was manning that gun?"

"Bear. And he is not responding to comm hails."

"You said it's venting life support? Probably didn't have a suit sealed up." Keel pulled one hand away from the flight controls to activate the ship-wide comm. "One of you guys better check on Bear!"

"Masters is already on it," Chhun responded.

Keel should have expected as much. The team had grown particularly close since they'd left the sanctuary of Mother Ree. Not there wasn't *already* a tight-knit bond before, but now... Now there was also a feeling that they were all that was left of the old Legion. That wasn't true, of course. There were loyal legionnaires stationed on planets along the edge, and a part of the Republic fleet had joined with them. But still, it felt like they were the last link to Major Owens and Legion Commander Keller.

So of course they would rush to make sure that one of their own was all right.

He was their brother.

And all they had left was each other.

"You picked up a tail, *Six*," Danns called over comm.

Keel spun a tight roll as blaster fire sizzled and arced around him. The hull absorbed one of the shots with a shudder. "Only one?"

"Three," said Danns. "Just didn't want to get you scared. Be a couple seconds before I can get 'em off you."

Keel was about to remind his gunners to watch their six when he heard Masters's voice come over the comm. "Guys, I could use some help here! There's hardly any oxygen left in the gunner's pit. Bear's unconscious and there's no way I can lug his big butt out of here by myself."

"I will assist," said Bombassa.

That would leave them a gun short, and while Ravi was capable of an astounding amount of multitasking, Keel knew from experience that when he was forced to fire too many weapons and focus on too many things at once, his effectiveness suffered. The hologram, or Ancient, or whatever he was, was like a demigod when he felt like using that blade of his, but he wasn't omnipotent.

The Black Fleet destroyer continued to launch wave after wave of starfighters. At first they had attempted to scramble bombers, but these were iced by Reaper Squadron so quickly that the commander of the destroyer had apparently put that tactic to bed. *Intrepid* was launching more fighters of its own, but all that did was make the battlefield more dangerous for the *Indelible VI*.

Keel found himself wishing that the wobanki were here with him instead of keeping an eye on Prisma back at En Shakar. Back during the raid on the Kesselverks Shipyards, he used to tell himself that the ship was just too crowded. Too many humanoids. But now those extra hands would've been useful.

"Vaped one of our pursuers," Chhun reported over the comm, his voice cool and efficient.

Same old Chhun. He might be a general now, but he was the same leej Keel had known back in the days when Captain Keel was still Captain Ford. Before Keel left his team behind in order to link up with an old retired legionnaire who taught him how to survive in the shadow of the Republic's seedy underworld.

"I'm about to get mine," Exo called. "Keep coming, you kelhorn. Stay still."

The burst turrets spewed their death and consumed another of the pursuing tri-fighters.

"That's right!" Exo crowed. "Keep on comin'! See if I don't dust every single one of you."

"It's like you don't even need me, *Indelible VI*," called out Danns as he vaporized the third tri-fighter. He roared even with the *Six* and turned hard starboard to wax another incoming fighter head-on. "Oh, who am I kidding? Everybody needs me. You got a clean path to *Intrepid*."

"Thanks," Keel said. "I'll buy you a drink when we're all back on board."

"That go for the rest of us?" Exo asked.

"You drink too much already," said Bombassa. "We have Bear out. He is alive. Taking him to the med bay now."

Leenah interjected. "I have the shields back up! They're barely hanging on, but it's something."

Keel turned to Ravi. "About time *something* went right."

The cockpit lit up in a brilliant green, and sparks and pops erupted from Keel's console, sending up acrid smoke in thin tendrils. More alarms sounded. Not just the persistent annoying kind, begging for attention. These were the big, booming, get-ready-to-abandon-ship type.

Leenah cried out over the comm, and an explosion sounded on her channel.

"Leenah!" Keel looked frantically at his shipboard display. "Show me shield maintenance!"

The display brought up the hard cam fixed inside the shield maintenance room. It was filled with a cloudy haze from the *Six*'s automatic fire containment systems. Leenah was struggling from the deck to her feet, her pink face smudged black.

"I'm all right," she grunted. "But I'm not going to be able to fix this shielding again until we get into a maintenance hangar."

"The Black Fleet destroyer is firing on us," Ravi said. "If they score a similar hit again, there is a ninety-nine point seven percent chance we will be destroyed."

Keel rolled and dipped down, diverging from the direct course he was on with the *Intrepid*'s docking bay. "Maybe they're just shooting at the destroyer and we got in the way."

Ravi shook his head. "One can hope."

"Yeah." Keel continued in a swooping, rolling pattern, not flying a predictable course. "You still doing all right, Leenah?"

"I'm fine, really."

She didn't sound fine. At least not to Keel. "You're sure?"

"Yes. But I think you're going to need to get a bigger med bay. This one is looking pretty crowded."

More green flashes lit up the cockpit. Not as close as the last one, but near enough to leave no doubt that it was the *Indelible VI* the Imperial destroyer was firing upon.

"This isn't fair," Keel grumbled. "Ravi, this is *not* a fair fight."

The *Six* looped and rolled, accelerated and turned in hard angles. Anything to keep from giving the destroyer's gun crew an easy shot. It was difficult for a capital ship to hit anything smaller than a corvette, but with enough gun batteries and enough open space, eventually they would get lucky.

"Wraith?" It was Chhun. "Talk to me. What's going on up there?"

"A little busy right now, pal. But suffice to say, the Empire really wants you dead."

"All right. Chhun out."

"Okay, change of plans," Keel said to Ravi. "Forget reaching *Intrepid*. You make the jump to light speed."

"I would not suggest this option, Captain. We have not determined the extent of the damage to the upper quadrant housing. If it is sufficiently breached, a jump to light speed could rip the ship apart without shielding. And, as a secondary factor, we are currently on emergency life support. Should this fail before we reach a certified repair facility, it will necessitate evacuation in the lifeboats."

Keel opened his mouth to reply, but Ravi continued.

"And of course there are not enough of these, because you took out half of the Republic-mandated quantity so that you could fit more charge for your blaster cannons."

"Are you finished?"

"Which I advised against."

Keel ground his teeth. "Thanks for the reminder." He fixed thrusters forward, putting as much speed as the *Six* had left in her to reach the relative safe haven of the *Intrepid*.

"Listen up, everybody," he said over ship-wide comm. "That Black Fleet destroyer has got it out for us and our shields are shot. I'm putting everything into reaching the *Intrepid*. We're either going to make it by the skin of our teeth, or we're all going out together in a blaze of glory. So now's the time to make good with your chosen deity. I'm talking about you, Masters. Captain out."

"Captain Keel?"

It was Garret.

Keel suppressed the urge to roll his eyes. The last thing he needed right now was to walk the kid through whatever existential crisis he was facing at the prospect of lying down on the wrong side of a graveyard.

"Tell me you've got some way to make this all better, kid."

"I do. And... you see, that's sort of *why* we're in the trouble we're in right now. I was able to hack into the Imperial destroyer's hangar operations. And I was going a little too fast, didn't cover my tracks as well as I should have, and so they know that I'm working from the *Six.*"

Keel veered up to avoid a flurry of laser blasts that were leading the ship. "Seems like overkill just because someone sliced their system."

"More like a last gasp effort to survive," Garret said. "You see, I've got their tractor beam pulling that explosive-rigged corvette into their main hangar bay. Once it's inside I figured I just blow it up."

Keel's eyes went wide. "Garret, that's brilliant! Do it!"

"Well... That's the other problem. It'll be inside the hangar in another fifteen seconds. But we're too far out of range to detonate the bomb. So you... kind of need to..."

"Garret, so help me, do *not* say *turn around and go back.*"

"Sorry."

Keel took a deep breath and stared up at the ceiling. He was calm. He would be calm. He would handle this.

Then he exploded.

"Gah! Ravi, why can things never be easy?"

Keel did a half loop and rocketed toward the destroyer. The heavy laser blasts emanating from the capital ship were now way off the mark thanks to the abrupt change in course.

"Yo!" shouted Exo. "Why in the nine hills are we turning around?"

Keel diverted everything he had into engines, streaking toward the ship as quickly as possible. "Forgot my wallet!"

"Ford..." Chhun said.

Masters sounded like he really was praying.

Keel saw the corvette slip inside the destroyer's primary hangar. Green blaster cannonballs seemed as thick as the stars themselves as they raced around the speeding Naseen light freighter. But that wasn't the only thing flying out of the capital ship. More starfighter wings, older models and bombers, were dumping out, all of them heading straight for Keel. And the destroyer had also started jettisoning escape pods. Just in case.

"Garret..." Keel said.

"Not much longer!"

"We... are going... to *die*!"

"Now!"

Keel imagined the beanpole code slicer pressing some oversized button he held in the palm of his hand. For a moment nothing happened. Then a dazzling light burst forth from every frame and window aboard the destroyer. The ship swelled and buckled and broke apart in a blinding explosion that engulfed the ships that had just launched from its bays.

"Turn around!" Ravi yelled.

Keel reversed thrust and threw the *Six* into a hairpin turn. The ship's flight controls felt loose in his hands, as if he were sliding on ice. A heavy, grinding clank sounded from deep within the engine room.

And then the *Six* lost all propulsion. It drifted through space, carried only by its momentum.

"Primary engines are down," Ravi said, silencing warnings and alarms as he frantically worked his station. "Secondary, too." The navigator placed his hands in his lap, then looked over at the safety harness that hung unused at Keel's shoulders. "I am thinking you should prepare for impact."

The blast radius from the destroyed Black Fleet capital ship was hurtling their way. Keel hastily fastened his restraints and then strained against them to reach the comm. "I hope at least this thing works."

He activated ship-wide and shouted, "Everybody, buckle up! We're about to go tumbling!"

Seconds later the shock wave enveloped the *Indelible VI*, sending the freighter end over end in a dizzying, raucous ride. Inertial dampeners—if they were even still online—were unable to keep pace with the whirling spin cycle that was the interior of the ship. Everything that wasn't bolted down or strapped in was hurled against a wall or the deck and then held there by centrifugal force.

Keel fought against the strain, telling himself not to black out. And hoping that Garret and Leenah had been able to get themselves strapped in. He owed them safety and protection, in spite of where they were and what they were doing. The legionnaires would be fine; they had on their armor. And the senator... well, Keel didn't give a rat's ass what happened to him.

Finally, the shock wave moved past, and the *Six*'s still functioning stabilizers managed to get the craft out of its spin. But the dizzying sensation continued in Keel's mind long after his ship had evened out.

He looked over to his navigator. But Ravi was gone, probably checking on the others in the ship. Thinking he should do the same, Keel unfastened his restraints and found himself floating up from his seat.

"Great. What else can go wrong?"

He activated the comm, unsure if anyone would even hear him. "Everybody all right?"

"Exo and I are fine," answered Chhun. "We're tending to Garret now. Something knocked him in the head pretty good, but I think he'll be all right."

Keel mouthed a silent prayer of thanks when Leenah's voice came over comm. "I'm okay too. I had already strapped in all the patients in the med bay, including myself, before we started spinning around."

For a princess, the Endurian was a practical type.

"Glad to hear it," Keel said, not hiding his relief, or caring what any of the others might think of it.

"Yeah, I'm okay," Bear grumbled. "But I think I actually felt better when I was passed out in a blown-up turret."

Masters groaned. "Guys... I puked in my bucket."

Ravi reappeared in the cockpit. "I apologize for my disappearance, Captain. I felt it wise to go through the ship and make sure it would hold until we can board *Intrepid*."

"Yeah?" Keel said as he swam around the cockpit. He wanted to see Leenah, but with the ship disabled, he had a duty to stay as close to his captain's seat—float as close in this case—until the ship was safely docked aboard *Intrepid*. He looked over his shoulder at Ravi. "And?"

Ravi made a circle with his thumb and index finger. "We are A-Okay."

The voice of Dax Danns chirped over the comms. "Looks like you're on one hell of a ride, *Six*. Everybody all right in there?"

"All accounted for," Ravi answered.

"Glad to hear it. All the Black Fleet is accounted for as well. Reaper Squadron will keep you safe until *Intrepid* gets close enough to pull you in."

"Understood," said Ravi.

"But I'll say this much," said the brash pilot, seemingly eager to talk now that the fighting had ended. "If the Senate and the House of Reason wanted General Chhun this bad before now... man, they are *really* gonna want him after this."

04

Safely docked aboard Legion destroyer *Intrepid,* Captain Keel went in search of Leenah and the rest of the crew. He put a self-assured half smile on his face. But he didn't *feel* like smiling. That was the closest he'd ever come to getting shot down and losing the *Six.* And if these missions continued… sooner or later, that was exactly what was going to happen.

He found the leejes, minus Bear, in the lounge. They were in various stages of undress, their armor peeled away, their mission over.

"How's everybody doing?" he asked.

"Been better," answered Exo.

"Oh, this is probably the best I've ever felt in my entire life," said Masters. He looked like he'd tried to clean himself up in the refresher, but he still had pieces of lunch stuck in his hair and clinging to the synthprene around his neck. "Thanks for asking, Captain Ford."

"Will we be able to leave the ship any time soon?" asked Chhun.

Keel crossed his arms and rocked on his heels. Every ramp was frozen in place from the damage. "Shouldn't be too much longer. Ramps are sealed up tight, but the *Intrepid*'s technicians are working on from the outside, and Ravi's taking care of what he can from within. In the long run, it's better to wait for them to fix it than to blow the emergency hatches. The *Six* has got a large enough repair order as it stands."

He continued on to the med bay, where Leenah was kneeling at the captured senator's side, removing the man's isolation hood. It must've been hell being under that thing, completely cut off from all sound and light, but still feeling the shakes and shudders of a ship in combat.

Served the traitor right.

As the hood came off, a pale face emerged, with red rings beneath eyes that looked around wildly. He appeared as though he were ready to vomit.

"Don't even think about getting sick," Keel warned. "I've just had the decks cleaned."

The senator closed his eyes and nodded. Quite agreeable for a would-be suicide bomber.

Leenah brushed the senator's forehead with the backs of her fingers. A brief return to compassion in a galaxy consumed by war. "He's not well."

Keel crossed his arms. "Probably how the Senate convinced him to blow himself up."

Exo, leaning in the doorway of the med bay, let out a rueful, one-note laugh. "And don't think we forgot about that, Senator. I say we have them run a Legion gauntlet on his way off the ship."

Leenah turned her head and scowled. "He's not long for this galaxy even without something like that. He needs to be transferred to the *Intrepid*'s med bay. It's much better equipped to handle someone with such an advanced illness." She looked imploringly at Keel.

"All right," said Keel, though he felt that Exo's idea was the better one. "I'll check with Ravi and see how much longer before we can get off the ship."

Ravi came over the comm. "I heard you, Captain. Doors will be down in two minutes."

Leenah gently wrapped her hands around the senator's emaciated arms. "I'll accompany you to the other med bay. Can you stand?"

"I'll help," Exo said, stepping fully into the room. Now stripped down to his synthprene undersuit, he seemed even more solid and muscular than when he was fully in armor. He grabbed the senator by the back of his red silk robe and hoisted him to his feet as though he were doing a one-armed clean-and-jerk. "Come on, Senator. Let's go get you healthy enough to stand trial so we can find you guilty of treason and execute you. Or you can just die here in the med bay. One way or the other, you ain't making it back to Taijing alive."

The senator's knees buckled. But he didn't look afraid—just weak.

Leenah stared daggers at Exo and then glanced sharply at Keel, as if asking him to intervene. What did she want him to do? The senator had tried to blow them all up. But Keel's mind was on something Exo had said. *Taijing.* The primary Sinasian world. Keel never paid much attention to who their targets were; he just piloted the ship and fired when necessary. The political mumbo-jumbo was Chhun's concern. But a Sinasian...

"Take it easy, huh, Exo?"

The hard-faced legionnaire stared at Keel in disbelief. "You serious?"

"I am," Keel said, taking control of the senator. The man seemed too light to be alive, all his vitality sapped by whatever galactic disease was eating him alive. "Leenah, can you stay with the senator? I want to talk to this legionnaire... privately."

"'This legionnaire'?" Exo grumbled.

"Just come on and help me find Chhun."

***

In the main lounge, out of earshot of the med bay, Keel stood with the two legionnaires in a tight triangle.

"I don't like the way you act around that Endurian," Exo said. "She's making you soft, bro."

"She's not making me *soft.*" Keel waved away the distraction. "You know what? Never mind. That senator is Sinasian."

"So what?" said Exo, clearly still hot.

"Cool down, Exo," said Chhun. To Keel he added, "So what?"

Keel shook his head. "You remember when you first joined Victory Company?"

"Of course."

"Well, right before you joined up, we had just finished a six-month stretch through the Sinasian Cluster. I was a second lieutenant, fresh out of the Academy. Prior to arriving, Pappy briefed us—you know, one of those informal briefings he would give to officers and NCOs before we arrived in a new world."

Pappy would usually pull up the House of Reason–approved informational and cultural presentation, then toss his datapad to the side and tell his men the real history of the planet or sector they were going into, so far as he was concerned. It drove the points crazy, but Pappy felt—and Keel agreed—that the best way to keep his men alive was to tell them the plain unvarnished truth of what they were getting themselves into.

"So according to Pappy, Sinasia had nearly launched a full-scale rebellion right under the Republic's nose. This was well before the MCR were making any serious waves. It fizzled out, but the thing of it is, the Sinasians *hate* the Republic that they've been forced to be a part of. And now we've got ourselves a Sinasian senator who's dying, who's apparently got nothing left to lose... and I'm thinking... maybe we can use that old Sinasian grudge against the Republic to help make our job a little easier."

Chhun laughed.

"What's so funny?" Keel said.

"Nothing about the plan. It's a good one." Chhun smiled. "It's just that this is the first time I've heard you refer to what we're doing in terms of 'we' and 'our job.' Did you stop counting the days until you could jump across the horizon and spend all that money you earned with your princess?"

Now Exo laughed.

"Glad to see how much I amuse the two of you," Keel said. "And yeah, that's still the plan. It's just that I can see that Kill Team Victory is never gonna get the job done without me. If you want something done right…"

"Okay," Chhun said. "Let's take the senator to Admiral Deynolds. We'll have a talk with him there."

"If he lives that long," said Exo.

Chhun frowned.

"Dude, I'm just sayin', he looks like he's gonna curl up and die."

***

"When the Dragon died," said Senator Van Cammack as he rose to leave, "we thought that was Sinasia's last hope. I did not dream to think… I am grateful to the Legion in this matter."

"We appreciate your willingness to see the validity of what we are attempting to do," Admiral Deynolds replied with a bow.

Two med bots led the sickly Sinasian senator—more like carried him—from Admiral Deynolds's private briefing room. Watching him go, Chhun could hardly believe the man had been able to stay upright for the ninety-minute negotiation that had just taken place.

Perhaps equally surprising, Keel had managed not to put his feet up on the table the entire time. But as the blast door shut behind the senator, he flopped back into his seat as though he were dropping onto his couch to watch a game of seamball. Leenah sat somewhat primly next to him.

"I told you that'd work," Keel said.

They had told Senator Van Cammack everything: that Delegate Kaar and Admiral Devers were involved in helping Goth Sullus attack Tarrago and destroy much of the Seventh Fleet; that the Battle of Kublar had been orchestrated by the Republic itself; that the House of Reason had violated every galactic law regarding artificial intelligence, resulting in the unleashing of the Cybar, which had led to a loss of life that was still being calculated. They'd shared with the senator every piece of intel and every dirty little secret in their possession. The very same information they would share with the entire galaxy—when the time was right.

Deynolds shook her head. "I'm not sure what we just did was constitutionally legal."

"Legal schmegal. You did great," said Keel casually, as though he were encouraging Deynolds about an audition rather than a treaty that would have a major impact on their continued mission to execute Article Nineteen. He looked to Leenah. "Didn't she do great?"

Leenah blushed at being included in the discussion. "I don't know what's constitutionally legal, but if the Republic had been more willing to make concessions like this—to hear the planets outside of the core instead of always telling us how wrong we were for simply being ourselves—the MCR would have never been able to recruit a militia, let alone an army."

Chhun could tell the mention of MCR didn't sit well with Admiral Deynolds. The admiral had already expressed her reservations about having Keel and Leenah in this war room. Chhun had no problem with Keel's presence—in fact he wanted it—but his crew didn't belong in this conversation, especially a crewmember who was former MCR. Leenah had sat in on the discussion with Van Cammack only because the senator had demanded that she remain at his side.

"Well..." Admiral Deynolds looked across the table at Keel and Leenah. "If the two of you will excuse us?"

Keel turned to Leenah and winked. "Sure. I need to oversee repairs on the *Six*, and then we'll figure out our next move from there."

"I'd like to get back and see Prisma again," Leenah said. "It's been too long."

Keel frowned. "Not my first choice, but yeah, okay."

"Actually, Keel," Chhun said as he and Leenah walked to the door. "Hang on for a minute. Just you."

Keel said to Leenah, "Go on, I'll catch up."

Chhun waited for the Endurian to give her assent and leave. Then he turned to Keel. "I'd like your thoughts on next steps," he said. "Once we release the holo the senator just recorded, Sinasia is going to be the next battleground."

Ford scratched his chin. "Who's the Imperial Legion's sector commander for Sinasia?"

It still amazed Chhun how his friend could so seamlessly switch between the smooth-talking, sardonic smuggler, Keel, and the all-business legionnaire, Ford, he'd first known him to be. There was probably some kind of psychological diagnosis in all of that, but Chhun had come to his own, non-professional, opinion: it worked. And if it ain't broke...

Ignoring the datapad that sat in front of her, Admiral Deynolds pulled out a pocket-sized datapad. "The sector commander is..." She swiped down. "... David Lawrence. I don't know him."

Chhun nodded. "I know Dave."

"You've only been a general for a few months," Keel said from behind a grin. "Already rubbing shoulders with the Legion's elite?"

"I don't know him personally," said Chhun, "but I know *of* him. My source on Utopion says he's loyal to the Legion—the real Legion—and he's ready to take the troops under his command to our side when we give the word."

"Your source, huh?" asked Keel.

Chhun and Deynolds exchanged a look. They were among only a handful of people who were aware of Imperial Legion Commander Washam's role as an informant deep inside the government. It was through Washam—Wash, as the man liked to be called—that the Legion had been able to get such reliable intel on where senators, House of Reason delegates, and Imperial Legion and shock trooper surges were likely to be. They took every effort to keep Wash's name out of people's mouths—and that would have to include Keel.

"Yeah," Chhun said. "And it's not that I don't trust you, but this source's identity is closely guarded."

"Fine by me, pal," Keel said, holding up both palms as if washing his hands of the matter. "Just feels funny being part of a top-secret talk with a Sinasian senator and then hear you get all cloak-and-dagger around me."

"Captain Ford," Admiral Deynolds said. She refused to call the man Wraith, much less Keel. "You were an agent for Dark Ops, so I know you understand the need for tight secrecy. No one was bandying about your name while you were out hunting for Goth Sullus."

Keel smiled, though Chhun knew he bristled at being called Ford. "Like I said, fine by me. Just don't put all your synth in one cargo hold is all I'm saying. Didn't work out so well for Legion Commander Keller."

Chhun looked down at the mention of Keller's name. The sting of his loss—and the loss of so many other legionnaires, chief among them Major Owens—was one that likely would never fade in his lifetime. Keller had gotten them *so* close to realizing Article Nineteen. In spite of the treachery of Nether Ops and the sitting government. In spite of the zhee being weaponized.

So close.

And then... everything fell apart all at once.

"Anyway," said Ford, "Sinasia. Republic SOP will be to send in Nether Ops, or whatever passes for intelligence under Goth Sullus, to destabilize things once they realize they've lost military control. Or maybe they just throw whatever forces they've got against Sinasia to see if they can actually stand up to whatever the Republic has waiting."

"No, I don't think that's likely." Admiral Deynolds traced her finger along the polished surface of the conference table. "With *Intrepid* and the rest of the surviving assault frigates and cruisers still loyal to the Legion ready to react, I don't think they'll make the mistake of forcing a head-on assault. They can't afford another full-scale battle after the losses they suffered at Utopion. We weren't the only ones severely damaged by that conflict. And Tarrago hasn't gotten close to producing the output they had hoped for."

"But you're right, Wraith," Chhun said. "We need to make sure Commander Lawrence is prepared, because the Republic isn't going to sit by once we set our plan in motion."

"I'm not sure I like the way you said *our* plan." Keel frowned. "Why do I get the feeling that 'our' includes 'me'?"

"I know you're eager to leave us so you can go see Prisma," Chhun said. He knew quite the opposite was true, which was why he said it. "But I don't think we can afford to lose you just yet. I need some more time to work this all out, but you're the closest thing to an agent we have, and if this goes the way I think it will, we're going to need you on Sinasia to work with the limited resources Dark Ops still has. I need someone on the ground to tell me where to point our kill teams."

Keel looked skeptical. "What exactly would you want me to do?"

"Just go to Sinasia, keep your ears open, and stay in contact," Chhun said. "That's all I'm asking. Feel free to work some jobs while you're there."

That last remark made Keel grin. "I know Sinasia well enough. Made a few smuggling runs from there back in the day. There's always plenty of jobs for a fast ship with a devilishly handsome pilot."

"Thank you," Chhun said.

"Don't mention it. But if the new emperor goes total war on Sinasia," Keel shook his head, "I'm not stickin' around for that, pal."

"Goth Sullus is going to have to choose his battles. He might control Utopion, and the core worlds might be happy to go along with him, but he doesn't have the resources to control what he calls his empire."

"Neither do we," Wraith pointed out.

Chhun smiled. "We're not here to control things. We're here to make sure the Republic has the opportunity to be what it should have been for decades now. What it was when it was first formed during the crisis of the Savage Wars. *And* we're here to make everyone responsible for what happened to the Legion pay for their part in it."

"Spoken like a true believer." Keel looked from Chhun to Deynolds. "Well, you probably need to talk about top secret things! And since I've got a ship that needs me..." He began moving for the exit. "That was a nice speech about Sullus, Chhun. When this is all over, you should think about making the transition into politics. You've got a knack for the rah-rah. And I hear the House of Reason will have a lot of openings before long."

One Republic News

The PLE journalist bot was in the middle of broadcasting a special interest story about two long-lost sisters separated at birth who were now reunited seventy years later thanks to the wonders of Republic facial identity software. It was the kind of feel-good story the Mid-Core seemed to love, so One Republic News's editors always made a point of scouring the holowebs for independent news stories such as this one that they could scoop up for themselves.

The bot was three minutes into its script, detailing all the ways the twins had nearly come into one another's lives only to fall just short—birthdays spent on the same amusement world but with different adoptive families, applying for the same House of Reason internship (neither was awarded the position), and perhaps most unlikely of all, sharing the same hyperspace cruiser on a layover jump from Spilursa—but the story wouldn't be finished. The bot received a directive to modulate its voice in order to report a breaking news story—something that had happened quite often recently, given the galaxy's turmoil.

"This is Kyle Cobb with a breaking news story," said the bot, taking on the form of one of the many holonews anchors it presented to viewers. "The Sinasian Cluster has declared its independence from the Imperial Republic.

We go now to an authenticated holo-recording of Senator Van Cammack."

The automated control center switched to a queued-up holo of the senator, who sat feebly in front of a Legion crest.

"I have been convinced that the House of Reason," he began, "in resisting the Legion's calls seeking the implementation of Article Nineteen of the Constitution, has made itself an invalid government."

The senator coughed weakly into a balled fist.

"Such resistance was not a matter of putting down a seditious force, but rather a naked attempt at maintaining power and control of our public institutions. I will no longer stand for such brazen disregard for the constitution of the Republic. Neither can I in good faith work with a government that has so soundly rejected its guiding principles.

"The people of Sinasia have felt the oppressive hand of the Republic ever since our unfortunate actions during the Savage Wars. Even though we were made part of the Republic in name, in fact we have lived as a people apart, constantly punished for the decisions of previous generations, though even the oldest among us were but infants in those times. In recent decades, the House of Reason and Senate crippled Sinasia with regulation and taxes, then carved up our planetary wealth for themselves.

"Still, I went to Utopion an idealist, eager to make Sinasia a full and equal part of the Republic." Senator Van Cammack looked aside, as though bearing all the weight of a life swelling with regret. "And I failed. I became part of the problem, doing what I was told to do in order to maintain my good fortune in the galaxy.

"But now my eyes are open. And what those eyes see is that every reservation the people of Sinasia have ever had about the Republic government, every suspicion they have had of House and Senate corruption, of self-dealing, of their derisive contempt for the peoples of the non-core worlds... every one of these fears is not only true, but worse than we could have even imagined."

Van Cammack gave another dry, weak cough.

"My time left in the galaxy is brief, but I would end it having done for Sinasia what it has most wanted for centuries. In a treaty that I have just negotiated with the Legion—the only valid government operating inside the Republic—I have ensured that Sinasia is now free of Republic rule. Sinasia has been sworn aid by Legion General Cohen Chhun should any parties misrepresenting themselves as the Republic threaten us harm or aim to force us to join them."

The senator looked straight into the holocam, his eyes full of fire. "People of Sinasia, today, you are free."

The newscast cut back to the bot, whose programming instructed it to sit quietly for three standard seconds, to better allow the weight of the package they'd played to register in the minds of the biologics who'd just witnessed it. The bot looked somberly at the holocam. "More on this as it develops. We'll go now to Liza Trah'farl with a history of Sinasian conflicts within the Republic."

05

Goth Sullus stood outside the door that led from his private chambers on Utopion to his adjoining war room. The place he'd specially constructed to be impervious to the endless bugging and spying that the Republic—*Imperial*—capital was rife with. *His* capital.

His *empire.*

Emperor Goth Sullus had agreed to take a meeting with his inner council. Leaders of both the Black Fleet and the fallen Republic awaited his presence, seeking his will. *Probing for weakness?*

Two massive shock troopers, all that remained of the Gray Watch that had sought to assassinate him in the failed coup attempted after the victory at Tarrago, accompanied him. Two would suffice. Enough to give him time to react to another attempt on his life, and few enough so as to be unable to harm him themselves.

Two trusted men behind him. A room full of vipers ahead of him.

He'd survived the first serious assassination attempt. The man who had been first to call Sullus emperor—Admiral Rommal—had also been the first to attempt to drive a blade between his shoulders. Goth Sullus had kept the man alive after, in the hopes of finding out the identities of the other conspirators, but no other faces had ever shown, and no probing of minds had given Sullus further revelation. And then Rommal died on board *Imperator*. A self-inflicted death, forced by Sullus's power. A belated execution for treason.

Did those waiting for him in the war room deserve the same fate? Sullus had no way of knowing. And that troubled him more than anything had in many years. More than when his old friend Tyrus Rechs had come to make good on a promise to destroy him for seeking the power to make the universe right. More than when his first open assault against the Republic faltered, requiring his direct intervention on Tarrago Moon.

And that moon... that was where it had started. The momentary lapse in his control, in his ability to manipulate the universe itself. As though a wet blanket had been thrown over his head, muffling his sensitivity to the phenomena known to him as the *Crux*. And it had only gotten worse since the Battle of Utopion. Now he could enter into only the least guarded of minds—and those were very seldom the type that contained anything worth knowing.

It was as though he'd gone suddenly blind after a lifetime of perfect vision.

Goth Sullus stood at the door, probing, seeking to know the will and thoughts of the men waiting for him inside.

Nothing.

Except... a voice. One he was growing more accustomed to hearing. One, it seemed, he almost yearned to receive counsel from.

We remain, Emperor Sullus. We still serve.

"Open the door," he demanded his guardsmen.

The two shock troopers, their gunmetal-gray armor shining as though shellacked by a master carpenter, activated the door controls, stepped through, blaster rifles at the ready, and stood aside for their master to enter.

The room fell quiet as Goth Sullus entered. He wore the armor. Rechs's old armor, made new. Made better. Helmet on, he scanned the assembled faces.

Delegate Orrin Kaar. Admiral Crodus. Admiral Ordo. Baron Scarpia. Imperial Legion Commander Washam.

Five men, a mix of the Black Fleet and the former Republic, who would each seek to forge the future of the new, *Imperial* Republic. Men who felt that this victory was as much theirs as anyone else's. They had fought and schemed. Killed and sent men to die. Spent fortunes. But they would know, when the time was right, that the Empire belonged to Goth Sullus alone.

There was never any other way.

"My lord Sullus," Delegate Kaar began, ever the politician with his flattery. "You honor us."

The House of Reason delegate stared unflinchingly at the emperor. Sullus knew that Kaar thought of him as nothing more than an equal, sharing in the spoils of a great new galactic order. "Emperor" was, to him, a vanity title.

Sullus hated the man.

No other eyes save Scarpia's looked upon Goth Sullus. The Black Fleet admirals remained timid around "the man in black," as they'd all come to call Sullus. And the new Legion commander looked as though he was on borrowed time—in a position of power due to the combination of a friend in a powerful position and the death of General Nero on board a Republic super-destroyer.

The men of Goth Sullus's high council waited until he sat in his chair—a veritable throne with high arms and a square back—before sitting back down themselves.

"I trust you have seen the holo of Senator Van Cammack?" Kaar asked.

Ordo cleared his throat. "My lord, we vetted the senator thoroughly. I'm confident he left with every intention of carrying out his mission to ensnare the rebellious Legion remnants. Perhaps they tortured him or—"

Sullus waved his hand, and the man in charge of Imperial intelligence fell silent.

"The navy stands ready to assault Taijing," Admiral Crodus said. The man had been eager to stage a full-scale naval operation ever since he'd assumed control after the death of Rommal. "Though Legion Commander Washam is unsure about the willingness of the defense fleet stationed in the cluster."

Sullus turned his head slowly to face Washam. "Elaborate."

Washam's eyes darted to Kaar as if seeking support. "Sinasia was... not a location many officers desired to be stationed at. As the appointment program grew, a special board was in charge of selecting where appointed officers would serve. This was designed to ensure the Legion did not isolate the appointed officers and maintain... independence."

"And what happened?" Ordo asked, stroking his chin, looking genuinely curious.

"The board failed in its primary mission and began to... sell off posts in the past few years. Transfers or assignments on core worlds and vacation planets were purchased for considerable sums." Washam shook his head. "The days of men like Admiral Devers serving in combat units at galaxy's edge ended not long after he was awarded the Order of the Centurion. With the exception of special units under the direct care and supervision of a local governor acting on behalf of the sector delegate or planetary senator... we have very few appointed officers beyond the mid-core, and none commanding in Sinasia, just a few on Taijing itself, but subject to Sector Commander Lawrence. He was decidedly pro-Legion when I last spoke with him, though he evidently did not commit legionnaires to my predecessor's seditious crusade against the House of Reason."

"And so you think he remains loyal to the Empire?" Ordo prompted.

"I cannot say for certain. Comm traffic to the planet is cut off. I have seen no evidence that Lawrence has instituted martial law or otherwise moved against the planetary government."

Sullus resisted the urge to scowl. The appointment program was both a blessing and a curse. It had eroded the Republic to the point where his Black Fleet was able to pose a threat. And the men appointed by the House of Reason were now the lynchpin that kept rank-and-file soldiers loyal to their new emperor rather than to what remained of the Legion. But he must now rely on those worthless men to fight his battles. He needed more men. Needed to rebuild all that he'd lost.

Orrin Kaar cut in. "Commander Lawrence may not be an appointed officer, but he would be a fool to refuse direct orders from his emperor. Sinasia will not be a problem. I am confident that we will put down any insurrection that might arise before a new, more loyal senator can be sworn in."

"I do not share your confidence," said Ordo. "I have no assets on Taijing or in Sinasia itself, but informants from nearby hubs say the Sinasians are responding quite positively to their newfound independence, with no reports of hostilities breaking out. That would seem to support Legion Commander Washam's interpretation of the matter: Commander Lawrence is complicit in all of this."

"I didn't say he was complicit," Washam interjected. "Only that there are no appointed officers commanding on Taijing. Comms are down, and Lawrence may well be awaiting orders from me, given the general chaos that followed the emperor's victory above Utopion. I will attempt to reach him again following the conclusion of this meeting."

Scarpia, made a baron for his service in supplying the Black Fleet, arched an eyebrow. "I'm not a general by any means," the kingly smuggler said airily, as though he were sitting on the veranda of some exclusive country club over a plate of treenahl caviar, "but I'd like to think of myself as something of an expert on handling... disloyalty. There are two options, gentlemen." He formed a 'V' with his fingers. "First, we end the relationship with Sinasia, using what leverage we have to make ourselves stronger for it. I made a small fortune with a former lover that way, though killing her outright would have been so much more satisfying. The second option is the more common. Make an example of them. Make them suffer. Let what happens to them serve as a warning to anyone who might think of doing the same."

Scarpia laughed at the thought and reached for a drink that wasn't there. He looked at the empty table distastefully. "That's my advice."

"A point well taken, Baron," Orrin Kaar said smoothly. "And in the case of Sinasia, a cluster of planets that has already attempted open rebellion once before in our lifetimes, there can be no debate: they must be destroyed. Utterly."

Admiral Crodus stood. "And at what cost? The navy is in no position to undertake such a campaign—not without great losses. And though Washam may be your lackey, I served long enough with General Nero—Oba, I wish he were here now—to know that our armies likewise are not capable of defending Utopion *and* successfully completing a multi-planet invasion."

Kaar rolled his eyes. "It's a wonder I was ever able to get the Black Fleet to attack Tarrago at all with this sort of cowardice in command."

"We will let the Sinasians go," said Goth Sullus, speaking for the first time since he'd entered the chamber.

Crodus sat back down.

Sullus continued. "They will be allowed to exist outside of the Empire. For now. But if they have not rejoined by the time our strength has returned, I will reduce their planets to ruin."

"My lord..." began Kaar. "This will be seen as a sign of weakness by the House of Reason... and the Imperial Republic itself."

"Empire," corrected Sullus.

Kaar frowned, clearly seeing a battle over terminology he did not wish to engage. "Semantics aside, my point stands. If you let them go, more worlds will follow suit. Mark my words. We will not be able to reconquer an entire galaxy. We need our worlds to know that leaving the Republic is unthinkable."

"I have declared the will of this empire."

Kaar let out a sigh. "My lord, you are thinking like a general without troops to spare. Rightly so. In those terms, I would not gainsay your decision. However, you now have far more weapons at your disposal. *Political* weapons. What if I were to propose a way to *soften* the Sinasian worlds in a manner that would cost the Empire no expenditures of military resources?"

Crodus folded his arms and snorted. "And what, pray tell, is that?"

"We open the worlds to the zhee for colonization. They've been busy enough invading their neighboring planets during the confusion. Imagine what they'll do when the Empire declares the Sinasian planets to be authorized zhee protectorates?"

The room fell silent.

Ordo nodded approvingly. "This... could work."

"I agree," said Admiral Crodus.

Only Scarpia voiced dissent. "The zhee are not to be trusted."

Sullus rose from his throne. "Have the zhee attack the Sinasian worlds. Crodus, Washam, Scarpia, keep your forces ready."

***

Sullus retired to his chambers confident in the plan and with a certain... increased respect for Delegate Kaar. For all the man's greasy political leanings, he had not reached the pinnacle of the House of Reason by being a fool. No, Kaar was the type of man who made use of fools.

And the galaxy was full of them.

The new emperor removed his helmet and placed it on a sideboard with a heavy thud—right next to the cutting torch he'd been given by that exceptional sergeant—then walked to an opaque window.

"Light. One third."

The blackened window grew smoky, and a third of the light from the daytime skies of Utopion entered his chambers. A steady stream of repulsor sleds hummed in the distant streets, and air speeders clogged the skies. But these endless traffic snarls were far away from the government campus, which had been engineered to look parklike and wild. An oasis in the midst of the most densely populated planet in the galaxy.

The buildings around Sullus's apartment were beautiful contrasts of black and white, depending on which alien stone slabs they were built from. They were centuries old, but Sullus remembered the time when these buildings— so much more elegant and breathtaking than the modern architecture that seemed designed to evoke a sense of vertigo, discomfort, or guilt—were under construction. He had been there. Here. Back then.

The Savage Wars Memorial was visible, not far from where he now stood. And somewhere inside that cathedral of polished black marble was a statue dedicated to him. Him from another time. Another person.

But just one.

Tyrus Rechs had several statues, each for a different one of his various aliases. Goth Sullus's old friend—his oldest friend—had been everywhere during the Savage Wars. So much so that as the Republic formed and grew around the Legion, he'd had to become more than one person.

"We could let them know," Sullus had once said. "Tell them how long we've lived. What we've seen. What we've done. They would treat us as gods."

He offered the comment with a laugh. A genial protection in case Tyrus took it the wrong way, as if to say, only kidding.

Only he'd meant what he said. The words he'd spoken meant exactly what Goth Sullus had wanted them to.

Only he'd been too insecure, too full of self-doubt at the time, to stand behind those words. He had not yet become the man who stood atop a burning galaxy, looking down upon the richest planet in all of history as its ruler, watching maintenance bots clean the spray-painted profanity off the side of the cathedral, profanity that slandered the warriors honored inside—men and women who had died in the greatest conflict the galaxy had ever witnessed.

No, back then, whiling away the wee hours in a starship that traveled through hyperspace at speeds that seemed so incredibly fast—and yet was so slow by today's standards—when he and Tyrus drank exotic scotch and spoke of times no one else could possibly remember, in that moment of honesty masked behind a laugh, Goth Sullus—Casper—had not yet reached the zenith of all creation.

"A god," Sullus whispered to himself, validating those words spoken so many centuries before.

A god. With the power over life and death. The freedom to choose who would live.

And who would die.

Like the zhee, when their purpose was finished.

Like those who sought to upset the natural order—cowards spitting upon warriors too far beyond the grave to smite them back.

Like... anyone who would stand in his way.

But you are not without mercy.

The voice—not his own—swirled inside Goth Sullus's mind. As though all the running waters of the universe whispered to him at once.

He looked down at his ring. Not a ring of power. Not some enchanted artifact, but a prison.

A mercy.

A prison. Holding those that had slipped into this galaxy. Those whom the Ancients feared so much that they abandoned everything in the hopes that somehow, someone would come to slay their darkest, most awful horror.

Goth Sullus turned his hand over, examining the ring.

The galaxy's savior stood victorious, though the galaxy knew it not.

In time they would.

In time…

A god.

But what sort of god? Surely not a conqueror.

The voices spoke to Sullus again. He bristled at their accusation.

"I have conquered the Republic."

Have you? You conquered us, yes. But is the Republic truly yours? Are you not allied with those you promised to upend?

"You know nothing of power. Or how to maintain it."

We are your servants.

"The Empire is fragile now. Alliances such as these are… necessary. But it will not always be so."

Not always, master. Not always. You will conquer again.

Sullus removed the ring from his finger and dropped it on the sideboard next to his helmet.

He *was* a conqueror. What did it matter if those who'd fought for him now whined like children told to wait for their dessert? He would do all that he intended. He had saved the galaxy once. He would ensure it would never again be left without one who could protect it. Who could save it.

Let those without the patience to see it be cursed. He was thousands of years old. The history of his ascendance was still being written. And in the end, he would stand above all.

06

"Getting in and out of Taijing has always been a big ask," Keel said to the man sitting across from him and Leenah. Legion Major Giles Endiffron. Appointed. "And that's *before* things suddenly got so tense here."

"I understand that," said the major, leaning forward and speaking in a low voice. "But we need a contingency plan. And credits aren't—"

He paused as a waitress delivered a steaming bowl of broth and vegetables. Keeping his eyes on the server, Endiffron sat in silence until she bowed and left the table.

Leenah pulled the bowl in front of her and began blowing on it, looking uninterested in the conversation.

"Credits aren't an issue," Keel said. "*You* said that."

"They aren't." Endiffron looked around, clearly nervous that he was being observed in the small, run-down dive of a lunch spot on the City of Ten Thousand Lily Pads, the capital city of the capital world of the Sinasian Cluster.

The reality was that the major had every reason to be nervous. He was a legionnaire, an appointed officer, and the word was out that Sinasia was no longer a member of the Republic. And that message had been met the thundering approval of virtually all of the cluster's populace. Every planetary governor had heartily endorsed their senator's decree, and makeshift militia were openly patrolling the streets, armed with weapons that—by Republic law—they weren't allowed to own.

Not in Sinasia anyway.

So far, things had been peaceful, but only because the legionnaires and marines remained inside their bases. They didn't go out on patrol. Didn't watch the major bridges connecting the larger floating "lily pads" to each other on this buoyant city ingeniously built atop the sea. They were safe and unmolested—as long as they minded their own business.

The Sinasians had declared their independence at least twice in Keel's memory—both during and after the Savage Wars. And now, finally, they were actually governing themselves. Third time's the charm.

But that wasn't what had the point sitting across from Keel so worried. It was the Republic's *response* to Sinasia's declaration of independence. The protectorate fleet—not a full battle fleet, just the kind used to defend a sector of space—had been recalled to Utopion, leaving only two armed cruisers overhead. No reinforcements had arrived. And the sector commander had disabled all outbound comm traffic and declared his intent not to get involved at the military level. It was technically within his right to do just that, at least until he received specific orders from Utopion to fight. But rumor was that he'd shut down inbound comms as well. So orders that *should* have come never could, not with the comms shut off.

All of that left Endiffron uncomfortably exposed. Stranded on Taijing with his peers.

But if the point major was being really honest with himself, he knew just how tense things were inside the new Imperial Legion. There were a whole lot more legionnaires who had enlisted the traditional way than there were men like him, who'd been granted their place through the generous placement of a senator or House of Reason delegate. And how long, really, would it be until those enlisted men joined the "other" Legion—the one calling for the toppling of the emperor? The one that had indicted the House of Reason under Article Nineteen?

How much time did he have before the house of cards came falling down?

"So credits aren't an issue," Keel said. "Good. Fifty thousand."

"Fifty thousand credits?" Endiffron asked, his face going from shock to anger.

Keel help up a hand. "You didn't let me finish. Each."

"This is ridiculous." The point stood up to leave, but Keel grabbed him by the wrist.

"Sit back down."

Leenah looked up from her steaming soup, her eyes moving from Keel to Endiffron as the tension mounted.

Reluctantly, the point did as he was told. Keel leaned in, eyes hot with anger. "You know who you're talking to, don't you?"

Endiffron's lip quivered, as though he'd forgotten and only now remembered. He nodded slowly.

"Say it."

"Aeson Keel."

"And you know who I work for."

The point nodded again. "The bounty hunter Wraith."

"You're damn right. Now you already dropped a thousand credits just to have the privilege of this meeting. So you'd best remember who you are and who *I* am, because Legion officer or not, I'll dust you right here if you ever show me that kind of disrespect again."

Major Endiffron held up his palms apologetically. "I'm sorry. I didn't mean any slight against you or," his voice quavered, "the Wraith. It's just that every other junk flyer I've talked to on Taijing hasn't asked for more than ten per passenger."

"So why not take off with them?"

Keel knew the answers. Because they'd run off with the money. Or try to earn double by threatening to hand them over to the sector commander. Or they'd kidnap them and see if they could extract a ransom from any rich relatives.

But Wraith didn't operate that way, and this point knew it.

Endiffron looked down. Leenah slurped her soup loudly, still looking completely indifferent.

"Yeah," said Keel. "Because it ain't exactly a savings when you don't have it and they want it all up front."

The appointed legionnaire lifted his head again. "Don't... don't you want it all up front?"

Keel shook his head. "Nope. I'm a realist. I know you're cut off from everything out here. And I know you've got deep pockets once you're off-world."

Instantly the point's face brightened. "I—we—can pay you forty thousand now. That's all we have. And then the rest in full once we reach Utopion."

Keel gave a lopsided grin. "Deal. How many again?"

"Seven of us. That are going." The point looked around again. "There are more... men... loyal to us. But they could never afford—"

Keel gave him a confused look. "If you've got others, why not take control? You said your commander has gone rogue and is fighting against the House of Reason." He bumped Leenah's foot with his boot. A sign for her to play her part.

Leenah's eyes grew wide. "Oba's ears! Could you *really* overthrow those traitors?"

"Ella," Keel said, as if bothered by his girl's sudden interruption.

"That would be so totally righteous!" gushed Leenah, playing the airheaded Ella to perfection, complete with mid-core accent.

This worked for a number of reasons. Partly because Leenah was beautiful, even by Endurian standards. But also because this was often what the galaxy had grown to expect from her race. Gorgeous princesses and princes with a desire for nothing but the ego boost that came from being the object of desire in a room. Dumb faux royalty eager to coast their way through life without ever breaking a sweat.

It wasn't true or just or fair. But it *was* making the point think about his own... romantic prospects with the Endurian sitting across from him. Because the Endurians were notorious for being all about free love—all the holoshows said so. It didn't matter if it was true or not. It was what the people wanted to believe. And that was truth enough in the Republic.

In the back of the establishment, a local band started to set up their equipment on a miniature stage which crowded them shoulder-to-shoulder. Their loop-drummer dropped his clap-cylinder, and it crashed noisily.

Keel watched the point as the man looked over at the source of the noise. This man was a mark. A type he'd seen endless times before. And what had started as an intelligence-gathering operation, his entire reason for being on Taijing, had the potential to be something much bigger.

The point turned back to the conversation. "I mean," he began, "I *could*. I've seen some action."

"Really?" Leenah sounded like she'd never heard anything so exciting as this.

"Yeah. Once or twice. We could take them down..."

"So why don't you?" asked Keel, pretending to be annoyed by the back-and-forth.

"I... I'm not sure we have enough men loyal to the Republic—sorry, the Imperial Republic—to be successful."

Leenah pouted, and Keel had to suppress a grin. She was doing a bang-up job at this. But then, she'd convinced *him* she was legitimate royalty back when they first met.

"Couldn't Wraith help?" she asked, caressing Keel's bicep.

He shrugged. "Wouldn't be the first time he helped appointed officers wrest control from Legion good ol' boys not willing to do what the House asked."

The point leaned forward. "You're serious? Wraith would help?"

"He might. If you've got the credits…"

"I do. *We* do. Yes. Absolutely we do." The point's eyes glazed over as though he were envisioning the grand reception that awaited him on Utopion for taking command and bringing Sinasia back into the Empire. They might even give him the Order of the Centurion for it. "If Wraith can help, that would be… amazing. But surely he can't take out an entire Legion garrison on his own?"

Keel raised an eyebrow. "Thought you said you had the guns to do that."

"Oh, yes. I mean, with the element of surprise… we can take control. The enlisted men will fall into line once the NCOs and the Legion commander are neutralized."

Leenah squirmed in her seat. "Oh, wow. This is *so* exciting!"

Keel almost flashed her a look to signal her to tone it down a bit, but then he saw the effect it was having on the point. He looked as though he was just waiting for Keel to get up so he'd have the opportunity to ask the Endurian for her commkey.

Well, when you've got a hot hand, you play it.

"You're telling me you already know who the traitors are," Keel said. "You know who's loyal to that group out on the edge that's been grabbing politicians for Article Nineteen."

The point scowled. "No one has actually *said* as much. But I believe so, yes. They fit the right profile, if you take my meaning. Disrespect to the House of Reason and the officers appointed to them—nearly to insubordination. More eager to kill the MCR than allow someone such as myself to negotiate a settlement. Always shouting 'ooah' and 'KTF'..."

"Yeah, I get it," Keel said, waving his hand. "Wraith can round 'em up, get 'em out of your way. But it's a big job. It needs a Republic-validated contract to make the arrests—best authorize lethal force if you can—"

"I can."

"Ooh!" moaned Leenah, as if the words sent her into a frenzy of excitement.

"And that order needs to be precise," Keel said. "Wraith will only grab the names you give me. And he'll shoot anyone who tries to stop him. That includes your buddies, so stay out of his way."

"Of course, of course." The point drummed his fingers on the table as the band began playing a somewhat unsettling mixture of S-pop and traditional Sinasian wood elements. "And... how much?"

Leenah gave a half-pout, half-frown. "Oh, grow a pair. Don't get cheap. This is so totally wicked!"

The point blushed. His tone was apologetic, yet masculine. Or at least what he must have thought of as masculine. The man was built more like a code slicer than an operator. "Oh, it's not that! I just wouldn't want to waste the Wraith's time if he's out of our combined price range. Our wealth isn't unlimited."

Leena frowned further, and began to lose interest.

"But we're still rich," the point quickly added. "Very wealthy."

At this Leenah perked up again and sent a gushing smile in the point's direction. That seemed to pick up his spirits.

Keel marveled at the performance she was putting on. He'd have to remind himself of today, lest he get wrapped around Leenah's little finger... if he wasn't already.

"I only work for Wraith," he said, placing his palms on the table. "I don't make the final call on anything that doesn't involve my ship—usually. But I can tell you how these things usually work: You get one shot. He doesn't negotiate, there's no dickering about price. You write up the order, include all the details, and put down a price that makes it worth his time. If you catch him in a good mood, or happen to want him to do something that helps him settle an old score—because the guy holds grudges like you wouldn't believe—he might do it for less than his considerable market rate."

"And what if we're too low?"

"Who do you think he holds all those grudges against?" Keel stood up and motioned for Leenah to follow. "If you lowball him, just pray that no one ever names you in a contract."

The point gulped, and nodded in understanding.

Keel took a step, then stopped short. "C'mon, Ella."

Leenah sat at the table, her chin resting on her latticed fingers, staring at the point dreamily.

"Ella... *today.*"

The point blushed and gave a fractional nod, as if giving the pink-skinned Endurian permission to blush and slide out of the booth to join her boyfriend.

That's rich, thought Keel. And though he felt a definite urge to grab the point by his non-regulation hair and slam his face into the table before leaving him to drown in Leenah's unfinished soup, the fact that they had this guy so thoroughly sucked in had left him in a forgiving mood.

Besides, it's not like *he* was really having to suffer anything. Leenah was the one who had to play like she was into this worthless pile of twarg dung. Keel hoped she wouldn't be too upset at him for bringing her into this little game.

Leenah joined him, and Keel faced the point once more. "All right, you have my commkey. Answer by nightfall or all you'll find if you ever try to reach us at that key will be a dead transmission. You've got your one chance to make good with Wraith. Don't blow it."

***

Keel and Leenah walked together down the crowded streets, doing their best not to stand out. Though Taijing was the capital world of the Sinasian Cluster, and therefore the most metropolitan and diverse, it was still relatively rare to see non-Sinasians on the planet. This was due to a combination of the Sinasian desire for homogenous seclusion and the Republic's heavy taxes and tariffs on all things Sinasian—including travel to or from its worlds. All part of a punishment for the cluster's choice to side with a contingency of Savage marines during the wars.

This wasn't the first time Keel had been in Sinasia. Most good smugglers found themselves invited to run the profitable lanes. High taxes and tariffs had a way of making folks rich—so long as they weren't the honest, law-abiding types. The other types—politicians, for one, and the night markets for another—made a killing. Basic economics.

"How'd I do?" asked Leenah as they weaved in and out of a sea of foot traffic. They'd tried locking arms to keep from getting separated, but most people forced their bluff, making them unlink arms or clothesline them.

"Good enough to make me jealous."

Leenah laughed and patted Keel's chest through his leather flight jacket. "You have no reason to be jealous, Aeson. None whatsoever."

"I dunno... that major was obviously a very powerful officer in the Legion. I'm only a captain—how can a guy compete?"

"I like you *despite* your being an officer in the Legion."

Keel shook his head. "I knew the recruiters oversold just how much those Legion dress blues would do for me."

Leenah rested her head on his shoulder.

They stopped to examine a fruit stand. Keel pointed to an oval-shaped piece of produce covered with two-inch spikes. "What's this?" he asked.

"Larupa," said a beaten-down bot on a small stool in front a credit box. It seemed to be the only one overseeing the rows of produce rolled out on carts on the sidewalk. "Very sweet."

An old Sinasian woman popped her head out of the storefront the fruit stand backed up to, and spoke in animated tones to the bot in her native language. The bot spun its head completely around to listen to her, then turned back to face Keel.

"If you buy one, you will get a second for half off. This is an unusually generous offer from my master, who is known to be among the toughest barterers on the Avenue of the Dragon."

"I dunno," Keel said, looking to Leenah. This was as close as they'd ever come to a date. It was funny how it took a covert Dark Ops mission for them to find the time. "What do you think?"

"It might be good..."

The old woman barked at the bot again.

"I am permitted to provide you a sampling." The bot carefully cracked the fruit open, then pulled out two wedges of what looked like white citrus with a green pulp. It handed one to Keel and one to Leenah. "Do not ingest the seeds. They cause hallucinations in most humanoids."

Keel hesitated, holding the firm and fleshy piece in his hand, but Leenah dove right in, chewing thoughtfully and then spitting a pea-sized seed into her palm. She tossed it in a nearby trash incinerator. "Try it, Aeson. It tastes just like the oulou fruit I used to eat back home as a little girl."

"I was just waiting to see if we were getting poisoned. You seem all right, though." Keel popped the fruit into his mouth.

Leenah punched him softly in the gut.

"What was that for?" he asked as he chewed.

"You know what for. Using me as a poison tester."

"Joking." He finished and sucked on his teeth. "Yeah, that's sweet all right."

"Are you pleased enough to continue with this transaction?" asked the bot.

Keel shrugged and looked at Leenah. He held the smile on his face even though the desire to do so had instantly vanished. In the distance, perhaps half a street away, was a man he'd spotted before they'd ducked in to meet with the point. He was wearing a loose hooded overshirt that hung sloppily over a pair of skin-tight athletic leggings—gray with a yellow thunderbolt. He was pretending to look at a table promising the best prices on holochits for movies that hadn't yet been released for public streaming.

"Yeah," Keel said to the bot. "We'll take two."

"Very good."

Without looking away, he spoke to Leenah out of the side of his mouth. "Listen carefully. I'm going to go inside. You pay, but don't wait for me. Keep walking on this street and then turn into the alley on your left. Do you see it?"

"Aeson, what's wrong?"

"Do you see it?"

Leenah nodded.

"Turn in that alley and try to at least get halfway down. I see a guy who I thought was following us before the meeting—don't look. And he hasn't moved on. Get into the alley, and if anyone tells you to stop, do what they say."

"Okay."

"Hey, can I go inside and use your fresher now that I bought something?" Keel asked the bot.

The bot swiveled its head back and presumably passed along the request to its owner. The woman, who had been leaning against the shop's doorframe, nodded and replied.

"You may use the refresher," said the bot, "but my master requests that when you go off-world, you tell others of the delights that await them on the newly reopened world of Taijing. You are a freight captain, are you not?"

"Most of the time," Keel said, moving toward the shop. He placed both palms together in the Sinasian style and gave a slight bow. "I'll let 'em know."

The old woman returned the gesture and stepped aside for Keel to enter.

Several aisles featured dust-covered cleaning supplies, non-perishable foods, and fourth-rate comms with flashy packaging rife with hip, young Sinasians. An end cap display featured some kind of anti-aging cream, an imitation of a popular core-world brand that used the same actress for its label and a remarkably similar name if not for an extra vowel.

Most everything here was the type of product that the rest of the galaxy would order by drone and have shipped to their home within minutes. But that was one of the nice things about technologically underdeveloped worlds—they still required people to leave their homes. It was quaint. And it also wouldn't last much longer. Not if Sinasia managed to stay independent and open up doors of trade that the Republic had long held shut. Well, held shut for everyone other than those connected few who'd scored lucrative import/export permits.

An older man, probably the husband of the woman out front, stood behind a counter at the back of the store. A wooden staircase on his left led up, probably to apartments above the shop, but the man pointed in the opposite direction. "Fresher," he said in accented Standard.

"Thanks," said Keel. "But I'm going up."

Before the old man could shuffle around the counter to protest, Keel had bounded up the stairs. He took them two and three at a time, hearing them creak and groan beneath him.

They let out into a hall with two doors, one on each end. He went to the door nearest the alley he'd pointed Leenah to, and knocked. There was no answer. Keel swore under his breath. This was probably the flat where the shop owners lived.

He returned to the stairs and went up to the third floor. More doors on this level. More apartments of a smaller size. The hall was full of the bubble-gum sounds of Sinasian S-pop. A surreal kind of music entirely dedicated to sounding cute. Every song Keel had ever heard in this style had a singer who sounded as though they'd sucked in a lungful of helium before approaching the microphone.

One of the doors was open, but that one was no good. He needed a window that would let out onto the alley. He knocked on the only door at that end of the building.

Again, nothing.

Keel pressed his ear against the door. He could hear a baby crying. This was also definitely the source of the blaring S-pop. He pounded on the door, hoping to be heard over the noise.

"Hey man, what you banging like that for?"

Keel turned to find a slim Sinasian man with a wispy mustache and smoked-lens sunglasses standing in the hall. He was carrying a sack of groceries, and a dragon pendant earring hung from one lobe.

"I need to get to a window?"

A rueful understanding crossed the man's face. "You in trouble, off-worlder? Maybe Chan is after you for dumping cargo?"

"I don't dump cargo."

"But you're in trouble."

Keel furrowed his brow. "You live here?"

"I live in the apartment above this one. You want to use my window, I let you. Costs fifty credits."

Keel looked up at the ceiling. The third floor was higher than he'd wanted to go, especially with how few of these old buildings had fire escapes. But Leenah was likely already turning the corner. And it didn't seem like the man tailing them had followed Keel inside. "Okay. Fine."

"Let's go," said the man carrying the groceries. He began walking up the next flight of stairs. "So, you don't dump cargo. That means you stole it, huh? Stealing from Chan is a bad idea."

"I don't work for Chan, but I'll keep that in mind."

"Yeah, sure, off-worlder. Every smuggler here works for Chan." They stopped outside the man's apartment. "Hope it was worth it."

Keel pulled out a credit chit and set its value to fifty. The chit beeped, acknowledging the value was withdrawn from one of his accounts and was now an untraceable currency. "I'm in a hurry."

"Okay, okay." The man set down his groceries and lined up his wrist comm with his door handle, causing the lock to click and disengage. He squeezed his way inside, then quickly leaned against the door to prevent Keel from following. He held out his skinny hand, palm up. "One hundred credits."

"You said fifty."

"Yeah, but if you stole from Chan, you can afford it. And if you want inside... you'll pay it."

The Sinasian's apartment must have had an open window, because Keel was sure he heard a scream drift up from the alley below. He pulled his blaster and forced his way inside.

"Okay, okay!" the man said, his eyes crossing as he focused on the blaster that was now inches from his nose. "Fifty is good."

But Keel wasn't concerned about the price. He walked right past the man, dropping the credit chit on the floor as he moved through a barely furnished apartment with piles of unwashed clothing gathering in the corners. He could hear voices coming up from the alley. Talking. And one of those voices was definitely Leenah's.

His blaster still pulled, Keel checked behind him to make sure the Sinasian flat owner didn't try anything stupid. But the man had retrieved his money and now had his back against the wall, only a quick few steps away from bolting out the door. For now he seemed content to stay out of the way until the stranger in his home was gone.

Miraculously, the old building had a fire escape to one side of the window. Keel deftly stepped onto it, careful not to make a clatter on the slatted metal floor.

He looked down.

The man in the hooded shirt was standing about five feet away from Leenah, who was clutching the bag with the fruit but otherwise standing her ground.

"Don't scream," the hooded man hissed.

"But you're frightening me," said Leenah.

Keel climbed down the ladder to the balcony below him. He was moving as fast as he could without making a racket.

"Where's your friend?"

"I don't know who you're talking about."

"Lady," the man said, his voice full of malice, "I'm not the kind of trouble you want. Don't play dumb with me."

"I don't have any money."

"I'm not looking for money."

The final ladder stopped about eight feet above street level. He would have to jump down the rest of the way, which would give the hooded man a chance to make his move before Keel could bring his blaster to bear. Ravi would have been able to give Keel his exact odds of success, but Ravi wasn't on this mission. He was running intel from the *Six*, and the docking bay was much too far off for him to be of much use right now.

"If you try to touch me, I'll scream," Leenah warned.

"I'm not after that either, but don't tempt me," said the man. "You're gonna come with me until we find your boyfriend."

A few things happened after that, all at once. Keel dropped from the ladder to the ground, immediately going into a roll that he came out of blaster up and on target. But it seemed the man had made his move, and Leenah had responded by swinging her sack of larupa at the man's face.

The man yowled in pain. One of the fruit's spikes had burst through the sack and lodged itself in the side of his face. He was angrily trying to dislodge it without causing any more damage. "You dumb bitch! I'll ice you for this!"

Leenah took a step backward as the man revealed a small hold-out blaster. He'd almost leveled the thing when Keel stuck the barrel of his own Intec x6 heavy blaster against the back of the man's head.

"Drop it. This is the only time I ask."

Frozen in place, the man said, "Who says? You the boyfriend?"

Keel deftly thumbed down the charge depletion dial and shot the man in the back of his knee. He fell in a heap, clutching his knee and swearing between screams. The larupa broke free of his face, taking a strip of flesh with it.

"I told you, only asking once."

The man had been twice lucky, though he might not have felt like it. First for Keel being interested enough in who he was so as not to put a blaster bolt through his skull. And second for Keel not using a full charge shot on his leg, which would have blown his knee right off.

"Here's another question I'm only going to ask once: Who are you with?"

"The... Legion. The real Legion. Article Nineteen."

"Wrong answer." Keel raised his blaster and aimed it at the man's head.

"Wait! Wait!" the man pleaded. "I just... I thought that was you. I'm Black Fleet. Working for Ordo. I thought... I thought you were with them."

This was far too easy. Which meant that the tail had an open comm and was waiting for backup. There was no telling if anything he said was valid, but Keel was sure he wasn't one of the good guys.

"I'm with Nether Ops," Keel lied, not wanting to give anything away if he was being recorded. "We're taking your emperor down for the House of Reason. So... that's still the wrong answer."

He shot the man in the head, then moved to grab a stunned Leenah by the hand. "C'mon, we gotta go."

07

"I know..." Leenah said, safely aboard the *Indelible VI*, "I know you have to do things like that. But, Oba, I hate seeing that sort of thing."

It had taken them forty-five minutes longer to get back to their docking bay than it usually would have. But Keel hadn't wanted to take any chances. He'd wandered down blind alleys, doubled back multiple times, drifted through dense crowds, cut through buildings, and even had Garret launch a stealth drone to watch them on the street until he was confident that no one had followed them. They'd paid a hefty sum to stay off the registries, and he wasn't going to blow that anonymity by being careless.

"I'm sorry, princess," he said, unfastening his gun belt and placing it on his workbench. "But that's what it takes to stay ahead of the people who make the galaxy a bad place for everyone else."

Leenah scrunched up her face. "Doesn't mean I have to watch it up close. *Most* of the galaxy doesn't watch it up close." She picked up her tool bag and slung it over her shoulder.

"Be happy I didn't take Rechs's slug thrower with me this time. Where you headed?"

Leenah opened an access hatch. "To fix the ship." She spoke as if that were the most obvious thing in the world.

"I thought they already did that on the *Intrepid*."

"Good enough to fly, maybe. But not good enough for me."

"Suit yourself," Keel said, smiling as Leenah ducked out of sight.

Leenah and Ravi had purchased six pallets worth of parts as soon as they arrived on Taijing—a damn expensive purchase, not only because of the cost of getting goods here, but because this stuff was much better than the sort of tech you could find in your average star port. But Keel had no doubt that whatever Leenah did with those parts would be well worth it.

"Just make sure we can still get her off the ground in a hurry if we need to," he shouted after her. "No telling what might come from that point."

Or the guy you dusted in the alley, Keel told himself.

The dead tail hadn't been Sinasian. So that ruled out local gangs or mobsters looking to find out what the new off-worlder was up to. And he had mentioned Ordo, who was Goth Sullus's head of intelligence, at least as best the Legion knew. Reports were that Nether Ops had been recalled and was undergoing a "loyalty evaluation." In the meantime, their work was limited primarily to the core worlds.

"Captain Keel." Ravi's voice came over the ship-wide comm. "Are you busy? You are just standing in place."

"I was thinking, Ravi."

"Ah. I had not considered this possibility."

Keel scowled at an overhead holocam. "Cute. What's up?"

Ravi abruptly appeared in front of Keel. Keel jumped and fumbled for the blaster in his gun belt, dropping the whole array onto the deck. "Gah! Don't do that, Ravi!"

Ravi arched a brow as Keel stooped to pick up his weapon. "I did not wish to communicate over comms. Just in case."

Keel strapped on his gun belt, thinking he might need it sooner than later. He pushed away his concern that the comms which were *supposed* to be locked down tight were now deemed untrustworthy by his navigator. "Communicate what?"

"The contract is in. I think you will be pleased."

Ravi motioned to a screen behind Keel's bench that usually displayed the freighter's various status updates and technical schematics. It now displayed a secure Republic order. A sort of contract the military provided to certain individuals such as bounty hunters and mercenaries. A way to get jobs out of the underground without having to go through the guilds. More secret. More secure.

Keel had once had one of these issued on his own head.

"Since when could this screen display anything but fuel cell readings?"

"Garret completed some spare-time coding." Ravi twirled his mustache. "The entire ship is now like one enormous datapad at your disposal."

Keel nodded. "Nice. Why didn't I employ a crew before?"

"You gave up after several failed attempts, including one where your co-pilot sold your ship to Dar Pulocke."

"Oh yeah."

Keel swiped through the boilerplate formalities of the order and got down to brass tacks. "Is this… is this legit?"

Ravi nodded. "Everything I have been able to discover through our usual holonet channels appears to be legitimate. Garret is going through his own testing, but so far is finding the same results. And if it is not real, it is the most elaborate honeypot I have ever seen. The time it would take to falsify so many data trails just to catch a smuggler who arrived on Taijing weeks ago and has no known connections to the Legion… The odds of it being a fake are negligible."

Keel chewed his thumb and moved toward the cockpit. "All right. Well, I know what my vote is. Let's see what the kill team thinks."

"I'll bring them up on comm."

"You'll what? Ravi, you said you didn't want to risk any of this over comms."

The navigator smiled. "Oh, no. The comms are quite secure. I just enjoy startling you."

***

"Mmmmasters here!" came the voice on the other end of the comm. "How can I help you, now that you've reached the most boring place in the world?"

"Masters, it's Wraith."

"I know. You're the only person who can reach us on this comm."

That wasn't technically true. Admiral Deynolds could also reach the secure comm Kill Team Victory had set up as they waited in a Taijing flophouse to see if they would be needed.

"I need to talk with Chhun."

"Ooh, I'm sorry. Officers below the rank of lieutenant colonel are not permitted to call upon the general directly."

Keel shook his head. Did this kid ever have an off switch?

"Just get Chhun."

The connection went silent, and then a slightly more serious Masters returned. "The general will be with you shortly. I think he's practicing looking distinguished for the holocams."

Keel was content to wait, but Masters, like always, was in a conversational mood.

"So, do you have someone for me to shoot?"

"I might have someone in mind, yeah. Goes by the name of Masters."

"Oh, ha ha. I might be on board with that plan, though. Let me ask you something, Wraith. You ever spend three weeks in a one-room apartment eating Legion rations with a guy like Bear?" Keel wasn't given time to answer. "Do you have any idea the kind of flatulence those ration packs produce?"

"I was in the same company as you, dimwit. Of course I know."

"But do you know what a steady diet of 'Meat Entrée'— the only one he'll eat—does? It's not pretty. Wraith, our toilet requires a hazmat suit. There's so much gas in the room right now that I can literally see the air shimmer. I'm sleeping with my bucket on."

Keel pinched the bridge of his nose. "Maybe you should go check on Chhun again."

"And what even *is* a Meat Entrée? What kind of meat? Does anybody know? No. And do you know why? Because *they* don't want you to know. I have it on good authority that when we go into a place and KTF, what's left behind is what's harvested for this particular menu item."

"Masters. Get Chhun."

"You probably don't remember, but after Kublar, every time we had meat it tasted fishy. Probably because we were eating Koob. Which is disgusting. And now that Ankalor is practically wiped from the face of the galaxy, do you know what Bear is pigging out on and then farting back out? That's right. Donk meat. And that might be worse."

"Masters—"

"So what I'm saying is, I *need* to go shoot some bad guys. Because I can't live like this, man. None of us can. I'm pretty sure Exo and Bombassa are going to rejoin the Black Fleet. It stinks *that* bad in here. And *another* thing— oh wait, here's Chhun."

Keel looked up at the cockpit ceiling and mouthed a prayer of thanks.

"Go for Chhun."

"It's Wraith. I've got something big out of to-day's meeting."

"Is that the one with the Legion-appointed officer?"

"Uh, yeah... What other meeting would it be?" Keel gave Ravi an incredulous look, but the navigator was busy measuring the improvements that Leenah had achieved in the *Six*'s timing cycles.

"Sorry," said Chhun. He sounded distracted. "It's just that I've got a lot on my plate right now. Things are really gearing up. I had to leave a briefing with Captain Bendele on the *Razor's Edge*. I think we're going to be able to add an entire company of legionnaires given the influx we're seeing of retirees, discharges, defections..."

"Well, this is going to be more of the same." Keel transmitted the orders to Chhun via a comm encryption so secure that Garret swore even he wouldn't be able to decode it.

"Okay, I'm not familiar with these," Chhun said. "Walk me through what I'm seeing."

"These are House of Reason–approved orders that points and other approved personnel can issue to non-military operators—typically smugglers, bounty hunters, what-have-you. It's a sort of off-the-record contract. Just about anything you can imagine except assassinations. They use Nether Ops for that."

"Unreal."

"Hey, don't knock it. Wraith made a lot of money cashing in on these when the points needed an MCR threat to go away and wanted it to look like they were the ones who got it done."

"So there's a lot of... I dunno, legalese."

"Skip to page three." Keel paused to wait for Chhun to catch up. "That's the name of every point serving under Commander Lawrence. I'm contracted to get them away from Sinasia and back to Utopion. That was what today's meeting was initially about."

"Initially?"

"Keep reading. There's another list of names on page seven. People they believe are loyal enough to help them mutiny and take control of the sector defense garrison. The points are willing to make a play if Wraith can grab the sector commander and some key NCOs and officers."

"So these are lists of who we need to put down." The excitement was clear in Chhun's voice.

"Exactly. All the points and those in bed with the House of Reason—the ones we need to take out in order to assure that Taijing's Legion garrison will be free of Republic meddling. So once we remove the loyalists... Taijing, and Sinasia, will have a Legion ally already on planet capable of standing up to any Republic attempts to put down their bid for independence. That's assuming you and Deynolds have made progress with the sector commander."

"Not directly," said Chhun. "But I've been communicating with him through my source on Utopion."

"Well, you'd better get your 'source' on the comm pretty soon to let him prepare the guy for what's coming. Because Wraith accepted the job."

"What? Alone? What if I told you Victory couldn't assist?"

"Scroll to the end of the agreement."

Chhun let out a whistle over the comm. "Five million credits. Is that legit?"

"Yeah, as long as I keep one of them alive long enough to make the transfer once they regain long-range comms. There's no way I could make Wraith say no to that. And we both know there's no way you're gonna pass up on this op. So tell Exo not to go all crazy."

"This is happening tonight?"

"Has to."

"Okay. We'll be ready."

"KTF," said Keel.

"KTF. Chhun out."

Keel turned to Ravi. "Well. Looks like we've got a gig."

"Just like old times."

"I'm going to get jocked up." Keel rose from his seat. "Respond to the point that Wraith accepts. It's happening tonight. And then tell him that we're taking some cargo out of here since they won't be needing our help any longer."

"What cargo?"

"Ravi, it's a lie. I just want him thinking that we're off-planet so he doesn't get it in his head that he can change his mind once the eleventh hour arrives." He paused at the door. "But... if you can find something that works for a quick buck, make it happen."

Keel felt good as he moved down the corridor to the main lounge. Almost plucky. It had been a while since he'd played the Keel/Wraith angle. Not since he'd started down the trail that had led them to Tyrus Rechs and, ultimately, where they were now. Ravi had put his finger on it: *Just like old times*.

He found he was looking forward to this mission. And maybe... to the end of this war. Then he'd finally be free to travel from one end of the galaxy to the other on his own terms. No more strings attached. Just a man and his ship.

And Leenah.

Who was waiting for him in the lounge.

"You've got an op?" she asked.

Keel raised an eyebrow.

"Ravi told me."

"But I just now—" Keel looked back down the corridor to the cockpit and shook his head. "I wonder if all the Ancients had such big mouths. Yes, we've got an op. But nothing to worry about."

"I'm not worried, I'm just wondering what exactly is happening. Is the mission a go?"

"Yep."

"And you're ready? Isn't it happening a little fast?"

"Oh, it's easy stuff. Find bad guys. Capture bad guys. Shoot bad guys. Not necessarily in that order, but with Exo around, who can say?"

"And when that's done…?"

Keel nodded slowly, understanding what she was after. "If this goes the way it should—and how could it not with me?—then we'll achieve our goal here on Taijing."

"And then we can see Prisma?"

Keel pursed his lips, not wanting to frown. Going back to En Shakar wasn't high on his list of things to do. He and the little girl got along better now than they did when they first met, but still, Keel wasn't keen on running back to say hello. And he *definitely* wasn't looking to adopt a space orphan. Not in his line of work.

But… it was important to Leenah. "Yeah. After that we should be able to see Prisma."

Leenah embraced him, resting her head against his chest. "I hope she's okay."

Keel stroked her hair-like tendrils. "It's not her you should be worried about."

08

"You're having a hard time concentrating, aren't you, Prisma?"

Prisma Maydoon looked down at the fist-sized stone before her, perfectly round with a stripe of white set against its deep gray like a blazing equator. She hadn't been able to make it budge a centimeter. Ever since she'd done whatever it was she'd done on the Cybar mothership—throwing people and things around as though her voice were a hurricane—she'd been unable to do... anything. She couldn't make this rock move. She couldn't move the tiny one Ravi had given her, either.

She had no control.

She had been stuck on the sanctuary of En Shakar, under Mother Ree's protection, for what seemed to her like years—though in truth it had to be far, far less than that. Time felt... *long* in this place. Stretched out. As though all the seconds and hours that so quickly evaporated and disappeared in times of joy and laughter—those happy days with her daddy, or even the time spent with Tyrus Rechs, those times that were somehow already gone and never coming back—weren't allowed to do that here. The seconds weren't permitted to flitter away. Every sinking sand of time gave its full measure.

And so it felt to Prisma like an eternity since Leenah had left with Captain Keel and the rest of those special legionnaires on the *Indelible VI*. She had been sad to see Leenah go. And even a little sad to lose Captain Keel, who wasn't as bad as she'd once believed. Though she could still think of lots of people she liked more. Especially Leenah. And Skrizz. And Crash.

The war bot was the only one she could talk to now, really. And he could get... boring when there was nothing new to ask him about. And here, where Mother Ree lived, nothing new ever happened. Unless you liked planting gardens and cutting leaves off and stuff. Which Prisma didn't.

Mother Ree said that it was precisely because En Shakar was so simple and peaceful that the people came to her seeking asylum. "An escape from the travails of the galaxy" was what she called it. But to Prisma it seemed like a place people came to to get bored and then grow old and die with dirty hands.

Prisma continued to concentrate on the stone, though she knew she wasn't really doing that. Because her mind went to Skrizz. She wondered where he was right now. The wobanki wasn't a gardener, so he spent the long days wandering through the lush greens of the sanctuary. Sometimes he went out to the cold parts, the ice caverns and caves. She knew this because he'd return late at night to her small hutch with frost around his face and whiskers.

He always came back. Even when he didn't let her see him before she went to bed. She knew he was just outside, tail swishing as he stood guard. Never relaxed or safe or easy. Just... watching.

And she would watch him through the thin pane of window glass. Try to make him out in the deep shadows of night. But only sometimes. Sometimes she would just lie in bed and think about everything that had happened. About Goth Sullus, and if he'd ever be punished for what he did to her. For what he did to her daddy.

Or was it she who was supposed to be punished? Had she done something wrong?

Was Goth Sullus sent to punish me*?*

Mother Ree moved in front of Prisma, her flowing white linen gown swishing like a breeze as she sat down before the girl, her legs crossed, her hands resting on her knees. She looked at Prisma with a face full of warmth and compassion. Understanding, even.

"Prisma," she said softly. "Did you hear me? I asked if you were—"

"I'm concentrating all I can!" Prisma snapped.

She instantly felt her cheeks flush with shame. The healer and keeper of the sanctuary had shown Prisma nothing but kindness. She'd shown her the most unconditional love she'd felt since... since her father.

But Mother Ree radiated compassion and loving kindness toward *everyone* who dwelled in her commune. All those people seeking to find something higher, better, more peaceful in a galaxy constantly ripping itself apart one planet at a time... they all received the *same* love. And somehow, that took something away from it. It made Prisma feel like she was just one of the crowd. That the affection Mother Ree showed her—as wonderful as it was—wasn't really for *her.*

It wasn't a special love.

It wasn't the way her father loved her. Or even the way Leenah loved her when she gave Prisma those big hugs and kind smiles.

"I understand," Mother Ree said, unfazed by Prisma's outburst. Her face never lost its warmth. Her eyes twinkled.

They were very pretty eyes. Mother Ree must have been gorgeous when she was younger. Prisma wondered if this kind, unflappable woman in front of her had ever been a real mother. Men would surely want to marry her. Tyrus Rechs had seemed to like her. Had she and Tyrus Rechs ever had kids? And if they did, where were they?

That was something she thought about lots. Even fantasized about. That Tyrus Rechs had a son, or even better, a daughter, who would come and get her, and then the two of them would go together to kill the man who had killed both of their fathers.

Goth Sullus.

But she couldn't find the nerve to ask Mother Ree that sort of a question. Because she was scared of the answer. Afraid it would be no. And Prisma would be alone again. Except for Crash. Who didn't count. Not exactly.

"When I was on that big ship," Prisma said, "I could move the pebble Ravi gave me almost any time I wanted. But ever since I got here, I can't... I can't get it to work."

"And moving this rock... is it something you *want* to do?"

Prisma drew up her legs and rested her head on her knees. "I dunno. Yeah, I guess."

"Prisma... what is it you want in life?"

To kill Goth Sullus.

"Just to be happy, I guess."

Mother Ree smiled. But not as warm as usual. More like she'd heard what Prisma thought instead of what she'd said. And it made Prisma sad. "Will sitting here all day trying to move the stone make you happy?"

"Probably not. Maybe. If I do it."

"Why don't you help Skyla in the infirmary? He told me that you're there quite often."

Prisma liked the infirmary. Not because she was eager to help and play nurse—though she gladly pitched in when Skyla told her to—but because she had a sort of… fascination with the very process. Dying. Healing. Some of the people there suffered from clear and obvious wounds. From war. Or disease. Others from… just… the cruelties of fate and humanity itself. But they were all broken in some way. On the outside or on the inside. Or both.

And though she didn't know why, there was something about the ones who walked that razor's edge between life and death—going from where she stood in the land of the living to the other side where her father and mother and Tyrus Rechs were—that captivated her attention.

So many people had tried to kill Prisma. And so many people had died around her. Some she knew, some she liked, but most… it was as if they never mattered.

Yet somehow, *she* did. Prisma Maydoon mattered.

And a quiet, wise thing deep inside her told her that at the infirmary, she would understand why.

***

The infirmary seemed to be the only place in Mother Ree's sanctuary—other than the docking pad—that had any sort of modern technology. Prisma figured that was why they hid it away from the gardens and the huts and the fruits and vegetables. Because maybe seeing the machines that kept people alive would remind those seeking sanctuary from the galaxy outside. And maybe that would make them sad. Or make them want to leave.

Mother Ree always seemed sad when people chose to leave.

Not all the gardens grew vegetables. There were big flower gardens with lawns and pathways and ponds that didn't have any food at all unless you were a bird or a bug. But that didn't matter, because these gardens looked and smelled wonderful. Greens and reds, deep ambers and bright yellows, cool blues, relaxing violets and whites. And scents that hung heavy as you walked by, and even came along with you, riding in the curls of your hair and reminding you of the glory of it all when you laid your head on your pillow later that night. Prisma liked those gardens the best.

Mother Ree said that the one type of garden nourished the body and the other nourished the soul.

The flower gardens were usually crowded; the people of the sanctuary often walked through them. But sometimes—like when a "brother" or "sister" left or when a new ship arrived—everyone would go to the landing pad out at the edge of the sanctuary, where the ice still ruled and the cold would whip around and stab you through your robes. And the garden would be empty. And Prisma would go and sit down on a bench she'd once sat on together with Tyrus Rechs, and she would try to remember the things he'd told her about shooting and killing and using her heart.

Because even though everyone else was off fighting against Goth Sullus and leaving her behind with Mother Ree "for her own good," Prisma felt that she would need those lessons.

Today the garden was crowded, and so Prisma only ran through it on her way to the infirmary, taking care to pass by the climbing Spilursan roses so she could take deep breaths of their intoxicatingly sweet aroma.

"You smell nice today," said Skyla, looking up from his datapad as she arrived.

"Thanks," Prisma said, feeling hot in her cheeks and knowing that she was blushing. "I went by the rose garden."

Though he wasn't as handsome as Masters, Skyla used to be a legionnaire medic. And there was something about legionnaires, Prisma noted, that just looked sharp. A confidence and directness. She couldn't explain it. She wished she could ask Leenah about it.

"I can tell," Skyla said. "Come by to visit anyone in particular?"

"Not really. Mother Ree said I should see if I can help."

"Hmm... well, patient twenty-three is due for a sponge bath."

Prisma wrinkled up her nose in disgust.

"Not a full body, Prisma," Skyla said, chuckling. "Crash helps me with those. He just needs someone to clean up his face and neck. He, uh... well, he just needs the help."

The explanation didn't compel Prisma to soften her look of disdain. It wasn't *just* the sponge bath part. She probably wouldn't even mind that. She didn't like patient twenty-three. Not at all.

"Instead of a sponge bath, you should just make sure he never wakes up again."

Skyla dropped his datapad to his side. "Prisma, what kind of way is that to talk about another living being?"

"Says the legionnaire who used to kill living beings for a job."

Skyla frowned. "That was different."

"No, it isn't. KTF, right? That's what Masters and his team of special legionnaires told me about. Hutch needs to be KTF'd. He's a bad man."

"Prisma..."

"He *is*! He kidnapped me and Leenah and Garret and Skrizz and Crash and I know he would have tried to kill us if all his men hadn't gotten killed by the Cybar."

"From what I understand," Skyla said as he moved down the hall, motioning for Prisma to follow, "Hutch got himself into his current medical state because he was try-ing to help you *escape*."

"Only because it was the only way out."

They stopped outside door number twenty-three. Not an automated door. There was technology in this building, but only the medical kind. The doors were still old-fash-ioned. With handles and hinges. Prisma thought it was fun to swing the doors open, though she was always careful not to slam them shut and disturb the patients.

"Still. He's here now, and he's completely reliant on our help. He's been in a coma for months. Honestly, I don't even know what the man's voice sounds like."

"It sounds like a jerk voice."

Skyla chuckled and then covered his mouth with his datapad. "I shouldn't laugh."

He bent down to get eye to eye with Prisma, even though she was as tall as his chest. Prisma didn't like it when adults did that. Crash called it feeling like she was being patronized. She didn't like being patronized.

"Prisma, one of the truths I found here with Mother Ree, when my time in the Legion was over and I was struggling to make sense of all the killing and all the men who died in my hands, was that compassion and love will never flourish in this galaxy so long as we're consumed with who deserves it. It's up to us to find those two wonderful gifts in our own hearts and give them freely. That's what will heal this galaxy, and that's what Hutch needs from you right now."

"I think he needs a blaster bolt to the brain."

Skyla stood up and let out a deep breath. He looked down on Prisma. Not angrily, more like... perplexed. As though he didn't know what to do with or make of the little girl—almost a woman—in front of him.

Prisma had seen that look a lot since her father died.

"Well, if you're not going to help," Skyla said, "you may as well run along."

"I'll help, I'll help."

There was nothing else to do.

Skyla smiled and led Prisma into patient twenty-three's room.

Hutch lay in a bed, white linen sheets pulled up to his bare chest. He was breathing on his own, and looked like he was sleeping. He had been "sleeping" ever since he was carried aboard the *Indelible VI* as they were escaping the Cybar. He still looked big and mean, though Prisma knew that eventually all those Nether Ops muscles would atrophy and he would end up almost as skinny as Garret. The corners of Prisma's mouth curled into a fractional smile at the thought. If the monster couldn't be put down, seeing him turn into a frail, helpless waif was at least something to be happy about.

Skyla fetched an antiseptic pouch and an absorbent rag from a standing cabinet and held them out for Prisma. "Okay, kiddo, you know the drill. Open the pouch and use the sponge inside to clean him off. Just the head and neck—and don't try to stuff it up his nose or squeeze any of the liquid into his mouth. It tastes terrible."

Prisma giggled, and the feeling that she was with a friend returned to her, though she hadn't realized until that moment that it had gone.

"When you're done, use the 'sorb rag to dry him off, then leave everything in that pan over there." Skyla pointed to a scratched and scuffed chrome dish on a moveable nightstand near Hutch's head. "Do you need me to stay around while you get started or can I go check on old Mrs. Renfree?"

Prisma did her best to look innocent. "Oh, you don't need to stick around. I'm sure we'll be fine."

The former Legion medic tilted his head, squinting appraisingly at Prisma. He folded his arms across his chest. They were still strong. Still Legion. "Now I'm thinking I should stay to make sure you don't try to suffocate him as soon as I walk out the door."

The thought *had* crossed Prisma's mind. But she had no intention of actually doing it. That wasn't who she was. Not really. Not for anyone in the galaxy except one.

"Suit yourself," she said.

She walked to Hutch's bedside, opened the antiseptic pouch, and pulled out the sopping sponge. It smelled of chemicals, somehow stale and fresh at the same time. Gently she slid it across his forehead, careful not to let the liquid stream over his brows and into the hollows of his eyes, the lids of which looked pink and gray, as though agitated and exhausted all at once.

When he'd first abducted them, and all through that mission with Andien Broxin to find the Doomsday Fleet, he had always been clean-shaven. So much so that Prisma imagined he must have used a laser-blade to remove the stubble more than once a day. But grooming devices like that were few and far between on En Shakar, and Hutch now had the makings of a respectable beard, if a tangled one. The compassionate thing to do—if Prisma were to follow the advice of Skyla—would be to comb it out for him.

She was about to ask Skyla if he had a comb when she noticed the thick streams of partially dried orange mucus. Understanding dawned on her. "Skyla," she said, wrinkling her nose, "did he throw up on himself?"

"Yes, Prisma. He's been sustained with nanitic hyper-nutrients, but today he had an upset stomach. That stuff on his beard is called bile."

"Well, it's gross."

"It is. And he can't clean it off himself."

Holding the sponge much more gingerly, Prisma attempted to dab at the drying fluid matted into Hutch's beard. She wasn't doing much beyond sending the antiseptic wash down his neck and chest in dribbling runoffs, but that was the best this killer could expect.

Prisma was *trying* to show compassion, but not all at once. And not for him.

"Skyla, you're a doctor, right?" she said.

"Prisma, you know that I am."

"Well, I've been having a sort of… *problem*."

"Like what?" asked Skyla, his voice calm and inviting. Professional. Curious.

"Like… my insides feel all grindy."

"Oh." Skyla took in a quick breath of air. "You mean your stomach."

"Sort of. More like just outside my stomach. It doesn't hurt, it just feels weird."

"Well, try putting something warm on it. Like a hot water bladder. And then let me, uh, know if it keeps up. And I can… ask Mother Ree about it if it continues."

Prisma thought it was strange that the sanctuary's doctor would need to check with Mother Ree about a medical issue. But maybe this was one of those other things people came to En Shakar for.

One of the soul things.

The helpful basso voice of KRS-88 sounded from somewhere down the hall. "Doctor Forster, are you available to see the patient you had me retrieve from the village? Though the medical software package Master Maydoon had installed in me is limited, my analysis suggests that she has no more than a few standard cycles to remain in runtime—that is to say, *alive*."

Skyla looked to Prisma.

"I'll be all right," she said.

The former legionnaire smiled and exited the room. Prisma could hear his voice down the hall. "For a war bot, you're mighty helpful in taking care of others."

"I am only a war bot when it is required of me, Doctor," Crash responded. "I much prefer it when I am not."

Prisma dipped her sponge back into the pouch, not because it was dry, but because it seemed it would take a lot more of the antiseptic solution to clean off nasty old Hutch. She wiped away the sheen of sticky sweat, and the bile and grime. And then she used the absorbent rag to dry him off.

And all the while she half hummed, half sang a tune that her mother would sing when it was Prisma's bath time. A lullaby that her grandmother had once sung to her mother, and her grandmother's mother had sung to her. But though Prisma knew the tune, the lullaby's words were lost to her. Because when her father tucked her in at night and she asked for the song, all he could do was hold her and hum it. He didn't know the words like her mother had.

And Crash never sang to her at all.

09

"What's the bot showing?" asked Bear.

Kill Team Victory, minus Chhun, was stacked outside of a mess hall inside Taijing's Legion camp. Infiltration hadn't been difficult. Most of the perimeter was guarded by marines, and they had the casual, disaffected motivation of people who had gone too long without seeing the reason for their sentry. Or too long without an inspection from a butt-chewing sergeant making the rounds.

Either way, Bear had led his team through a blind spot nestled between two guard towers. Masters disabled the perimeter fence's sensors, and they slipped inside, trusting their Dark Ops armor to keep them invisible to passive scanners.

Once inside, they played it casual. Rather than looking like a kill team breaching the base, they swaggered around like a kill team who owned the place. Which would be a familiar sight to any regular leej, marine, or basic who'd shared acreage with Dark Ops. The fact that Taijing was currently without a Dark Ops attachment was someone else's problem.

The intel Wraith had provided said that the gathering of points and point-friendly legionnaires would be in the mess hall. The stated purpose for this gathering was an optional "sensitivity training" regarding the zhee, in response to the "Slaughter on Ankalor"—which was how the House of Reason was referring to what Legion Commander Keller had done.

That was the cover that Major Endiffron had created in case anyone asked him why he and his fellow points and their friends were gathering together. Though no one did. No one cared.

Still, it was a great cover. Bear had to give the point that much. That it was House of Reason training meant that the points and their ilk would feel compelled to attend. That it was optional meant that they'd be the only ones.

Bear remembered back to his days in the Legion. Before Dark Ops shielded him from so much of the politics that trickled through to the rank and file. It had been bad enough when the House or Senate would force legionnaires to watch holovids when their buckets booted up and then answer multiple choice questions designed to address whatever social outrage was trendy on Utopion at the moment. Special courses on the right way to show concern for natural disasters. Learning to avoid micro-aggressions such as offering good thoughts or prayers instead of monetary donations to a House of Reason–approved charity. Things like that.

The guys always hated that stuff, and would usually draw straws to make one unlucky leej watch the show and write down the answers for all—unless a point was around to order them to do it "the right way."

But no self-respecting leej would be seen dead at an optional zhee sensitivity training. As for the points who were there right now—being seen dead there was a distinct possibility once the kill team breached the mess hall.

"Room's pretty full," said Masters, observing the bot's feed in his bucket. The small bug-sized machine had crawled in through the ducting system and was showing row upon row of legionnaires—some in armor, some in their casuals—sitting and listening to a point talk to them about something. "I'd say maybe a hundred."

"That's a lot of traitors," Bear grumbled.

"This could be more than the four of us can reasonably control," said Bombassa, who was watching the corners for any surprises.

"Which is *why*," Exo said, "we oughta be tossing in fraggers instead of ear-poppers."

"Do they have weapons?" said Bear, ignoring the comment.

"There's a stack of rifles against the far wall of the mess hall. Points following point directives, even it means disarming their own dudes."

"But they did bring them," said Bear.

"Yeah, and a few are holding." Masters sent visuals from the bot to his team's buckets. "Not a lot, but that's where to find them."

"I'm *sayin'*," insisted Exo, "it's time to KTF. We go in hard and we can put these points down before they know what hit 'em."

Bear shook his head. "We go in hard, and with this many, some will make the exits. That plus an alarm and the sound of our blasters means that we could end up in a firefight with our own guys. No. We stick with the plan."

Exo hissed but didn't press the issue.

"I'm going straight for the point doin' the talkin'," Bear said. "The rest of you keep those sorry excuses for leejes covered. Focus on the ones who're armed. But don't kill 'em unless you have to. Do I have a copy?"

"Copy."

Bear nodded to his team, then rolled away from the wall and kicked open the old-fashioned double-hung swinging mess doors. The doors banged against the walls, and the assembled points and other legionnaires jumped in their places and turned to see the racket.

"Down!" thundered Bear. "Everyone down!"

Chairs skidded as the men inside the mess dropped to their stomachs. No one even attempted to make a move for the door. And Bear knew why. There was no KTF in this group. These were soft men born of low standards. Points whose chief skill was keeping their heads down. And leejes who would dutifully do what was asked of them by the points who ruled over them. Just like they immediately did as they were told when a Dark Ops team burst in and shattered their world.

The rest of the kill team poured inside, rifles up and moving straight toward the few armed legionnaires.

"Weapons down!" ordered Bombassa.

Masters and Exo repeated the command with shouts of their own, their voices an assault in and of itself.

The armed points dropped their weapons and joined the rest of the men on the ground.

That left Bear standing in the middle of what he guessed were the ringleaders. Officers in Legion fatigues who had been holding the "sensitivity training." It didn't take long for one of them to give Bear some lip.

"What is the meaning of this? You have no authority to—"

Bear clocked the man in the jaw with the butt of his rifle. He was unconscious even before the back of his head hit the floor in a way that made Masters think he would forget his name and periodically wet his pants for the rest of his life.

"Nobody else talks!" shouted Bear in that wild, deep, and magnificent way that only he seemed able to achieve. A voice that you could feel as much as hear.

Another point standing near Bear opted for a different tactic. He took off at a run. But he wasn't able to outpace the big legionnaire's tree trunk of an arm as he grabbed the point by the collar and slammed him hard against the ground. Bear placed his boot on the man's neck and leaned in hard enough to make the runner's eye's bulge and his face turn crimson.

"Nobody else moves!"

And that was that. Now all the kill team needed to do was wait for Wraith to complete his part of the mission.

***

The Legion base on Taijing seemed to be operated more by marines than actual legionnaires. Though in Wraith's opinion, large elements of the modern Legion weren't much better than marines with shiny armor when it came to fighting. That wasn't an insult, it was simply a fact.

The gap between marine and legionnaire was as thin as Wraith had ever seen it. And it all stemmed from Devers's rise to fame.

Standards had declined, equipment was cheap, and the warrior culture was looked at as suspect, something deemed toxic by a galaxy of soft-handed hedonists eager to declare themselves experts on whatever topic presented itself through the milieu of pop culture and the state-run news cycle. Points were everywhere.

And then the vogue thing became reality holoshows on a point's home planet showing the point's grit in passing Legion training. It was something that most of them could never do in reality, but reality holos were the opposite of reality. And that fiction led to the Legion instructors being replaced with more points—until the whole thing became a shell of what it used to be.

But it looked good for the holocams.

Which wasn't to say that there weren't still real leejes who knew how to KTF. It's just that a lot of them got out of the Legion or ended up stuck in Goth Sullus's shock trooper corps... or went down in Legion Commander Keller's attempted assault on Utopion.

Talk about a big gamble gone bad.

Still, Wraith had been ready for the possibility that a hard-nosed sergeant was overseeing the base's perimeters. But other than a handful of leejes, who seemed busy talking, it was a marine-run operation inasmuch as perimeter defenses went.

Which was to say, getting inside hadn't been difficult.

Wraith's armor, for those familiar with such things, was every bit the work of art that the *Indelible VI* was. It was a modification of his Dark Ops kit, albeit with an after-market helmet he'd paid a fortune for, itself an illegal slice of another Dark Ops bucket. It kept him invisible to virtually all scanners and sensors, absorbed blaster bolts that would punch right through the standard-issue kit, and shrugged off blunt force by vibrating away the energy at point of impact into the entire unit.

It was next-level, and it looked it.

It still showed enough of the Legion style to get gullible points and insecure legionnaires to believe his frequent cover of being a Dark Ops leej on a secret mission—but it was unique enough to stand out in the seedy underworld of mercs, bounty hunters, and assassins. A world he'd risen to the very top of, not counting Tyrus Rechs.

But Rechs was dead. The Wraith was still very much alive.

"I'm inside the wire," he called to the kill team. They remained in the shadows of the demilitarized buffer that sat between Taijing and the base. Though a higher number of Sinasian citizens than ever before had been creeping into that buffer zone, setting up shops and stands in a city that had long ago eaten up every square inch of free space.

"Copy. We're making our move in fifteen."

"Copy."

Wraith moved through the shadows, moving from building to building in a slow, frog-hopping path that would lead him to Legion HQ. Because that was the one place he could count on finding the Legion commander.

The HQ building was a flat-roofed square of reinforced impervisteel and duracrete, designed to take a direct hit from an orbital bombardment. The building sat on a grid to itself, with a fifteen-foot interior blast wall behind it, a comm station on one side, and two combat sleds parked on the other side. Two legionnaires guarded its front entrance, each carrying an N-6 blaster rifle. There was no telling how well they knew how to use them.

Wraith approached from the comm station side, hugging the back of the windowless building as he slowly crept toward the HQ. "Okay, Ravi, time to earn your keep."

"I cost you literally nothing and have saved your life on multiple occasions."

"I bought you those TT-16 bots that one time."

"One time. And only after I had to remind you incessantly."

"Yeah. You never shut up about it." Wraith moved from the cover of the comm building into the open street, then he slipped behind the HQ building in the narrow alley between it and the blast wall. "I also pay you with patience, Ravi. And kindness. So earn it back already."

"Hoo, hoo," laughed Ravi. "Do you know why I am laughing? I am laughing because you actually believe this to be true. Hoo, hoo, hoo. Stand by."

Wraith waited for Ravi, but in standing by he didn't remain still. His passive scanners told him through the HUD that no biologics were nearby except for the guards on the opposite side of the building, so he took three big steps and jumped against the blast wall. He planted his foot a little over a meter up and activated the jump-assist jets in the heels of his boots—just enough to launch him another four feet up as he leapt from the blast wall back toward the HQ.

The jump jets wouldn't let him fly—he didn't care to bog himself down with the fuel tanks necessary to make that happen—but they were enough to give him the extra oomph during acrobatics like this without having to weigh himself down with a strength-augmenting exoskeleton. He'd always preferred speed to strength. In a world with blasters, being fastest meant something. That's how he'd gotten the drop—twice—on Tyrus Rechs.

The second jump had him within grasping distance of the HQ roof, but his HUD was picking up a distortion right along the edge of the roof that might have been an infrared perimeter alarm. So he jumped again, bouncing from the HQ back to the wall. The final jump saw him clear the rooftop edge by a wide margin and land squarely inside.

No alarms, and no motion from the guards. And any holocams recording the area would have shown nothing but a gray blur—a bug flying up close, or some other incidental interference.

"I'm in position, Ravi. Is the Legion commander inside?"

"No. They are summoning him as you theorized they would."

Wraith nodded. All that was left for him to do was lie low and wait. Ravi had called into the HQ via a direct comm line—spliced courtesy of Garret—and had posed as a Sinasian warlord concerned about a potential riot and march on the Legion base. Nothing like that was happening—at least, not so far as Wraith was aware—but the actions of the Legion commander to this point suggested that getting into an open conflict with the Sinasians was the last thing he wanted.

Minutes later Legion Commander Lawrence—alone—strode down the street toward the HQ building. He walked at a dignified, though hurried pace. A sheen of sweat around his temples suggested that he might have jogged part of the way.

Wraith crept to the edge of the roof, directly above the two guards.

The legionnaires snapped to attention at the arrival of the Legion commander. "Sir!"

"Sign me in," Lawrence said, placing his palm on a biometric pad mounted outside the headquarters' primary blast doors.

Wraith jumped down from the roof, dropping an elbow on the top of one of the legionnaires' shiny helmets, and nearly splitting the cheap thing with the impact. As the kid went down, Wraith lunged for the other guard's rifle. He grabbed its barrel, forced it away from both himself and the Legion commander, and pulled the legionnaire wielding it off-balance with a ferocious tug. The guard stalled on the tips of his toes to keep his balance, but Wraith sent a forearm shot to the side of his bucket, sending the face of the helmet around to the side of the man's head. With a spin, he grabbed the guard's arm and used the momentum he'd generated to slam his back into the blast doors.

The second sentry was out at the feet of the Legion commander, who was moving for his sidearm.

But Wraith was too fast. He drew his own blaster and shoved the weapon under the Legion commander's chin, pressing his back into the blast doors and pinning him in place.

"Do it, Nether Ops," spat the Legion's sector commander for the Sinasian Cluster. "Send me to hell. You'll find me and a company of legionnaires waiting to beat your ass once you join us."

Wraith removed the pistol from Lawrence's chin and tapped him gently on the shoulder with its barrel. Up until that moment, he hadn't been sure where the Legion commander stood. He hadn't sent his resources to support Legion Commander Keller during the Article Nineteen crisis. His men didn't fight on Ankalor or, luckily, in the Battle for Utopion. But he might not have been able to, given the number of points and loyalists in his ranks. That had certainly been the case elsewhere.

But now, well... Lawrence's supposed final words let Wraith know he was a real leej.

"I'm not here to send you to hell," Wraith said, a ghostly sandstorm of a voice drifting from his external bucket speakers. "I'm here to spring you and your leejes from it."

10

Chhun sat restlessly in his office aboard the Legion destroyer *Intrepid*. Lately, his life had somehow turned into a series of never-ending meetings and comm discussions. He'd moved up in the world. And he was doing what needed to be done. But he would probably never shake the itch to put on a bucket, slap in a fresh charge pack, and KTF.

He'd wanted to stay with Kill Team Victory while they were embedded on Taijing—but they didn't need him. They needed an additional *fighter*, yes, but not him. Not with Wraith and his crew providing support. And not when that extra man—*General* Cohen Chhun—was constantly needed elsewhere.

His datapad flashed. Again. Reminding him that there was an active duty roster of legionnaires that he kept meaning to review. It periodically interrupted the device's sleep screen just to let Chhun know it was still there. And waiting. Bear should have a say in that one, of course. About who the next man on Kill Team Victory should be. And Chhun should be prepared for that meeting. But he knew he wouldn't be. That roster was going to remain as unread as ever now that Bear's team had returned to *Intrepid*.

There just weren't enough hours in the day.

Chhun threw his head back and looked up at the ceiling. "Why did I become a general?"

He knew why. Because the Legion had been in tatters after what happened on Utopion. Because Admiral Deynolds was the de facto leader of what was now the Legion Navy. Because they were all in this together after Article Nineteen had stalled. Because Deynolds had pushed hard for Chhun to take the role and do what he could to bring together the disparate legionnaires stationed throughout the galaxy.

In a way, it was no different from Kublar. The need was there, and Chhun did what was needed, even though it swept into something he'd never imagined he'd be doing. And just as on Kublar, his only aim was to save his legionnaires.

Except this time, *all* of the legionnaires were his legionnaires.

This time, the Legion itself was fighting for its survival.

Still, the battle was going as well as he could have hoped for. Steadily, the Legion had regained its strength. Points and so-called "loyalists" had gradually been purged from a number of Legion bases and naval vessels, and the *true* loyalists—those who were loyal not to the power brokers of the moment, but to the Constitution of the Republic—had taken command. You could argue that the Legion now even held primary sway over galaxy's edge, although Goth Sullus and his empire had certainly maintained an iron-fisted grip on the core worlds.

That Sullus seemed willing to let Sinasia go wasn't surprising, given the losses both sides had suffered during the

Battle of Utopion. The unholy attack of the sentient machines—a prime example of unchecked House of Reason power almost destroying the galaxy—had left no one in a position for a winner-take-all fight. Because that's what it would be.

Chhun wasn't prepared to subject his men to those stakes either. Not yet. Not while there remained options.

And with the way Sinasia was going, those options appeared to really be opening up.

Wraith and the kill team had managed to neutralize every point and every loyalist on Taijing. Legion Commander Lawrence had declared his loyalty to the Legion and Article Nineteen in a public holofeed and then ordered the points to face court-martial for crimes of treason. Their rank-and-file lackeys—indoctrinated kids that went through Academy believing that men like Silas Devers were the heart and soul of the Legion—were dishonorably discharged.

Most of them would probably go home and stay there. A few would find their way to the Black Fleet. But that was okay. Because after all his talk about destroying the Republic, Goth Sullus had proved himself to be more than willing to work with the political machine to hold on to power. And that had riled up more than a few legionnaires who'd initially been swayed by his mission.

Exo was still hot about it.

The chime on Chhun's door sounded.

"Come," Chhun called.

The door swooshed open and Bear, still in his armor save for the bucket, stepped inside. "General."

Chhun nodded. He didn't want to be called "General" by a man he'd fought beside and bled with, but he knew there was nothing else for them. "Good to see you, Bear." He motioned for the legionnaire to sit down. "I've got to admit that I haven't had time to adequately look over the duty roster for your kill team."

Bear grunted. "All due respect, sir, that's about as surprising as getting the snaps from a Taijing hooker."

Chhun failed miserably at hiding his smile. "That obvious?"

"You're trying to do the job of a kill team leej, and Major Owens's old job, *and* be a general. You're not an AI, man. These things take more than a few seconds."

Chhun nodded appreciatively. "That being said, your team can't get by on just four legionnaires. I thought about folding you together with Kill Team Warbird and going with a ten-man unit."

"Warbird's been doing good work. We don't have enough Dark Ops to consolidate and still get what needs doin' done. But I do have a suggestion if you're open to it."

"You read the list?"

"Hell no."

Chhun chuckled. "Okay. Then...?"

"Reactivate Sticks."

"I'm sorry, did you say Sticks?"

Bear nodded. "Yup. He was medically discharged, but he's found his way back to *Intrepid.* Lotta leejes are finding their way out to the edge to join the fight after what happened."

Chhun nodded. That much was true. So much so that Admiral Deynolds had been forced to contract work to outside code slicers—a somewhat sketchy but harmless bunch connected to Keel's crewmember Garret—just to keep up with the background checks. Not that it would be too difficult for Nether Ops to sneak someone in if they wanted to. Which surely they did. And had. Nether Ops had more than enough crooked legionnaires on their payroll.

But between Legion bases like the one on Sinasia joining the cause, units shedding their points and tracking down the Legion on the edge, and the influx of recently discharged or retired looking to grab a rifle and KTF, Chhun continued to see an unexpected inflow of reinforcements. Enough that he was really thinking about how they might bring about Article Nineteen.

"Can he still go?" he asked Bear.

"Well, it's been a few months since his injury. But his legs are working, yeah. And he hasn't forgotten how to fight."

Chhun gently rapped his fist against his chin in thought. "Bear, there's a reason legionnaires with cybernetics are discharged. If someone tossed a bot-shocker in the room, he'd go straight down like a paralytic."

Bear held up both hands. "I know, General. But finding men who are kill team ready..."

Finding *anything* was hard work right now. Even if you had it, you didn't know where it was, or in what condition, or who could get it where it needed to go. He and Admiral Deynolds were trying to rebuild a galaxy-spanning Legion from the tattered remnants that were left after the Battle of Utopion, and though he was encouraged by the constant influx of returning leejes and ships, every new element had to be organized, integrated…

If Cohen Chhun was going to make this work, he needed to let go.

"Bear, I trust your judgment. He's on the team if you say so."

The big legionnaire nodded, looking surprised at how easy that was. "All right. I'll let the boys know."

"Good. After that, I want you to link up with Kill Team Warbird. Wyatt McMillan is the lieutenant there. I want you to get me some names for a leej who could fill Major Owens's role."

Bear looked at Chhun with confusion. "I usually work with Marko, Warbird's team leader."

"I understand that, but this needs to be done by the officers in charge. That's McMillan and that's you. Congratulations, by the way."

"You're… making me a lieutenant?"

"That's right."

"All due respect, sir, but becoming an officer sort of makes me want to kick my own ass. I'm just fine stayin' an NCO."

Chhun smiled. "I wasn't thrilled about it when it happened to me either. Stunned is more like it. But looking back, it needed to happen then, and it needs to happen now. The NCO has been the backbone of the Legion—the only thing that kept us an elite fighting force as men like Captain Ford went to Dark Ops and points kept filling the commissioned spots." He drew an invisible circle over the top of his desk. "This? This right here that we're building? The Legion needs men like you serving in its officer corps. When we take back this government, it will be years before we have capable men graduating from the Legion's officer schools."

Bear shrugged. "I didn't follow half of that, but yeah, I'll do it, sir. Of course. Thank you."

"You're welcome." Chhun made a note in his datapad to update Bear's credentials. "How's the rest of the team? Haven't had the chance to talk to any of them in a while."

"About the same," said Bear, nodding. "Exo has been telling everyone lately that—"

A chime sounded from Chhun's datapad. He pulled it out of his pocket. "I'm sorry. I have to take this right away. Dismissed."

"Okay," Bear said, rising from his seat. "Good talkin'."

Chhun nodded and stepped into his inner office, already speaking to whoever was on the other line. "Go for Prime."

"Wanna bet on the game this weekend?"

That was the phrase used by this particular agent to let Chhun know that he was calling from a safe location, with no reasonable presumption that his secure line had been compromised.

"My wife would kill me," Chhun said, giving the response indicating that all was well on his end.

"That was masterfully done with Sinasia and the senator and Legion Commander Lawrence," said the informant.

Chhun sat down and watched the holofeed of his outer office. Bear had left the room. "I think so, yes. Of course, none of that would have happened without your giving us the intel, Legion Commander."

"Don't call me that," replied Legion Commander Washam. "I ain't no kelhorned Legion commander. Call me Wash. My *friends* call me Wash."

This was the tenth time at least that Legion Commander Washam, the Dark Ops spy implanted on Utopion in the aftermath of the war on Psydon, had told this to Chhun.

"Only because you insist, Wash."

"I do. I do insist. An old man ought to be able to insist on a few things. Ought to have earned that much."

Chhun smiled. Wash was hardly geriatric, but Psydon had been a long time ago, and the sharp features and dark hair of the man who'd fought through those jungles that Chhun had seen through old holo-clippings had been replaced with wrinkles and white hair.

"We keep losing former legionnaires, by the way," Wash said. "Heard an entire company killed their point OIC and commandeered the freighter they were on."

"We brought them in last night, yeah."

"Goth Sullus... he broke a lot of hearts in that outfit of his when he didn't immediately break the House of Reason. Now everybody that thought they were doing the right thing is seeing the Legion declare Article Nineteen and Goth Sullus siding with the government to stop it. You'll find a lot more deserters if they get the chance."

"That brings its own concerns. With so many new men, we can only screen them but so much. I'm wary of Nether Ops agents infiltrating."

"Don't be. Nether Ops is neutered for the time being. They were all recalled to Utopion to work as a sort of secret police. Everyone investigating each other for signs of treason. What Sinasia did… a lot more systems want to do the same."

Chhun didn't see how *every* Nether Ops agent could have successfully left the field, but what Wash was telling him matched up with Wraith's report from Sinasia. The spook he'd run into had been a Black Fleet man, not Nether Ops.

"Well, I know you didn't call just to chat about deserters," Chhun said.

"No, I didn't," said Wash. "They're comin' for Sinasia."

"So Kaar was lying when he gave that sorrowful farewell speech about how Emperor Sullus was a man of peace seeking prosperity for the Imperial Republic? I don't believe it."

"You're being sarcastic."

"It's hard not to. I'm a legionnaire."

"Well, for what it's worth, Kaar wasn't lying. I've known him a long time, and he rarely lies, if you can believe it. He's the type that tells just enough truth. And in this case, the truth is that the Black Fleet and the Imperial Legion *aren't* coming for Sinasia."

Chhun was confused. "So… who's coming for Sinasia?"

"The zhee."

Chhun ground his teeth.

"See, before old Mad Dog Keller went Legion on Ankalor, the zhee were given a lot of things they shouldn't have gotten. Armor, weapons, and cruisers that were *sup-*

posed to be used in the fight to retake Tarrago. And now we know why the House of Reason didn't make that happen."

"Yeah, they've been using them to invade Republic worlds from what I've heard."

"That's the truth. Almost as soon as word got out that all sides took a licking on Utopion, they started gobbling up their neighbors. But Goth Sullus is going to compel them into focusing on Sinasia instead, and it won't be pretty."

"Compel? How?"

"He's given them quiet warning to immediately abandon all worlds they've invaded using Republic-acquired tech... or face his wrath."

"Empty threats don't do much when it comes to the zhee."

"Not an empty threat, General Chhun. He's... unbalanced. I can't put my finger on it, but he's not ordinary. They believe him. They're afraid of him. He in effect told them to attack worlds outside the Republic or he'd bomb their home worlds. And he's sending one of his Black Fleet favorites to oversee."

Chhun nodded. "So then we need to be ready to defend Sinasia from the zhee."

"Better yet, you need to prepare a trap that will wipe the zhee off the board for good. At least as a naval power. Which is why you need to convince the zhee that you're occupied elsewhere. They'd want Sinasia even if Sullus hadn't told them to go after it—it's part of their grand purpose. But they don't want to get into another fight with the Legion. Not after Ankalor.

"No one is sure what to believe about the size of the Legion still out on the edge, but the popular theory is that you're at max consolidation and content to just go from planet to planet causing trouble. So if they see you in a conflict at, say, one of the planets that no longer has naval protection thanks to Admiral Crodus recalling their defense force…"

"…they'll assume we're done with Sinasia," Chhun concluded. "But we can hide enough elements in the Cluster to spring an ambush."

"Bingo," said Wash.

"So we at least partially withdraw and become a headache elsewhere. I assume you have a specific planet in mind?"

"Of course I do. And it's a big one. Not just a diversion. More like the next domino to fall. Get in contact with the leadership on Cononga. They want out. They'll invite you to help. And you'll still be within striking distance of Sinasia once I get word of the zhee mobilization."

Chhun knew a little about Cononga. It was a world that had never forgotten what the Legion did for it in the Savage Wars. And when one country on the planet became a Republic protectorate, a small squad of legionnaires had fought alongside their local militia against some invading neighbors. And now the entire planet was in the Republic, and it had been renamed for the single nation that had brought them there.

"Okay, thank you, Legion Commander. I'll begin preparations to make the best use of this intelligence."

"It's Wash," corrected the old appointed legionnaire. "And I'm not the Legion's commander. But… it needs one. And it ought to be you. Call for the selection. You'll see. Oba's beard, Chhun, you have no idea how much what you're doing is resonating with the galaxy. They already see you as Keller's replacement."

Chhun shook his head. "I'll take that under advisement, too."

"Wash out."

Chhun powered off his datapad and leaned back in his chair. His work pile had just gotten considerably larger.

11

The flower gardens had been busy all day. Every time Prisma wandered from her small hut, she found the others in Mother Ree's sanctuary pitching in to tend or provide or meditate or... whatever else they did to find themselves at peace. They were all nice enough, but they seemed weak to Prisma. They seemed broken.

In many ways, En Shakar was the paradise it was supposed to be, warm and abundant. But it was also a prison, and Prisma found herself feeling like a captive. And unlike all the other prisoners, she didn't *need* to be here. She wasn't afraid of the galaxy. Or the dark.

I can't let myself need any of this, Prisma thought. *I have to be ready to leave as soon as I can.*

She was almost a woman—even though her body didn't show as much indication of that as she wished it would—and someday soon, she would be free to forge her own destiny.

It had been four days since she'd last tried to move the stone on the floor of Mother Ree's humble home. Mother Ree didn't seem to mind that she hadn't gone back to try again. Prisma had seen her a few times, and the matriarch of the sanctuary at En Shakar just smiled as she always did, without so much as a word of rebuke.

And that made Prisma appreciate Mother Ree—and, at the same time, distrust her. Just a little bit.

Because when Ravi had told her to continue to focus on her abilities, he had made it all seem so important. And Mother Ree seemed to agree. But if it was so very important, why wasn't anyone making her do it?

Maybe it was just a trick Mother Ree was attempting to pull. Some sort of reverse psychology. That would be fine. Mother Ree could ask Crash how well *that* worked. The bot had reprogrammed itself to not even attempt such tactics with Prisma anymore after one "exasperating" night—Crash's word—when Prisma had shown him just how ineffective his manipulations were. But that was long ago. So long ago that at the end of the night Prisma's daddy had come home and carried her to her room in his arms. Free from the "serious trouble" the bot had threatened would come.

With no privacy to be had at the gardens, Prisma decided to visit the infirmary again. Maybe Skyla had something else for her to do, so long as it wasn't another sponge bath for Hutch.

She pushed open the simple double doors and slipped inside. The scent of antiseptic solution greeted her nostrils as she waited in what passed for a lobby—a ten-by-ten room with hand-carved and smoothed wooden furniture harvested from fallen trees at the edge of the sanctuary.

Prisma listened quietly to see if anyone was about. She knew better than to yell on arrival like some little kid coming inside from playing all day, announcing her presence. But all was quiet. Normally she would hear Crash's voice or the low tone of Skyla speaking with a patient.

She padded softly down the hall, peering inside a few rooms as she went. She found Crash in an empty room, folded up in his recharge position. The infirmary and the frigid landing pad were the only places on En Shakar where the bot could power up. This place was not designed for his kind.

But it somehow fit his... nature. And he had clearly taken to it. When he wasn't spending time with Prisma— usually because Prisma said she wanted to be alone—he would help plow the fields or assist Skyla with the sick.

"Don't you enjoy it here, young miss?" Crash had asked her just the night before. "If your late father had known of this place, I calculate that things would have been much different."

"Mother Ree couldn't have stopped Goth Sullus."

The bot's optical processors focused on the rude wooden ceiling of their hut. "Do you think not?"

"Yeah, I do."

"It seems difficult for me to consider such violence in this place as what befell your late father and my former master."

"Crash, can we talk about something else?"

"I apologize, young miss. It was insensitive of me to—"

"No. I don't care about that. It doesn't bother me. I just don't want to talk about this place. It's boring. I want to leave."

The bot's gears whined in the darkness. "I... see."

Prisma had thought about asking Crash if he liked En Shakar. But she already knew the answer. And it seemed like doing so would only... hurt the old war bot. If such a thing were possible.

And now he sat stooped next to a recharge station, optics unlit. Likely dreaming of a long runtime on this simple world, free from violence and harm.

My war bot's a pacifist, Prisma thought with a roll of her eyes.

She moved on down the hall, and paused by Hutch's open door. The big man was still locked in a sleep he might never awake from. Prisma stared at him for a long while, trying to remember what other faces had accompanied his. All those men who had died fighting Goth Sullus and then, later, fighting the Cybar.

None of those faces came to her clearly. Only Andien's. She seemed too nice to be with men like that.

But people weren't often what they seemed.

The last room in the hall belonged to the aged Mrs. Renfree, whom Crash had pronounced as having only days more to live. She was still hanging on, slouched over in her bed, impossibly thin and gaunt. When Prisma looked at her, she felt like she saw more skull than face.

The old woman looked up, somehow sensing her visitor. "Hello, little girl." Her voice was trembly and wizened.

"I'm not little," Prisma answered. And she wasn't. At least, not how the old lady made it sound.

"I was a little girl once."

Prisma nodded. The thought wasn't an impossibility to her mind. She understood that people aged. Were young, then old, then dead. If they were lucky. Some only got the first and the last.

"It was during the Savage Wars."

Prisma nodded again, unsure what to say. "I'm sorry." It was the best she could do.

"It was an awful time to be a child. Just awful."

For a woman expected to die soon, Mrs. Renfree seemed talkative, though her voice was light and breathy. As though just speaking the words was equivalent to taking a morning jog.

"But it's always difficult being a little girl."

"Oh."

A hand gripped Prisma by the shoulder. She shouted in fright and wheeled around.

"Relax, Prisma," said Skyla, smiling. "It's only me." He looked past her to Mrs. Renfree. "Are you and Mrs. Renfree... talking?"

"Sort of."

Skyla looked as though he didn't believe it. He stepped farther into the room. "Hello, Mrs. Renfree."

"Hello, little girl," the old woman replied in the exact tone she'd greeted Prisma with. "I was a little girl once."

Skyla turned back to Prisma and spoke in a low voice. "She's suffering from a combination of severe dementia and delirium. Mother Ree has her drinking a tea that helps keep her calm, but she's at the end now. Her mind... it's not all there any longer."

"It was during the Savage Wars," said Mrs. Renfree.

Prisma frowned. She wondered how many times the old woman had repeated this speech. She felt a certain melancholy and realized that she'd actually hoped to talk to the old woman about... well, about life. Being a little girl and then... not being one.

"Have you seen Crash?" Skyla asked.

"He's down the hall, recharging."

"Okay," Skyla said. "I'm going to see if he can power on. I could use him for some translations."

Prisma nodded.

"Goodbye, Mrs. Renfree," Skyla said, and then strode down the hall.

"It was an awful time to be a child. Just awful."

Prisma leaned against the wall and muttered, "Well, that much hasn't changed."

"They would kill our parents and then take us on board their big ships."

Prisma's head jerked up, as did the hairs on the back of her neck. "What?"

The old woman stared straight ahead, as if lost in a memory, her vision distant. "They needed the children. *Wanted* the children. They would murder all the grownups. Mothers, fathers. Sometimes little babies too if they couldn't walk yet."

Prisma swallowed and fought away the fear that was rising from the pit of her stomach.

"On *my* ship," the old lady continued, only now the room seemed thick and heavy. Dark and foreboding. Like it had aboard the Cybar ship when that terrible voice told everyone they would die. Like it had that day when Goth Sullus arrived and murdered her father. "The ship they took me to, they would peel away all your skin. I remember the blood pooling in the bottom of my cell. I remember screaming as a Savage scientist rolled back the flesh on my arm like he was pulling up my sleeve."

Prisma tried to back out of the room, but found nothing but the wall behind her. "I... I don't want to hear this."

Her hands groped for the door. She couldn't turn and look, couldn't look away from the old woman, who seemed in a trance. The room felt warm and dark, as though the light from the windows could no longer come fully inside.

"And he put... things on my arm. Sometimes they were alive. Sometimes they were machine. But they always hurt. They hurt so much."

"No," Prisma said, shaking her head. She wasn't just hearing this story. She was seeing it. She was *feeling* it. "No. Please."

"At first, I prayed for the Legion to find our ship." The old woman's head snapped suddenly upright, and she stared straight at Prisma with a deadness in her eyes. Her voice strengthened. "And then I prayed for death. And then I *begged* for death."

The saucer of tea by Mrs. Renfree's nightstand was rattling as if an earthquake shook the ground beneath it. A pressure built inside of Prisma's eardrums, and she felt they might burst.

The old woman began rising from her bed. Not standing up—elongating. Almost floating.

Prisma's hands kept swimming behind her to find the door. She couldn't turn. She couldn't run. But she could fall out of the hellish room if she could just find the way. Outstretched fingers groped blindly, knocked over a vase on a shelf, sent it crashing to the floor with a smash.

"Prisma?" yelled Skyla, his voice approaching from down the hall. "Prisma, are you all right?"

He entered the room, and Prisma broke free of the old woman's spell and buried her face in his stomach. "*Skyla!*"

"Hey, hey," he said, patting her back gently. "It's all right. It's just a vase. Accidents happen."

Prisma sniffed, hot tears flowing freely now that the grip of fear had loosened. She pulled away, aware of the wet stains she'd left on Skyla's shirt.

Mrs. Renfree sat slouched on her bed, as aged and harmless as ever. "It was an awful time to be a child. Just awful."

"Come on," Skyla said, ushering Prisma from the room. "I'll clean this up later."

Prisma allowed herself to be herded into the hall.

Crash was waiting outside. "Are you quite all right, young miss? You look distressed." The bot held up a finger. "Ah, I take it you spoke to Mrs. Renfree. Young miss, speaking to an individual with such severe dementia can be unsettling, especially to those such as yourself and other children who are not used to the—"

"Crash, I… I don't want to talk right now."

"Ah. Very well, young miss."

The bot followed Prisma and Skyla as they walked down the corridor.

Mrs. Renfree's voice was a distant whisper. "But it's always difficult being a little girl."

Prisma looked in Hutch's room as they passed. He'd shifted in his bed.

12

The knock on Prisma's door woke her from a deep and troubling sleep. Dreams of Savage Wars atrocities raged in her mind.

"Prisma," Mother Ree called from outside. "It's time to get up. We're sending someone on."

That meant they would have a ceremony for someone who had died inside the sanctuary. They'd held the ceremony a few times since Leenah and the *Indelible VI* had left her here. There were no graveyards on En Shakar, so a procession would carry the deceased's body to a funeral pyre, a sea of hands floating the corpse to its flaming end. The entire village was expected to come out and pay witness. Only the very sick would stay indoors.

"Okay," Prisma said, getting out of bed. The floor felt icy to her feet. She looked for Crash, only to find that the bot had already left. He seemed more and more independent. More at home at the sanctuary. "Where's Crash?"

"May I come in?"

"Sure."

Mother Ree pushed open Prisma's door. There were no locks on En Shakar. "He arose early to assist in building the funeral pyre."

"Who died?"

"Mrs. Renfree."

Prisma's breath caught. "Oh."

"Did you know her?"

"No."

"I think you would have liked her. She was a very kind woman."

Prisma threw on her warm robes. The procession would end up near the icy outskirts by the landing pad. "Have you seen Skrizz?" she asked.

"I have not."

The wobanki had been gone for a few days now. Even when Prisma looked out her window at night, she didn't see him. This was the longest he'd ever disappeared without checking in.

Prisma knew that Skrizz didn't particularly like being stuck on En Shakar either. She wondered why he hadn't left along with the rest of them. But Leenah had said that the big cat felt a sense of responsibility to Prisma and that he wouldn't leave until that changed.

Maybe she could convince Skrizz to leave and take her with him.

A din of crowd noise unseated the quiet still of Prisma's rustic hut.

"It's my time to take the place at the head of the procession," Mother Ree said. "Do make sure to come."

"I will," Prisma said, though until she'd been forced to give her word, she had considered slipping away and enjoying the gardens in solitude. Maybe she could creep out of bed tonight if it stayed warm. The gardens were usually pretty empty at night.

Mother Ree opened the door, ushering in more noise from the crowd that carried Mrs. Renfree's shell. They were singing, banging drums, and clacking together hollow sticks, but not in a random, uncontrolled way. It was a sort of symphony. Hopeful and bittersweet. The clanging percussions of life and death.

Prisma stood at her doorstep and watched the procession move past her down the street. There were about one hundred people living on En Shakar—though she'd heard that in times past as many as two thousand had lived here. And though all species were welcome, the current residents were mostly human, and the few non-humans were all biologically very close to human—like Kimbrin. There were none of the more exotic species, like the tentacled Tennar.

Skyla was at the back of the procession. He wasn't part of the swaying, undulating center that stretched and reached to hold the dead old woman above the crowd, surfing her to the fate that awaited her material body. He trailed behind by a few paces, arms held out, face and palms to the sky.

Prisma skipped to the side of the former legionnaire. "Why are you doing that, Skyla? Are you worshipping Oba?"

He looked down and smiled. "No. Oba is a Republic god."

Prisma knew this. "Yeah, so?"

"So that means he-she is only as old as the Republic."

Prisma stared blankly.

Skyla smiled. "Prisma, don't you think a real god would be *older* than that?"

Prisma hadn't thought much about the issue. Oba was just the respectable deity that people worshipped in whatever way they saw fit. And the Republic seemed pretty old to her. "Maybe Oba changed his name when the Republic took charge."

"Maybe."

"So you worship *old* gods. Like the zhee gods?"

"Definitely not."

The procession made the turn down the simple dirt road that led to the landing pad. The towering funeral pyre could be seen in the distance, a wooden sentinel oiled and ready for a body and a spark.

"Do you worship the Ancients?" Prisma asked.

"Seems like any real god would be older than them, too."

"No one's older than the Ancients."

"Hmm."

"Tell me!" Prisma punched Skyla in his side. Playfully. Almost flirtatiously. She wasn't sure where the impulse to do so had come from. It hardly fit the proper decorum for a cremation procession.

But Skyla didn't seem to mind. "I honestly don't know. And because I don't know, I ask this god to allow me to worship them—or him or her or it; again I don't know—the way they truly are. And truly desire. Not the way I want or imagine them to be."

"That makes sense."

"I hope so."

The two walked side by side, Skyla in his pose of spiritual connectivity, Prisma in a more leisurely manner. She watched the people in front of her and spied for birds and other small animals in the trees that encircled the sanctuary village.

The elevation increased, and it grew colder the higher they went. Prisma could soon see her breath puffing out as she leaned forward into the slope. At the crest of the hill, ice crystals towered above them. It was remarkable, even to Prisma, that this sanctuary could be so awash with verdant life in a near-tropical valley, yet it was all hidden by towering glaciers, and its landing pad was accessible only by traveling through a fantastic and beautiful ice cavern.

When Prisma once asked Crash how it was possible, he mentioned something about geothermal heating. The phrase didn't entice her to find out more. It sounded boring.

The procession came to a halt by the funeral pyre, at the very edge of the cold. Prisma's shoes crunched in a thin layer of permafrost. New snow had been cleared away to form knee-high banks. Crash had probably taken care of that.

Ahead, Mother Ree was saying something, but Prisma was too far away and couldn't hear it above the howling wind in the ice caves.

And then the fire started, which was the one thing about all of this that Prisma was interested in seeing. The pyre's blaze swirled high into the air and melted the frost in a wide radius. Prisma could feel a bit of its warmth even at the very back of the procession.

The people of En Shakar, of Mother Ree's sanctuary, were quiet and still as they watched the flames lick their way along the dry, oil-coated wood. Soon it began to snap and pop, and its crackling reminded Prisma of a distant time spent out of doors with her mother. Or maybe it was her father. She didn't remember which; she had been so very young.

Not like now.

The sound of a ship's repulsors came bouncing through the ice tunnels. The glass-like passage into the sanctuary made every starship that went through it sound like it was flying down a bottomless pit, its engine noise making echoes upon echoes.

Prisma pressed excitedly through the crowd. Was it Leenah and the *Indelible VI*? Had they finally come back? To at least see her, if not take her away outright. It had been so long.

She couldn't quite make it to the front, so she tried to climb up an old snowdrift that had hardened to ice long ago. Her boots struggled to find a grip though, and she slipped. "Whoa!"

"Easy, Prisma," Skyla said, catching her elbow and saving her from a nasty fall. He held her hand to keep her steady as she climbed up again. "You sure you don't want to just sit on my shoulders?"

"Oh, please," Prisma said, rolling her eyes. "I'm not a baby."

Her anticipation grew as the repulsors continued their howl through the tunnel. But it vanished, replaced by a sting of disappointment, when an old Grendel-class hauler appeared in view. It wasn't them. It hadn't sounded like them, either. She'd just... hoped.

The ship sent up billowing flurries of snow as it settled on its eight articulating landing gears, and the cold rush of air sliced through Prisma's robes. But she didn't turn away. She only bared her teeth against the frost and watched.

Maybe something happened and they had to find a new ship, she told herself, going to that place where she imagined the most fantastic thing she could in spite of the evidence before her, just to stave off that awful feeling of being left alone again.

Mother Ree approached the ship as its boarding ramp extended. And then out stepped the ship's captain, who was definitely not Captain Keel. The man was dark-skinned and looked kind, but he was not Bombassa either. He was much shorter than Bombassa. He began helping out people who looked wounded, some with skinpacks on.

The look of war, Prisma told herself. *Refugees.*

She hopped down from the frozen snowdrift. They hadn't come. She was still alone. And there was nothing for her here.

At least... not while there were so many people around.

***

The sun had gone down and the people had moved to the fellowship hall near the center of the sanctuary. There was always a big meal with all the best food when someone new came to En Shakar.

Most of the people that had arrived today would have to stay for a long while. They were from a planet named Qadib, and they had suffered the blaster wounds and missing and crippled limbs that came from open warfare. The zhee had called for genocide there, wanting the planet all for themselves now that the Republic was in so much turmoil, and these were the lucky ones who'd gotten away. Although Skyla said some of them probably wouldn't live much longer, and many who did would bear the scars and disfigurements of their experience for the rest of their lives.

So lucky was a relative term.

The disfigurements could mostly be fixed by cybernetics and advanced tissue therapy on more medically advanced planets. But Prisma didn't think they would leave En Shakar. Although the captain might. Something about him told Prisma that he didn't intend to stay with the refugees and live out the rest of his life in peace. Not yet, at least.

What interested Prisma more than the captain was his ship. And it was there that she headed under the cover of darkness, wearing an extra robe to keep the cold away once she reached the landing pad.

Crash was supposed to be keeping an eye on her, but of course he was busy assisting with the meal. Maybe his newfound independence here in the sanctuary was a good thing. Maybe he'd finally found a place for his soul to have rest.

And Crash *did* have a soul. Prisma knew it.

And Skrizz... even if he weren't still missing, he wouldn't have stopped Prisma from slipping away. Why would he? It seemed to be the only thing the wobanki ever did himself. And Skrizz wasn't the parental type anyway. Protective, sure. But parental? Not in his makeup.

Halfway up the hill toward the ice caves and the landing pad, Prisma paused to turn and look back at the village.

The fellowship hall seemed ablaze with the cheerful light of oil lanterns. The sounds of laughter and conversation drifted up to her, and she could imagine the rustic aroma of the stews the sanctuary's cooks had specially prepared. They would have baked treats, too. Pastries and cakes. Fruit pies.

It was too bad she would have to miss out on those. But what she was doing meant more to her than a sticky dessert ever could. No matter how much her stomach tried disagreeing with its low rumbles.

And beyond the fellowship hall were the gardens. They were empty and looked soft and cool in the night. It would have been a good night to go there. She could be alone. She could sit on the bench she'd once shared with Tyrus Rechs. She could sit there and think.

Only that wouldn't do either. She had to get to that landing pad, and she had to do it tonight. Any other time would likely be too late.

The ship still sat on the landing pad, looking like a spider with its eight landing struts. Prisma knew that these models were designed to land on uneven surfaces. They were popular with asteroid miners and galactic explorers. They were also ugly as sin.

Temperatures had dropped below the usual cold with the setting of the sun, and the outer hull of the ugly hauler was covered with a thin layer of frost that obscured its dingy, matte-green paint. Prisma padded through a thin dusting of snow, hoping the wind would obscure her tracks. As if doing her bidding, a sharp gust arrived, sending the flaps of her gown-like robe flapping. She pulled the cloth in tight to shield against the biting chill.

As she reached the front landing strut, she approached cautiously, recalling how Captain Keel kept an automated self-defense system in place for his ship. She didn't want to end up riddled with blaster cannon holes. But no hidden guns dropped down menacingly and no warnings sounded as she walked under the hauler. This ship had no secrets. It was exactly what it appeared to be. That was refreshing. It seemed that nothing in Prisma's life was ever that way, and she found satisfaction in an ugly green ship being nothing more than an ugly green ship.

Now she just had to find a way inside it.

Garret had once told her about a Republic master code that allowed legionnaires and other government officials to enter most private ships built in the last twenty-five cycles. Technically it was perfectly legal and possible for the ship's owners to disable application of this master code, but it was so buried in the various AI and software features that it was usually left alone.

But what *was* the code? Prisma couldn't remember. The skinny slicer had always been talking about techy minutiae. She realized now how useful it would have been to really listen. She had a good memory. She probably would be able to recall the code if she'd paid attention.

Well, she'd figure something out. She wasn't about to just turn and go back down into the village.

As it turned out, she didn't need to figure anything out at all. When she reached the location of the ship's boarding ramp, she must have triggered an auto-sensor, because the hull opened with a hiss and sent out a flat gangplank that periscoped down to the frozen landing pad. Warm, yellow light shone out from the ship's interior, cutting through the darkness like a sunbeam.

Prisma hesitated. Part of her wanted to turn around and go back, but that part was not as strong as her will to continue forward. To seize the opportunity that stood before her.

"Hello?" she called out, taking a few tentative steps up the ramp. "You left your ship open."

Never mind that she had been willing to break in—or at least attempt it. If someone was on board, Prisma didn't want them to think she was a raider. Because now she didn't have to be. And she'd never wanted to be. It had just seemed the only way.

She listened for an answer, but heard only the gentle scattering of the powder-dry snow being pushed across the landing pad.

And then she heard something else. A faint crunch. It was so light that she questioned whether she'd heard anything at all. Except it sounded like a foot in the snow, somewhere in the dark beneath the ramp.

She stood still and strained her ears. But the sound didn't repeat. And somehow that was more worrisome than if it did. Because now she could only replay the sound in her mind. Had it been so quiet after all? Now she re-membered it as being deafening, like whatever had made it was huge. A giant foot or a massive, serpentine body moving through the snow, heading straight for her.

You're being silly, Prisma told herself. She wasn't afraid of anything anymore. Not least some imaginary monster conjured up in the night.

She forced herself up the boarding ramp with a slow, dignified walk, her head held high. If anyone spied her, she wouldn't have them thinking she was a frightened girl running for her life.

The ramp opened into an airlock. Prisma preferred the types of ships where boarding ramps went right into a lounge or central room. Those seemed cozier. But this ship was all about necessity and business, and its designers hadn't seen the need to impress anyone when they walked aboard. A single door, about as wide as Prisma was tall, with a transparent impervisteel viewing port, sealed the airlock from the rest of the ship.

Prisma turned around and looked down the ramp, seeing only as much as the lights inside the airlock illuminated. Small flakes of snow traveled their confused, spiraling path along the wind, passing through the light just long enough to shine before disappearing once more into darkness. Her heart was beating faster than it ought to, she thought, and her mind fed her images of some horrible tyrannasquid appearing with beaks and tentacles at the base of the ramp, writhing upward to ensnare her.

But there was nobody there.

With the airlock sealed, it was unlikely that anyone aboard had heard her friendly calls from the foot of the ramp. So she pounded a hand against the glass, then stood on tiptoes to look inside. The window was an inch or two above her eye level; she was short for her age. Or so she imagined. She hadn't exactly spent much time around other girls her age.

She took in the ship's interior as her breath fogged the glass. Nothing was flashy. The deck plates were simple rectangular grates. Everything from benches to counters to stools looked like it folded up into the wall to clear space. As though the design concept for the hauler had been based on a cramped Utopion apartment in the alien districts.

"Hell-looo!" Prisma called, knocking on the airlock door once again. She couldn't see anyone inside.

To her right was an override door release, a large handle like a flight throttle. She grabbed hold of it and pulled it down. It gave her a little trouble, but she was pleased to be strong enough to activate it.

The door slid open, releasing a rush of warm air. It felt nice, and as Prisma stepped inside, she appreciated the sudden temperature change. She glanced back down the ramp again—still empty. All the ship's warm air was rushing out to escape into En Shakar, and the captain probably wouldn't like that, but she didn't want to close the door behind her. It seemed like if someone found her on board, it would seem less suspicious if she didn't try to cover her trail. She would seem more innocent. And that was a tactic, she had often found, that kept her out of a good deal of trouble.

She listened carefully once more, but heard only the soft thrumming of the ship's life support and central servers. She was all alone, and felt secure in the silence.

She would need to reach the cockpit to do what she had planned. Which meant that she'd have to figure out where the cockpit was in this old hauler. It wasn't obvious from the exterior, which meant it was probably some-where at the top of the ship.

For now, she was in a hold of some sort. It was empty save for a few repulsor crates stacked in a corner, a thin layer of dust suggesting they were full of equipment the captain and crew kept around for themselves. Probably emergency repair parts. Keel had those on his ship, too, but he didn't let them get dusty. A small workstation stood beside them—really just a console and table with a bolt-ed-down bench. But it had a datapad sitting on it.

The trip to the cockpit wouldn't be needed after all.

The datapad powered on slowly. It looked to be a pretty old model, and someone had managed to crack the screen. Its corners felt unnaturally smooth and worn, and there was a bit of black grime at the edges of the screen protector that had been placed over the damaged original screen. With as cheap as these things were, Prisma won-dered why its owner had hung on to it for so long, and in such condition. Sentimental, maybe.

There was no lock screen, and Prisma found she had full access to the pad's entire suite. She pulled up the comm. A device as old as this would probably have a severely lim-ited range, perhaps only inside the ship itself. Unless...

She pulled up the comm's connection listing, and sure enough, she found a strong sync with the ship's in-ternal hypercomm. Which meant that she could use the old hauler as a relay and hope that it could find a comm station somewhere nearby that could get her call out free and clear.

She punched in the commkey she'd memorized. She'd paid attention when *that* was given to her.

The old datapad brought up an antiquated loading screen with a comm logo that Prisma had never seen before. She wondered when this thing was last updated. But she was soon rewarded with a connection light. Now the person on the other end just had to answer.

A tired face appeared on the datapad's screen. *Leenah.* There were sleep lines beneath her eyes. The call had woken her up.

"Leenah!" Prisma shouted. She sounded to herself like a little girl, but she didn't mind. Because for the first time in what seemed like ages, she was happy.

"Prisma?"

"Yeah, it's me!"

Leenah smiled and repositioned herself in bed, causing her own datapad to sway around and cast the glow of the screen on rumpled bedsheets.

Prisma frowned. "Where are you, Leenah?"

"In bed."

"That's not your bed. That's Captain Keel's."

Leenah gave a patient smile. "Prisma…"

"You're not supposed to do that until you're married. My daddy always told me that."

"Look," Leenah said. She panned her datapad around, showing an empty bed. "Captain Keel isn't here. He's on a mission to a place called Cononga. It's just me watching the ship until he gets back. Well, and Garret. But he's not in here either. Not in a million years."

Prisma realized how much she was frowning and softened her expression. "Oh." She sat down on the floor and wedged herself beneath the workstation.

"Prisma, are you okay? How are you calling from Mother Ree's?"

"A ship came by today with some refugees, and the captain said I could."

"Well, it's wonderful to see you, Prisma. I've been aching to get back there, but it seems like the *Six* is destined to be everywhere in the galaxy but the place I most want to be."

"Where's that?" Prisma asked. She thought she knew the answer, but she was afraid that Leenah might name some exotic locale where she could be beautiful and with Captain Keel. Or back home or...

"With you, silly."

Prisma giggled. Which bothered her. It sounded like a little girl's laugh. And she was almost a woman.

"Aeson thinks that after he hunts down..." Leenah stopped herself, as though she just realized she was being too free with her words. "After he finishes this assignment, our next stop will be to see you."

"And bring me with you?"

The smile didn't leave Leenah's lips, but it was a pained look now. "I'm sorry, Prisma. I wish, wish, *wish* that were so, but until the galaxy stops losing its mind... it's just not safe for you. Not like it is with Mother Ree.'

Prisma wanted to fight this. Wanted to ask why *Leenah* wasn't staying with Mother Ree if the galaxy was so downright dangerous. Besides, things didn't seem any worse than when Goth Sullus and his murderous henchmen killed her father and forced her to flee her home to go mix with opportunistic smugglers and criminals.

But that would cause a fight. A fight Prisma would lose. Leenah, more than anyone, seemed always able to turn away Prisma's anger and diffuse her swelling urge to be obstinate. And in the end, none of that was what Prisma wanted. It wasn't why she'd come here.

"Leenah?"

"Yes, Prisma?"

"Did your mother ever..." For a moment Prisma's mind hovered there, aware of the litany of possible questions she could ask—she *wanted* to ask—about everything from love to attraction to how to navigate her own body. But what she asked surprised her. Because it was so simple and old and spoke of a deep longing that the coming of age hadn't quite squelched or driven away. Because it never can fully be driven away. Deep down, it's always there.

"... did she ever sing to you?"

"Like when I was little?"

"Yeah."

"She did. It was a song called 'My Princess, My Girl.'"

Prisma bit her lip. She had to summon all her courage to ask her next question. Even though it ought not to have required any. But the world, she found, had a way of making the ought-nots into painful realities.

"Would you sing it to me?"

Leenah laughed and rested her mouth against her palm and the top of her wrist, casting a sidelong glance. Maybe like it was a little silly. But before Prisma could backtrack,

Leenah lifted her head in a way that looked almost regal. "I can. But I need to sing it in Endurian. It doesn't sound right in Standard."

Prisma nodded.

And then Leenah closed her eyes and began to sing. Haltingly at first, and a little off-key, but she soon found the rhythm and the melody.

Prisma hugged the datapad to her chest as Leenah sang, so many light years away. Tears streaked down her face. She wiped them away with the sleeve of her robe, careful not to make a sniffle or sound that would take Leenah away from her singing. Beautiful singing. The best Prisma had ever heard, because it was the purest. It was sung with love. Sung from the heart.

Leenah must have felt that connection, too. She repeated the song, softly singing words that Prisma didn't comprehend, but fully understood.

Prisma stopped wiping away the tears now. She pulled the datapad away from her chest and watched through watery, blurry vision as Leenah sang to her, her eyes welling with tears of her own, her voice threatening to crumble with emotion.

When she finally stopped, Prisma whispered an emotional, croaking, "Thank you."

And then footsteps came rapidly up the ramp and through the airlock.

"Hello?" a man's voice called.

"I gotta go!" Prisma said, and she turned off the datapad before Leenah could reply.

13

"Anybody here?" called another male voice. A pause. "Nothin' looks outta place, Cap."

"All right." The first voice. It sounded cautious, but not overly so. "Probably the wind and snow playing haywire with the external door sensor."

Prisma heard boots walking along the deck. Two men. And a third, not wearing boots. Or at least not wearing boots that made as much noise as the others.

She pushed herself deeper under the workstation, hoping that whoever it was would pass by without noticing her. And leave the way open for her to escape. A tall order, but it was better than being caught with someone else's datapad in her hand.

"And the airlock door," the one referred to as Cap said—obviously the dark-skinned captain Prisma had seen helping carry refugees to Mother Ree. He seemed nice, but Prisma reminded herself of just how often things weren't what they seemed. "You're sure you left it in the open position?"

"I'm sorry, Cap. I don't remember. Thing's been sticking so much lately that I might have."

"That'll have to do. We can do a sensor sweep before we rack up for the night. Wouldn't want any creepy-crawlies stowing away." The captain shuffled his feet somewhere in the unseen distance. "Now then, stranger. The ship is what she looks like. Luminoh Adventurer—Grendel-class exploration and mining vessel. I call her *Julie's Honey* for reasons that are my own. Like I said before, I don't need a crew. These Adventurers were designed for one-man operations. But that don't mean I ain't willing to take on a good hand like Tommaso here."

Prisma could hear the captain all right, but when whoever he was speaking to responded, she couldn't make it out. It sounded like they were mumbling in a low, hushed voice.

Then the captain spoke again, and she could hear clearly once more. "All the better because I aim to leave tonight. No pay. You work off your transit fees on the jump to Gerk. You stay on after that and I'll cut you in on the next job."

This seemed to agitate the prospective crewman, because now they were speaking much more loudly. So much so that Prisma became aware that the language being spoken wasn't Standard, it was Wobanki.

She rolled out from under the workstation. "Skrizz?"

The wobanki was standing just outside the airlock with the ship's captain and another man. All three jumped.

"Oba's saints in heaven!" the captain said, covering his heart. "You nearly sent me to the final dock, little girl."

Skrizz's ears went down flat, and he purred something. Something that Prisma was either too upset to understand or simply hadn't learned yet in her time learning the catman's language.

"Skrizz," she said, "are you leaving?"

"*Eh wabba la sha-sha.*"

"Is this little one yours?" asked the other man—the captain's mate.

Skrizz gave a half-purr and swished his tail.

"I'm not little," Prisma said. "And Skrizz doesn't own me and I don't own him. But you need to answer my question, Skrizz. Are. You. Leaving?"

The wobanki looked from Prisma to the two men, then nodded. "*Jebb oppa ru sah.*"

Prisma gave a slow nod. "Then I'm coming too. I'm not gonna stay here any longer."

"Uh, sweetheart," the captain said, bending down to look her in the eyes in that patronizing way she hated. "I can't take you."

"I'm not your sweetheart."

The captain's mate laughed, hiding his mouth behind his palm.

"Well, that's all right. You may not be my sweetheart, but I am the captain of this ship. And I'm not taking a little girl off of En Shakar unless Mother Ree gives me a real good reason to."

"And *that* is something I will not do." Mother Ree appeared at the top of the ramp, just behind the others. Her voice was stern, and with the wind whipping up her robe and hair, she was as close to angry as Prisma had ever seen her.

"Why not?" Prisma demanded.

"Because it's not safe. Because I vowed to protect you here."

"Yeah, well, nobody asked *me*. No one ever does!"

Mother Ree's voice grew softer. "Prisma, Captain Pereira has made his decision clear to you. As have I. If asking what others want means so much to you, now you have it. We both want you to stay here."

Prisma flushed with anger. She balled up her fists.

The datapad at her feet moved—just a few centimeters.

"Prisma..." warned Mother Ree.

"Fine!" Prisma exploded. "Fine! Why should anybody else in the galaxy care what I want?"

And she ran. Out of the hold, through the airlock, and past Mother Ree. Not knowing where she would stop, except that it would still be somewhere on En Shakar.

***

The sound of the ugly freighter could be heard as far as the flower gardens, which was where Prisma ended up, though her legs had grown tired from running long before she'd arrived. It was where, deep down, she knew she'd go.

She sat alone on the stone bench where Rechs had spoken to her about how to kill a man. Had talked to her about the things in your mind that would try to stop you, like some pre-programmed code of ethics. And how to get around that mental block in order to make sure you didn't let them kill you first. There were other things, too. How to deal with that first rush of guilt and why it was a good thing if it never fully went away.

"Do you still feel guilty when you shoot people?" she'd asked him that night, in the garden with the moon making the white bell flowers around them glow as if fairies lived inside.

"No," he'd answered.

Now she sat alone in the same place, listening until the ship had traveled so far into the ice caverns, so far away from the sanctuary, that the sound of its repulsors died away completely.

And she was a little more alone.

She sat there like that for a long time, angry at Skrizz, and then returning to her fantasy about finding the orphaned children of Tyrus Rechs and having a new family who would see that justice would be done to that wicked murderer of fathers, Goth Sullus. And then her mind grew fatigued. She sat and stared at the blue moss at her feet, zoning out completely. The cold stone bench had long been warmed by her body heat, but she was anything but comfortable. Her legs were on the verge of going to sleep, and her tailbone was numb. She didn't feel good. She felt like her insides were scrunching and pinching together. It felt gross.

And she knew why. She knew what was happening.

She could barely remember her mother. And her father, who had ushered her from one safe house to the next after her mother died... he hadn't talked to her much about what it meant to be a woman. But she'd watched holos. The documentaries about the human body and how things worked. She was not so sheltered as to not know what life would bring to her as a part of her growing up.

And now it was here.

Her legs ached and begged for her to stand. Her heart ached for different reasons. She wanted to cry, but held on to a vow that she would not. She would never cry again. Not if she could help it. Though somehow she doubted she'd have too much choice in the matter.

But you do have a choice.

Prisma heard the words clearly. She looked around the empty garden, searching for someone among the flowers and dwarf trees. "Hello? Is somebody out there?"

No reply came back.

Prisma's eyes were adjusted to the dark, but she saw not so much as a leaf swaying. She couldn't tell where the voice had come from. It was almost as if it had spoken inside her very mind.

"I have a choice," she repeated to herself. Though she was sure the thought was not her own.

Yes.

And then Prisma had a sense that this voice was indeed distinct, and coming from somewhere on her left, where the creeping wilburs emerged from a fish pond to open their flower pods and release their heady plum and red wine aroma in little bursts of phosphorescent pollen.

A man stood there, in the midst of those plants. His face was concealed beneath a hood. He seemed like a shadow. Seemed to be standing in the pond itself. No, not in it. On it. He looked like he was standing on the surface of the water.

Prisma stared at the man for a time, her mind aware that she should get away, or at least exhibit extreme caution. But she felt no fear. She was perfectly at ease.

"Who are you?" she asked.

"Your life is not without choices, Prisma Maydoon." Now the man spoke aloud. She could hear his voice clearly. It was strong and rich, confident but free from arrogance. It reminded her of Ravi, but without the accent. "You should know that."

Prisma wrinkled her brow. She certainly didn't *feel* like she had choices. It felt like everything in her life had come upon her whether she wanted it or not. When was the last time she'd done anything but react to what was happening around her?

It was when you went to find a bounty hunter.

Prisma didn't know if the thought was her own or spoken by the stranger standing among the creeping wilburs, but it was true. That was the last time she'd attempted to control her own destiny. And she'd managed so much. She'd almost managed to have Goth Sullus killed. If it hadn't been, if it hadn't been for...

If he hadn't failed you.

Prisma shook her head and looked over to the stranger. The back of her mind continued to tell her that she should be alarmed, but she felt perfectly safe and at ease. "No, he tried. He destroyed everyone just to get to Goth Sullus."

"They've all failed you, Prisma," the man said. "But when you made your own choices... you didn't fail."

Prisma looked down at her feet again. Unsure what that meant, or if it was true.

"Young miss." The voice of Crash came from somewhere distant in the garden. "Are you there?"

Instinctively Prisma looked to the stranger standing on the pond, feeling as though by his reaction, she might know more of his heart.

But he was gone.

And that left Prisma unsure what to think. Was he a friend? He hadn't made her *feel* as though he was an enemy. He seemed to... seemed to *care*.

"I'm over here," she said, not wanting to shout, and trusting the bot's audio sensors to detect her voice.

The large war machine came stomping down the garden path, his metal feet clanging against the flat stone slabs or sinking into the mossy ground whenever he stepped off the path.

"There you are, young miss."

"Here I am."

Crash stood several meters back, his optics scanning the surrounding garden. "Are you alone? I thought I heard a distinct voice aside from your own."

"Just me."

"Ah." The bot lumbered closer. "Mother Ree suggested that I find you. She intimated that you would be upset. You do not seem upset."

"I'm fine," Prisma said, but her throat distorted the words. A lump formed, and her body released a cocktail of hormones and emotions sure to make her cry. But she would not cry. She would not.

Crash seemed to sense this. He stood next to her and extended his hand toward her face, only to pull it back as if unsure what to do. Finally, he brushed her cheek with the back of a hand that had killed untold sums. "It will be all right, young miss."

The bot's hand felt icy on her face, as though he'd just finished using his frame to plow snow away from the landing pad. Prisma instinctively moved her head away from the robotic fingers.

Crash folded his fingers into a soft fist and dropped his arm to his side. He seemed… sad.

"Thank you," Prisma said, not wanting to hurt her oldest friend. And wondering how it had come to be that such a possibility had ever even entered their relationship. "For saying that."

"Of course."

Prisma stood, her legs shooting pins and needles in protest and her numb feet offering no help with balance. Her seat felt wet and sticky. And she knew why.

Crash noticed as well. The bot's optics whined and zoomed in the quiet of the garden night, examining where she had been. "Oh dear, are you hurt, young miss? I detect—" He stopped himself. "Oh dear."

He looked down at Prisma, his optics and processors all whirling at once, trying to navigate a myriad of decision trees. Clearly Prisma's father had not programmed KRS-88 for this particular eventuality.

"Young miss, it would seem you have started your—"

"Crash, I know. And I don't want to talk about it."

"You are… all right?" The bot's optics zoomed in, as if ready to study Prisma's face for signs of deceit. "My general human biologic software package suggests that the onset of menstruation in pubescent females can be a traumatic experience."

Prisma fought a fresh rush of hormones calling for her to cry. She killed the urge, replacing it with a roll of the eyes and a head tilted upward in exasperation. "Crash. Never talk about this again."

"Very well, young miss." He paused as if to consider his words. "Very well... Prisma."

The pair walked back to Prisma's hut. The rest of the village had gone to bed, and all was quiet.

Skrizz was waiting for Prisma at her front door. He hadn't left after all. He'd decided to stay. Here. With her.

She stopped to face his towering form. She reached up on her tiptoes and stroked the big catman's furry neck, eliciting a purr that Skrizz seemed unable to keep inside and less than pleased to have made.

And then Prisma went inside to clean up and prepare for her life. A life with choices. The stranger had been right about that.

She was no longer a little girl. She was a woman. With only a wobanki and an ancient war bot to help her on her way.

14

Bear sat with his kill team on a docking sled being pulled through the *Intrepid*'s docking bay to their staging area. The sailor driving the sled flipped on something old, a steady strum of a bass guitar making introduction for a slightly nasal singer to belt out an odd half-sing half-rap about falling to pieces. The legionnaires bobbed their heads in unison to the beat as the sled snaked through full companies of legionnaires who'd gathered from across the galaxy to join the rebellion.

Outside the massive main docking bay's shields, the blue-green planet of Cononga loomed. The planet had long been loyal to the Legion—even more than they were loyal to the Republic, some felt—which was why, after the Battle of Utopion, Goth Sullus had specifically sent the newly legitimized MCR army here to occupy Cononga for the Empire.

But that was before Sinasia's successful—for now— bid for independence had shaken things up out on galaxy's edge. The president of Cononga had happily responded to Chhun's outreach and was eager for the Legion to liberate his people as they had Sinasia.

The Legion was showing itself to be bruised but not broken. And lately, Chhun had been on a roll. In recent days alone he'd orchestrated a stunning defeat of an

Imperial destroyer and three MCR cruisers in an ambush outside the Ackabar system days after it had departed from Sinasian space.

Star systems were taking notice.

"Let's go," called Bear as he jumped off the still-moving sled. The rest of the kill team followed, hopping from the mover as it slowed in front of their shuttle.

Sticks staggered just a bit, but found his balance in an instant.

"Need some oil for those knees?" joked Exo.

"Somebody call a tech!" shouted Masters.

"I got it," said Sticks, his face registering no pain or annoyance, just an icy cold determination to KTF.

Squadrons of Raptors and tri-bombers were already streaking toward the planet. The light show of the initial planetary bombardment—requested by Cononga's government and approved by Admiral Deynolds, who was only too happy to oblige—had already wrapped up. Now the featherheads were going down to clean up and make sure the dropships and shuttles had clear landing paths.

Word was that the Conongan militia had already begun engaging the MCR and shock trooper forces. And now the Legion was here to make them pay.

"Marines!" Exo called to a platoon of recon marines. Hullbusters still loyal to the Republic. "Cononga is all jungle once you leave the cities. Bring extra water."

The marines cursed back that they knew what they were doing.

That elicited a belly laugh from Exo. "Just sayin', man!"

"How 'bout us?" asked Masters. "Will *we* have enough water?"

"We're fine," said Bear. "Our mission is to secure the presidential palace in Noi. No jungle fighting this time. Tell me you paid attention to the briefing."

"Thank Oba," said Masters. "Because I'm not sure that Sticks's bot legs can handle the humidity. They'll rust up. And then we'll have to carry him."

"You couldn't carry me if I let you," said Sticks.

Exo chuckled. Bombassa just sat by passively, looking eager to get going.

Bear ignored the banter. "Fighting is going to be most concentrated in the city. MCR and Black Fleet can't hold the countryside. That's a death trap out there. Farmers'll eat 'em for dinner. So the faster we secure that palace, the better, because you can bet it'll be the fallback point for the bad guys once the pincer closes on them."

The kill team nodded.

"Okay. Buckets on. Let's rock and roll."

***

"I think I'm gonna puke, Sergeant!"

Sergeant Arlen Vix shook his head at the young legionnaire. Their combat sled was hurtling toward Cononga inside a massive transport shuttle, along with four other sleds and a main battle tank. They were in reentry and rattling around like sea foam in an ocean wave.

"First!" shouted Vix, his nerves bringing him to yell even though that was unnecessary over L-comm. "Take off your buckets if you're gonna puke. And second, be happy we're not on Ankalor any longer!"

After Legion Commander Keller had brought the Legion to the zhee home world to show the donks that Article Nineteen meant the games were over, Vix and his leejes had found themselves among the thickest fighting, right in the heart of Ankalor City. And then in the aftermath, they had been charged with maintaining order on the world. But after the Battle of Utopion, the legionnaires who served at Camp Rex found themselves stranded. They just barely survived an invasion of cybernetic killing machines, and only because they all inexplicably shut down.

That had turned Ankalor into a scrapper's paradise. Which, all things considered, wasn't the worst thing to happen to that backwater planet. At least it gave the zhee some kind of productive industry. It was now a decent place to make credits if you didn't mind the occasional holy killing and cannibalism.

But Vix and his leejes sure as hell didn't want to stay there. And when they heard General Chhun's call to gather at the edge, they didn't hesitate for a second. None of them, at the time, really knew what was left of the Legion. The *real* Legion, that is. Not that *Imperial* Legion full of "loyalists" and lackeys serving that point SOB Washam.

But even if all that was left of the Legion was General Chhun, an N-6, and half a charge pack, they'd have joined up. He was Legion. They were Legion. That was all that mattered.

And now the whole of Task Force Grinder was about ready to KTF in the effort to strengthen the Legion's growing foothold in the galaxy. Each planet that successfully defied the Imperial Republic brought them another step closer to Article Nineteen. And vindication.

"Thirty seconds to touchdown," called the Navy pilot flying the lumbering shuttle.

The sled drivers gunned their repulsors, drowning the bay in noise and sending anything that wasn't tied down flying. A final check before preparing to roll out. The combat vehicles groaned against the magnetic stasis plates that held them firmly in place.

"All sleds reporting green for launch," Vix's driver called out over the squad comm.

The shuttle dropped, sending Vix's stomach into his chest.

"Ten seconds!" called the shuttle pilot.

"This is it!" yelled Vix. "Don't puke! Don't puke!"

"Touchdown! Get out of my bird!"

The transport shuttle's massive armored cargo doors fell down into a ramp, flooding the three waiting combat sleds with Conongan sunshine. As one, the drivers revved to maximum acceleration, screaming out of the shuttle the moment the loadmaster gave the final "Go!" to announce that the stasis plates were off.

Vix watched the scene unfold through his forward monitor. His sled gunner had already begun firing at the shock trooper lines waiting to greet them from dug-in positions. "Don't let up!" he shouted. "KTF! Don't let up!"

The white smoke trail of an aero-precision rocket roared past Vix's sled, bending upward before impacting the smaller, second dorsal wing on the back of the shuttle. That wouldn't be enough to take the big craft down, but it did leave it belching black smoke and lumbering for altitude.

"Sket, that was close!" called Vix's gunner, who had no doubt felt the force of the missile passing by, it had been so close to the turret.

"These guys shoot better than donks," Vix called out. He pinged the driver. "Gotta give the featherheads a chance to get out of here. Take us through the line!"

The driver, already at max acceleration, drove them directly toward the foxhole from which the missile had launched. Shock troopers and uniformed MCR soldiers dropped down as the craft roared through their sandbags and went right across the line.

"Drop doors!" shouted Vix. They were getting out to do it the hard way.

With the sled decelerating, but still very much in motion, plowing the lush greens of the agrarian fields outside the city, Vix called out his legionnaires' numbers—including his own—as each man ran off the ramp.

Behind the lines, they hugged dirt and sent blaster fire into the shock trooper positions. The sled driver kept going, circling the entrenched commandos and popping bafflers to keep what missiles they had confused.

Vix dodged blaster fire to instruct his men where to concentrate their firepower. These next few minutes would be crucial. They were part of a larger force of mobile cavalry designed to neutralize the outer defenses that would threaten their rear if they dropped directly inside the city—as legionnaire drop troopers were now doing. If they were held up—or worse, repulsed—those leejes inside the city would have no one but the Conongan militia to provide support in the street-to-street fighting. It was a battle they would win, Vix was sure of that, but the fewer casualties, the better.

This wasn't going to be a campaign of unlimited resources.

The shock troopers were holding fast. Vix had heard that some of these were former legionnaires. Maybe, maybe not. Vix had come across plenty of leejes who'd joined and then left the Black Fleet. There was widespread disillusionment over what Goth Sullus and his admirals promised, and what they actually delivered. But whoever they were—former leejes or MCRs or mercs or militia—they were fighting well enough to cause a delay, even with tanks booming on one side of them and legionnaires and combat sleds behind them.

And then Vix heard one of the most glorious sounds any legionnaire ever hears in combat. And one of the most frightening. The low growl of a buzz ship, the slow-moving armored flying tank capable of chewing apart just about anything unlucky enough to find itself in its leisurely sights.

"Got a target for me, Legionnaires?" called the pilot.

"Paint your targets for me, Grinder," Vix told his men over the squad L-comm.

His HUD filled with pinpoints showing where his men were shooting, and probably a few other spots that they weren't able to get effective fire on, but would like shredded all the same. Vix packaged the data and transmitted it to the buzz ship pilot.

This was joint warfighting. This was what things looked like when the Legion was free to use all its resources at once. No questionable muscle-flexing like Keller and Hannubal had done on Ankalor. No points tying hands behind their backs. Just total KTF.

"Received. Enjoy the show."

The buzz ship waggled its wings before leveling on a strafing run along the dug-in lines of shock troopers. Those Imperials and mids who recognized the sound and knew what was coming attempted to flee their positions. Vix's leejes cut them down. The rest were torn asunder by the blistering firepower of the buzz ship's main cannon. It chewed a line through the landscape, exactly following the HUD readout to avoid friendly fire. By the time it pulled up, the mids and shock troopers were less than meat, and the legionnaires were whooping and shouting oaths.

The ship again waggled its wings before buzzing away to find new prey. And Oba help them when it did.

"Mount up," Vix called. "We're rolling on Noi. Time to bring some freedom to these kelhorns."

***

Intel was absolutely right about the fight on Cononga. The Black Fleet space defense was gone—pulled away for reasons known only to the Republic. Armor was minimal to non-existent, having been annihilated by a combination of orbital bombardment and bombing runs. And there wasn't much resistance left to speak of in the countryside.

But the capital city of Noi was a whole other matter. The Black Fleet and MCR ground forces were still holed up there.

And they had a sket *ton* of anti-aircraft emplacements.

Bear wouldn't have minded Legion intel being wrong about that. He would have preferred flying into the city without taking insane amounts of fire. But now that the Republic and points were out of the new Legion... Intel didn't seem to get much wrong at all. And that meant the pilots of his shuttles had their hands full as they roared in low and loud on their way to the presidential palace.

Arcing lasers of battery fire sizzled past the open side doors of the drop shuttle, punctuated by explosive detonations of flak—because the old-fashioned method of blowing holes in aircraft never really went out of style.

"Seems welcoming," Masters quipped over L-comm.

But nobody laughed. It was tense and hot and dangerous, and no one on board the shuttle was ready to unbottle a laugh. This was how Dark Ops teams experienced total party kills. No amount of training can get around shuttle-sized fireballs and the deathly embrace of gravity.

The legionnaires held on tightly to their speed ropes, ready to kick the thick black cables over the side and descend onto the palace rooftop as soon as the ship came to a repulsor-assisted hover.

"Ten seconds," called the pilot, one of the best the Legion had at its disposal. A warrant officer three named Richard "Rooster" Gallo. He'd flown in the famed Gothic Serpents wing for years, where he made near-impossible insertions seem like nothing. But today his voice sounded tense. Almost worried.

Considering what he was flying into, and through, he had good reason for worry. But there was nothing to do but put up with it or destroy the capital. And blowing up a country's president and citizenry wasn't exactly the best way to assist a planet seeking your help.

"No delays!" Bear yelled. "When this bird gets over the roof, ropes out and you right behind."

"Bingo, KT!" called Gallo.

The kill team kicked out their ropes and jumped out of the shuttle without any hesitation. They watched the roof speed up toward them, taking in everything in real time.

Bombassa landed.

Then Exo and Bear.

"Incoming missile!" called out the pilot, with Masters and Sticks still burning down to the ends of their ropes.

The shuttle swayed, tilting on its axis to let the dumb-fired rocket streak past cleanly. But the motion caused the ropes below to twirl like a kid spinning a rock on a string.

"Hang on!" Bombassa shouted.

Masters and Sticks halted their descents, gripping the ropes tightly as the momentum of the sudden shift swung them out wide. It was all they could do to keep from flying off and plummeting into the concrete streets several stories below.

"Stabilizing," out Gallo called, the strain evident in his voice. "Hang on..."

The ropes slackened in their extreme spin and began to tangle into each other, which could be just as bad.

Masters and Sticks slammed into each other at what felt like thirty miles per hour.

"Whuf!" shouted Masters as he struggled to keep his grip.

But Sticks lost hold of his. Luckily his lateral momentum had been absorbed by Masters, and he went straight down, landing feet-first on the rooftop some twenty feet below.

Masters immediately took up his descent, zipping down to join the others before the shuttle had the chance to send him flying away again.

"We're clear!" Bear called out as soon as Masters hit the roof and he was sure that no one was caught in any of the coiled ropes.

"Good luck, boys," Gallo replied, then banked his shuttle hard so that it seemed to fall away from the roof, roaring down the middle of the street before darting up and away to gain altitude and navigate the blur of anti-air fire that nearly choked out the sun.

"How are we?" Bombassa asked, rushing to Sticks's side. "Functional?"

"I'm good, yeah," said Sticks. "Legs are showing some damage but should be operational." He stood up, and immediately some kind of pneumatic liquid—blue and milky—sprang from his boot. "Dammit."

"That," Bear said, pointing to the leak while trying to keep eyes on the roof. "What's that mean?"

"It means I'm gonna be a step slow," said Sticks, clearly frustrated. "It should self-seal, but if I run out of that juice,

I'm gonna have a forty-pound piece of dead machinery stuck to my leg."

"Let's hope that doesn't happen then," said Bombassa, helping Sticks up and handing him his rifle.

Exo and Masters were already at the rooftop access door, stacked up on either side. The roof, though it had blaster emplacements and sandbags, was empty. It seemed everyone in the Conongan militia was in the streets, fighting it out with the shock troopers and mids. Legionnaires arriving in drop pods were further adding to the chaos.

Things were going according to plan, but Victory needed to secure the palace and keep the president safe. The Empire might not be able to hold this planet, but there was no telling what they might do before losing it. And killing the president… that might be just the thing to dissuade other worlds from attempting an uprising of their own.

"We're up," called Bear. "Blow it."

Exo had already set charges around the steel door. He called out, "Clear!" and blew the thing wide open.

Masters darted inside, rifle ready, looking down his weapon's holographic sight as he stormed down the stairs. Soldiers died in places like this, but there was nothing to do but keep moving forward prepared to KTF any hostiles that made the attempt.

The metal stairs resounded with footfalls as the kill team descended, filling the stairwell like liquid, each man's blaster rifle searching for a target.

"Do we have comms with the president yet?" Bear asked the central comms officer stationed aboard *Intrepid*.

"Negative."

The team reached the door letting out onto the third floor.

"We haven't been able to tell them we're coming," Bear informed the team. "So keep frosty and don't count on any friendlies holding their fire."

Exo checked the door. "Unlocked."

"Banger," Bear ordered.

Exo cracked the door, tossed in the device, and pulled the door back tight.

"Go!" shouted Bear following the blast.

The kill team pushed through, spreading out and clearing corners in a central hall connecting to several bedrooms. One by one they called the rooms clear.

"No sign of anybody on this level," Bombassa reported, returning from the last room in the hall.

Bear noticed Sticks limping. "How's that leg holding up?"

"Could be better." The legionnaire looked down at his damaged cybernetic limb. More fluid was pooling at his feet. "Guess there's a reason they discharge you when you get past five percent cybernetic."

That might or might not be a wise rule in other circumstances, but at the moment, the Legion needed every man they could get. And a man like Sticks was more capable with a peg leg than five fully functional soldiers working for the MCR.

"Bad luck," Bear said. "Happens. Find a window to get on overwatch and see about helping out the militia until the sleds arrive." He looked around at his men. "Who's humping the N-18?"

"I got it," said Masters. He dropped to a knee and pulled a rectangular case from his back. "Thing almost went through my spleen when we crashed on the ropes."

"I'll set this up," Sticks said, taking the case and hobbling to the nearest bedroom. "Don't forget me on the way out."

"Kill Team Victory, this is *Intrepid*."

"Go for Victory," said Bear, sharing the comm broadcast with the rest of his team.

"We're receiving stand-down demands from a Republic major demanding a cease-fire. Says he has the Conongan president and his family hostage. What's your status?"

"Just cleared the third floor. No hostiles."

Bombassa cleared his throat. "Perhaps they are moving?"

"Check it out," said Bear.

Bombassa and Exo jogged to the stairwell and slowly opened the door. "Nothing."

"Keep an eye on it."

Down the hall, the elevator dinged.

"Uh-oh," said Masters.

The door opened to reveal six shock troopers armed with N-6 rifles, all of them clearly expecting the floor to be empty. It seemed the kill team had been only minutes ahead of their foes, who must have moved up through the building from street level.

The shock troopers immediately swung their weapons, but Masters was ready for them. He sent blaster fire on full auto into the elevator. Their armor mitigated its effects, but no armor could hold up to heavy blaster fire indefinitely. The troopers in the front were pressed into their comrades behind them, and Masters's continuing fire pinned them in the confined space.

Bear pulled a pump-action surge shotgun and sprinted for the side of the elevator doors, keeping wide of any enemy fire that might find its way out of the narrow opening. He slammed the wall outside the door, his burly shoulder lighting up the down arrow.

Like a donk holy fighter trusting the four gods to guide his shots, he stuck his shotgun around the corner blindly and sent deafening blasts of energized plasma slugs ripping into the shock troopers until the doors closed, cutting him off.

"Did we get 'em?"

"Maybe half," said Masters. "You kept killing the same two guys up front."

Bear grunted and set his legs apart in a power lifter's stance. He grabbed the seam of the closed doors and began to pull them apart, growling from the strain. Once he'd pried it open enough for the doors to shut off their auto-close function, he leveled his shotgun again and sent more fire into the cables controlling the elevator's descent.

It snapped on the second blast, sending the elevator car into a freefall for a brief moment before the screeching of emergency brakes halted its fall. A blaster bolt came through the car's roof and up the shaft. Bear dodged back and grumbled.

"Still didn't kill them?" asked Masters.

Blaster fire erupted from the stairwell.

"Shock troopers are pushing up the stairs!" Exo shouted. He tossed a fragger into the stairwell. "Frag out!"

"We need to get down to the next level quickly," said Bear. "Masters, get me a peeper. I need to see what's happening on the floor below. Sticks! Get some more fire on that stairwell."

"On it!" The legionnaire had to practically drag his dead limb as he rushed out of the room he'd set up in.

"Exo!" shouted Bear. "Bring me a det-brick. A big one."

Masters pulled out a spherical observation bot and activated it. The small machine hummed on tiny repulsors. "You break a window in there?" he asked Sticks.

"Yeah," shouted the legionnaire between shots down the stairwell.

Using his HUD control interface, Masters guided the bot through the room Sticks had just left. It glided over the discarded N-18 and through the broken window, then decreased altitude until it hovered outside a window the next level down. "Sending the feed to your HUD."

Bear examined the live holorecording playing in a small window in his visor. "And this is right below us?"

"Yeah."

He hustled back to the elevator shaft and held out his hand. "Exo, the det-brick."

"Whoa," said Masters. "You're dropping a whole det-brick on the top of that elevator just to dust three trapped shock troopers? Isn't that excessive... even for you?"

"Not gonna blow up the elevator," said Bear, pressing the powerful brick of explosives flat on the floor and inserting its ignitor dial.

"Dude. What are you doing?" asked Exo.

"This is an old building. Wood and plaster. I'm gonna blow a hole in it."

"You're going to kill us is what you're going to do!" Masters shouted.

Bear looked up at the legionnaire and activated the ignition delay. It beeped urgently. "Better take cover then."

The three legionnaires ran for the far end of the hall and ducked into a side room. Bombassa and Sticks pulled themselves away from the stairwell and moved into the same room to await the blast.

An explosion with all the intensity of a tank firing its main gun in the living room shook the palace. The lights went out and the third-floor hallway filled with black smoke that drifted into the room where the legionnaires had taken cover.

"That'll do," said Bear. He sprang up and moved back into the main hall.

"Holy strokes," mumbled Masters.

The blast had blown a hole in the floor as Bear had intended, as well as an equally large hole in the ceiling. Flames licked a few sections of exposed wood, walls were reduced to their studs, and bedding and feathers were everywhere.

"Lock up the stairwell door," Bear said.

Bombassa placed a wedge beneath the door. The device attached itself to the bottom of the door and the floor with self-screwing fasteners. Whoever was on the other side could kick it for days—it wasn't swinging open. They'd need to cut or blast their way in.

"Banger out!" Exo called. He tossed an ear-popper into the hole in the floor. The subsequent flash and bang lit up the opening below.

"Let's go!" Bear called, reaching the edge of the opening and sending blaster fire down on a shock trooper struggling to regain his footing below.

The rest of the kill team did the same, dropping targets from the hole in the ceiling. Except for Masters, who hopped down onto on a pile of beams, crumbled plaster, and light fixtures, and began to move through the floor, dropping targets and trusting the rest of his team to follow.

He was the first to reach the president, who was struggling with a uniformed Republic officer over a blaster pistol.

Masters dropped the officer with a blaster bolt to the temple.

The president whirled around and held up both hands.

"All good, my man," said Masters. "Sorry about your house, though."

"Secure the rest of this floor," Bear called. "Make sure you clear the stairwell." He hailed *Intrepid* on his comm. "*Intrepid,* this is Vic One. Package is secure."

It was unusual to go through the Legion destroyer overhead for communications, but Admiral Deynolds had felt that the ship would be in the best position to coordinate the battle orders, with Chhun observing from the ship's war room. And truth be told, this had been as smooth an operation as Bear could ever remember. Every sailor, marine, soldier, and legionnaire was operating seamlessly as a united Legion.

"Copy, Vic One. Stand by for exfiltration. Combat sleds are en route to your location. ETA is ten minutes. Say again, ETA is ten minutes."

"Copy." Bear switched to squad comms. "Ten minutes until go-home." He turned to the president. "We'll get you to a more secure location to oversee the situation shortly."

Exo walked up. "Stairwell is secure. Don't know about the ground floor."

"Are your family and staff accounted for?" Bear asked the president. "Is anyone on the floor below? Perhaps hiding upstairs?"

The president shook his head, thick, shining strands of black hair bobbing across his face. "No. We were all on this level. We tried to get down to the vaults in the basement, but... they stormed the compound so quickly."

"They knew you were their only shot at making us slow down," Bear said. He didn't add how foolish he thought it was that the president hadn't already gotten himself to a secure location *prior* to the start of fighting. But Cononga had never been known for its tactical acumen. Their men showed grit, but they didn't think like fighters. "Are there hostiles on the ground floor?"

The battle was still raging on the streets, with blaster fire everywhere. And some of it certainly *sounded* like it was either just outside or right beneath them.

"I don't know. They barricaded us on this level. They got past my guards..."

"Masters. Can your peeper get us a view of the next level?"

"Bot's dead, boss."

Bear turned on his L-comm. "*Intrepid,* this is Vic One. I've got word that all friendlies are accounted for in the palace on the second floor. First floor is unsecured and presumed hostile. Say again, first floor of the palace is presumed hostile."

"Copy, Vic One," said the comm relay man. "Connecting you with Task Force Grinder, en route to the palace."

"Copy."

Sticks hobbled from a room with a middle-aged, almost elderly woman whom Bear assumed was the First Lady. Her black hair held streaks of peppery gray. She looked around at the dead mids and shock troopers with a mix of horror and contempt before getting eyes on her husband and hurrying to embrace him.

"Any other family members we should prepare to take with us?" Bear asked the Conongan leader.

"No. My daughters are studying off-planet." He seemed proud to say, "University of Utopion, one of the mid-core campuses."

Exo scoffed. "*There's* a few hundred thousand credits you ain't never gettin' back."

"Vic One, this is Grinder One." That would be the officer in charge of the combat sleds. Regular army. Or at least the part of the army that believed in what the Republic was supposed to stand for. "We're pulling down the street and seeing blaster fire exchanged between the first-floor windows. Hard to tell who's shooting at who right now."

"It's not us, Grinder One. Might be Conongan militia. I cannot confirm."

"Roger. We'll drive in a little closer and see how they like some cav showing up."

"Copy." Bear let an ear-splitting whistle pass through his external speakers. "Rides are here. Get ready to move. Presidential staff and servants are gonna have to stay put. The sleds'll leave some leejes to keep the building secure."

The rattle of blaster fire from beneath them picked up in intensity.

"Vic One," called the lead combat sled over L-comm. "Whoever's inside is not pleased to see us. Be advised, we are set to engage. Say again, we are engaging hostiles on the first floor beneath your position."

"KTF," returned Bear. "Just keep your aim low."

"Copy. KTF."

"Everybody get down," Bear called to his team. "Shootin's about to start."

The kill team dropped to their stomachs, keeping their blasters pointed at the potential access points, just in case the mids and shock troopers had been successful in circumventing the barricades emplaced throughout the palace. The president and his wife covered their ears as a furious volley of blaster fire erupted from the twin cannons mounted on the tops of the combat sleds.

"How big do you guys think the repair bill is gonna be on this place?" Masters asked.

The barrage of heavy blaster cannon fire died down. Legionnaires from the sleds would be storming the building now, making sure the pathway was clear for the kill team and their VIPs.

"Vic One, we got 'em all cleared out and have the floor secured. Sergeant Vix is inside waiting to escort you to designated exfil sled."

"Copy that," said Bear. "You know, I always liked you basics in the cavalry."

The driver sounded like he was smiling on the other end of the comm. "We're the Legion's basics now, Vic One."

15

Captain Vampa stood with her arms folded under her breasts as she coolly appraised the bridge crew of *The Bloody Horde*, the lead zhee battle cruiser now bearing down on Taijing.

She'd had her misgivings about this assignment. She'd been drawn away from the much-needed refits being completed on her *Revenge*, currently in orbit around Tarrago. She'd wanted to demand—respectfully, of course—to stay and oversee that work. But her position within the Imperial Black Fleet wasn't secure enough for her to go around making demands. And... this order came from the emperor himself. Or so she'd been told. Word was Goth Sullus had chosen her specifically, rejecting the handful of names that had been put forth by his advisors, to lead the zhee war fleet in action against the upstart Sinasians.

Maybe because of that trick she'd pulled at Tarrago?

Regardless, the Sinasians, and the galaxy, had a lesson to learn. Extend yourself beyond the control of the emperor, and you face whatever whirlwind the galaxy has to throw at you. Any calamity that comes your way... you're on your own.

Or you could submit... and be protected by the Empire.

She was here to make sure that the whirlwind, in the form of the zhee, succeeded in teaching that lesson.

"Admiral Halood," called out the zhee executive officer from his station near sensors and comm.

The admiral had eschewed the standard position of every Repub and Imperial officer—standing near the combat information TACAN table—in favor of posturing near the helm, staring forward at his target as though he possessed some singular sense of vision revealed only to him. As though he were "leading."

Halood did not turn to face his XO's address. That was not done in zhee society.

The XO continued braying out the latest report from the sensor sweep. "Negative hostile assets in-system. Target clear for approach... standing by to commence combat operations at your call, Most Noble Son of the Brass Trumpet."

In lieu of the brevity of rank, the zhee liked to use some type of ceremonial ancestral noble title system.

Because that will make things easier, thought Vampa.

The admiral, in full zhee dress, flowing white robes, and gem-flecked turban, raised a hairy muscled fist and drove it forward at the planet.

Vampa, to the rear, shuddered. Visibly. Something that would have gotten her smacked right across the face had she been a zhee mare and not surrounded by her command staff and a guard of the emperor's finest shock troopers, all heavily armed.

As it was, the zhee wisely chose to not notice this egregious disrespect.

True, the in-system TACAN looked too good to be true. Which was what made Vampa nervous. Very nervous. But she was a commander, and she'd flown a dozen different ships into similar situations. Sometimes she'd been wrong, and sometimes she'd been horrifyingly right.

Like that time at Breeda. She was a Republic captain on a light shuttle pulling a standard supply run out to some leej outpost when suddenly the small ship was in over its head and running from three pirate raiders. She'd barely gotten out of that one, and with no room to spare.

There was no reason this situation couldn't turn into a Breeda. In a heartbeat. Of course, instead of a single light shuttle, she was now flying with ten zhee battle cruisers, courtesy of the fall of the Republic.

Somehow that didn't make her feel any safer.

The zhee had been making the most of their new muscle. On their own, they'd been acting like a pirate fleet, raiding defenseless worlds and taking down corporate freighters with escort Q-ships. And calling these engagements "battles."

They had yet to fight a real one.

And that was a reason she'd been sent here, today, right now.

Because the emperor expected a fight. With that weird uncanny sixth sense of his.

She'd tried her best to give the zhee some basic knowledge of tactics beyond rush, point, and shoot. But their palpable insolence had made it clear they wouldn't be taught how to fight by a mare from an unclean race such as the humans. The admiral had turned away with a snort. She'd finally worked through a shock trooper liaison—which is to say, a man—and managed to force the lesser officers to sully themselves enough to learn how to *almost* fight as a team in the event the fleet of powerful late-production battle cruisers saw real action.

"Identify your targets and capabilities. Then coordinate effective fire to take out their anchor ships," she'd told them—through her male interpreter, who repeated her words verbatim in the exact same language and tone.

That had been met with stony coal-eyed silence.

Then one of the less-arrogant zhee, a junior officer who'd seemed willing to learn, or at least willing to listen, asked, "But then who will get the honor of the kill?"

Honor of the kill? Vampa shrieked inside herself bitterly. Thinking, *There's no honor, or even glory, in space combat. What you get is to not die today.*

She told them that. Skipped the ridiculous male interpreter and *told* them that. Hectored them to the point that she moved from pedantic into nigh-hysterical. One of her aides had to step in and let her know that the message had been received.

She'd never been a good teacher. She was a better master.

"Our neck is on the line out there too," she came back at them in the briefing room almost like she was going to physically attack them. "Any of you break that formation, and you expose a weakness within the design system of these technological monstrosities you still haven't figured out even after they were gifted to you on a silver platter! And once that gets opened up, we're all dead! Us and you!"

Again, her own staff had to pull her back from the edge of insanity. Reason returned, and she straightened her

Imperial black officer uniform. No decoration for saving the fleet's butt at Tarrago and making the dream of empire come true that day.

But you didn't see her asking for any of the glory.

The irony was not lost on her. Some cold, calculating, ever-watchful side of her saw that too.

Now, entering the Sinasian cluster among the Suwaru nebula—seven planets, thirty-six moons, and over four hundred stellar bodies of consequence—she had an uneasy feeling that anything could go wrong in the next few minutes.

Pirates.

A rogue Repub fleet looking to settle a score.

Mines.

Local resistance using fast attack ship swarm-style tactics. She doubted the zhee could keep up with a frenetic running firefight.

They'd lose a ship. Maybe even a few.

And how would she look in front of the emperor then? She'd been sent out here to make sure they ruined someone. If they took losses and still ruined someone, then maybe it wasn't all so bad. But if they took losses and nothing got ruined... then that was a failure, and maybe the next time *Revenge* put out to do some Imperial pirating of its own, she wouldn't be in command on the bridge.

So... success was critical.

If she had some fighter cover, or some long-range scouts, she could sweep the local moon. Perfect place for a fleet to be hiding out and waiting to pull something tricky.

"Advise the zhee—" she had just begun to say when the grand zhee admiral barked out, "Prepare for orbital bombardment. Target civilian population. Independent targeting."

Not a bad move, thought Vampa. *But not yet. Clear your sectors, you idiot!*

"Contact!" shouted a zhee sensor officer a minute later. "Lone Republic destroyer. Inbound on course track zero-seven-three."

Vampa leaned over the TACAN table and brought up the sensor contact. The latest Repub data analysis still loaded with the ship's data core cross-checked the hostile signature against known ships.

A moment later the word "Intrepid" appeared along with a briefing on weapons and shielding, crew and other data.

"Message from target!" roared another zhee with barely contained anger.

The admiral should be announcing battle stations, thought Vampa.

"I will hear it," snorted the Grand Son of the Western Brass or whatever the zhee admiral was calling himself this afternoon. He conveyed an air of royal indifference toward anything temporal.

Static and interspace distortion popped and crackled as the in-progress transmission played.

"... Admiral Deynolds of the Legion Expeditionary Fleet commanding the *Intrepid*. Stand down and leave this system immediately. It is currently under protection of the Legion in accordance with the rules of Article Nineteen. Stand by to face..."

The woman's voice was calm, cool, and in control, and Vampa didn't like it one bit. Deynolds was a pro. Worst thing you could face in a situation like this.

The zhee admiral ordered the transmission cut off.

He turned about in a fuming rage.

No doubt, thought Vampa, *because his will is being opposed by a "mare."*

The incoming ship was not breaking off and in fact had increased to attack speed.

Well, thought Vampa, *good luck, sister. Feels a little desperate.*

"Target has launched torpedo!" shouted the sensor officer.

Against ten state-of-the-art Aegis-linked battle cruisers, a single torpedo wasn't going to do mu—

Except they aren't Aegis-linked at the moment, Vampa thought. A chill shot through her extremities and her heart began to skip. The stupid admiral had ordered the fleet to bombardment. Meaning they'd switched off Aegis in order to target individual tangos on the world below.

"We've got a second torp running!" shouted one of Vampa's aides, who'd stationed himself near sensors. The zhee sensor officer had read both targets as one instead of doing an acquisition solution before engaging the PDC fire control teams.

"Switch over to point defense posture. Reactivate the Aegis system!" shouted Vampa from her place at the rear of the bridge.

No one moved.

The zhee were braying at each other in their harsh, nasal language, spit flying as both torpedoes streaked in at the battle formation.

Vampa turned to the electronic warfare station and saw that it was completely unoccupied. She motioned for her staff to get it up and running, and knew there wouldn't be time.

The zhee battle fleet was arranged in three wedges of three ships each, all following the lead battle cruiser *Bloody Horde* toward Taijing. The two powerful SSM torpedoes fired from the *Intrepid* streaked past the *Horde* and slammed into the *Divine Zephyr*, the leader of the central wedge. With the zhee fleet not at battle stations, the torpedoes didn't even have to evade point defense fire, and they blew through the almost nonexistent power to the defensive screens.

They savaged *Zephyr*'s bridge and engineering in one swift strike. The mighty ship was blind and dead and began to drift from her place within the wedge.

Standard SSM reload time was two minutes.

"The crazy mare!" shrieked the zhee XO. "She's going to ram us!"

Which indeed was exactly what it looked like the Legion destroyer *Intrepid* was about to do. *Intrepid* was a smaller class of ship than the super-destroyers or the massive Black Fleet dreadnoughts, which gave it certain advantages in attacking the zhee battle cruisers. The cruisers had been designed to compete with much more powerful ships—for no reason anyone in the House of Reason had ever managed to adequately voice, because other than the other even more powerful Repub Navy ships, there *weren't* any other big ships. And now *Intrepid* shot through the zhee formations at reckless speed, her turrets raking the cruisers' hulls as they passed.

The *Intrepid*'s point defense cannon systems were switched to engage a larger class of targets than just incoming missiles and fighters, adding additional firepower to the sudden assault.

Vampa drew her blaster pistol and motioned to her troopers to do the same. Instantly, and without hesitation, they did.

"If you want to live, do as I say!" she shouted at the bridge crew.

The zhee's claws went to their knives and personal weapons.

But the admiral reacted differently. Perhaps he saw that they were in over their heads. He hadn't survived the homicidal promotion plan of the zhee hierarchy by being strong and dumb. He had some sense in him.

"Tell us what your plan is, woman," he snuffled.

"Order all ships to come about to starboard. Engage the Aegis and prepare for ship-to-ship combat. In other words... go to battle stations now!"

The admiral brayed that this should be done, and with no other ship hitting another ship, the maneuver came off within thirty seconds.

Save for the *Divine Zephyr*, which was now dead in space.

Rescue operations, surmised Vampa, were beyond this bunch.

The next tactical picture presented a lone running Legion destroyer and nine battle cruisers giving chase.

"Range to engage with turret fire?" shouted Vampa.

The zhee checked with their admiral to make sure that they could comply with this request. Once permission had been granted, a lone target acquisition operator called out the answer.

They weren't close enough.

"Why not the torpedoes?" huffed one of the zhee officers as though attempting to disparage her tactical skills.

"Not on a fleeing target. Too easy for them to evade, or just outrun. Only on closing targets."

Duh, thought Vampa.

The zhee wanted a kill. Wanted to avenge the insult to their fleet. A fleet that had easily decimated every "opponent" they'd managed to face so far.

They'd finally been punched in the face. And now they wanted blood.

But Vampa wasn't having any of it. She was screaming at the admiral to back off and return to hit the planet. Return to mission but under Aegis-link guaranteed safety. Chances were the *Intrepid* was reloading and just begging for the zhee battle fleet to come closer to the moon she was running for. Deynolds would try the torpedo trick again because she'd gotten away with it the first time.

Every commander Vampa had ever known would do that.

She was trying to tell them that when the first zhee stabbed her quick as a cat. Cut her deep across the thigh with his wicked *kankari* knife. And suddenly, right there on the bridge of the *Bloody Horde*, a firefight broke out in full between the Imperial escort and the zhee bridge crew.

Whatever was going on, whatever would happen next, Vampa had lost control, not to mention blood, she thought as she began to go into shock.

The shock trooper captain grabbed her and pulled her back into the fold of armored soldiers. They retreated from the bridge to the speed lift and took it down to the hangar deck and the waiting shuttle. But by this time half the troopers, and most of her staff officers, had already paid for this escape with their lives.

***

The zhee admiral, having retaken control of his own bridge, and fleet, ordered pursuit on the lone Legion destroyer.

The first sign that something was wrong didn't come in the form of another inbound charge and torpedo drop from the Legion destroyer. It came when the *Mad Demon's Kankari* exploded. Suddenly and without warning.

"What has gone wrong now?" cried the admiral.

Zhee scrambled to read the sensors as best they could, trying to determine why the lead battle cruiser of the port wing wedge had seemingly self-destructed.

Comms to the wounded battlecruiser yielded nothing but screams and unheeded damage klaxons. Escape pods were already flinging themselves away into space and boosting for one-shot jumps to nearby Repub naval bases because no one had bothered to go in and change the navigational escape protocols.

"Mines!" said a zhee junior officer who'd taken some time off from interstellar looting and pillaging to understand sensor contacts better.

"The demon mare dropped mines all over..."

"What do we do?" asked the grand admiral. He leaned over the mass of officers staring at the displays.

"Full stop?" ventured the junior sensor officer. "They could be motion-activated. I suggest diverting max power to our sensor systems to see how many they are. If that is your will, Oh Grand Immenseness."

The admiral thoughtfully studied the displays without any comprehension whatsoever. Then he nodded, shaking his great muzzle.

"Do it!" he barked. "Full stop now! Max power to sensors!"

A hushed silence fell over the bridge as orders were relayed. The zhee fleet fell to a dead stop.

The sound of distant blaster fire and explosives could be heard as the Imperial shock troopers continued their desperate escape.

"Data coming in now..." mumbled the young zhee officer who'd figured out the sensors. "By the sand god's muzzle!" he brayed.

Sensors revealed a picture of near space. Small dots were closing in from every direction.

"Are those... fighters?" asked the grand admiral ignorantly.

No one said anything. Because the answer was not good.

"Warning..." announced the ship's AI. "Proximity alert."

"What is that?" asked the admiral, sounding more like a scared zhee colt than the Most Noble Son of the Brass Trumpet. But no one noticed. They were all scared.

"The mines..." said the junior officer. "They're closing in on us."

The first one made contact with the battle cruiser *Call of Death*. Then three more gravitic mines swarmed in on the wounded ship, rupturing her hull in direct contact explosions. Precious atmosphere and crew were swept into the void as more mines closed in like sharks to a sudden feeding frenzy. Zhee crews were ill-prepared to deal with damage control, to say the least.

Then the *Brass Djinn* flared and exploded, taking her sister ship *Rage and Fury* with her. The *Supreme Vengeance* tried to power her engines up and escape, but succeeded only in drawing the swarm of mines directly to her main drives. Her engines rippled, bloomed, and detonated, sending debris and plasma-burnt hull plating scattering across her surviving sister battleships.

And more mines were still coming in, as though appearing from cloaked deployment systems along the last known trajectory of the Legion destroyer *Intrepid*. The mines raced in toward the stricken battle cruisers like locusts falling on a field at harvest. Proximity alarms raced like a heart going into tachycardia.

The zhee admiral could only bray impotently about ungodly demon mares as no less than twenty mines struck the flagship and exploded.

***

Lieutenant Kat Haladis held her breath. The Imperial shuttle was hovering off the hangar deck of the flagship, but still within the wide internal bay. Out beyond the bay was nothing but destruction as the hangar opening presented an apocalyptic view of the disintegrating zhee battle fleet. Ships turned, broke in half, burned, or exploded. Mostly exploded.

"Go now!" shouted the shock trooper captain. "Punch it and get us out of here!"

Kat ignored him, her green eyes flickering between the shuttle attitude controls and the hyperdrive calc computer interface below the jump throttles.

"We're gonna roast in here if you don't get us out now!" pleaded the trooper captain, still in his armor. He tore his helmet off.

Medics were screaming for more plasma at the rear of the shuttle. Vampa was fading on the deck back there.

"What are you waiting for, Lieutenant?" shouted the hard-core trooper in his best drill instructor's bark. Right in her face.

"Gotta wait for the jump calc, Captain! We exit the ship now, mines will hit us too."

Suddenly the entire zhee battle cruiser started exploding all around them. Smaller ships inside the hangar were flung loose from their moorings. Cranes wobbled and collapsed. Even the hull was on fire, consumed as though being eaten by a school of vicious Gendaar piranha-snakes.

"This is it!" shouted the trooper captain.

Kat held position, dancing the ship with throttle and yoke to maintain a picture of the hangar exit within the field of view inside the shuttle cockpit.

"C'mon..." she told the jump calc.

It flicked over to fifty-eight-percent green.

"Good enough," she whispered. Then... "Hold on."

She slammed her hand onto the jump throttles and pushed the controls full forward. Hyperspace opened up... and they were gone.

A second later the entire zhee flagship went up like a powerful firecracker going off right at the center of what remained of the mighty zhee battle fleet. The nearer ships exploded in response, and the rest surrendered to the swarms of mines closing in from every direction.

Other than the Imperial detachment sent to advise and assist... there were no survivors

16

The Nether Ops agent known as X stood on the outskirts of Rawl Kima's largest city, Kahl. Once considered a backwater despite its proximity to the core, the city and planet had become a hub of military activity thanks to the legitimization of the Mid-Core Rebellion once it had been folded into the Imperial war machine.

X was always deliberate about referring to the new order on Utopion as the *Empire*. Even though its official name was the Imperial Republic and simply saying "Republic" was, for the present anyway, still considered acceptable. From his—admittedly limited—interactions with Goth Sullus, X had come to realize how much the man was captivated by the term.

Empire.

And emperor.

So if X wanted to see through his plan to find his way into Sullus's inner advisory council... if he were to lift Nether Ops from its current place as secret police testing loyalties in the core worlds... he would be an Empire man.

At least until that went out of fashion. Because, in the end, the secret to longevity and the way to win the game was to stay on the side with the power to keep the world turning. That was once the House of Reason, until for a brief moment it looked as though the Legion might have the goods… until they didn't and it was expedient to throw in with Goth Sullus.

Which had always been a contingency.

X was grateful that Sullus had chosen not to end his life. But being on the outside and looking in on this new government… this was certainly *not* part of X's plan.

Of course, there were contingencies for this, too.

There were always contingencies.

Steadman Pawoe, the gray-skinned reporter with red eyes and a pinched ridge of skin running along his jawline, shuffled his feet nervously in front of X. "I don't know," he said yet again. "I don't know about this. It seems dangerous."

"My dear fellow," X said, clapping the journalist on his shoulder, "it *is* dangerous. But it's also likely your last opportunity to maintain whatever shred of journalistic credibility you once held."

Steadron curled back his upper lip in disgust. His star had fallen quite a long distance. There was a time when he enjoyed the heady heights of awards and toasts for his work embedded as a war correspondent with the zhee, showing the galaxy the unyielding resolve they'd shown toward those with a bigoted phobia against their peaceful religion. But more recently he'd found himself serving as a usually drunken correspondent from the planet Ankalor. And that wasn't even rock bottom yet. This was all true and indisputable. But clearly, X's comment had him bothered.

"Don't talk to me about my credibility. I remain a verified journalist who produces at minimum two articles every week."

X raised his eyebrows in a diffident stare. He patted his shirt pocket for something, he didn't know what. Perhaps a pipe. It seemed like a good time to smoke a pipe. But the act was for appearances rather than to retrieve any actual item. There was no pipe.

"My boy, that periodical you write articles for will publish the rantings of anyone who submits a screed obeying at least some basic rules of grammar. They pay micro-credits, and only *if* you pass a few million impressions. Your work has nothing to do with 'journalism,' and we both know it."

X paused to see if Steadron would argue the point. If he would, then he'd made a bad choice and would need to cut bait now to minimize his time spent away from Utopion. The path to power involved being in the thick of things there. The wars had gone cold. For now.

Steadron seemed unable to muster a reply.

He knows it's true.

Deep down, they all did.

X continued. "Now, I have arranged for this bot to send your report back to the Spiral News Network—your old stomping grounds."

Steadron looked at the journalist bot. Its cameras were deployed and its antenna was up, ready to record and broadcast.

"But how can I be sure of my safety?" he asked. "The rumors about Goth Sullus don't paint a portrait of a man brimming with mercy. He doesn't seem the forgiving type, and *surely* this will be a blow to the coalition he now leads. I want some sort of guarantee that I won't be held accountable for reporting the situation."

X smiled genially as he picked at his fingernails, though they were already immaculate. "Steadron, there are an untold number of reporters who would *literally* kill to have the opportunity I'm offering you. In fact, my agents have witnessed them doing just that. These are young, fresh faces not yet ravaged by decades of hard drinking and even harder living. That is to say, they don't appear on the holofeeds looking as... *dignified* as you. But they know what a story like this would do for their careers. They comprehend that a story like this would catapult them into the upper stratosphere of their profession."

Steadron looked down, his lower lip sticking out as though he was holding back bitter, angry tears.

"But none of them are standing here with me today. And do you know why, Steadron?"

Steadron shook his head.

"Because of the *story*, old boy. A story such as this, when told by a no-name reporter hungry for a slice of the pie, desperate for fame and galactic recognition... well, sure, it would make a lot of noise. It would seem amazing to those who heard it. Scandalous. Incredible. And also... unbelievable. Because the upstart *needs* the recognition, and everyone knows it. 'They'll probably retract it later,' people will say, '*after* they've made a name for themselves.'"

X looked up wistfully. "Ultimately, the story would be disregarded. Denied. Painted as the ravings of a partisan profiting from the advertising. So the people ignore it as they wait for another, more trusted source, to corroborate. And believe me, once this is out there, the sources I've given you will change their tune.

"But *you*, Steadman. They already *know* you. And though you are now, quite rightly, a laughingstock, in the backs of their minds they remember that there was a time when you risked life and limb as a correspondent to tell the galaxy what was happening out there on the edge. They trusted you then, and they want to trust you again. When *you* tell the story, it will be as much about your redemption as it is a piece of news capable of winning you more awards at this late stage in your career. You'll be a part of this story, Steadron, in a way that no other reporter could be. The man who fell hard and then made good."

Steadron swallowed hard, and X could see in his eyes that he would do his part. He was right about Steadron. He was right about most things.

"All right. I'll do it."

Like a director, X oriented Steadron to the bot and pointed out its holocams. "You look fantastic. And Steadron, I believe you'll find this to be the best decision you've ever made. You're going to be a star again."

Or he'll be executed.

But in either case, X was guilty only of telling the truth. He didn't end up needing to give assurances Goth Sullus would not come down on the reporter. Honestly, he had no idea how Sullus would react. It might be with wrath. Or he might just ignore it. The emperor did seem to have a larger picture in mind. Gone was the day of petty revenge played out in the media.

But none of that really mattered to Steadron, X knew. Not deep down. The opportunity to again be in the public eye, to enjoy the accolades of his peers, was simply too much to resist. That was why X had sought him out. That was how X would set in motion the next piece on the game board.

His game board.

This would get him on the emperor's council. Make no mistake about it.

"This is Steadron Pawoe with a special report for Spiral News: *Unrest on Utopion*. Multiple sources inside the House of Reason and Senate have reached out to me expressing mounting concerns over Emperor Goth Sullus's inability to suppress the rogue faction of legionnaires still attempting to enforce Article Nineteen even after it was declared void by Delegate Orrin Kaar and Imperial Legion Commander Washam.

"These sources also state that more planets are sure to leave the Republic following the successful bids for independence of Cononga and the Sinasian Cluster. Those considering secession were only further encouraged by the Sinasians' defeat of the zhee, which I have been told were sent to invade the planet under the direction of Emperor Sullus himself..."

***

Goth Sullus entered his council room in a rage, though one wouldn't know it from his outward appearance. Temper tantrums and petty outbursts revealed themselves as cracks in the facades of weaker men. His was a more potent emotion, a cold anger silently waiting below the surface. One forged from dispassionate reason—and not the farce that the pathetic Republic House took as its namesake.

You wanted to be emperor. And you took the first opportunity.

Sullus ground his teeth from behind his helmet. The voices often aggravated him. But his servants in the ring spoke the truth. He had grown intoxicated with the idea of an empire—though he had fought the urge—from the moment Admiral Rommal bended knee and declared him emperor.

And that was why you had him destroy himself with the Imperator.

Perhaps. But it was also to stop the threat that had used the Cybar as their vessels. It was always, first and foremost, because of that. He had saved the galaxy. And now he would rule it so it would never again need saving.

And indeed, we are your servants.

The room was full of men bickering, each voice vying to outdo the others. Recriminations and blame for the solidified losses of Sinasia, Cononga, and now virtually the entirety of the edge. Even much of mid-core had declared independence from the Imperial Republic, or signaled that they soon would.

The Legion's victories had been embers set against kindling. That reporter—he had fanned the flames. And the Legion marched on in its quest to institute Article Nineteen.

Though the arguments were heated, all fell silent when Goth Sullus strode into the room. They looked at him somberly, then their eyes darted to the man standing behind him. X. The Nether Ops agent who'd brought Sullus to this point of no return. A resourceful man, if cravenly self-interested. A man who would help Sullus solidify his base of power on Utopion.

You don't need any of them. You have us.

"My Lord Sullus," said Delegate Kaar. "I should like to know why *he* is allowed in this room."

"A pleasure to see you again, Delegate Kaar," said X.

"This man is treacherous," Kaar said, not attempting to hide his sneer. "He has shown a repeated willingness to destroy countless lives in the hopes of somehow proving his blundering decisions correct. He is no friend of this government."

X dabbled about, looking in his shirt pocket. "There is a certain degree of irony in that statement, Orrin—"

"Delegate Kaar." The man insisted on the honorific.

"Yes, Delegate Kaar. A man unable to deliver what he promised to our emperor." Sullus could see that X was playing to the gallery now. "Emperor Sullus was to lead the Empire to new heights, and you would ensure that the Senate and House of Reason supported him. And yet..."

"*I* cannot control the depletion of our militaries! I cannot stop the flow of desertions every day from both the Imperial Legion *and* the Black Fleet. Entire companies deserting their posts. Battleships seized and given to our foes, who are so myopic as to only desire Article Nineteen. These are an enemy blind to the fact that the Republic that once was is gone, and a new order exists under *our* emperor."

He lies. He sees you not as his master. Not as we see you. He sees you as a tool to achieve his own power. Can you not see it?

Goth Sullus held up a hand. "Admiral Ordo. Your network of spies has been unable to slow the advance of the Legion. And it is clear we have in our ranks a traitor. Tell me who."

Ordo cleared his throat uncomfortably. "My lord, the Legion has remained out of our grasp, and our agents sent to infiltrate their ranks have all been, ah, eliminated."

Perhaps it is Ordo? Those dealing in falsehoods are treacherous, master.

"The traitor among us?"

"My lord… I have no evidence to suggest—"

Goth Sullus held up a hand to silence this man who had been with him for years. He turned to X. "You are now in command of Imperial intelligence. Do not fail me."

X smiled. "I won't. I'll find the traitor, Emperor. And I'll have the reporter, Steadron, eliminated. My men already know where he is broadcasting from."

Ordo looked down, stunned.

"Leave us, Ordo," Sullus said. "X shall give you further orders."

When the admiral had left the room, Legion Commander Washam raised his hand.

This one is a friend of the delegate's. Trust him not, master.

"The Imperial Legion stands ready to mobilize from Utopion at your command, Emperor Sullus."

"Send them to Ankalor."

"My… lord?"

"The zhee must be punished for their failure. Their time draws to a close. Admiral Crodus, mobilize on one of the other three zhee worlds and destroy it from orbit. I desire the use of nuclear ordnance. A lesson for the rest of the galaxy."

"My lord Sullus," Kaar interjected. "This will surely erode the support you have from the House of Reason and Senate! Do not let the actions of a minority of quarrelsome senators sway you from the path you are on!"

Sullus paused, then slowly removed his helmet. "In the Savage Wars, there were two men. A general and an admiral. The general's strategy for defeating the Savages was nuclear destruction of every world they conquered. But the admiral protested. There weren't enough worlds to bear the cost of such a ruthless strategy. The galaxy was a smaller place then."

Sullus placed his fists on the conference table and leaned forward, staring at Kaar. "The galaxy is a much bigger place now. The zhee will keep three of their precious home worlds. And they will stay in line forevermore."

You are Goth Sullus. You are a conquering emperor.

Kaar shook his head. "This action will result in open warfare against this government. And may I remind you that after the disaster that was the Battle of Utopion, we are *not* in a position to maintain galactic order!"

The power you need can be yours, master. We will show you. Let us show you.

Kaar railed, giving his most impassioned delivery. Decrying this course of action. Now was not the time for Emperor Sullus to abandon the principles of the Republic. He must stand with the House of Reason. Rebuild. Wait. Have patience.

"How?" Goth Sullus asked the voices. His servants in the ring.

"I beg your pardon?" asked Orrin Kaar, clearly confused.

Show us, master! Show us that we serve a conquering emperor. A savior.

Goth Sullus reached out, channeling the Crux around him, probing at an atomic level for Kaar's spine. Seeking to bend it, to snap it. But it was all so vague and damp. And he could not.

He could not.

We see, master. We see your desire. Grant us leave to bring power to you, master. Grant us leave. Grant us leaaave...

The voices practically begged.

"You have my permission."

Kaar was apparently under the impression that Sullus was acquiescing to his impassioned speech. "I... see. Yes, well—"

And then Goth Sullus moved across the table in a blur, his gauntleted hands wrapping around Kaar's neck. He lifted the delegate off of his feet, watching his eyes bulge wildly and his face turn crimson.

"I have no further use for the House of Reason and Senate." The strength-enhancing armor that had once belonged to Tyrus Rechs held Kaar dangling two feet above the floor as he slowly strangled. "I declare them both... dissolved."

And with that, Goth Sullus broke the neck of the first of the Mandarins. The first among equals in the House of Reason. Because he was a conqueror.

Because he alone was emperor.

17

Pete "Paren" Micale didn't know a whole lot about the planet Ochnia. He knew it was far enough from the core to be considered part of galaxy's edge, but it was closer to a cluster of mid-core worlds known as the Bahnner Row than it was to the next closest edge world. And he knew it was the home of a Republic training grounds for marines and Republic naval personnel who needed combat training. Personnel such as the destroyer liaisons who embedded with legionnaires. And the Wet Sox, commando teams who worked exclusively in underwater warfare. That was technically still the navy's purview even after it had reached the stars.

But that's not what had brought Paren to Ochnia's sandy beaches and rugged mountains. Not Camp Erol or any of the numberless businesses around the base that served its marines, sailors, and families.

He was there because of the carnage.

Not that Paren was the sort who reveled in the stuff like one of those Bronze Guild bounty hunter nutjobs. But the aftermath of carnage often presented opportunity.

The galaxy was in flames. Especially after that last big blowup at Utopion between the Legion and the Republic and the Black Fleet... and the machines.

It was the machines that interested Paren.

Because these bots—which no side officially claimed responsibility for unleashing on military and political targets like Ochnia—these bots were a credit mine. The official narrative was that the bots were an alien race called the Cybar that had timed an attack when the Republic was at its weakest. And only Emperor Sullus had been able to fend it off.

But that was all narrative. And in the end, it didn't matter anyway.

Because however it happened and wherever they came from, those bots all shut down at the same time. Right in the middle of the slaughter and the carnage. The holonets were awash with survivor stories. Humanoids who were looking down the tri-barrel of one of the big war machines, waiting to die, when the bots just... stopped.

And right away, Paren realized that bots this sophisticated and capable weren't just the average servitor model that you could pull out of the back of a speeder and then strip for a few hundred credits or maybe re-sell for a couple thou. As long as you knew a code slicer who wouldn't get you tripped up. These bots had processors, frames, joints made from some of the most precious metals in the galaxy. They had military-grade tech that could be sold on the night markets for more money than Paren was used to making in a year.

And they were just lying around for the taking on ravaged worlds like Ochnia. Waiting for the first scrapper with vision to come and change his life.

Paren was the first on Ochnia. Because he remembered the marine base. And he figured... *there's* a spot a lot of people aren't going to get to for a while. Not anymore. Not with the Republic's new Imperial Legion and what remained of its fleets stretched so thin. Especially not once the Legion showed how hard it was to kill and started arresting every senator and delegate who dared leave core space.

Two days after the Battle of Utopion, as they were calling it, when the bodies were still rotting in the sun, Paren landed on Ochnia with a Titan-class freight hauler, a spare pilot, and fifteen drusic bodyguards armed to the teeth. He'd sunk his entire life's savings into the venture. His apartment, his interest in an asteroid mining company, his old ship—which was much nicer than this one—everything. And he'd landed with barely enough to keep the drusics paid for five weeks.

The stench was pretty awful then. Paren felt bad for all those marines and their families.

Even a scavenger has a heart.

You could see the pattern once you'd been on planet for a while. The bots had landed all around the small hospitable region of Ochnia—where the base was. They moved in like a tightening circle, killing everyone in their path. And near the center of that circle was where all the survivors made their last stand. That was a pretty good spot for salvage. Under normal circumstances, it would have been a scrounger's dream come true. Lots of Republic weaponry. Lots of bots, but most of them had holes through their heads or mainframes.

But the exact center... that was the motherlode. It was also the saddest place. The place with the most bodies.

Where the bots had begun a systematic execution of anyone who remained.

And then... they shut down. Frozen like statues.

But not before their work was finished. Ochnia wasn't one of the places where survivors found Oba and a newfound belief in the miraculous.

No.

Ochnia wasn't one of those places.

On Ochnia, they were no survivors.

One day a week, in those early days, Paren and the drusics would gather piles of decaying corpses and burn them. The rest of the week was for scrapping. Until the ship was full and the pilot—a man Paren trusted like a brother—went off to make that first fortune. Which he did. And when he came back to pick up the next load, every man and drusic on that expedition was set for life.

It wasn't long before more enterprising scrappers arrived on planet. Paren had added drusics in that time. Had his own army, practically. But he wasn't greedy. This bounty the galaxy had given him wasn't solely meant for him. He let the new scrappers work the outer rings, salvaging the bots destroyed early in the conflict. Paren took only a fifteen-percent cut. Which was downright generous.

He didn't do much picking anymore. He had people working for him. Truth be told, there wasn't all that much left. Maybe enough work for another six months or so, then that would be the end of it. And then? Maybe he would develop Ochnia. He was making almost as much from selling scrappers supplies as he was from selling the dwindling scrap itself. And it wasn't like the Republic cared about Ochnia.

It was too far away for them to care. That was the little secret that was just now getting out as places like Sinasia went independent. The Republic's arms were just too short to box with the edge.

"Sir," said P1-PP, his servitor bot. "Breaking news, if you would like to hear it."

Paren never thought he'd own a personal bot. But now that he had one, he didn't see how he could live without it. "What's it about, Pipp?"

"Highlights from an emergency State of the Empire address. It seems Delegate Orrin Kaar is dead."

Paren raised his eyebrows. "Really?"

"Yes, sir. And the House of Reason and Senate have been dissolved."

"What!"

Something about the casual way the bot said this was almost comical, and Paren found himself laughing. "Yeah, put it on, Pipp."

"I have synced the holocast to your datapad, sir."

Paren pulled out the device and watched as a man with a handsome, well-traveled face addressed the holocams from the center of the Hall of Reason, which was ominously empty. A graphic beneath his visage read "Baron Scarpia." And he was speaking shocking things to a galaxy that had been in shock ever since Goth Sullus notoriously attacked the shipyards at Tarrago, which seemed now like ages ago.

"... His Highness the Emperor Goth Sullus has already done more for the galaxy than most could ever hope to comprehend. To those who have sought to use the former government as a shield for their own iniquity, a swift retaliation is in store. To those who have longed for security—for safety—Goth Sullus and his Empire will usher in a peace that will endure every bit as long as the Savage Wars..."

Paren read a streaming ticker that gave summations of what he'd missed.

> *House of Reason & Senate dissolved. Delegates arrested. Senators sent to home planets.*
>
> *Goth Sullus to Legion: "The Empire will not allow Legion influence in the mid-core."*
>
> *Scarpia: "We have armies awaiting activation that will restore order to the core and mid-core."*
>
> *"Delegate Orrin Kaar – A Life of Service" ... tonight at 7 UST.*

Paren shook his head. "This is... unreal."

The fall of the Republic. It was the most shocking and alarming thing he had ever witnessed. And it would hold that distinction for all of thirty seconds.

"Master," said Pipp, gently tapping Paren's shoulder. "Master, I—"

Though he was absorbed by his datapad, it wasn't the bot that got his attention. Rather it was the noise all around them as he stood at the center of the great salvage yard. The killing fields of Ochnia.

The massive Cybar war machines were reactivating, the red glow returning to their long-dormant eyes. And as the machines still intact came online, they arose, like skeletons rising from their graves to join the ranks of an unholy army.

The big machines marched past Paren, whose eyes were wide and mouth agape. They moved toward the docking pads Ochnia had built under Paren's direction. Big discs of impervisteel capable of receiving some of the largest freighters in the galaxy. A construction project that had made a self-made man even wealthier.

The Cybar, their numbers reduced to the size of a platoon at half strength after the long salvage, filed by more scrappers, who dropped their tools and cutting torches, leaving the flames to burn unattended at their feet. The drusics gripped their weapons but gave up ground, letting the machines move past them as well.

It wasn't until the Cybar reached the landing pads that Paren heard blaster fire. Thick and heavy, but brief. A five-second battle and then... silence until a heavy cruiser lifted off, refueling hoses snapping, the ship's repulsors stretching them to their limits, as the Cybar flew themselves from the place of their massacre. As the Cybar left Ochnia.

18

Prisma felt a new confidence that had been lacking before that night on the ship and in the garden. One that she hadn't known was missing.

Whoever the stranger was, he was right about her having a choice. Prisma alone could choose her path. Others might not agree with it, might seek to stand in her way. But anything getting in the way of her decision was a passing thing. It would last only so long as the person in opposition was able to contain her or control her.

And she could outlast them. She was young. Not a little girl, but young. With energy and hope. She had come through so much, weathered storms of violence and heartache unknown to most. And that... that was a source of strength. It made her realize that... she could handle it.

She could handle anything.

Including the stones Mother Ree had placed before her.

"Prisma... I'm amazed," gushed Mother Ree. "To see this sort of improvement is remarkable."

Prisma had been causing six stones, smooth and round as billiards, to race around the room in concentric circles, none of them breaking loose. They moved as a single unit.

"Thanks," she said, lining the rocks up in a row and then "releasing" them from her thoughts. "I had a breakthrough."

"I should say so," said Mother Ree. "Prisma, you've been almost a completely different person since that night last month."

Prisma felt so, too. And she felt good because of it.

She smiled and stood, bending back down to collect the stones. "It's about control."

Mother Ree arched an eyebrow. "Well, you're controlling the stones quite well. I think Ravi will be impressed."

Prisma smiled. "Not the stones. Myself. I didn't work before because, even though I could harness whatever it is inside of me that lets me do this, I didn't want to."

"And now you do?"

Prisma nodded. "Now I do." She placed the stones in a wooden box on the dresser.

Mother Ree took her by the hands. Mother Ree's hands were always warm and felt so smooth. "Why? Tell me why you want to now."

"Because wherever I choose to go when I choose to leave, I think that knowing how to do all of this will help me."

The smile faded from Mother Ree's face. "You're still wanting to leave?"

"Well, not right now. There's no ship." Prisma winked. "But someday I will. And I'll know when that day comes because it will be the day I've chosen to go."

"Prisma, you seem to be talking a lot about choice. About destiny."

"Not destiny." Prisma began to walk toward the door.

"Just... what you choose."

Prisma turned. "Yes."

Mother Ree began to give her the look. The one that would be accompanied by bending down to a knee and looking her in the eye to tell her some truth from the adult world. Only she didn't do that. She didn't bend down, didn't lower herself. She stood in place, meeting Prisma's stare. "Whatever your choice may be," she said, "others might not have it so."

"I don't care about them. And that doesn't matter." She could see that Mother Ree did not comprehend. The stranger had not visited her. "Mother Ree, can you move the stones?"

Mother Ree cast her eyes down furtively and shook her head. "No. What you and Ravi can do is well beyond me. I only know that, whatever it is, it's a part of the same thing that lets me bring comfort to those who come to En Shakar."

"Then I'll tell you. The choices I make are all I'll ever truly own. Whether those choices result in me getting what I want doesn't matter. When my father was being killed, I could have chosen to save him. I could have stood up and fought."

"Goth Sullus would have killed you, Prisma," Mother Ree said, imploringly. As if she wanted the girl to see the reason in her words.

"He might have. Or something else might have happened. But he couldn't have stopped me from *trying*. He couldn't have stopped me from *choosing* to save my father's life." She slipped through the open door, then turned back once more. "And I'll never let anyone take my choices away from me again."

***

"Prisma, you're back!" said Skyla, looking up from inspecting a bandage wrapped around one of the sanctuary members' hands. The woman had gotten cut with a spade wielded by an inattentive gardener. "How many days has it been since I last saw you? Nine?"

"Twelve," answered Prisma. She smiled at the bandaged woman. "Hello, Faith. How's your hand?"

"Better, thanks."

Skyla helped Faith down from the examination table. "Keep applying that poultice each night before bed, just to make sure any infection stays away."

"I will, doctor."

"So, what brings you here?" Skyla asked Prisma when his patient had left the room.

"Here to help."

Skyla rubbed his chin as if considering this. "Here to help. And that's all? No ulterior motive? Like, say, the fact that Faith usually brings in sweet rolls after she has a checkup?"

"Nope." Prisma shook her head. "I want to be the kind of person who helps others, and this is where I chose to do it."

Skyla nodded approvingly. "All right. I can go along with that. So, let's see what I could use help with..."

"Don't say another sponge bath for Hutch."

Skyla laughed. "Nope. Crash took care of that earlier this morning."

Prisma tried to envision the nearly eight-foot-tall robot, built to take on entire platoons of soldiers, gently wiping down an invalid. "You're kidding."

"Not at all. Crash is a remarkable machine."

They stepped out the door and walked toward the end of the hall.

"He's my best friend," Prisma said.

"Seems kind of sad for a bot to be somebody's best friend."

"Didn't say he was my only friend."

"Right. You pal around with that homicidal predator, too, don't you?"

"Yes. And you."

Skyla stopped short and looked confused. "Who did you think I was talking about when I said 'homicidal predator'?"

Prisma laughed. She was pleased with the way the noise sounded. "How old are you, Skyla?"

"Too close to thirty," Skyla said, stopping to open a hall cabinet. "How old are you? Exactly."

He'd asked her this once before. But Prisma hadn't cared to answer. This time she felt different. "Too close to twenty."

Skyla smiled. "Did that medicine I gave you help out with your, uh..."

"It did. Thank you."

The legionnaire nodded. "So, Prisma, I'd like for you to count everything in this cabinet and enter the number of each item in this datapad. Every bag and box has a unique identifying number, and the datapad screen is organized just like the cabinet is arranged. So 0001-A1SP are skin-packs, and they're on the top shelf to your left." He pointed. "Just count 'em, enter that number in the datapad, and move on to the next item. Sound good?"

"I think I can handle it."

"Great!" Skyla turned and began walking down the hall.

"Where are you going?"

"Lunch! I've got some time to do it now that you're here to help."

Prisma shook her head. "Nice."

Skyla called out over his shoulder, "Don't get sarcastic with me or I won't bring you anything back."

"Oh, no," Prisma called after him. "That would be terrible."

It wasn't how Prisma would have spoken to the man just a few short weeks ago. But it was how she'd chosen to speak to him now. It was who she was. Who she wanted to be. She wasn't a little girl any longer. She might be short, she might be young, but she was a woman. And her choices were her own.

***

Skyla returned with a sandwich made from a seedy bread that smelled like cake. "Here, kiddo."

"Thanks," said Prisma. She took a bite before saying, "I finished up. We're all out of tamir root. But that's okay."

"How so?"

"Because when I was helping in the garden yesterday I helped dig up at least three bushels of it. It's drying now in the smokehouse."

Skyla nodded. "That's good. We need it to—"

A sudden clang sounded from a room down the hall. Both Prisma and Skyla jerked their heads toward the noise.

"That's odd," said Skyla. He began to move down the hall.

Prisma followed, eating her sandwich along the way. "Someone else here?"

"Not that I know of. I—"

And then Hutch was standing in the doorway of his room, wobbling from weak legs too long confined to a bed. He ground his palms into his eyes, as if attempting to rub away his disorientation. "I..."

"Whoa, easy there," Skyla said, jogging toward the Nether Ops legionnaire and grabbing his shoulders in an effort to steady him. "You're going to want to sit back down."

Skyla was a big man. A legionnaire. But he looked skinny next to the hulking Hutch. Even after months of inactivity. So much for atrophy.

"No, I..."

It was clear that Hutch remained in a cloud. He probably thought he was still aboard the Cybar mothership. Still attempting to escape. Fighting for his life.

But as Prisma approached, she saw something that made her blood run cold. She dropped the sandwich on the floor, a large bite still in her mouth. Hutch's eyes had flashed a brilliant turquoise, and just beneath the surface of his skin, binary sigils lit up, glowing in undulating patterns of neon yellow and magenta.

He barreled past Skyla, knocking him into the wall, lunged at Prisma, locked thick, powerful hands around her throat, and began to squeeze.

Prisma felt her feet leave the floor as she held on to Hutch's forearm in a desperate attempt to pull away. Her head felt as though it was going to explode. She tasted blood mixing with the partially chewed sandwich in her mouth. She couldn't scream. Couldn't even choke out a gurgle of a cry. And there was no air. She hadn't even had the chance to suck in a surprised breath before the attack begun.

The monster before her held her in his hands as though she were nothing more than eggshell.

She could choose not to die. But that was a choice of inanity. An impossibility.

She was being killed. Slowly. One second at a time. The hands clamped tighter and tighter, and her eyes threatened to burst from her skull.

Prisma chose. She chose to fight.

With what strength she had left, her legs, already flailing, now attempted to kick Hutch as hard as they could, wherever they could, with the hope of connecting with his groin—anything to force him to let go. She reached out with her hands and clawed at the Nether Ops legionnaire's face, drawing blood with claw marks that might have impressed Skrizz if he were here.

Why *couldn't* he be here right now?

The wounds on Hutch's face dripped red blood mixed with silver mercury. He only squeezed harder.

"Prisma!"

Skyla slammed into Hutch, his shoulder thudding into the larger man's side just below the ribs. All three of them went sprawling, but the blow was enough for Prisma to break free of Hutch's grip.

She fell hard on her back, nearly aspirating the ground-up pieces of bread in her mouth as she gasped in fresh supplies of air. This brought about a violent coughing fit that left her incapable of doing anything except repeatedly evacuating her lungs, her face inches from the floor, palms flat on the cold stone.

Mere feet away, Hutch and Skyla were locked in a violent struggle, each man using their Legion training to KTF the other. Because that was how it would be. One of them wouldn't survive this fight. And if Prisma had to choose, was forced to bet her life on the outcome... Hutch was going to kill Skyla.

The two men were a tangle of arms and legs with Skyla straddling Hutch, attempting to land elbow strikes while avoiding being swept away. It was a stalemate as the Legion-honed personal defense combat techniques sought to neutralize one another. But that would only last for so long. Prisma could see just how much Skyla was struggling against the Hutch's muscular bulk.

She pulled herself out of her coughing fit and looked frantically around the hall for something she could use to help Skyla. All she could find was a handmade pedestal with a vase of Spilursan roses set on top of it. She grabbed the pedestal by its leg, sending the vase to shatter on the floor, and lifted the small table like a cudgel.

"Skyla! What should I do?" Prisma kicked Hutch in the side of his head, thinking that at least that much would help. But the blow didn't even faze him. There was murder in his eyes, which alternated between a dead black and the glowing blue she'd seen earlier. Whatever the bots had done to him on that ship, it seemed to have claimed him as one of their own. He was... post-human. A cyborg almost.

As Prisma attempted a follow-up kick, Hutch broke an arm free from his struggle with Skyla and reached out to grab her planted leg. He yanked, and sent her tumbling onto her back.

The air left Prisma in a rush and she hit the back of her head on the stone. Her body strained to suck in more air. She put a hand behind her head. It came away bloody.

"Prisma, run!"

Run.

Hutch's impervisteel-like hand groped again for her, stretching to reach her while Skyla struggled to hold him back. It was as though Hutch was a machine whose only programming objective was to kill Prisma Maydoon.

But he wasn't like the replicants she'd seen on the Cybar ship. He wasn't like the fake, look-alike Leenah that they had sometimes sent to pry secrets from her. Prisma had seen Wraith destroy one of those replicant machines. It didn't bleed. Not the way Hutch was doing now.

Hutch wasn't a machine built to look like a man. He was a man who'd been turned into a machine. Like the man's body had been a cocoon, and now, for some reason, he was awake—and changed.

And he was going to kill Prisma if she didn't get away.

"Run!" Skyla yelled again.

His movements were slowing. His energy was fading. Whereas Hutch seemed as strong and fresh as ever.

Prisma crab-walked backward, out of the reach of the Nether Ops killer's grasping fingers. She wanted to do something. Desperately.

"Crash!"

She screamed for her bot, her oldest friend, in the hopes that he was near enough to pick up her voice on his audio sensors. Because as big and bad as Hutch was, a motivated war bot would tear him limb from limb.

"Crash! Help us!"

No answer came. No heavy footsteps. No synthesized threats of death and violence. There would be no salvation. Not if Prisma stayed here.

Hutch was able to keep Skyla at bay with just one arm now, and the other was moving to take hold of the dropped pedestal.

"Dammit, Prisma, run!" Skyla yelled. He sounded tired, nearly at his end.

Prisma turned and began to run. Just as Hutch grasped the pedestal. Just as he swung the blunt wooden object into Skyla's neck and collarbone.

Run. Don't let his death be in vain. Run.

Prisma streaked toward the exit. She could hear behind her the wet thud of Hutch striking Skyla again and again with his newfound weapon. Pausing at the exit, she turned to give her friend one final look. To see him one last time. Because he deserved that much, didn't he? To be looked on with compassion one more time?

Skyla was dead. A battered, pulpy mess. Half of his face caved in. A rapidly growing pool of blood shimmering beneath his limp body.

Hutch drew himself up. The pedestal was now nothing more than a club, its round tabletop scattered in fragments, gathered against baseboards, embedded in Skyla's corpse. He began to walk toward Prisma. With each step he picked up speed until he was nearly at a run.

Prisma's legs threatened to betray her. They rooted her in place as though some magical force prevented them from moving, from taking her away from the infirmary, away from the killer. But with an effort, they finally responded. She pried her feet off the floor and ran outside.

There were people out there. In the sunlight. Lost souls who'd found peace in the sanctuary of Mother Ree.

"Help!" Prisma shouted, simultaneously desperate to avoid the thing that pursued her and feeling guilt at drawing others into this life-and-death conflict. "He killed Skyla!"

The passersby paused to look at the raving little girl. And in that moment, the closing moments of their lives, they seemed to realize that she was not as young as she once was. Hardly any taller, but older somehow. And had she ever been that young to begin with? Did they ever even know? Or was she just little Prisma, who Mother Ree told them was scarred and stunted, emotionally and physically, and in need of the love of the sanctuary?

Whatever they thought they knew, she was different now. They could see that. Three men steadied themselves, prepared to meet whatever might come through the other side of the infirmary door. Men who had spent the final years of their lives in blissful labor, planting and harvesting, enjoying the simplicity of honest, hard work. Men who had not been made soft by a life of on-demand entertainment and technological dependence that seemed designed to keep people from doing anything for themselves.

Prisma fell behind this new rank of protectors. Stood with a pair of women. One old, almost grandmotherly. The other still young enough to bear children.

Did all these people know one another? Was this the worst kind of nightmare for them? One that involved not just danger to oneself, but to the ones you loved?

Prisma hoped not. She hoped they were passing strangers, chosen out of chaos to face the coming whirlwind. Confident in the safety of their loved ones in some other, distant place. With that one final assurance, at least, to keep them warm.

"No," Prisma said, realizing what her calls for help had consigned these souls to face. "No... run! Everyone! Run!"

But they stood firm. Even the women.

And Hutch burst from the door like a charging beast. An ogre emerging from its cave. He spent no time analyzing what stood before him, and he gave the three men no opportunity to react to his arrival. His club swung from head to head, caving in a skull with each stroke.

By the time the first man had fallen, Prisma was already running. Not to the gardens, or the town, but *away*. Toward the landing pad. She could not lead this demon to slaughter any more of the people of En Shakar.

Her legs propelled her at a speed she didn't think herself capable of. They burned in protest, but it seemed even the slope of the hill leading to the frozen outskirts was unable to slow her.

The women screamed behind her.

Prisma didn't look back.

She ran. Thinking of the ice and what it would do to her. She was furiously racing toward the frozen caves with just one robe, no food, and no water. Running *from* death... *to* death.

It was not a great choice. But it was still a choice. A choice between her immediate death and one that would take time.

And she chose to live as long as she possibly could.

19

The ice caves were beautiful. Even while running from Hutch—in the moments when she'd steal away into a cavern to catch her breath—Prisma was aware of the beauty surrounding her.

The light of En Shakar's nearest star diffused through the cathedral ceiling of natural wonder above her, sending blazing waves of radiant shine through the clearer sections of ice like light through a prism. The effect washed the floor with color, so it looks like she was running across a rainbow. The effect was breathtaking, with crystal clear ice formations contrasting against white, frosty spires and aquamarine marbling that ribbed the caves. If she had to die, she would be hard pressed to find a more beautiful place in the galaxy for it.

She thought of the day her father died on the dry, barren hardpan that was Wayste. It was a death unbefitting a man who had done so much for the Republic. Unbefitting her father.

The memory—and the lack of justice for that event—triggered a fire within Prisma that warmed her and kept her going. To keep putting distance between herself and Hutch. The big man seemed no faster a runner in this new life than he'd been in his old.

The best legionnaires aren't usually the body-builder types. Masters had said that once, when explaining why he was so much better than Bear at being a legionnaire. And though it had clearly been said in fun, Prisma noted that the others seemed to agree with this assessment in general, if not specifically about the two men specifically. Big muscles meant you could lift big things, but a legionnaire was expected to excel in a multitude of arenas. They were a well-rounded lot. The best warriors the galaxy had to offer.

Prisma wished those warriors were coming for her now.

But that wasn't going to happen. No one would come to save her. If she was going to survive, it would be because of her own resourcefulness. Her own choices.

She continued her run through the cavern, padding her growing lead over Hutch, looking for someplace where the solid walls of translucent ice offered a tributary away from the main tunnel.

Looking for somewhere to get lost.

***

Prisma sat shivering on an ice shelf, hidden behind a virtual wall of giant icicles that went from ceiling to floor, forming columns to enclose her little alcove. She'd found this place deep inside a winding cave that branched off from the main cavern. And it wasn't the first branching tunnel she'd come across. It was the third. To take the first seemed too obvious.

She was well hidden. She hoped. But the cold was getting to her.

She pulled her robe tightly about her, trying to trap in whatever warmth she could. The running had made her tired, and she knew she needed to rest. But it was when she stopped moving that her hot perspiration began to feel like ice against her skin, and the chill came over her in earnest.

It wasn't all bad. She had her boots on, and considering how often she went barefoot in the sanctuary, that was a stroke of good fortune, if not a minor miracle. She didn't know how long it would take for something like frostbite to take hold of her toes—Crash could have given her an exact range—but surely after what had to be, what? Nearly two hours in this icy cave? Bare feet subjected to the ice for that long would definitely not be doing well.

The even better news was that there was no sign of Hutch. And hadn't been since she'd first seen him enter the mouth of the ice cave as a distant figure. Once she'd gone around the main tunnel's natural curve, she'd lost sight of him completely.

Prisma had been listening for sounds of his pursuit, straining to hear above her own panting breaths. She'd heard nothing. And now that her breathing had calmed and she was completely silent, all she heard was a dripping somewhere nearby, echoing throughout the cave, magnified. An ice melt. That would supply her with water, at least. That would keep her alive a little longer. If she could just survive the cold.

It was warmer on the shelf than on the ground. Not warm, but warmer. She had once read something about how the cold did that. It was in some holomag she'd loaded onto her datapad about survival and fun facts of the galaxy. Cold air went down, warm air went up. So all the cold was resting a few feet below her makeshift nest.

Curling herself into a tight approximation of a ball, she tucked her head down deep inside her clothing, shivering and struggling for every bit of heat she could find and preserve. But she didn't cry. And she wasn't scared.

The distant star still scattered its light through the translucent ceiling of the great ice cave, giving the air around her a warm glow like moonlight.

She fell asleep.

***

"Prisma..."

The voice woke Prisma from a dreamless sleep. Her heart raced, and fresh adrenaline pumped through her system, blocking out the cold and the soreness from lying on the ice shelf for so long. She'd been asleep for... a while. The character of the light shining down through the ice had changed. It was weaker now, much later in the day. It would be night soon.

And then things would get very cold indeed.

But staying alive even that long was hardly a guarantee. Because the voice that had just called her name belonged to Hutch. Prisma was sure of it. And yet it was distorted, as though his voice box had become an electronic speaker that was shorting out as it processed the vowels in her name.

"Pri-i-i-sss-m-m-a-a-a-a-a..."

He was close. Somehow he'd followed her into this blind tunnel. How? Was it blind luck, or had she been asleep long enough for him to thoroughly scour each snaking fork from the main cavern? Maybe there really was nowhere to hide. Maybe she'd gone as far as she could.

The alcove she'd chosen was as good a hiding place as any she was likely to find. It required squeezing between the column-like spires of ice and then moving into a dark stretch, where some sort of mineral flow interrupted the transparency of the freeze above. Prisma could just barely see a thin vertical strip of tunnel from her frozen bed, and she was confident that anyone looking inside would not be able to see her.

Unless they stepped in to investigate.

And Hutch wouldn't fit through the gap.

He gave another robotic catcall. "You're here, Prisma-a-a-a. We know you're here."

We? Who is we? Were there more like Hutch? Had he... done something to the people in the village? To Skyla and Mother Ree?

Visions crowded Prisma's mind—visions of a village of cybernetic zombies, all with the single purpose of slaying her. But though her heart raced, she forced the thoughts away. What would be, would be. The fear of the thing would give her no advantage.

She thought about the stones she'd moved. And then she looked up at the icicles hanging all about, shimmering spikes that could cause untold damage.

Let them come.

And they did. Or at least, Hutch did. Prisma watched as the Nether Ops foot soldier crept alone past the alcove she'd retreated into. He was still holding his makeshift club. His arms were red with dried and congealing blood. Prisma wondered how many of the villagers had died to paint that tapestry of horror on his massive forearms.

"Pri-i-i-i-sm-a-a," Hutch called. The glow was still there beneath his skin, as though his veins had become processors and switches, and it pulsed, accentuating each syllable with a spectrum of neon that seemed to belong perfectly in the wondrous ice caves.

He didn't know where she was. Prisma knew that now. He was trying to bait her, trying to goad her into fleeing into the open. He was guessing, probably had been the entire time he'd been searching since losing sight of her.

She lay still. For a long time. Long enough that the adrenaline wore off and the cold of the ice shelf sucked away her body heat like a vampire. But she had to be sure Hutch had moved on. Then she could double back and put more distance between herself and the killer.

Because eventually Keel and Leenah would come back in the *Indelible VI*. And there was no way she'd miss their arrival. She only had to hold on long enough—stay hidden well enough—and then she would find herself safe.

Only what if they didn't come in time? It had already been so long since the *Six* was last here. Even the call with Leenah was weeks ago.

You will only survive on your own.

Prisma heard the voice clearly in her mind. It wasn't her own; she was sure of that. It belonged to the man in the garden. The man who had told her that she had a choice was now telling her how she could survive.

And she believed the voice. For so long—her entire life—she had been dependent on others. Her father. Crash. Tyrus Rechs. Leenah. How much longer could that go on? How many more people would have to rotate through her life as protectors? And at what cost?

The thought didn't escape Prisma's mind that some of these protectors had already died for their loyalty.

Feeling as though enough time had passed, she carefully slid off of the ice shelf. At first her robe stuck to the surface where the warmth of her body had made a thin layer of moisture, freezing it to the ice—but then the cloth pulled away with a gentle ripping sound that seemed to fill the quiet alcove.

Prisma stood still, like a gorbanite relying on the camouflage of savannah grasses to keep it hidden from predators. There were no other sounds. Not footfalls in the icy tunnel beyond. Not the schizophrenic calls of whatever Hutch had become.

His true self, Prisma thought. The man from Nether Ops had been a monster *before* all of this. Now he was simply unable to hide it.

Numb toes wriggled inside her boots in an attempt to gain feeling as she quietly eked her way toward the ice columns that enclosed her alcove. They seemed now more like jail bars, and Prisma wondered if she hadn't locked herself in a prison of her own choosing. She stopped just before those bars, cautiously listening for any sign of trouble in the main tunnel, not more than a meter away.

Her breath puffed up tiny clouds of fog.

Nothing.

There was nothing out there.

Wiggling her fingers, Prisma took a step toward the opening.

"Hello there!"

The face of Hutch appeared in the gap between the columns. The blue glow in his eyes flashed with an epileptic pulse that made Prisma freeze in place. Then those same eyes lit bright red as the Nether Ops leej reared back, club in hand, and sent it smashing against a column of ice. Cold shards flicked Prisma in the face, breaking her from whatever trance Hutch's flashing eyes had put her in.

The big man swung again, and the ice groaned in protest. It was solid, thick as a man's waist, but it couldn't last forever. She needed to get back. To get away.

Prisma scrambled to the back of her alcove, diving through the shadows and stumbling over the slick, misshapen floor.

All the while Hutch battered and abused the bars of ice that kept him from his prey. A mammoth blow sent a huge section of one of the columns tumbling to the ground, sounding like a sheet of plate glass and concrete rubble.

The savage killer attempted to squeeze himself through the newfound opening, but it was still too narrow for his giant frame.

"Pri-i-sm-a-a!" he shouted in that awful techno-vocal speech, his arm and shoulder reaching through the opening he'd made, head pressed against the columns of ice, eyes blazing red. "Ou-ou-ours agai-ai-ai-ain!"

The sound of Hutch wailing echoed in pursuit of Prisma as she backed further into the unexplored darkness at the rear of the alcove. Back here, beyond the ice shelf, was utter blackness that even the cavern's diffuse glow could not penetrate. Prisma held out her arms, unable to see what was in front of her, moving forward, hoping—

Her palms struck a wall of solid ice.

A crash of shattering ice sounded behind her once more. "N-n-n-ooo-o-w!" he roared, as if possessed. And truly how could he be anything but? "The-e-e-e time i-i-is n-o-ow!"

Prisma could tell by the sound of the voice that he was inside the alcove. He'd squeezed through.

He would reach her soon.

She groped desperately, sidestepping, searching for an opening in the ice wall, a crevasse, a hidey-hole, anything. She planted her right foot and the ground beneath her gave way, sinking her into a bone-chilling pool of slushy ice water. Her fingernails scraped against the wall as she flopped into a sort of split, one leg sprawled on the floor, the other sunk in freezing water to her thigh, her hands numb against the ice wall, bracing herself from falling in even further.

This was the source of the dripping sound. She could hide here. Slip under the water until Hutch determined that she must have gone another way. But she knew to do that would be to invite sure death through hypothermia. Her leg already felt numb, her heart weak. The sudden shock of cold was wreaking havoc on her nervous system.

Pulling herself up from the pool, Prisma pressed her back against the ice wall, hidden in the black of the shadows. Her wet boot was already freezing to the ground.

The red glow of Hutch's eyes slowly approached.

Can he see in the dark? She wondered if whatever had turned him into... this... had given him such abilities.

But if so, Hutch didn't let on, didn't train those glowing red eyes on her. And he was silent now, as if his instinct to kill was all that was left of him. He was stalking her, closing in.

And then those eyes turned toward her.

He *could* see her. Even in the dark, he could see her.

And he was coming directly for her.

"Miss Prisma!" called a voice.

Crash! The bot had come looking. But his booming voice sounded distant, almost feeble. There was no telling how far away he was. Prisma felt her sudden hope wink out as quickly as it had sparked. *Too far*, she told herself. *Too far to help.*

And then she became aware of another presence in the deep and shadowy alcove. At first she thought—hoped—it was Skrizz, arriving undetected and on his own terms, as the wobanki so often did. But then the voice spoke to her—spoke to her in her mind—and she knew it was the man from the garden.

Choose, Prisma. Whether you will live or die, choose it right now!

Hutch hurled himself toward her, his red eyes arcing through the darkness.

"No!" Prisma shouted, holding out her hands to fend off the attack.

A sensation came over her, filling her entire body. It was a feeling she'd only had once before, with Ravi on the *Indelible VI* when the flew over Tarrago's moon and he asked for her help.

Hutch's glowing red eyes were suspended in midair. Frozen in place.

But as Prisma watched, she realized that he wasn't frozen. He was still hurtling toward her... just very, very slowly. Almost imperceptibly. And in the glow of his eyes she saw minuscule fragments of ice—bits of crystalline powder that had swirled into the air with his leap. They, too, moved slowly, lazily. Dust motes in a red sunbeam.

Time hadn't stopped. But it had slowed to nearly the same.

Sensing a presence, she looked to her right and saw the man. He appeared as a shadow so black that it stood out even from the darkness itself. Utterly absorbing the meager light emanating from Hutch's red eyes.

"What... what is this?" Prisma asked.

"This," said the man, "is your salvation. The Ancients called it the hastening of time."

"How am I doing this?"

"With my help."

Prisma didn't immediately understand, but then she again thought of Ravi and that time aboard the *Six*. He had helped her use whatever this ability was that she possessed. And now the stranger was helping her do the same.

"In time," the stranger continued, "you will find in yourself the ability to do such things without help. You'll never need anyone again."

"I don't... I don't understand."

Suddenly the stranger was standing on her opposite side, and much closer. "Of course," he said, "the hastening of time cannot last forever. And I cannot make your next decision for you. What will you do, Prisma?"

"Do?"

"To this man. Corrupted and infected by a malevolent race known as the Cybar. Made a vessel for their purposes. What will you do to him now that you are free of the restraints of time and fear?"

Prisma thought about this. She could run. Move around Hutch and find Crash. Get away from this dead end she'd found herself in. Or...

She remembered the icicles.

"This man," said the stranger. "Do you know how many innocents he killed in the name of a greater good?"

Prisma shook her head.

"*He* does. And he feels no regret. This type calls the killing 'how the steaks are cut.' Isn't that nice? Doesn't it feel so wise and necessary? A matter of survival. It would all be so noble, were those steaks not leaving behind wailing mothers and orphaned children."

The word "orphaned" caused a pang of hurt in Prisma's heart.

And anger.

"And do you know," continued the stranger, "what this man would have done, had he completed his mission? His original mission, on the *Forresaw*? Would you care to see? I warn you, it is not for the eyes of a child. It is not for the faint of heart."

Prisma was not a child. Nor was she faint of heart. "Show me."

And then the stranger was in her mind. Like a visitor stepping inside. His presence felt warm, though what he revealed, which came to Prisma like a buried memory, was anything but.

She saw herself. Dead. A single blaster bolt having left a cavernous hole in her head. Garret was dead too, executed the same way. And Skrizz. Crash lay in a disassembled heap on the deck.

And then she saw Leenah and Andien Broxin. They had both been executed as well. But these two... were naked.

And Prisma knew why.

Her anger grew. And the icicles above her head rattled.

New visions came. The Cybar fleet arriving over Utopion. Hutch reporting to an older man, who shook his hand and took him to someone. Someone important.

And then she watched as Hutch and the man approached Goth Sullus. Saw them kneel before him. Saw Goth Sullus bid them rise and then look upon his fleet as it orbited his newly conquered world.

And Prisma's anger grew hot enough to melt the ice caves themselves.

"Knowing this," the stranger said. "What would have been. And knowing what was—the death of your friend in the village. The deaths of so many others who fled here to *escape* the galaxy's lust for violence and mayhem. Knowing all of this, Prisma... what do you choose for this man?"

Prisma did not need to think about it. She answered with a single word, her voice as cold as the air she breathed.

"Death."

The ceiling above crackled and showered down ice as she pulled loose eight-inch spikes and sent them hurtling faster than blaster bolts through Hutch's suspended body. The ice daggers tore through him, sending a spray of that pulsing, silver mercury and red blood in torrents onto the icy floor.

Time suddenly caught up with itself, and Hutch's corpse crashed into Prisma, knocking her back into the wall. They plunged together through the slush and beneath the icy water. It was deep and dark and wide. So big that Prisma immediately realized that she could find no walls, and no way back up.

Hutch's body floated down, down and forever away as Prisma felt frantically for the surface, for the opening through which she'd fallen. She was so cold that she felt her lungs might burst. And she was tired.

So tired.

Sleep came to her in the blackness. And with it, a peculiar warmth.

20

"Wanna bet on the game this weekend?"

Chhun was so relieved to hear the words over the comm that he nearly forgot to give the counter. "My wife would kill me. Holy hell, Wash. What is going on?"

"I have no idea," Wash answered. He sounded tired. Looked it, too. Like all the years he'd been carrying had caught up to him at once and dug in deep among the wrinkles and lines of his face. "In fact... I'm surprised that... anyhow, I'm sorry I couldn't check in sooner. Things must be very turbulent."

"No. Take care of yourself. You have to be careful."

"I'm doing what I can."

Chhun nodded. "The House and Senate: dissolved?"

In a way, this was exactly what the Legion had wanted. To a point. The Republic was to reset. To be made right again. But this...

"I saw it happen. Goth Sullus killed Orrin Kaar with his own hands. The senators have all returned to their home worlds—at least the worlds that will take them back. And the House of Reason... I think he'll execute the lot of them by the end of the week."

"But you're still in command of the Imperial Legion?"

"For whatever it's worth and for however how long, yes. This army is a mess, though. The appointed officers all look up to me—that was the plan—and they'll do what I ask. But we've lost so many former legionnaires—to you—that what's left of the shock troopers are the psychopaths and those who were never Legion to begin with. Though I'll tell you, if Goth Sullus had done what he just did when he first arrived on Utopion, I think it would be a different story."

"How serious is he about wanting only the core and mid-core worlds? Because it sounded like his threat was also a concession to leave the edge, and the Legion, alone."

Wash rubbed his hand across his mouth. "You're asking me to make a judgment call about someone who, in my opinion, is insane. But my take is that he knows the core, not even the mid-core, is all he can hold with the forces he has. He's asking for a breather. But he'll come for the edge once he has the strength for it."

Chhun nodded. "I think we have a shot at Utopion. Not another direct assault, but... so many former legionnaires have been seeking to join us out here that if we could just get them to stay put and find a way to arm them... we'll have armies already on planet."

Wash laughed. "Sorry. None of this is funny. But it just strikes me that the way the Legion might win this thing is by taking on the tactics we've been fighting against since Psydon."

Chhun smiled and inclined his head. "What doesn't kill you, right?"

"Right. So, I've got two potential operations for you now. Guns and ships. In four days we'll begin a new campaign designed to put the galaxy on notice. Targeting the zhee. Admiral Crodus has orders to nuke one of the zhee home worlds from orbit. Glass it completely. They've settled on Nidreem. I'll get you the window once I know it."

"Holy hell."

"Yeah. And I'm to order a landing on Ankalor to finish up what the Legion started. Goth Sullus has ordered a takeover of the planet. Ankalor is to then become an Imperial world, and I told him I don't have the men, but he says he'll provide."

"Are you serious?"

"*He* is. Absolutely."

Chhun eased back into his chair and let out a tense sigh. This was starting to feel too unpredictable. Too much to process. In an instant, Goth Sullus had gone from the second incarnation of the House of Reason to a despot with a battle plan that would have made Legion Commander Keller and General Hannubal balk due to its aggression.

The question was, should Chhun try to stop it? *Could* he even stop it? Exposing the Legion fleet to save a planet of zhee—a species that would sooner enslave the galaxy than live peacefully in its midst—seemed... idealistic. Naïve. On the other hand, he knew from his time stationed on planets with heavy zhee migrations that they weren't *all* that way. Some of them seemed as trapped and helpless among the terrorist tribes as the rest of the people forced to share a planet with them.

"You said guns and ships. What did you mean by that?"

"I can tell you where the Imperial strike force is planning to consolidate before the jump to Nidreem. Your admiral ambushed the zhee fleet pretty well, and here's a chance of further weakening the Republic's Navy. Maybe snag a few more vessels for yourself. That's what I meant by ships."

"And the guns?"

"After we take Ankalor, I'll arrange for the weapons stockpiles to move your way. In huge quantities. Much faster than what you can do through smuggler rings—that'll take years even with the money the Legion has from those synth mines you took on Herbeer."

That was true. Though it hadn't seemed important at the time, the Legion taking full control of the synth mines meant they were now the only entity in the galaxy capable of exporting the valuable material. One of the first things Chhun had done was send more legionnaires to reinforce the notoriously inhospitable planet, and Admiral Deynolds had a dedicated task force set up to fend off pirates. It was even more secure now than it had been when the Republic and Gomarii were running it.

Guns and ships. Chhun didn't see a way that they could swing both of these opportunities. They weren't *that* large of a force. At least not yet. "All right," he said. "Guns. It seems like it's only a matter of time before Goth Sullus begins a new push, and we need to be ready. When you find out what he's talking about as far as adding to your fighting force, you'll let me know?"

"I will. KTF, Legion Commander Chhun."

"KTF. Chhun out."

***

Captain Keel cycled down the *Indelible VI*. No sooner had the cloud of super-heated gases vented from the ship than a collection of men wearing after-market body armor and military-grade blaster rifles encircled them. Still more men—with less armored but obviously packing—pushed repulsor crates in a row outside of the *Six*'s cargo hold.

"You guys ready to go?" Keel asked over comm.

"Yeah, we're good," replied Exo from the ship's hold.

He and the rest of Kill Team Victory were on an outing to acquire surplus N-4 rifles and fraggers from some scumsack who'd been stockpiling them. Sticks, unfortunately, was no longer with them; after the trouble on Cononga he'd voluntarily pulled out of rotation, deciding he could be of better and safer use elsewhere.

"Okay, so listen up," Keel said, not yet lowering the ramp to let the kill team legionnaires—who wore black T-shirts, cargo pants, and a few leather jackets, all looking like a crew of hard-nosed spacers—down onto the docking pad. "This job was arranged by Wraith. So unlike the last one, you don't try to play it cool. There's no feeling-out process. If anyone gives you lip, you bust their ass. Because that's what Wraith would expect of you."

"I like Wraith more than you," Masters said.

"I'll tell him you said so," replied Keel, smiling.

Leenah leaned forward from her seat behind Keel. "That didn't just make you sound like a crazy person. Not at all."

"Havin' second thoughts, babe?" Keel asked, before getting up to make his way to the back of the ship. He was already wearing Wraith's armor and now picked up his bucket from Ravi's seat, his arm going right through the spectral navigator.

Ravi sighed in frustration.

"What? It's not like you feel it."

"Yes, but it is rude."

"Ahh," said Keel dismissively as he pulled the bucket over his head.

His HUD came to life and painted a battle map. The crates outside certainly *looked* like they could carry the goods. But by Keel's count, there were only about half as many as there ought to be.

"Lower the ramp and let the boys out," he told Ravi.

"Ramp is down. Shall I deploy the burst turrets?"

"Not yet. You'll give 'em a heart attack, Ravi."

"Very well."

Wraith left the cockpit, grabbing the bullpup NK-4 he preferred to carry when operating up close. He tapped into the exterior holofeeds from the cams positioned outside his ship, activating audio to hear how the kill team handled the situation.

"Bro, what the hell?" Exo shouted at the armored merc who stood at the head of the column. "Twenty crates was the deal. I see ten."

As always, Exo sounded hot and angry. Wraith didn't think the man was acting. He deserved an award if he was.

Mercs tensed, their hands gripping their weapons a little tighter, their eyes darting to one another, seeking courage. The kill team, though not holding outright, hadn't attempted to be subtle about the bulges inside jackets and underneath shirts.

The lead merc, a kimbrin wearing armor still detailed with MCR insignias, shrugged and looked to the others, attempting to settle them down with a hand-wave. This was a pattern that Wraith had noticed. Former MCR soldiers were raiding their supply depots and offloading weapons to the highest bidders. And with the galaxy in the state it was, there were a lot of bidders.

Exo walked up to the kimbrin until he was eye to eye with the merc leader.

The kimbrin, nearly a head taller, looked down disdainfully at the plain-clothed legionnaire. "Deal *was* for twenty crates. Half payment up front, half on delivery. So when I get the other half, so do you."

"Oh yeah?" Exo said, rubbing the scar on his face with the knuckle of his index finger. "I didn't realize that's how you played the game."

"It's how I—"

The kimbrin didn't finish his sentence before Exo's fist struck him square in the jaw. The blow knocked the merc flat on his back, and Exo followed up, getting right on top of him and pounding his face with repeated punches. "You think this is a game? Huh?"

It looked like Exo was channeling the vitriol he felt for every point in the galaxy.

Wraith hurried to the ship's ramp.

The other men delivering the cargo went for their weapons. But the kill team was quicker, and soon every last merc had at least one blaster or auto-pistol aimed at his head.

Exo stood up, breathing heavily, hands bloody from the damage he'd done to the kimbrin. "Where's the rest?"

No one answered. The mercs just shifted uncomfortably.

"I said, where's the rest!"

Still no one answered.

"Bear," said Exo.

The big legionnaire, the real-life leader of the team, stepped forward and cracked his knuckles. Since their op on Cononga, during the time they'd been traveling with Keel accumulating munitions for the Legion, they'd realized a few things. First, that when it came to talking, Exo was much more frightening to the sort of scum they dealt with. And second, when Exo called the Bear forward... things got even scarier.

"Come here!" Bear grabbed the kimbrin by his chest plates, hauled him to his feet, and held the wobbling former mid in place with one hand. He slammed his armored fist into the merc's stomach until his after-market torso plate cracked and splintered.

One of the other mercs moved slowly to swing his blaster rifle around, but found himself in the sights of both Bombassa and Masters.

"Naughty, naughty," scolded Masters.

The merc froze and went back to watching his team leader get battered to a pulp.

The kimbrin had both eyes swelled shut. He vomited a mix of blood and what looked like half-digested insects.

Bear gave a half-disgusted "Huh," then hurled the kimbrin over a pallet, sending him crashing hard onto the deck plate.

"Where's the rest?" Exo shouted.

A merc in full armor, complete with helmet—an expensive kit—stepped forward. He removed the helmet to reveal the face of a human. "I'm the one you want to speak with. I authorized this sale."

"You Brisco?" Exo said.

"Indeed I am," said the merc in an almost academic voice. "And I can't say I'm pleased with how you've treated the head of my security team." He made a "tsk" sound and shook his head.

The man had been making something of a name for himself. It wasn't exactly impossible to get ahold of Legion-level weapons; lots of two-bit thugs and bottom-feeding gunrunners could scrape together a few N-4s or N-6s. But Geoff Brisco, who according to the rumors was a player in the MCR before it became legitimate, was one of the only guys out there selling in bulk.

"Where's the rest?" Exo asked.

"That depends on whether I believe you or not."

"About what?"

"About whether you're really working with the Wraith." Brisco looked around. "His name was on the bid. But these things can be falsified. And weapons purchases certainly would be a... *new* venture for the man."

Exo turned his head and looked to the side as though he couldn't believe what he was being told. "Look. I'd say you got more than enough to worry about right now with what's in front of you, whether Wraith is here to dust you or not. I want the full order."

"As I thought..." Brisco said, a self-satisfied smile on his face. "Half is all you'll be taking. I do apologize if my battered friend led you to believe otherwise. And I'll still be expecting the full amount. The price has gone up."

"Bear."

The big legionnaire took a step forward.

"Oh, I don't think so." Brisco held out a hand. In his palm was a detonation switch—though to what, wasn't apparent. "The time in my life where I'm willing to take a beating has long since passed. Stop right there. Or don't, and see what happens."

Bear halted. The endgame was to get the weapons. Not go to war with a gunrunner.

"It seems that the zhee are quite frantic following the drubbing they took at Sinasia," Brisco continued, still wearing that self-satisfied smile. "They're buying up everything they can right now. My entire warehouse is spoken for. And they're paying *four* times what your contract specified. So in giving you half of your order, I'm being rather generous."

"We had a deal..." Exo said, the warning clear in his voice.

"Deals change, whoever you are. Now if you'll kindly..."

Brisco's voice trailed away and his face went pale at the sight of Wraith walking down the ramp. He moved his jaw up and down, trying to speak, but no words came out.

"My cargo," Wraith said, his voice the synthetic moan of the damned, whispering through the air.

"I—I..." Brisco stammered.

"All of it," said Wraith.

Brisco's eyes darted around wildly, brimming with fear. He nodded and brought up his wrist comm. "Bring the other ten. Change of plans."

"*All* of it," repeated Wraith.

The gunrunner looked confusedly at Wraith.

"What you sold to the zhee. All of it."

Brisco shook his head fractionally, the mathematical reality of his financial ruin playing out in his mind. "I..."

"You tried double-crossing *me*." Wraith referred to himself in a manner that suggested he knew exactly the thoughts that raced through Brisco's mind. They were the same fearful reactions he'd seen countless times before. The Wraith had come, and ruin was all that could ever await those he refused to pass over.

"I didn't know. I thought it wasn't you. I thought—"

"Your cargo for your life." Wraith raised his blaster, at once calling Brisco's bluff and making it clear that the moment of decision was now.

Brisco spoke into his wrist comm again. "Bring... bring all of it. Everything." There was a chatter of back talk that made the man's face grow red. "Yes, I said all of it, damn you!"

"Scan before loading," Wraith said coldly to Exo. "Kill anyone who delays us further."

And with that Wraith turned and walked back on board the *Indelible VI*.

21

Prisma awoke softly, as though it were a Sunday morning and she'd found herself warm and burrowed inside of smooth covers. She blinked her eyes, taking in her surroundings. A campfire blazed cheerily in front of her. The air was warm and slightly damp—almost humid, really—and seemed alive with chirps and glowing streaks that fluttered by. She was no longer in the ice cavern, but she was still underground. The space around her was lit by large incandescent mushrooms, some as tall as evergreen trees.

Beyond the fire was the icy melt, lapping against a shore.

Prisma propped herself up on an elbow. Her drying clothes were arranged near the fire, and she was zipped inside loose-fitting coveralls and tucked under a metallic emergency blanket with nano-elements to keep her warm.

"She is awake now."

Crash was speaking to someone. Crash was here.

Prisma was unsure if she was dreaming while in the final throes of drowning in the frigid waters.

"Crash?"

The bot approached and folded down on itself as if squatting by her side. "Are you quite comfortable, Prisma?"

"Considering."

"Yes. Indeed. I was worried for a while that you would not awaken, that your runtime was at an end. But I needn't have. You recovered spectacularly."

Prisma furrowed her brow and looked at the ground beneath her. It was composed of pea-sized stones that shifted with her every movement. And she was wearing gloves now, the sort that pilots sometimes wore when flying.

"Did you dress me? Where did you get all this?"

"There is a craft nearby. Very old." Crash paused, looking up. "Yes. She is quite well."

"Who are you talking to?"

"Skrizz. I am able to communicate with him through my built-in comm array. Though the connection is quite weak. He was assisting me in tracking you. The Nether Ops agent left quite the blood trail behind."

Prisma sat up all the way now. She was beginning to feel too hot beneath the blanket, and tossed it to the side. "Why isn't he here?"

"Wobanki are not good swimmers." Crash's optics zoomed in and out. "Though I believe he would have gone in after you had I not. And he would have died because of it."

"I didn't think you would be a good swimmer either, Crash."

"I am not. However, I am completely waterproof, an important feature for a war bot. I was able to dig into the ice pack over my head and hang on. I found you floating against the ice."

Prisma felt suddenly hungry. "How did we get... here?"

"I detected a slight current and pulled you toward it. It seemed that you had drifted closer to this shore than to the hole you fell through, and I believed time was a critical factor in maintaining your runtime."

Prisma sat before the fire, considering this. It seemed so surreal. Everything seemed like it hadn't happened. Or if it had, it had occurred decades before.

Decades. How could she feel so old? How could she, who'd not yet made it midway through her second decade of life, so clearly know that feeling?

But she did. She knew the sense of time long past. Of decades... and more.

"Young miss—I apologize—Prisma. What is 'Morghul'?"

"Hmm?" asked Prisma. She'd been lost in her thoughts and hadn't quite heard.

"You were saying it in your sleep: Morghul."

And then an ocean of remembrance flooded Prisma's mind. She recalled that which she'd never known. That Goth Sullus had failed the galaxy. The man he'd once been knew it. But Goth Sullus was all that remained. And no one would stop him. Not Ravi, not Keel, not the Legion. No one.

Except her.

If...

If what?

If I go to Morghul.

The stranger, the man who had shown her what she was capable of, would teach her. Train her.

On Morghul.

And she would return. The only one capable of destroying Goth Sullus. Because the man he was, was dead. Like Tyrus Rechs. Like her father.

But not like her. Because she had chosen to live.

"Where's the ship?" Prisma asked, standing up abruptly.

"Er, Miss Prisma, I do not believe you are well enough to—"

"The ship, Crash. I need to see it."

Crash gestured toward a path lit by the glow of the luminous mushrooms. "It is a ten-minute-and-thirty-two-second walk from here. Though the return trip takes slightly longer because of the incline."

"I have to see it."

"I advise strongly that you keep your strength."

Prisma began walking. She would leave the bot, if she must.

But Crash followed, speaking to Skrizz over the comm. "Yes, we are going to look at the ship. Ah! An excellent idea. I should have thought the same."

The war bot quickly caught up to Prisma with its great strides. "Skrizz suggests that we see if the craft is operable. After all, someone managed to fly it in here. So it stands to reason there is a way out. I quite agree with him. And we would be unable to swim back without you again losing consciousness. Unless we can find some sort of re-breathers aboard the ship."

"Tell Skrizz that—" Prisma began.

Crash stopped in his tracks.

"Crash, what're you doing? Come on. Tell Skrizz—"

"I cannot tell him anything if we continue moving, Miss Prisma. We are at the extreme end of our communication range. I will have to relay any message you have for him from this spot."

Prisma took a deep breath. "Tell him we won't be coming back. Or at least I won't. Not for a long time."

"Oh," said Crash. The machine sounded heartbroken. Like he didn't want to leave but knew he must. Refused to do anything but. "I... see."

"And I want him to tell Leenah something: I love her. And I'll never forget her."

Prisma began walking up the path again. Then stopped, her back still facing the only other person in the galaxy she truly loved: her war bot. "And Crash... it's okay if you stay here. I want you to be happy."

She looked back to see the war bot standing taller than she ever thought possible.

"Young miss. I would find no happiness without you."

Prisma nodded and trekked ahead, leaving the bot to deliver her parting message to Skrizz, trusting that the wobanki would see it delivered.

The ship was as old as Crash had promised it would be. The hatch was open, and she paused to inspect it, worried that the war bot might have damaged it in getting inside. But all looked well.

"VN-708," Prisma said, recalling the model of the ancient craft she had no memory of. "Tratt and Kleider drive," she said to the glowing mushrooms and the strange creatures of light that zipped and flew around her. She looked up at the ship's two ionic engine thrusters, hoping that the years had not been so cruel to them as to have left them inoperable. She would need them. At least long enough for her to make the jump.

There was no reason she knew any of this. But the stranger had wanted her to. It was he who had led her here. Had he wanted, he could have helped her stop Hutch in the infirmary. Could have saved Skyla's life.

But he wanted her *here*.

And so she was. But not without the knowledge that the stranger, for as good as he made her feel, and as kind and warm as he seemed, was a being of cunning. One of tricks.

But was Ravi not the same?

In the end it didn't matter. She made her choice.

Prisma stepped inside the relic, instinctively moving to the hyperspace stasis bay, a rarity on modern ships used to traveling in the known galaxy. But she was heading to the unknown. To a place of monsters.

The stasis pod read active. Prisma nodded and moved to the canopy.

She had made it through half of the pre-flight check when Crash arrived.

"Prisma, how did you learn to—"

"That seat is optimized for bot interface," Prisma said, motioning for Crash to port in. "I'll need you here to oversee things while I'm in stasis."

The craft's engines hummed to life.

"Stasis?"

"It's a long jump." Prisma began to enter coordinates into the ancient nav computer, which beeped and buzzed as it struggled to locate her destination on any known star maps. These were coordinates that others had spent lifetimes searching for, had died to discover. They marked the location of a forgotten planet that held such secrets that the last man to find it was promised death waiting for him out on the edge when he returned.

But no one would be waiting for Prisma.

Crash examined the feed. "This reading says the jump will take four and a half standard cycles."

"Closer to five," Prisma said, still not fully aware of how she knew any of this. But it was the truth. "Pre-flight reads go all across the board."

"Yes," confirmed Crash. "It is as if the ship sat here waiting for our arrival."

Prisma looked over at her bot. "It has."

She sealed up the ship. *Leenah's Love*. She would name it *Leenah's Love*.

The old VN-708 lifted gently, though its old repulsors howled, a side effect of being a primitive version of repulsor technology. Landing lights revealed a narrow opening in the cavern.

"Take us through there," Prisma ordered Crash, not trusting her own ability to fly. What she'd accomplished just in getting off the ground was a surprise, and she didn't wish to push her luck.

The war bot navigated through the rocky cave vent to the surface of En Shakar. They continued upward, leaving atmosphere, the ship bumping worse than Prisma had ever experienced on any modern vessel.

For a moment, she thought about the freedom she'd just obtained for herself. There was an entire galaxy ahead of her. She had her own ship, a war bot, and a confidence that she could control her own life.

Why not just find Leenah and the rest? Why not tell them that she would join them in their fight to destroy Goth Sullus and the Republic that had abdicated its responsibilities to him?

If they said no—and they would assuredly say no—she could do it on her own. They wouldn't stop her.

But then she thought about Tyrus Rechs. And *his* failure to stop the monster.

No. If she was ever going to see her vengeance through, this would be the only way. Bitter and painful as the path might be. She was leaving a life behind. And so was Crash.

"Are we clear to make the jump?" she asked.

"We are." Crash looked at her through his glowing optical receptors. "And are you quite certain that you wish to go through with this? There is no turning around once we've committed halfway. I calculate enough fuel to reach your destination and no more."

Five years. Whether she went all the way or turned around at the halfway mark.

Five years.

"I'm sure, Crash. Make the jump."

The bot nodded and pulled the activator, causing brilliant needles of starlight to swirl around the latticed cockpit canopy. And quietly, so faint that Prisma barely heard it, Crash said, "Goodbye."

"Okay," Prisma said, rising from her seat. "I'm going to go into stasis now."

"Already?"

"Sorry, Crash."

"I... understand. I will see you when you awake, Miss Prisma."

"See you in five years, Crash."

"Yes. I will see you then."

Prisma walked to the ship's stasis chamber. It was an advanced model—another thing she knew without knowing how. It could effectively lock her in time, slowing her growth to almost negligible levels, so that she would be in five years almost exactly as she was right now. Reducing days to mere minutes. Making a trip of years seem to last only months.

But Prisma sensed that what was in store for her would not be easy. And though she was a woman, her body was ill prepared for the trials that lay ahead.

She brought up a programming screen on the side of the glass-domed chamber and began punching in menu options and pathways that she should not know. Navigating software that predated her parents by... well, the answer to that she *truly* didn't know.

With a series of confirmation beeps, the screen blinked and turned green. The canopy hissed open, inviting her to slide inside. Prisma removed her coveralls, feeling the ship's chill against her bare skin.

She climbed a metal ladder painted yellow, just three steps, and entered the pod. It was cushioned, and the cushions warmed as she pressed against them. The lid closed around her, and the pod filled with a white vapor that obscured the ship's overhead lights. A soft, gentle music surrounded her.

Prisma's eyes grew heavy. A scene of a green meadow with undulating grasses bent by the wind played before her, superimposed on the canopy lid, it too getting lost in the fog that seemed to drift down from the mountain in the background of the holographic image.

Prisma had chosen to age on the trip. Her body would grow, muscles stimulated and trained to achieve peak physical fitness by the end of her voyage. It was a potentially dangerous choice. If the ship malfunctioned—and if Crash malfunctioned along with it—she would continue to age as they floated through space, their emergency beacons begging for rescue. She would die an old woman, never again leaving the pod.

But the choice had been hers to make.

22

It would have taken the average dock crew hours to load the *Indelible IV* to maximum capacity, with crates of blaster rifles, charge packs, fraggers, ear-poppers, AP missiles, and more.

But here, now, it took all of thirty minutes. Because of who they were working for. And because of what delay meant.

Sometimes, Keel was almost frightened by the reputation he'd developed for himself—for Wraith—in the galaxy's underside. A lot of it had been exaggerated whispers, the sort of legend that grows from real-life achievement whenever someone rises to the top. But a lot of it was real.

People *had* tried double-crossing Wraith. Had tried to push him. And those people were all dead. Because that was how it had to be.

Doc had taught Keel that. Back when he was still a Legion captain trying to blend in and do the job Dark Ops had sent him to do. Back when he'd been imprisoned on a local backwater after his first attempt to get some intel. He'd been naïve then about what the Legion had become. Or parts of it at least.

Major Owens had sent Doc in to get him out and provide a little on-the-job training. And the old leej took him under his wing. Taught him how not to scream military whenever he stepped into a cantina. Helped Aeson Ford become Aeson Keel. Helped LS-33, call sign Wraith, become *the* Wraith.

Fully loaded, the *Six* jumped into Ponterran space. It was probably the proximity to Ponterra that had made Keel think of Doc, whom he hadn't thought about in a long time. The last he knew, the old man had taken up residence out here. The two had parted ways when it was clear Keel didn't need the old man anymore—and even clearer that the old man wanted to go back to living out the rest of his days in obscurity.

Now there was nothing for Keel and the *Six* to do but await the *Intrepid,* which had left to escort a Taijing freighter with a massive Samurai mech to Herbeer. The Samurais were relics from the Savage Wars, the fathers of the modern HK-PP mechs the Republic used, and could still go toe to toe with anything out there today. Now one of the massive things was serving as a guardian of the synth mines, further protecting the lifeblood of the Legion's finances.

Another major victory for Cohen Chhun. The way he had managed to assume control of the Legion and keep the boys getting paid while simultaneously growing the force... it really was something to behold.

And to think, Keel had known him way back when.

They'd both come a long way.

"Any word from *Intrepid*?" Keel asked Ravi.

"Nothing yet. They are only two hours late. Which, given the size and logistical requirements of the destroyer, is not unusual."

"Yeah. I remember Tarrago."

The destroyer hadn't shown up at all during the raid on the shipyards. And though Keel understood the reasons why, he still hadn't quite let go of the mistrust he'd developed as a result. Just because everything worked out all right didn't mean being stranded like that *was* all right. Not how he saw it.

The cockpit door swished open, and Masters and Exo took seats behind Keel and Ravi.

"Hey," Keel said to Exo, "I've been meaning to tell you. That was nice work back there. Really this whole trip. I could've used a guy like you back when I was out hunting for the big bad wolf."

"Yeah, well, once the House of Reason goes down," Exo said, stretching his legs out, "we can talk price."

"How about me?" Masters asked. "Do you want me to join your crew like Exo? Or am I too sexy? It's that, isn't it? You'd feel intimated with me always around. No, I understand. The captain of a ship needs to be either the most handsome guy or the most ugly guy. And if Exo is on the crew, we know who the ugliest guy would be. And if *I* were on the crew—"

"Sorry, Masters," Keel said. "Guys who can fire a blaster are a deema a dozen out here. But Exo is the type who makes people think real hard about using those blasters. Can't teach that."

"*You* were taught that," interjected Ravi.

Keel shot the navigator a withering stare. "No, I wasn't. It was innate."

"I could do what Exo does," Masters insisted. "Easy. How hard is it to act like you're always passing a kidney stone?" Masters scowled and impersonated Exo. "Yo, get outta my face, bro. I'll kick your ass. See? Easy."

"Not bad," said Keel with a half grin. "If you'll work for less than Exo, you're on."

"Psych," said Masters. "No way. I'm Legion for life. My life's goal is to reach Sergeant Major and then just do exactly what I do now, only no one will be able to shut me up." He rubbed his hands together. "It's going to be glorious."

"Yeah, I'm definitely getting out of the Legion after the House of Reason falls," Exo said. "No way in hell I'm stickin' around for Sergeant Major Masters."

"Hey, I have a question," Masters said, leaning forward in his seat. "What exactly did you do in your time away from the kill team to make criminal kelhorns look at you *like you're the most frightening thing in the galaxy*?"

Ravi laughed, "Hoo, hoo, hoo."

"Seriously," continued Masters, "were you like just killing everybody out here? Did Major Owens given you a license to kill? And then revoke it because you wouldn't stop murdering bad guys? What gives?"

"KTF in the private sector," Keel said nonchalantly. "That's all."

"Yes, this is all," said Ravi. "You systematically destroyed not one, but two multi-planetary crime syndicates because they short-paid you."

"It was the principle," Keel said.

"And then you also burned down a Republic governor's home—with him inside—for putting out a contract for your arrest when you refused to assassinate his mistress."

"He had it coming."

"And you impaled a colony of Gomarii and left them to rot on Grevulo."

"Technically the slaves did that."

"Hoo, hoo, hoo."

Masters shook his head. "Dude. You're messed up."

The comm chimed and Leenah called out, "The four of you need to come back here."

"That sounds ominous," Masters said, springing to his feet.

Keel got up and gently shoved the legionnaire back down into his seat. "Captain coming through, Masters. And I *am* the most handsome on this ship. You have a too much of a baby face."

Masters looked up innocently with his eyes as wide as they could possibly go. "How *dare* you!"

He got up again only to be pushed back down by Exo. "Move."

"Rude," Masters said, rising one more time only for Ravi to pass through him entirely.

"Aaaand weird."

The lounge of the *Six* was occupied by the other members of the kill team plus Leenah and Garret. A holo-projection was rendered at the center of the room, flashing a pale blue against the deck.

"What's this?" Keel asked. The team looked as somber as he could ever remember. It was the same look they'd worn after hearing the voice of Major Owens giving his final transmission before he died at Utopion.

"Goth Sullus has dissolved the House and Senate," said Bombassa gravely. "And he has scheduled the execution of every House of Reason delegate for tomorrow."

The holonewsfeed was showing a scene of mayhem. The House of Reason, in session, had been interrupted by a mix of shock troopers and those machines that had attacked military installations and strategic ports throughout the galaxy during the Battle of Utopion. Affronted and terrified delegates were being rounded up at gunpoint. Some could be seen fleeing for exits, only to be shot dead before they reached safety.

"Holy sket," said Exo. "Those war bots are working for Sullus?"

"Duuude," Masters said. "Dude." He shook his head. "Dude..."

"Stop sayin' dude," grumbled Bear.

"Holy strokes," said Masters.

Bear shot a laser-like stare at the sergeant, then went back to the holofeed, shaking his head. "This is bad news, man. Those bots are bad news."

"What they're doin' doesn't look so bad to me," said Keel.

Bear looked over at him. "You saw what they did on Gallobren, Captain. Total genocide."

Keel knew well what the machines were capable of. He'd fought through scores of them to rescue Leenah and his crew. He turned to Ravi. "You said whatever was controlling those bots was... what did you say?"

"Nullified," answered the Ancient navigator.

"Yeah. So what gives?"

Ravi closed his eyes for several long moments. Then reopened them and shook his head. "I do not sense a return of their former rulers. Goth Sullus achieved that much."

"Maybe he found a way to reactivate them," Exo said, not taking his eyes off of the images before him. "And now he's makin' good on what he promised us when we signed up for the Black Fleet."

Bombassa and Exo shared a look.

"It's damage control," Bombassa said. "The legionnaires of the Black Fleet have abandoned him in droves. Goth Sullus desired the power of empire more than the justice of the cause he called us to in the first place. He's trying to stop the defections."

"Well, if he'd'a done this right at the beginning—like he did with that point space rat Devers..."

Masters raised his hand. "Is there any way the two of you could *not* talk about your conflicted feelings in whether you should be shooting *with* me or *at* me?"

Exo shook his head. "Nah, bro. We're all good. It's like 'Bassa said. Sullus knew what buttons to press to get us to sign up. Maybe even believed all that stuff. But as soon as he got a whiff of victory—victory that *our men*"—Exo pounded Bombassa on the chest—"died to achieve, it went straight to his head. Everything was about *his* empire. And then to find out he was workin' with the House of Reason and Nether Ops and the points the whole time...? Nah, screw that guy."

Garret, who had stood at the back of the room leaning up against a bulkhead and furiously swiping through his datapad—likely looking for forum rumors—spoke up.

"So how do you do Article Nineteen now? What's the plan when there's no House or Senate left to depose?"

It was a question that no one on board the *Indelible VI* knew the answer to.

23

As Kill Team Victory filed out of the *Indelible VI* into *Intrepid*'s docking bay, they found Legion Commander Chhun waiting at the bottom of the ramp. The men hesitated for a moment, then straightened and saluted as memory kicked in.

Keel could see that Chhun wasn't exactly thrilled about the moment. Not because they showed him any disrespect, but because of the awkwardness of it all. Chhun had once told Keel that he hoped never to be awarded the Order of the Centurion, because doing so would alienate him from his fellow legionnaires in Dark Ops. Well, he hadn't been given the Order, and the result seemed about the same.

"Excellent work these last few weeks," Chhun said, returning the salute. "I mean that."

The kill team stood still for a moment as though there was something they wanted to say to Chhun. Probably about what they'd seen from Goth Sullus and the state of the galaxy. But they kept those thoughts to themselves.

"Thank you, sir," said Bear.

And then the team carried on down the ramp, off to work out or do whatever else they had planned now that they'd returned to their home ship and dormitories.

"No fun, huh?" Keel asked as he leaned against a bulkhead near the ramp, legs crossed at the ankles, his blaster still slung low on his hip.

"How's that?" asked Chhun.

"Being the boss."

"Oh. Well, I was their team leader before. So I'm used to it."

Keel gave a half grin. "Sure. Well, I'd grovel at your feet, Your Majesty, but I've already got one princess on board and couldn't really stand for any more royalty, even Legion commanders."

Chhun laughed, and it seemed to Keel that the legionnaire was happy to have someone speak to him as an equal. As a friend.

Which was a good thing, really. Because Keel felt just about done with the Legion. Not with the cause or the boys, but with the everyday life that was necessary to keep an army in fighting shape.

He'd felt that sense of purpose, that desire to right galactic wrongs that day on En Shakar when they learned of the Legion's fall at Utopion. They all had. But for Keel, the feeling had been more than quenched in the subsequent months of raids, fights, smuggling deals, and dogfights. And now the dissolution of the House of Reason and Senate... that was the last piece in the puzzle.

He had an overwhelming urge to go back to living life on his own terms. His independent spirit—trained out of him during his time in the Academy and while fighting for Pappy with Victory Company—was now stronger than ever. That spirit, which had first started to reappear when he went out into the cold for Dark Ops, had grown like instinct as he made his own way in the galaxy.

He could never have become Wraith—or even Keel—without that. And he wasn't keen on going back to the old ways.

To Chhun's credit, he'd never asked him to. Not since it was presumed he would go on a kill team rescue op for Major Owens on Herbeer. Chhun had given the *Indelible VI* an incredible amount of leeway and freedom to select its missions from a myriad of options always on the table as Dark Ops struggled to rebuild itself from the terrible losses the organization faced.

"Nice work getting all of this," Chhun said, looking around the interior of the *Six* as though he'd forgotten what it looked like. "I've got a newly developed angle on enough weaponry to supply twice the number of legionnaires we have. But this haul will definitely make a difference in the fight."

"The fight?" Keel crossed his arms. "Cohen, it sounds to me like the fight is over."

"You're talking about what Goth Sullus did?"

"And what he said." Keel pushed off from the bulkhead and strolled toward his friend. "Buddy, let it all go. The core *deserves* whatever they get. They created the environment that let the House of Reason flourish."

"Maybe," said Chhun, nodding. "But how about the mid-core?"

"Well, maybe they're getting a raw deal. But the galaxy is full of winners and losers."

The men were dancing around the meat of the issue. Playing a game of polite conversation. Avoiding the points that required gut checks.

Chhun showed the resolve that Keel expected of him. "Goth Sullus is a tyrant. He attacked Tarrago without regard for military or civilian life. He killed legionnaires. You said he did the same thing on Tusca. He sent the zhee to Sinasia. He killed Major Owens. I have a duty to the Republic to protect it from people like him."

"And how does that play out when there's no Republic left to defend, huh, pal?"

"I still have a duty to the Legion. And so do you."

"Ah." Keel looked away, feeling like he'd been hit with a cheap shot. "I've done *plenty* for the Legion."

"Not saying you haven't."

There was a moment of silence between them, filled by the humming of the *Six*'s instruments as they exchanged data and catalogued everything they'd need in order to soar among the stars once the hold was emptied of its contents.

"What about X?" Chhun asked.

"What about him?"

"Wraith, he's responsible for the deaths of hundreds of thousands of legionnaires. Not directly, but by his actions. Pappy. *Chiasm*. All gone because of him. And for what?"

Keel's jaw clenched. The Nether Ops kelhorn had done the Legion dirty. All out of his own sick sense of self-importance. He epitomized the saying, "Legion don't make you Legion."

Because some guys passed the training, but never became legionnaires.

"Listen," Keel said, doing his best to sound reasonable. "If you ever get a chance to dust the guy, call me up. I'll be more than happy to help. But what you've done rebuilding the Legion from where it was at after the Battle of Utopion... it's special, Cohen. Don't throw it away on a fight that doesn't need to be fought for a cause that can't happen any longer. Let the galaxy move on."

"So... you're going?"

Keel frowned. "To En Shakar. Yeah. Leenah's been after me to get her to see Prisma again. Doesn't sound like the kid is handling things too well there. Maybe could use a visit."

"I'm not going to try to stop you..." Chhun began.

"Oh, I was worried," said Keel in mock alarm.

"Because," continued Chhun, his hands up in a disarming pose, "I agree that you've done a lot for the Legion. More than anyone had any right to ask. I, uh... I read your files. One of the many new privileges that come your way once you're voted Legion commander. You went through a lot for us. And you should know that it's appreciated."

Keel looked away. This wasn't something he wanted to talk about. "Yeah, well, some of that was a long time ago."

"Doesn't change the fact that you're, in my opinion, the best the Legion has."

Keel nodded but didn't smile. "I feel the same way."

The two men laughed.

"You're free to go, and I know you didn't need my permission for that." Chhun looked around the ship. "Oba knows you'd just blast out of here if someone ever tried to keep you around. But I'm really hoping you can do one more job for the Legion. For me."

Keel pulled his hand down his face. "What?"

"It's why I arranged to meet in this system. I need you to make a pickup on Ponterra. It's paid for, and it was expensive. But I was hoping you could get it."

"I thought you said you had enough weapons from your new deal."

"Not like this. It's a MARO."

MARO. Massive antimatter reaction ordnance. Like the bomb that took out *Chiasm* a lifetime ago.

"Holy hell, Chhun. Who are you planning to use that on?"

"No one in particular. I just don't like the idea of one of those being out there for someone else to use. Like on Kublar."

"Pick up a MARO. Why not just send a shuttle since you've got a destroyer in the system?"

"Legion paid for it, but the seller doesn't know that. I don't think they'd have made the deal if they suspected. And I can trust you not to screw it up."

Keel kicked the decking with the point of his boot. This was going to make Her Highness Princess Leenah royally upset. If she heard about it. But like Chhun, Keel didn't like the idea of a MARO being on the market for the next psychopath to pick up and detonate inside a destroyer full of legionnaires. Or in the middle of a city.

"I'll do it, but on one condition."

"Name it."

"That shuttle you can't use to pick up the MARO? Use it to get Leenah to En Shakar. She's waited long enough and I can't ask her to wait more."

This didn't look like it pleased Chhun. "I can't... I can't use a military shuttle to facilitate a civilian reunion, Wraith."

"Sure you can," said Keel, sidling up to Chhun to put his arm around the man. "You're the Legion commander. Who's gonna stop you?"

"You're not going to agree to make the pickup unless I do this, are you?"

"Not a chance."

Chhun sighed. "Fine. Life would be a lot easier where you're concerned if I could just give you an order."

Keel smiled. "You'll always be Sergeant Chhun to me, pal."

***

"Just like old times, huh, Ravi?"

The *Indelible VI* had made entry into the Ponterra atmosphere and was now gliding above an old-growth forest cut through with deep dark rivers and streams. Cleared fields of farmland interrupted the wilderness, the crops a uniform yellow that complemented the orange and red hues of the forest. They'd arrived during this section of the planet's autumn, and the wood smoke Keel could see rising from the chimneys made him yearn for simplicity.

And though life was rarely ever simple, flying the *Six* with just him and Ravi seemed close enough.

"We will reach the designated spaceport in ten minutes."

It was an old smuggler's trick, entering atmosphere well away from the desired spaceport and then coming in with sensors on full beam. It had only taken one run-in with pirates lying in ambush for Keel to learn that one by heart.

"Ravi... did Leenah seem a little too eager to take that shuttle without me?"

"Hoo, hoo. Now I am playing master of the heart?"

Keel frowned and nudged the flight controls starboard to avoid a monolithic pine tree that rose high above the rest of the forest canopy. "Ah, you're right. She's crazy about me. Who wouldn't be, amiright?"

"I can think of several."

"You know what? I'm in such a good mood that I'm going to let that slide. I'm showing restraint, Ravi. Restraint."

"You do seem to be in high spirits, Captain."

Keel set the controls to auto and leaned back in his seat. "I am. For two reasons. First, because all this fighting is done and we can get down to living life on our own terms. And two, because it's nice to get back to the way things were. Just the two of us."

"Garret is also on board."

Keel looked around the cockpit, as though expecting the code slicer to be physically in their midst instead of holed up behind a datapad in some corner of the ship. "He is?"

"Yes."

"Huh. Well, you get the point."

The comm pulsed blue. Keel leaned forward and flipped it on. "Yeah?"

"This is Port Alpha, Ponterran Security Agency. Identify."

Keel gave a grin. "This is the freighter *Whisper of a Summer's Dream* requesting permission to land at docking bay..." He muted the comm. "Ravi, what's our bay?"

"I cannot believe you used those credentials."

"The bay, Ancient one."

"26-E."

Keel went back to live comms. "Sorry about that. Docking bay 26-E."

The comm fell silent.

Keel and Ravi exchanged a look. The navigator raised an eyebrow.

"Everything all right, Control?" asked Keel.

"*Whisper of a Summer's Dream*?" the traffic controller asked.

Keel smiled. "I just fly it, Control. They didn't ask me what to name it."

The agent on the other end of the comm chuckled. "You're clear to land, *Whisper*."

"Acknowledged." Keel turned to Ravi. "See? No one trying to run a fake registry would pick a name like that. That's why I picked it."

"There is an increased likelihood that, due to the memorability of your name, a special inspection will be ordered. Four percent."

Keel shrugged. "As long as it's *before* we've got a mega-bomb in the hold, who cares? We're running clean right now."

Ravi cleared his throat.

"*Mostly* clean," Keel amended. "Just fly us in. I'm gonna make sure the seals on the armory aren't reading anything." He stepped out of the cockpit only to return a beat later, holding his finger up like a ward against his navigator's laughter. "*Only* because it's due. I'm not worried about getting inspected."

***

Only two humanoids met Keel at the docking bay. A human who looked like he'd been across the valley once or twice and stopped to get drunk at every dive bar along the way, and his surly drusic bodyguard, an older male whose black fur had turned silver with age. The ape-man didn't appear to have lost any size or strength to the years.

"You're at 26-E," the human said.

Keel looked around the docking bay as if unsure of this detail. "Yeah. Looks like it."

"Lemme see your auth manifest."

Keel tossed him a rugged datapad that showed the R-verified credentials Chhun had brokered to his falsified registration. "Here you go."

The man looked down at the datapad. He had a red, almost glowing alcoholic's nose with pink eyes to match. The drusic snuffed out two clouds of vapor from his nostrils.

"Yeah, all right," said the man. "You know how this is gonna work, right?"

"Not at all," answered Keel. "Blind shipment in almost every way. I'm supposed to get here, get loaded, and then get off planet and meet the next guy at—"

"Ah ah ah," said the man, waving his hands in the air as though banging them on a window. "I don't need to hear about what happens when you dust off, spacer. And I don't *wanna* hear it. Fathom?"

Keel shrugged. "Sure, I guess."

"He guesses." The man looked over his shoulder at his drusic friend. "Got ourselves an amateur over here."

Keel looked down as though he were wounded by the remark. "Hey, I'm just doin' what I was told."

"Yeah, all right. You got any idea what you're haulin', kid?"

Keel shook his head. "Nope. Like I said, blind shipment in more ways than one. You could put a bomb on my ship and I wouldn't know it. Can't even access the hold. It's all slaved to the manifest. Which you've got and I'm locked out of. Is that normal? Like, will the guy in—sorry—will the next guy be able to get the cargo out?"

"Unbelievable, this guy," the man said to the drusic.

"He's an idiot," rumbled the big alien. "So let's load it up and go already. Paren ain't payin' us by the hour."

The man gave Keel a squinty smile. "All right, spacer. So this is all in order and... we just gotta get you loaded up. Give us a couple hours and then come on back. Here." He flipped a credit chit at Keel, who acted as though he barely had the reflexes to catch it. "There's a girly bar about ten blocks east of this avenue. You can pass the time there. On us."

Keel inclined his head as if to say, "Whatever you say," then strode out of the docking bay, hands in his jacket pockets, whistling Mendella's cover of "Holographic Love" out of order and off-key. Usually he wouldn't stand for *anyone* loading his ship without his being present. But since, luckily, he'd brought Garret with him, the coder would keep them from getting anywhere except the cargo hold. Besides, they were already putting a bomb on board capable of cracking a destroyer in two, so he wasn't sure what else he'd worry about.

Come to think of it, maybe Chhun had sent him because he didn't want to risk a freight full of Dark Ops leejes blowing up midway. No... probably not. Chhun didn't think that way.

Ravi was waiting for his captain outside the docking bay. "I must compliment you on how well you come across as having utterly no clue."

Keel scowled. "Thanks."

"Please tell me we are not going to pass the next two hours at the less-than-gentlemanly establishment suggested by those two?"

"Nah. Figured we'd just walk around."

Ravi moved to keep up with Keel, who was walking quickly across the street. "Perhaps you will be open to an alternate agenda."

"What's that?" Keel asked, not breaking stride. He danced around a pair of long-haired Republic advocates coming out of a galactic-wide kaff franchise, the purple streaks running through their hair a dead giveaway that they made their living as citizen lobbyists. Professional protestors jumping from one hot topic to the next. Who knew what the outrage of the hour was on Ponterra. Maybe the dissolving of the House and Senate. But probably something more farcical, like free health care for household pets.

It was all Keel could do to keep from "accidentally" bumping into them and knocking the overpriced dessert they tried to pass off as kaff out of their hands.

"Since you are on the same planet, I was thinking you could visit Doc."

Keel halted. Pedestrians flowed around him like a creek around a boulder. "Ravi, I'm not sure that's a good idea."

"You don't think he'd be happy to see you?"

"I don't think he's even alive. He was old back *then*."

"But if he *is* alive…"

Keel shrugged. "Yeah, why not. But there's no way of knowing—"

"Yes, he is alive," Ravi said with a singular nod of his head. "I checked. And he is living in this district."

"Convenient," Keel said from behind a glower. "He just *happens* to live in the same district as our drop location?"

"No. This is why I changed the pickup location."

Keel shook his head. "The way you manipulate me into things, pal…"

"Not manipulating, Captain. *Guiding*."

"Fine," said Keel, his lighthearted mood fading fast. He looked back to find the two purple-haired advocates and see if their drinks were still close enough to swipe out of their hands and frowned anew when he saw how far away they'd gotten. "Which way?"

Ravi pointed to an intersection. "Eight blocks there and then a left, and then three blocks, and then a right."

Keel stepped in front of an enclosed speeder, which had to slam on its brakes to keep from hitting him. He pounded on the hood.

"Leave the street level for walkers, you jerk," Keel shouted.

Why repulsors cruised the roads when they could just as easily move in one of the aerial grids above was a mystery to Keel. And something of a pet peeve. He ignored the driver's retort and hopped up on the curb.

"Let me guess," he said to Ravi. "You already told Doc we're coming."

Ravi laughed. "Oh, no. I want there to be a surprise."

"Swell."

The two moved along the sidewalks. Keel stopped in front of an Endurian-style grill. "Let's go in here," Keel said. "Those two at the docking bay gave me a free lunch, so I may as well take it."

As they ate, Keel gave Ravi the rundown of all the reasons the Legion would be crazy to push into the core now that Goth Sullus had eliminated the big problem of the House of Reason. But Ravi, though he never gave a counterargument, seemed less than convinced.

Military and political ideology aside, Keel was glad the meal and conversation managed to eat up some time. He was still going to visit Doc, he just wasn't sure he wanted the visit to be a long one. And having a loaded ship to get back to was as good of an excuse as any to get going when the time came.

As he and Ravi neared their destination, it became clear that Doc lived in one of the rougher neighborhoods. The bustle of commerce that had greeted Keel near the docking bay was replaced here with relatively empty, dirty streets. The few people he saw tended to be congregating on cement stairs leading up to rundown tenement buildings.

A speeder hovered by blaring Hool diss tech, an odd variant of electronic music first popular among the Hools, though created by Hildaarians, where each song insulted the listener directly. The most popular artists plugged into their listener's social media and synthesized tailor-made diss tracks specific to the individual.

The galaxy was a crazy place.

As the diss tech faded, it was replaced by the sound of shouting voices.

"Doc!" the voices shouted.

No, not voices. One voice. Echoing. Multiplying. A trick of all the uninterrupted duracrete.

Keel picked up his pace.

"Doc!" the voice yelled again. "We know you're in there, old man!"

Keel turned a corner and saw five men, all wearing black trench coats, all armed. They were gathered in front of a squat, one-story building with barred windows. It looked to be a converted garage for the boarded-up building—maybe an old deli—adjacent to it.

"Why do I feel like this is the place?" Keel asked Ravi.

"Surprise," the navigator answered.

24

Keel strolled casually out in the street, moving toward the thugs who had surrounded Doc's home. In all their yelling, they were oblivious to his approach.

"Odds?" Keel asked from the side of his mouth.

"Certainly you are not considering shooting these men in the back?" Ravi said.

"I'm considering it, yeah."

"Eighty-five percent, but I do not recommend such action for a number of reasons. I cannot account for lookouts, backup, body armor beneath those long coats, Ponterran police responsiveness—"

"Fine," Keel said. "We'll do it your way. Happy?" He moved ahead a few more steps and shouted, "Hey! Is Doc in?"

The five goons whirled around. Two had blaster pistols, and both were now aimed at Keel. Two other goons waved batons menacingly and the last raised a glistening machete.

"Whoa," Keel said, putting up both hands. "Not looking for trouble with you. It's Doc I'm after."

"Who're you?" snarled a large man with a crooked nose and brownish-green teeth.

"I'm Keel, and this is Ravi," Keel said, hitching a thumb at his navigator. "And we're not looking for trouble with you. Doc owes us money and I'm here to collect before the next job takes us off planet."

"How much money?"

"Oh, it's not like that," Keel said, still holding up his palms. "He swiped the pay-key on a job I completed, and I need to get it back from him before some code slicer re-routes it to his account. I mean, look at this dump. He doesn't have any money *now*. I just need to find out where he hid it."

The thug held up a finger, keeping the pistol in his other hand pointed at Keel. "If I was you, I'd turn around and forget about all that. We got here first, and Doc ain't gonna live long enough to tell you about no pay-key."

"He, uh…" Keel began, making his voice break ever so slightly. "He owe you money, too?"

The thugs formed a semicircle behind their leader.

"This ain't about money, off-worlder. He killed one of us. Killed a Wingo. And that don't fly on Ponterra."

Keel suspected as much. Which was why he'd been ready to drop the men before they'd even seen him. These were gangbangers, probably terrorized the neighborhood Doc lived in. And Doc being Doc, he'd probably had enough one night and put one of them down. And now the others were out for payback.

"Ravi?" Keel asked.

"Forty percent."

"Three shots."

"Oh. Forty-five percent."

Keel frowned, then pointed to one of the gangbangers holding a pistol. "Could you... could you step to your left? Just one step."

The thug looked in confusion at his fellow hoods, then back to Keel. "You retarded or somethin'?"

"Just one step," Keel repeated. "I wanna see what's behind you."

The man obeyed, and they all turned around to see what Keel was talking about. And in that split second, Keel pulled his blaster.

It was already out of the holster and firing by the time Ravi said, "Seventy percent."

Three shots ripped into the clumped gangbangers. The first struck You-Retarded-Or-Somethin' in the chest, went straight through him, and slammed into the chest of the man behind him. The second shot struck the leader in the forehead, blowing out the back of his skull. The third took out thug number four, another chest shot. Keel let the fifth banger run, his machete clattering to the street and his trench coat flapping behind him as he retreated.

Keel took a step forward, only to hear a voice from the window shout, "You dumb sonofabitch! He's the worst of 'em all and you're lettin' him get away!"

Keel rolled his eyes, but stopped and lined up the fleeing thug in his sights. He was at least sixty yards away now. Keel sent a single shot that slammed home between the thug's shoulder blades and put the man dead on the street.

There were no sirens.

Keel holstered his weapon. "Satisfied, Doc?"

"He was runnin' for backup!" Doc shouted through the metal bars of his window. "You don't let a loose end like that hang out. You finish the job, Leej!"

Keel walked up to the window bars. Through the broken glass, Doc's home looked ransacked and filthy. And Doc didn't look so fresh either. His hair was thin and completely white. His face was sagging with age. Gone was the hard jaw line that had been barely hanging on when Keel first met him.

Doc was an old man.

"Y'know, I could've just let *them* finish the job," Keel said. "The least you can say is thank you."

Doc revealed through the bars a surge shotgun that looked too heavy for him to even lift. But he pumped it all the same in the smooth, practiced motion of a man who'd spent his life using firearms. "I was just gonna get them close enough so I could blow their damn heads off. I'm not gonna thank you for help I didn't need."

Keel pinched the bridge of his nose. "Old age certainly hasn't softened you up."

"The hell with that. I used to be the nice guy, you know."

"The nice guy, I know," Keel said, speaking over Doc's sentence as he finished it.

Because that's what Doc always said. *I used to be the nice guy*. And maybe that was true once upon a time. But as long as Keel had known him, Doc had been the hardest of the hardasses.

Doc's gaze rested on Ravi. "You bring the ship, Ravi?"

"Yes, Doc. It is good to see you again."

"Huh." Doc moved away from the window toward the door.

Keel followed his motions from the outside, reaching the door just as Doc swung it open. He tried to step inside the house, but Doc pushed him back and slipped outside. He tucked the shotgun inside a bugout bag and pulled a ball cap over his white hair.

"Oba's balls, Keel. What the hell you tryin' to do? You don't hang out at a place like this. Not with five bodies in the streets. We're leavin'."

"We?"

"You're damn right, 'we.' I was gonna kill 'em *inside*. Someone had to hear that Intec hand cannon you're packin'. Now I gotta burn this pad and find a new one."

"How? How were you going to kill them inside?" Keel asked, walking with Doc and Ravi past the carnage and disappearing into an alley. "Were you gonna invite them in for tea and cookies?"

"No, I was gonna leave the door unlocked, make like I was having a heart attack, and then shoot 'em all in the head from the blind I have behind the wall."

They snaked through alleys and side streets. No one was out. And still, no sirens.

"That's stupid," Keel said. "That wouldn't have worked."

"It woulda worked."

"Ravi?" Keel asked.

"Having not seen the blind... a percentage is not reliable."

"Assume it's a good one," Keel snapped.

"You're damn right it's a good one!" said Doc.

"Thirty percent."

"See?" Keel said, holding out a hand toward Ravi.

"Hell, he don't know," grumbled Doc.

They continued to move through the alleys, dodging tipped-over refuse pods awaiting automated pickup.

"We oughta just take the main streets," Keel said, hopping over a puddle of what was definitely not *just* water. "Still no sirens."

"Cops don't run this district," Doc said. "Wingos do. Right up to the docks. They're who we're tryin' to avoid."

As if on cue, two men wearing the same long black trench coats as the gangbangers Keel just dusted turned a blind corner to stand in their path. One had a blaster pistol and the other a full-auto blaster rifle.

Keel and Doc instinctively jumped for cover as the blaster rifle sent sizzling bolts down the center of the alley.

But Ravi acted faster than Keel even had time to process. His azure robes flowing, he closed the distance between himself and the thugs in a flash, caused a sword to materialize in his hands, and sliced the two men nearly in half with one stroke. He disappeared and rematerialized next to Keel and Doc.

"Holy hell," said Doc. "When did he learn to do that?"

"Recently," Keel said, moving toward the two dead men. "C'mon!"

Doc paused to look at the dismembered bodies. "He do this all the time?"

"No. Only when he feels like it."

"Yes, this much is true," Ravi said. "And I feel it is important for us to get to the *Indelible VI* without the delays a prolonged gun battle would create."

"Oba's balls, what I wouldn't have given to have him on my kill team back in the day."

They found their way to the better-patrolled streets of the docks without further trouble. It was earlier than the time Keel's contacts had told him to return, but it had been long enough that they should have finished loading the MARO—unless they were out to milk the clock. But Keel didn't think so.

And in fact, they entered docking bay 26-E just as the man and his drusic companion were making for the exit.

"You're early," the man said.

"Yeah," answered Keel. "Got bored."

The two parties kept walking, Keel's crew toward the *Six* and the loaders toward the door. They kept a respectful distance from one another, putting crates and tool chests between them. Everyone liked to play it safe after a deal. Just in case.

"Who're these two?" asked the man.

Keel looked at Ravi and Doc. "Friends I met on the town."

The drusic snorted. "Not the type I would've picked up at the girly bar."

Doc was incensed. "Why, you kelhorned—" He pulled the shotgun from his bugout bag and pumped it to prime a surge blast.

The drusic and his friend both went eyes wide and scrambled for the exit.

Doc wasn't the type who pulled unless he meant to use it. He sent a blast at the two that smashed into a drum full of coolant, sending oily blue rivulets into the air. The loaders yelped and sprinted from the docking bay as Doc pumped the action a second time.

"What the hell are you doing?" Keel shouted.

"They insulted us!" Doc yelled back. "Always make 'em pay! You know that, Leej!"

Keel dropped the ramp to the *Six*. Now there *were* sirens. "That's not what that means!"

"It's what it means to me," Doc said as he passed Keel on his way up the ramp.

Ravi followed sheepishly.

Keel scowled at his navigator and held out a menacing finger. "This is your fault."

"I confess I had forgotten how he can get."

Keel nodded mockingly and did a nasal impression. "I forgot how he can get."

He ran inside and slammed his fist against the ramp-return button.

Doc was inspecting the inside of the ship. He'd already tossed his bugout bag on Keel's workbench, sending Keel's blaster's cleaning tools over the side.

"You stay here," Keel ordered, then ran up to the cockpit.

Ravi was already warming up the *Six* for departure.

"Guys?" It was Garret over comms. "What's going on? I heard blaster fire outside and now there's a mean-looking old man asking me a bunch of questions when I came out of the fresher. He's calling me a stowaway. I think he's going to hit me."

"Don't talk to him," said Keel. He flipped on the ship-wide comm. "Doc, the kid's with me. Leave him alone and strap yourself in for takeoff."

Keel switched the comm over to the Ponterran controller. "This is docking bay 26-E. Someone is shooting outside my ship and I'm requesting immediate clearance to take off. I fear my life's in danger."

"Identify yourself," said the controller.

The cockpit door swished open and Doc stepped through just as Keel said, "This is the freighter *Whisper of a Summer's Dream*."

"What the hell kind of fem name is that for a ship?" Doc growled.

Keel spun around. "I have reasons!" He returned to face forward and help Ravi initiate the takeoff sequence. "And I meant for you to strap in *back there*. Away from me."

"With the geek? No thank you."

Keel ground his teeth. Doc had taught him a lot about living outside the Republic's "respectable" side, but those lessons had come with a caustic price. Especially toward the end. And now it seemed that those qualities had grown rougher with age.

"*Whisper of a Summer's Dream*," squawked the comm, "we have holocam footage of a shooter making an unprovoked assault on two humanoids."

"It was provoked," grumbled Doc under his breath.

"He appears to have boarded your ship."

"Uh, no," said Keel, acting like he was surprised to hear it. "Couldn't be in here. Just me and... my... bot. Maybe he's hiding under the belly? I'd better take off so you can see him better."

"Do *not* leave the docking bay. We're sending tactical police to your location."

Keel tried one more time. "I'd really rather not stick around..."

"Stand by for tactical police, *Whisper*."

Whirling in his seat, Keel said, "Why couldn't you have just let it slide?"

"Because!" Doc shouted.

"Fine." Keel took hold of his flight controls. The docking bay was accessed through an enclosed tunnel that kept the noise away from the streets outside. "Garret?"

"Yeah, boss?"

"Can you make sure those docking tunnels don't close on us?"

"Not a problem, boss."

Keel turned to his navigator. "Ravi, we're taking off."

"They will send interceptors after you if they believe you are running."

"We'll outrun 'em."

"And may I remind you of what we are carrying, should any errant shots get through our shielding before we can sufficiently accelerate?"

"Oh, yeah." Keel frowned. "Okay, new plan."

He switched on the comm for Ponterran Control. "Oh, no! This is *Whisper of a Summer's Dream*. You were right! He's on board! He says he'll kill us all if we don't take off right away. Me and... the bot."

"You're damn right I will!" shouted Doc, doing his part. "Don't think I won't! I just iced five Wingos and you ain't nothin', fancy boy!"

"*Whisper*, this is Flight Control! I'm transferring this call to the Ponterran police."

"Sorry, no time!" Keel switched off the comm. "Punch it, Ravi!"

The ship took off, its running lights lighting up the dim tunnel, shining on a sealed blaster door ahead.

"Keel..." said Doc, sounding concerned.

"Don't worry."

The ship raced closer.

"Keel..."

And then the doors spread open allowing the *Indelible VI* to shoot through. Each subsequent door opened behind it.

"Nice work, Garret!" said Keel.

"Thanks, boss. I had to divert the Ponterran sanitary mainframe to allow—"

"Not the time!"

Two Preyhunters had emerged from connecting tunnels behind them and were now pursuing the *Six*. So far they were keeping a respectful distance, but Keel wondered how long it would be before the police found out what had really happened.

"Huh. That kid's all right," Doc said. "Opened all those doors like that? He's all right."

"Don't tell him in person," Keel warned. "You'll frighten him."

The comm pulsed blue. "*Whisper*, this is the Ponterran tac police. You are to power down immediately and surrender yourselves for arrest for attempted murder."

"Looks like the drusic and his pal talked," said Keel. "Everybody hang on."

The *Six* surged forward as Keel threw additional power into the engines, causing the rest of the tunnel to streak by in a blur. Then they were shooting out of the tunnel and out over the autumnal forests they'd passed on the way in, leaving the Preyhunters in their backwash.

"I remember this ship being fast," said Doc, "but not like this."

"This is thanks to Captain Keel's mechanic and love interest," said Ravi.

"Huh," said Doc. "So you finally put together a crew that wasn't twarg-dung crazy."

"Imagine that," Keel said.

He piloted the *Six* out of Ponterra's atmosphere and disappeared into the unending folds of hyperspace.

25

Chhun sat at his desk—loathing how much he'd been chained to it—as he spoke to Wraith over hypercomm.

"Cargo's secured and we're on our way to the drop-off," said Wraith, on audio only due to the limitations inherent to communicating with jump drives active. "Should be a couple of days."

"Thanks. For doing that. I mean it."

"Haven't done anything yet," Wraith answered. "Cargo could still blow us up before the trip is finished."

"Well," said Chhun, "assuming you don't wind up a scattering of atoms across the galaxy... thanks."

"What the hell did he just say?" asked an unidentified, and grouchy, voice in the background on Wraith's end. Chhun could hear Ravi quietly answering the question, though he couldn't make out the words.

"Who's with you, Wraith? This is supposed to be a secure comm."

"Oh. He's good. He's with me. Former Dark Ops. You'd like him." Wraith paused. "Okay maybe not like him, but he *was* Dark Ops."

Chhun hesitated, but assumed in the end Wraith would just tell whoever he'd picked up whatever he wanted to, classified status be deviled. That fact didn't present him from sighing.

Evidently Keel heard the sigh. "Relax, pal. He loves the Legion. He'd probably have joined up with you already if he wasn't such an old fossil. Did you decide what the Legion's going to do about Goth Sullus?"

This wasn't something a Legion commander should be speaking about with what amounted to an independent contractor. Even after all the extra security Wraith's code slicer had put in place around all comms to and from the *Indelible VI*, it wasn't proper.

But at the same time, Chhun didn't feel like he had much of anyone to talk to. He was Legion commander. Which wasn't to say he was without peers. There was Admiral Deynolds, of course, and a few of the Legion generals who had made their way to rejoin the diaspora centered around the *Intrepid*. Even a couple of sector commanders. They had all weighed in with their analysis and opinions.

And they were roughly split. Some wanted the Legion to hold the line and make the mid-core into a buffer between the edge—which Goth Sullus *was* ceding to them— and the Imperial center that was the core. Others wanted to take the fight to Sullus. To make him pay, along with Nether Ops, the only vestige of the House of Reason that had survived the purge, according to their intel.

And what all that really added up to was…

… the decision belonged to Chhun.

"I haven't fully decided. Sullus controls Tarrago. We control Herbeer. Even if the fighting were to stop, we'd be looking at an arms race. Both sides would just be even more destructive when we finally do cross paths."

Of course, the "new status quo" scenario assumed that all the non-edge planets would just play along with the dictates given by the leader of the Black Fleet. Which they wouldn't. Not all of them. Ten worlds had announced their independence from his empire within hours of his claiming the core and mid-core. That was the funny thing about politics on the galactic stage. The haves always assumed that the have-nots would just go along with whatever they decided.

But Chhun knew better. He knew firsthand just how easy it was for defiance to take control of a population. Even when that resistance was a lost cause. Men would forever motivate other men to fight. War was a constant. As sure as any other natural law in the galaxy.

"Well, it sounds like you're comin' around," Keel said. "Last time we talked you were ready to march on Utopion straight away."

" I still want to hear from a few more people. But if I *had* to make a decision right now... yeah, we'd fight."

"Can't say I'm surprised. You'll do the right thing for the Legion."

"Glad you think so. How about you?"

"I do the right thing, too. For me. KTF, Legion Commander."

"KTF. Chhun out."

Chhun picked up his datapad and checked his planner. Wash was past due for a check-in, but that was all right. He needed to keep a low profile. Besides, Chhun didn't really need Wash to tell him what had been going on on his end; Chhun could already see that for himself.

The Imperial conquest of Ankalor, for one thing. It had gone off without a hitch. Wash had deployed his shock troopers and their MCR support teams efficiently—not that there was much resistance to be had among the donks. The Legion had, after all, done the heavy lifting over there already.

And as promised, the flow of firearms and other munitions had begun—right under the noses of the Empire. Weapons were being moved into key underground resistance groups manned by current and former legionnaires living on Imperial planets. Particularly Utopion.

A chime sounded in Chhun's office. His next appointment had arrived.

"Enter."

He'd spent some time thinking about how a Legion commander should grant access to his office, and "enter" was the best he'd come up with.

Bear poked his head in. "You wanted to see us, Legion Commander?"

Chhun stood. "Come in, Victory."

The entire kill team was there. Bear still hadn't replaced Sticks—who was organizing some former legionnaires for a resistance cell near the Chorbarrio Void—but Chhun had someone in mind.

Bear led Masters, Exo, and Bombassa inside, and they all saluted sharply.

Chhun saluted back. "Guys, that's... you don't have to do that. Not in private like this. I know you're saluting the rank, but I wanted to talk to the four of you on more equal terms."

"What, like you're givin' us a promotion?" Exo said. "Yo! Legion Commander Exo up in here! And I *do* expect to be saluted."

Chhun smiled. He and Exo went way back. Farther than anyone else on the team. Farther than Ford, even. It was nice to feel that bond again.

"You all know about Goth Sullus and what happened on Utopion."

"Old news," Masters said, walking around Chhun's office as though it were his own. Picking up décor and inspecting it and then placing it back down far less delicately than he ought.

This, too, was a bit like old times. But not the sort that Chhun was eager to bring back. "Masters, careful with that stuff. Some of it has been with Legion commanders since the Savage Wars."

"I'm not gonna drop anything." Masters continued with his hands-on tour of Chhun's office.

"Is Utopion what this is about?" Bear asked. "You got plans that involve us? Because, yeah, I want to go there and KTF."

"Yes and yes." Chhun leaned against his desk, crossing his arms. "Right from the start, Admiral Deynolds and I have been working on growing our forces. And since we couldn't very easily train new legionnaires, we felt like our best option was to reactivate former leejes who could still put up a fight."

"Guys like Sticks," said Bear.

"Yeah, and a whole lot more. Vets who went home, but whose heart is still with the Legion." Chhun reached back to knock on the surface of his black, polished desk. "All those arms deals you did with Captain Ford? Those weapons have been put in the hands of cells of legionnaires throughout the mid-core and core. And they're waiting on me to say when the shooting should start."

"Dude!" Exo exclaimed. "Hell yeah!"

Chhun suppressed a smile. "Our single biggest cell is on Utopion. Lots of leej private contractors, bodyguards, plus the guys who just wanted to live where the action was."

"How large is this force?" Bombassa asked.

"Big enough that I feel confident that we have a shot if we want to take it."

Masters was rummaging through a bureau and found a datapad. "Hey, what's this?"

Chhun winced. He'd forgotten to lock that one and knew exactly what was on it.

"Is this a boooook?" Masters asked. "Are you writing a book, Legion Commander Chhun?"

Masters held the datapad as though unsure how to read it, rotating the screen in a mock attempt to make the words line up straight. "'The galaxy is a dumpster fire.' Catchy opening."

"That's—" said Chhun. "Put that down. Psyops thinks getting my memoirs out there will serve to increase our recruitment of former legionnaires. It's all in there. Kublar, Devers, Tarrago. I couldn't even have written it down if I wasn't able to clear the classified info personally."

"Hmm," said Masters, ignoring Chhun's request to set the datapad aside. "Lots of acronyms. That's gonna confuse the casual reader."

"It's not for the casual reader," Chhun said through gritted teeth as the rest of the kill team chuckled. "I wrote it for leejes who know how to KTF."

"Yeah… but still." Masters began to swipe the datapad. "How long until I show up in this story? I'm concerned that you didn't include me on page one. The reader will suffer."

Chhun stepped forward to take the datapad away forcefully. "Hand it over."

But Masters dodged away, still trying to find whatever he was looking for. "You said you didn't want to be treated like a Legion commander. So, no, I'm not giving this back until I've dropped a copy on my own datapad. I like to read before bed."

"Masters," Chhun said, not quite chasing the legionnaire around his office, though Masters was making it clear that he was willing to run if that's what it took to keep away.

Finally Masters walked backward into Bear, who snatched the datapad out of his hand and tossed it to Chhun.

Masters gave Bear the stink eye. "Oh, you are such a suck-up." He strolled over to Chhun. "If you want my advice about writing…"

"I really don't."

"… then what you need to do is turn this into a romance novel. I'm not kidding. Ladies of numerous species can't get enough of legionnaire romance stories."

"I take it back," Chhun said. "I'm the Legion commander and I take it all back. Everyone salute and leave before Masters says another word."

Masters held out both hands as if framing a marquee. "He was a legionnaire whose only joy was war. She was a lowly Republic Army supply clerk. Captured by mid-core rebels, they must escape the steamy jungles of Psydon. But there's no escape from the steamy lust that erupts in the acclaimed novel… *KTF Me*."

The legionnaires groaned at the punch line.

"What? I think that would sell great. I could be the cover model, because, have you seen these abs?" Masters lifted his shirt.

Chhun laughed and shook his head. This was nice. And deep down, he knew that it would be the last time in a long time life would be this way. A part of him wanted it to just keep going. Wanted Major Owens to bust through the door and tell them they had an op and to jock up. Wanted things to just go back to the way they were before everything fell apart.

But that wasn't going to happen. And it was up to him to make right what had gone so terribly wrong.

"Listen, guys. This… what I'm going to say next… it's not usual and it's not going to be a habit. Command is split about whether we keep fighting or strengthen up out on the edge. And that means it's my call."

Kill Team Victory was now sober, each man waiting quietly to hear what Chhun would say next.

"I remember that day when we heard Major Owens's last words. It was just us back then, ready to take on the Black Fleet and House of Reason by ourselves. And so now I'm asking just us to decide how far we take it.

"The House of Reason and Senate are gone. And if they come back, it's not going to be the same. Goth Sullus followed through on his threat: he executed every member of the House of Reason on Utopion as of four hours ago."

"If he had done this right away..." Bombassa said. But he shook away the thought. "Legion Commander, when Exo and I left Utopion, our mission was to find the girl Prisma Maydoon and use her to take the fleet at Ungmar. Operation Indigo." The tall legionnaire took in a deep breath and exhaled slowly. "I was *also* undergoing a separate operation—one that Exo was not aware of. It was called Reliance. My purpose was to determine whether the fleet was capable of stopping Goth Sullus."

"You serious, bro?" Exo asked. He didn't sound upset, just surprised.

"I am. It quickly became apparent that Goth Sullus lusted power above all else. The talk of empire seemed to intoxicate him, from the little of him I observed firsthand. There was an attempt on his life shortly after Tarrago. It was only because I had been ordered away that I wasn't slaughtered with the rest of the legionnaires who sought to take control of the Black Fleet."

"I take it your vote is to fight then?" asked Chhun.

"It is."

Exo nodded as though he were listening to a song. "Yeah. Me too. A lot of good leejes died on Tarrago and he threw that all away. Like trash. Ain't no difference if he did the right thing later. Like when Devers brought us charge packs back on Kublar, remember?"

Chhun nodded. Admiral Devers had pitched in during that final battle, when it looked like a last stand was all Victory Company had left. But as soon as he was safely aboard the *Mercutio*, he was back to his former self.

"So yeah, KTF."

"KTF," echoed Bear. "Just tell us what happens next."

"Masters?" asked Chhun, not necessarily because he wanted to, but because he felt everyone on the team needed a say.

"Hmm? What was the question?" But before anyone could answer, the mercurial legionnaire smiled and said, "I'm in. Of course I'm in."

"All right," Chhun said, rubbing his hands together. "We've got a small window during which there's a reduced fleet at Utopion. Sullus has plans for them to further punish the zhee."

"Oh yeah?" said Exo. "Maybe I should change my vote."

"I didn't say we were going to try to stop him." Chhun tried to smile, but couldn't. The sting of what had happened to Kags, Fish, and Twenties would never leave him. Never. "We'll be slipping into Utopion to link up with the Legion resistance that's been arming, waiting to be activated. Admiral Deynolds will show up when we start shooting. Things go well, we'll get support from the Lex Fleet. If not, it's up to the assets we already have on Utopion to take Sullus out."

He brought up holomaps showing the layout of Utopion's capital. They were incredibly detailed, the diligent work of Wash.

"Okay. Let's start putting together some attack plans..."

26

X was finally feeling back in his element. He had consolidated enough Nether Ops agents to have a serviceable task force that he could trust. Men and women from the Carnivale. For that was the purpose of the Carnivale: to keep options in front of X.

There were other Nether Ops agents on Utopion too, of course. Goth Sullus had dictated that the House of Reason pull on every string found in every delegate's pocket until the bulk of the agency was back on the planet. Most of them were assigned to new department heads, who in turn were working for Admiral Ordo.

A rival.

But a rival with the tools X needed. Because most Nether Ops agents, at the end of the day when the wounds were tended to and the blood rinsed away down the swirling drain of a sink, were men and women doing a job. That was all.

It was all it *could* be. All it *had* to be for these very human agents with very human emotions to cope with what they did for a living. And so trading in one boss for another really didn't seem all that troubling.

Those in senior positions put their minds to work determining how to find their equilibrium in the new order and resume their treks to the top. Those in the field obeyed orders. Or they didn't and went underground. A few killed themselves.

All that was common enough.

But X couldn't get by with common. He needed uncommon commitment. The type he'd groomed for service in the Carnivale. Men like Hutch had been. Willing to murder their own grandmothers had X asked it. He would never have asked it without a good reason. But Hutch's kill team... they would have done it.

And there were others like him. Dispersed into the various bureaus under Ordo's flaccid leadership. Just waiting for X to call them back in.

And now he had.

Because the favor of Emperor Sullus was a panacea. That's what those adjusting to empire didn't yet comprehend. The emperor was all. And X had found his way in.

Just a few leaks to the press created the sense that things were falling apart but *he* could help keep it together. And... favor shined down on him once again.

As it ever did.

Because in the end, what he was doing was good. A greater good. One that normal men with their moralistic notions of decency could never comprehend. Never wanted to comprehend.

X was the finest man he knew of. And he knew himself to be a cold-hearted killer. But so was everyone. There was a savagery inside of man that few ever faced. The difference was, X *used* his. And employed others who did the same.

For the greater good. In the Carnivale.

"Allison," X said into the ether of his office comm. Allison was his secretary, though the paperwork said "personal assistant." She had a good name for a secretary, X thought. "What's the word from Rawl Kima? Did they get anything out of him?"

"The report just came in, sir. I was preparing a memo just as you called."

"I can have it now, orally."

X looked out the window. He didn't like the view as much from the Imperial Palace. Too close to the hustle and bustle of downtown Utopion. He preferred his old haunt, drafty though it was. Away from the distractions. But, to serve the emperor required being near the emperor.

And the die had been cast, and X very much served this emperor. The benevolent dictator. Who had torn down a putrid House of Reason and a bloated Senate. Just as X's game theory had suggested would happen. Goth Sullus was the man for the hour. And now it was up to X to keep the momentum going. Because the man of the hour was never without his enemies.

X paused, and allowed himself a fractional smile. He had been right. About everything. About everything he'd done, every life lost, every betrayal. He was right. History would forget all of that. History would look back fondly on the untold lives he'd saved in reaching this point, this moment in his professional career.

He was right.

"The journalist was arrested and sent for interrogation by agents known to work for Admiral Ordo," Allison said, dutifully reading her memo. "Carnivale kill team five was able to neutralize the journalist before the transfer was completed, and they escaped off planet without detection."

"Thank you, Allison. That's smashing news."

X drummed his hands on his lap in triumph. Steadron was a potentially harmful loose end. X probably should have neutralized him long before Ordo went seeking him out. But it's never wise to throw away your toys until you're quite sure you're done playing with them.

"Tell me, Allison—hadn't you planned on taking a long lunch today?"

"No, sir."

"Well, take one anyway. I intend to."

The smile was evident in his secretary's voice. "Thank you, sir."

***

There was a slight mist out. Not enough to demand a ride in a speeder, but certainly sufficient to soak X's scalp. Still, it felt rather invigorating, as did the brisk pace he kept up to a decidedly underappreciated Feltish café in precisely the right part of the wrong part of town.

They knew him by sight there, the owners. Though not by name. Still, when X came up, they waved and smiled and prepared a minute cup of kaff. They waited for X to pick his pastry. He liked variety when it came to baked goods, though the ellian fritters were always a cracking choice when nothing else stood out.

That was what he had today. He sat by a window, wishing it were the sort of day fit for spending time outside, legs crossed in the breeze, picking up the scents of Utopion. Watching tourists pointing out the little street-front café and eagerly taking a table of their own, so they could have the pictures of themselves for later days. Days of remember when.

X sat and looked out the window. Thinking of spring. He'd finished his kaff and was seriously contemplating another. Though more than one always made his heart flutter.

But he'd selected a particularly thick and sweet fritter. So sweet that the kaff was necessary to keep him from being overpowered. And yet... he couldn't stop eating it. The devilry of a baker put Nether Ops to shame.

One more. He might as well have one more.

And then his heart fluttered for reasons beyond caffeine.

On the corner across the street was a run-down hovel of a bar. Indistinguishable on Utopion from all the other little dive bars that necessarily filled a city—and what was the planet except for one enormous city? A city that could do so much for a man and then just as easily destroy him. Except this bar was known as a Legion bar. The sort of place where old cranky legionnaires went and groused about age. Or argued. About anything. Sports, tactics, wars, politics, who had the better company emblem. Anything.

X didn't patronize bars like that.

But he recognized a man emerging from it. Legion Commander Washam.

And the Legion commander, one of the first appointed officers in the Legion... well, he certainly wasn't the type who would patronize such a bar either.

Or at least, he *shouldn't* have been.

Because those former legionnaires—of any age—though they argued about everything, they all agreed that points didn't belong in their bar. And the times when a point wandered in only to be thrown out on his rear... those were the moments that defined a whole year for these once and former heartbreakers and lifetakers. An existential moment that made tolerable the squalid lives they now lived. Away from brothers, from war, from anything except the nagging pain that no doubt followed them around like a ghost. The lot of the soldier returned home.

Such was a defining moment for an old leej.

And this was an... edifying moment for X.

It was the moment he decided that Legion Commander Washam needed to be watched.

***

Goth Sullus stood in One Voice Park, beside the Imperial Palace. For years, the lush, spacious park had been touted as a welcoming place where members of the public could encounter delegates and senators on their strolls—much to the dismay of the delegates and senators.

But now it was part of the Imperial Compound, off-limits to the public.

This was one of many changes to Utopion during Goth Sullus's short rule. The Senate Building had been locked up tight. The House of Reason had been renamed "the Imperial Palace." And along with One Voice Park, these central government buildings now formed what was known as the "Imperial Compound."

Sullus had not changed the name of the park. It was fitting. His was, after all, the one voice of the Empire.

But now the park was empty, Utopion's citizens kept on the other side of energy gates. The beauty of the landscape, the twin waterfalls fed by the river Eebris, the lagoons, the lush green of its lawns and trees that wrapped around the Imperial Palace and the former Senate Building... these were spoils belonyging to the Empire.

To Goth Sullus.

He stood looking out over his conquered land of promise. But he barely noticed the park or its beauty. He saw only the two thousand Cybar war machines arrayed before him.

"Is this all?" he asked.

"I beg your pardon, my lord?" asked Legion Commander Washam.

"There should be more."

"I... am unsure how Admiral Crodus was able to, as you say, reactivate them at all."

Should be more. Yes, master. There should.

This was the voice from whom Sullus had sought counsel. One he'd grown more and more dependent on as he solidified his empire. His enduring peace for the galaxy.

"Leave me, Washam. I will arrange the use of these war bots."

Washam bowed deeply. "Of course, my emperor."

Though Goth Sullus could not probe the man's mind, he sensed that Washam was thankful to be departing. The

Cybar had caused untold amounts of harm to the galaxy. Seeing them up close and on Utopion would indeed be unsettling, had Goth Sullus not been their conqueror.

Alone with the ring and the voices it conveyed. The spirits behind the Cybar. Demons, he'd once called them. When he had been naïve. They were others. Not Ancients. Others. And they obeyed him.

He had conquered them.

"This is all you bring me when I grant you leave to serve your master?"

You defeated us, master. You alone. This is all that remains of the Cybar.

The machines had served their purpose from the very instant of their arrival at the palace: they had caused panic in Utopion. At first because the populace thought the influx of ships running customs meant an attack. And then because of what stepped out of those ships.

But the Cybar paid no attention to the people of Utopion. And soon it was clear that they served Goth Sullus. As did the rest of the galaxy.

As did the House of Reason, whom the Cybar, along with Sullus's Imperial Legion, had captured. And executed. Every last one of them. Dead and incinerated.

And the grand irony of it all was that these self-important men and women, who for so long thought themselves the ultimate power in the universe… they died not mattering. Utopion carried on. As Goth Sullus had known it would.

But Utopion was not all that the galaxy contained. And these Cybar… they would be of little use beyond the planet itself.

"These will not be enough to defend the core against the Legion."

No, master.

"You have failed me."

No, master. Give us time, master.

"Time to build more Cybar for your emperor?"

No, master. You defeated us. You conquered us. We cannot build more. That is forever lost.

"Then... how?"

Silence.

Did you feel that, master?

Goth Sullus felt nothing. The Crux was as closed to him as it had been before he'd made the journey. It was maddening. He gave no reply.

The zhee screamed in their final moments. By your hand, conqueror, they are vanquished.

Goth Sullus felt nothing. But a tiny voice in his mind asked him why. Why he had done what he had done. Why he had failed to comprehend that such an act, even to the zhee, would only harden the hearts of the galaxy against him further.

Unless he *broke* their hearts of stone.

With fear.

Fear would save them. Because fear would preserve their emperor in his rightful place. And only Goth Sullus could save the galaxy from itself.

Let us come, master. We will serve you, master. We will fight for you.

Goth Sullus stood captivated by the allure of his own ascendancy. As emperor. As conqueror.

He would use his spoils to expand his territory.

"Show me."

And the others, the demons, entered his mind. And they revealed to Goth Sullus wonders to behold.

27

Kill Team Victory landed on Utopion in civilian clothing with nothing more dangerous than the knife tucked into Bear's pocket. The weapons they would use to fight their way to the Imperial Palace were in the hands of the Legion Underground waiting for them.

"Look at 'em all," Exo said, watching the anthill that was the streets of Utopion flowing with humanoids. "Just lost their government as they knew it, just nuked the zhee, and it's like nothin' even happened."

They had arrived by public transportation after taking an economy starliner to the Utopion System. Each man had a false ident registry, but only Chhun had to wear an uncomfortable facial reconfiguration mask. Something popular with Nether Ops. Dark Ops always had the luxury of their buckets.

"How you feel, Chhun?" Bear whispered.

"Like hell." He'd been in the mask for hours. Word was you got used to it after thirty minutes, then your face started screaming by the two-hour mark. And yeah, that had been about right. "How do I look?"

"You've never been handsomer," Masters said. This was because the mask had distorted Chhun's face to look improbably like Masters's. Or so Masters kept claiming.

Still, it was a necessary discomfort. Chhun's face had been all over the holowebs as the Legion's rising general and new Legion commander.

It was only because of his position as Legion commander that Chhun was allowed to undertake this mission. Because there was no one who could stop him. Sector Commander Lawrence would assume Chhun's role while he was away.

Getting in the fight wasn't what was expected from a Legion commander, but it was what Chhun felt he had to do. For himself, for his men, and for the Legion.

Everybody would fight. Including him.

Especially him.

The transport sled slowed as it pulled into a massive station that floated high in the air, level with the top floors of some of Utopion's tallest buildings. When the ride came to a halt, the doors hissed open and crowds of passengers hurried off to catch a transfer, grab a speeder, or take one of the lifts down to the surface level.

Chhun and his team were walking toward Terminal N when the miniature comm in Chhun's ear beeped an incoming transmission. He pressed his finger into his ear as if scratching an itch.

"Wanna bet on the game this weekend?"

"My wife would kill me," Chhun answered.

"Hopefully your trip went well," Wash said. "Take a seat next to Kaine. He'll be on a bench looking at a datapad underneath the Terminal N Private Speeder sign. Wearing a red ball cap. Say his name."

"I see him." Chhun motioned for the kill team to stay behind as he went forward and took an unassuming seat on the bench next to the man Wash had described. "Kaine."

The other man nodded, got up, and walked away, leaving a duffel bag behind. Chhun grabbed the bag, slung it over his shoulder, and started walking.

"Got the bag."

"And now you're armed," Wash said. "Welcome to Utopion. Wash out."

It was illegal for private citizens to own weapons in Utopion, just as it was illegal to carry them on public transportation and any inbound spaceships. The kill team had gone through customs upon arriving in their economy liner, and they were clean then, so the assumption was that they'd stay clean. So Chhun walked without concern past shock troopers armed with N-6 rifles watching for weapons being smuggled *into* the transit hub, all the while carrying a duffel bag full of blaster pistols.

Goth Sullus had made a lot of changes, but tightening Utopion security hadn't yet been one of them.

They took a speedlift down to the street. No one was joking or chatting now. That levity had been replaced with the cool professionalism that came with being on mission. Passing that checkpoint, taking the handoff of weapons… it served as a mental cue that the rest of their time on Utopion was on the clock.

There were holocams on the speedlift. There were holocams just about everywhere on the planet. Except for some of the poorer neighborhoods. There, cams were installed at the entrances of buildings, but missing were the bots hovering overhead with a watchful eye. The House of Reason had ruled it discriminatory to have excessive cams on neighborhoods below the Utopion poverty line.

They walked down grimy, unwashed streets that smelled like humanoid waste. It had rained earlier, and that seemed to have activated the stink of the city. A drunken human male was lying across the sidewalk, his head on the street as the kill team passed by. Chhun could hear him vomiting as they passed.

He took the opportunity to look around, and saw no one but the drunk.

"This alley here."

The team disappeared into the alley, and Chhun crouched behind a large garbage capsule. He dropped to a knee and unzipped the bag. It was full of blaster pistols and charge packs. Each legionnaire retrieved a weapon and two packs and concealed them. Chhun crumpled the bag into the trash capsule and followed his men back out of the alley.

It took all of thirty seconds.

Looking left and then right, Chhun continued up the street. A black enclosed speeder drifted alongside the team and came to a stop. Its doors opened and the driver leaned out. "This the way to Front Street?"

That was the signal. The legionnaires quietly piled into the vehicle. The sled surged down the street.

"So you're my VIPs?" the driver said, watching the legionnaires in his rearview mirror.

The speeder was large enough to seat seven. Exo, Bombassa, and Masters sat in the third row behind Bear and Chhun. The driver was alone up front.

"Looks like it," Chhun said, holding his blaster out on his lap. "You Legion?"

"I suppose," the driver said. "Name's Trevor. Trevor Martin."

"How do you mean, you suppose?" asked Bear.

"I was out. Making a good living collectin' contacts for the Bronze Guild. Lotta former leejes go into that line of work. Then I saw what happened to the Legion. Heard the new Legion commander, what's his name, Chhun, call for support. And I'm back in. Sort of."

Chhun squeezed the grip of his blaster at the sound of his own name. Everything was as he'd arranged with Washam, but there was never any way to be sure about anything. Especially on Utopion with its preponderance of Nether Ops spies.

Evidently Bear was feeling the same way. He communicated his concerns with Chhun with a series of sidelong looks.

"Why come here?" Bear asked. "Legion's been getting flooded with former leejes looking to re-up."

Without turning around, Martin held up a hand. He flexed the fingers enough times that the mechanical whir of cybernetic servos could be heard above the hum of the speeder's repulsors.

"That's why. Too much machine for Legion standards. Not bounty hunter, though." Martin put his hand back on the wheel. "Anyhow, I had a job on Utopion, ran into some buddies who were part of the Underground. They said it didn't matter if the only part left of me from birth was my head—they needed guys who could still KTF. And I can still KTF, sirs."

"Sirs?" asked Chhun.

"Didn't figure they asked me to pick up five privates."

"Where we goin'?" Exo asked from the back seat.

"Not supposed to say," Martin answered. "You might be Nether Ops."

Bear let out a grumbling laugh. "Was thinkin' the same thing about you. Did they warn you about Nether Ops? Most leejes—most of the galaxy—don't even know they exist."

"Nah. I was Dark Ops before. Until I lost my arm fightin' MCR."

"Sorry to hear it, Leej," Chhun said.

"Hey, at least I survived. The ones that need to feel sorry are the shock troopers that get in my way once this all goes down."

"Ooah."

Bombassa's deep voice boomed. "Someone is following us."

"Yeah," said Martin. "Saw him. Was gonna give it one more turn to be sure."

Chhun leaned forward. "You were Dark Ops. You know an alley divide?"

"Sure do."

"Turn here. Bombassa and Exo, right side."

The sled turned at the last second in a hard left that strained its repulsors, then it accelerated down the road, sending the legionnaires back into their seats. They traversed two blocks before Martin slammed on the brakes, stopping next to an alley.

Behind them, the speeder made the turn and began accelerating. They were being followed. There was no doubt of that now.

"Go!" Bear ordered, and Exo and Bombassa jumped out of the sled and ran into the alley.

Martin took off. The pursuing sled, all black and unmarked, slowed at the point where Exo and Bombassa departed. Two men in civilian clothes armed with blaster rifles got out and went down the alley where the legionnaires had run, then the sled resumed its pursuit.

"So far, so good," Martin said, drifting around a corner and cutting off a sled that had just started to creep forward with the change of a hovering traffic bot. "Assuming your boys can handle their part of the plan."

"They're Dark Ops," Chhun said. "They can handle it."

Martin nodded. It was clear that the driver had been honest about being Dark Ops himself. He handled the sled masterfully, a product of graduating from the Dark Ops driving courses. Every leej in Dark Ops knew how to drive offensively and evasively. They knew how to drive tactically, how to shoot while driving, and how to use their vehicles when engaged in a firefight outside.

Chhun hoped it wouldn't come to that. He wanted Martin to escape and then pick up Exo and Bombassa on the other side. The two leejes would continue to move in the same direction until they were picked up. How far and fast they went was up to them and up to the threats and conditions they faced. But Chhun had confidence that his men would be a match for whoever was following them on foot.

The chase continued. This was a poor district, one that butted up against the alien districts. Less crowded, less policed. Martin put some distance between his sled and that of their pursuer, but not enough to lose them. Each legionnaire inside had his pistol ready, prepared to use it if the opportunity presented itself.

"I see two guys in that sled," Masters called out. "Driver and front passenger seat. Passenger is carrying a subcompact."

That would provide a considerably higher rate of fire than the pistols the legionnaires had acquired.

"Trevor, do you have anything in the vic we can use?" asked Chhun. "Pistols aren't gonna cut it."

"Got a SAB in the back. You might be able to get it if you crawl over the rear row. It's heavy."

"On it," Masters said. He started climbing over to retrieve the unwieldy but high-cycle weapon.

Chhun was about to say that he didn't want to open fire unless they had to, when a blaster bolt crashed into the rear window a foot and a half away from Masters's head. The glass shattered, and Masters dropped back into his seat shouting, "Holy strokes!"

"Did you get it?" Bear shouted. He and Chhun had ducked behind their seats and were peeking around the edge to get a look at the trailing sled.

The man in the passenger seat was leaning out the window and sending wild sprays of blaster fire at the back of the sled. Bolts smashed into the buildings that raced past the speeding sleds. Martin swerved and weaved to keep the vehicle a difficult target.

Masters was crawling on the floor of the sled. He reached under the seat and grabbed the SAB. "Hey, I got a pretty good shooting position right now. Can you pop the back door up on this thing?"

Their vehicle was a larger sled, the sort that felt like it had been built on a truck frame, and the back window and gate appeared to be one unit.

Martin, who had been speaking urgently into a comm united attached to his shirt collar, pressed a release button, but nothing happened. "Nothing doin', man. Won't open while I'm in drive. And I'm not stopping."

"Here," Bear said, moving toward the back.

Blaster bolts continued to streak past, one of them smashing into a taillight and sending red shards of composite onto the street. Bear ducked and sent two shots with his pistol toward the pursuing vehicle. The sled veered, dodging the second shot but suffering a hole in the front windshield from the first.

With the pursuing sled's driver in evasion mode, and his gunner back in the passenger seat, Bear sent a blaster bolt into the rear door release. The door flipped open, giving Masters a full view from beneath the seats.

He opened fire immediately, sending an overwhelming stream of blaster bolts at the pursuing sled's windshield. Red hot bolts tore up the hood and ate through the acryliglass, peppering driver and passenger alike.

The sled veered hard left, moving onto the sidewalk before the vehicle's automated braking system took over for the driver, bringing it to a stop to keep it from crashing into a building.

"They were driving a factory sled!" Masters called out. "No after-market armor or AI overrides."

"So are we!" Martin yelled back.

"Ahead!" Chhun shouted.

Two metallic gray sleds crept out of opposite alleys to hastily set up a blockade. Four armed men, all of them looking military but dressed in plain clothes—jeans and athletic jackets—jumped out and primed N-6 blaster rifles.

"Belts!" called Martin before redlining the accelerator.

Bear and Chhun strapped themselves in, knowing that all that would come next was either a full reverse or a full-on charge. And they weren't moving backward.

As the legionnaires' larger sled raced violently toward a collision, blaster fire burned pockmarked holes into the hood. The defenders were attempting to disable the sled's repulsor housing before impact.

They continued racing toward the blockade, building speed.

At the last second, Martin swerved slightly to slam the front of the sled directly into one of the Nether Ops shooters—or at least Chhun assumed they were Nether Ops—a guy who stood in the pocket to deliver blaster fire for a few seconds too long.

The impact pinched the man's legs off as he was violently crushed between a speeder traveling eighty-eight kilometers per hour and the luxury sled he'd driven in on.

There was no time to delay. Immediately Chhun, Bear, and Masters were up and sending fire into the other Nether Ops agents, who'd ducked and scattered. Bear dumped half a charge pack into a burly operator with a barrel chest wearing a coyote tan synthprene undershirt. He went down hard, as did the man next to him, who was dropped with three shots to center mass by Masters.

Chhun channeled the ghost of Wraith, who they could have used in a fight like this, with head shots into the two remaining operators on the passenger side. That left three on the other side.

But there was no need to take them on. The force of the speeder collision had created a gap wide enough for Martin's sled to push through, and he was already engaging the accelerator and roaring past. He dropped a fragger from his jacket casually out the window as he did so. Blaster bolts chased them until the grenade detonated, perforating the remaining men.

Now there were sirens in the distance, and observation bots would be racing in once the proper sensitivity screeners determined if their use would be an acceptable action of Utopion's local government in consideration of the maligned lower-class community where the commotion was taking place.

Things wouldn't be like that for long. Chhun didn't see Goth Sullus hanging on to the House of Reason's over-legislated governing. Not after he'd been willing to kill all its members. But for now, things were running the way they always had. And that meant they were afforded time they didn't deserve.

"Okay, we're clear," Martin said into his comm. He peered through his fractured windshield, straining to read the street signs projected above him. "Turning east onto New Justice Avenue."

Chhun looked outside. People were gathering, looking at the wreckage they'd left behind. And noticing the damage to their sled. "We need to get out of this sled and leave. Then get Exo and Bombassa."

"Yeah." Martin pulled the sled over. "Leave the SAB."

They all leapt out, and Martin dropped a thermal fragger in the middle of the sled. Then the four men walked quickly down the street as the fragger burned hot, quickly consuming the sled in impenetrable heat.

"Keep walking," Martin said, ignoring the spectacle behind them.

Chhun could feel the heat against his back. Everyone on the street was drawn to the flames like moths, watching the sled burn. Only the legionnaires were moving upstream in the opposite direction.

A pair of sleds—one old and maroon, the other white and shiny—pulled up beside the team.

"Here we go," said Martin.

The doors opened, and the legionnaires split up among the two sleds. Chhun with Masters. Bear with Martin.

The sleds turned on opposite streets, leaving the scene to find Exo and Bombassa.

28

"Hold it!"

Bombassa and Exo had made it halfway up the alley before they heard the warning from the other end. Blaster fire followed. Meaning that whoever called for them hadn't meant for them to stop and go peacefully. They'd meant to get a still target.

But the Dark Ops legionnaires hadn't complied. They turned a corner in the alley as the bolts sizzled past, destined to hit whatever was in their path.

Shooting in a city was risky that way. Maybe the bolt slams into the hard exterior of duracrete and impervisteel building. Maybe it hits a utility box or a parked speeder. Or maybe it goes right on through a window and hits some kid or wife sitting down for dinner. Ruins someone's life.

Whoever was shooting at them—and Nether Ops was on Bombassa's mind—obviously didn't care.

"We have to keep clear of bystanders," Bombassa said, sprinting beside Exo, covering ground with ease, his footsteps echoing along the alley. The buildings on either side went up twenty stories at a minimum. Small for Utopion, but this was a district trapped in the past. It was a ghetto. It was where the rich and powerful in Utopion kept those who decidedly were not.

Almost every planet in the core had places like this. Even Utopion. In spite of all the rhetoric of poverty being a thing of the past. Of the poorest among the city having access to every right owed to humanoids. Despite the free stuff given to people who were anything but. People who hid inside because what was outside was falling apart around them.

But the elites Utopion kept them around. They had to. Because the rich wouldn't serve themselves. And bots couldn't do everything.

Exo was taking two strides for every one of Bombassa's, and just barely keeping up. "Yeah, well, them shootin' at us oughta keep folks from comin' out for a stroll."

They reached a side alley that cut off from the wider one. A thin passage between two buildings that made up one half of the city block.

"Down here," Exo said.

Bombassa followed. They needed to find a place where they could either stand and eliminate the threat chasing them, or slip away and rejoin the others. They hoped their earlier maneuver had served its purpose, stalling the pursuing vehicle for long enough to allow Chhun and the others to lose it.

The narrow alley was strewn with empty boxes. Exo peered back around the corner to see if the pursuers were catching up. He saw them, moving with rifles ready. Slowly. Not wanting to spring into an ambush. Which was smart, because he and Bombassa would be happy to provide one.

"How 'bout these boxes?" Exo asked, nudging one that looked large enough to hide them.

"What would you do, if you were them?" Bombassa asked.

"And I came here?"

Bombassa nodded.

"Probably shoot up the boxes," Exo said. "Yeah, let's keep looking."

They moved farther down the alley. The walls were made of brick. Old walls. Old buildings. Steel doors were inset periodically, trash capsules waiting outside for sanitation bots to pick up as they hovered through on collection day.

The two legionnaires began to test the doors to see if they would open.

"Locked," Bombassa said with each failed attempt. Exo did the same from his side of the alley.

They were rapidly reaching a point where they would need to make a decision. Ambush and evasion had been their best choice thus far. But sometimes you just had to run.

The two Nether Ops shooters turned the corner behind them, rifles ready.

"Exo!" Bombassa warned, pulling his pistol and hunching into a shooter's stance. He squeezed off two shots that both went wide as the Nether Ops leejes dropped to a knee and took aim.

This was a bad situation. Though both legionnaires were efficient with pistols, their opponents had superior weapons at medium and long range. They needed to find an exit.

"In here!" Exo shouted, pushing open a door on his side of the alley and disappearing into the darkness inside.

Blaster fire arced down the alley and over Bombassa's head. He sprinted low across the field of fire, feeling the bolts sizzle just behind him as he, too, flung himself through the open steel door.

Inside was a showroom of rock bottom. The air stunk from too many different types of incense and whatever else the people inside were smoking. The overhead lights were out, and the only illumination came from a few emergency fixtures that painted the shadowy room in a red glow.

A young man lay in the middle of the floor, clearly dead from an overdose. A few feet away sat a topless Endurian, mascara tears running down her cheeks, her arms and shoulders raw and bleeding from self-inflicted wounds. She compulsively scratched and picked at her skin from a bad H8 high. As Bombassa's eyes adjusted, he saw that there were other users lounging about in a drug-induced stupor, motionless except for the shallow rise and fall of their chests. Some sat propped against the wall, others were strung out on ragged and filthy sofas that looked as though they'd been pulled out of the gutter. In one corner a group of alines with pink eyes gathered around a holo-display playing pornography.

"Flophouse," Exo said, giving a name to the obvious. He examined the door. "Doesn't lock."

Assessing no threats, Bombassa moved to a corner window that was covered with some kind of metallic foil painted black. The corner stank of urine and feces, making it no wonder that so much incense burned here. He wrinkled his nose and peeled the light blocker away, bringing in a streak of daylight that somehow made the room seem even more squalid than it had in the dimness.

"Hey, man," shouted one of the addicts. A guy not yet wasted enough for light and darkness to no longer matter.

Exo strode over, pistol in hand. "You shut up and pretend we ain't here or I swear to Oba this is your last high."

The man held up his hands. "I'm cool, man. I'm cool."

"Here they come," Bombassa whispered, his pistol barrel pointing up as he peeked out the window. He hoped that the blaster rifles were all these two had. No flashbangs or fraggers to toss inside. They weren't dressed in a full military kit, so Bombassa figured his luck was about even.

It turned out to be slightly better.

The men came into the room hard, blasters firing on full auto. The few junkies with enough clarity for self-preservation scrambled to the back or dropped to their stomachs. Some, like the Endurian, took fatal blaster hits. But most just lay in wonder, watching the unexpected but oh-so-beautiful light show dance just over their heads as they lay in chemical ecstasy on the feculent floor.

Exo and Bombassa were in corners, pistols ready. But the Nether Ops men knew enough to swing their weapons to those blind spots as they entered. Their arrival had been a show of strength, and it seemed to Bombassa that they either thought their prey had attempted to squirt out the back or believed they could overwhelm them with the ferocity of their attack. Whatever the case, the legionnaires were ready.

Each man from Victory Squad squared up against one of the two Nether Ops agents. As Bombassa's man swung his rifle—still spewing blaster bolts—toward him, Bombassa didn't have a clear shot without the risk of hitting Exo. So he kicked the agent's arm savagely, redirecting the spray of blaster fire, and followed up by grabbing the weapon and wrenching it down and away, clattering to the floor.

Seeing the pistol in Bombassa's hand as it swung around, the Nether Ops agent threw up his wrist to strike the weapon and keep it out of the kill box. Then he showed trained footwork of his own, kicking the weapon out of Bombassa's grip and leaving both men without firearms.

The agent charged Bombassa, attempting to bully him into the filth-stained corner. He was a strongly built man with broad shoulders, but shorter than Bombassa by a foot.

With his large hands, the giant legionnaire grabbed the charging agent around the neck. He was able to feel the tips of his fingers touch as he began squeezing, strangling. The Nether Ops agent's eyes grew wide with the realization of his mistake and the growing pressure inside his skull.

Bombassa used his height advantage to force the choking man down onto his knees, allowing him to apply even more pressure. He had done this before, once. Not to a humanoid, but back home. The home he had joined the Legion to get away from.

There, in that forsaken hellhole, it had been a large predatory cat. Like a lesser-evolved wobanki. Bombassa could see the beast now, its yellow eyes and snarling fangs, bubbles of snot inflating and popping in its nose as it scratched and clawed Bombassa's arms. But those hands of his. That vice-like grip, it held on to the beast. Because to let go was to die.

The Nether Ops agent—unable to reach Bombassa's body as the legionnaire extended those long arms—beat against him the same way the cat did. No claws in a man, but his nails were drawing blood.

And what was true that day back on his home world was true today: to let go was to die.

Exo had an easier time. His agent had had the disadvantage of having to swing around the open door in order to clear Exo's corner. Exo put a single shot through the man's head before he had time to get his blaster rifle close. His target eliminated, he moved to Bombassa, who seemed so focused on choking his man out that he was oblivious to the knife the remaining agent was pulling from his beneath his pant leg.

Pistol in hand, but with no safe shot in such close proximity to Bombassa, Exo ran to the fray. As the agent drew the knife free, Exo grabbed his arm and snapped it back, popping the elbow out of joint and causing the weapon to fall to the floor.

Exo picked it up and stabbed the Nether Ops agent repeatedly with quick thrusts into his exposed back, seeking to deflate the lungs or pierce the heart.

The man died, and Bombassa returned to his senses.

"Rifles," said Exo, tossing Bombassa the nearest one and crossing the room to pick up the other.

This would go a long way in evening the fight if any more Nether Ops dogs were coming. Harder to move through the streets without attracting attention, but staying alive was the order of the day.

"Let's take the back exit," Bombassa said, but the *whoosh* of a rocket answered. It hissed through the open door and exploded on the far wall beside Exo, sending chunks of concrete flying and filling the room with smoke.

Both legionnaires went down with the noise. Dropping on instinct to avoid what they could of the blast.

Bombassa felt no pain and sensed no loss of motor skills as he hugged the floor. His ears were ringing and he knew he had to get up. More missiles, more men to clear the building... something. Something was coming. Staying down wasn't an option.

He struggled to his feet, keeping hold of the blaster rifle. "Exo!"

"Yeah," shouted the other legionnaire. "I'm good!"

And then blaster fire streaked through the open door, cutting Bombassa and Exo off from one another. A Nether Ops agent, or perhaps a Utopion police officer—he wore a black tac suit but no full armor—burst into the room. A partner was hot on his heels.

Bombassa dropped them both and then checked his charge pack. Low, but it was two packs taped together. He released, flipped, and reloaded. "Exo! The back! Let's go!"

More blaster fire came sizzling in, just barely clearing the bodies of the two newly dead men lying in the open doorway.

As Bombassa moved back, he sent short bursts of return fire, if only to keep anyone else from coming in and to give Exo a chance to get to the back of the room with him.

He was nearly out of the room and could see an open door that let out onto a street. He had to reorient his mind to the fact that this was the row house's front door—he and Exo had entered from the back.

Exo was pinned by the onslaught of blaster fire. From Bombassa's vantage point he could see the source—a man in a tac suit spraying blaster fire from a kneeling position, his armored kneepad sending ripples in a puddle.

Bombassa lined up his shot and sent two bolts into the man, neck and head. "Exo! I'll lay it down for you!" He switched his selector from single to full auto.

Just as the odds changed. Just as a banger bounced into the room not ten feet from where Exo was pinned.

Bombassa was just barely able to spin himself out of the room and behind what he hoped was a thick wall when the grenade exploded. Even with the protection, his hearing went immediately. Total deafness. The flash, though he'd shut his eyes, left him feeling dazzled, as though he'd stared at an overhead light for too long. He blinked, but everything looked burnt-out before him. Nothing was in focus.

Calling for Exo would do no good. He couldn't hear himself, and Exo sure wouldn't. The room would be filling with men. But leaving Exo wasn't an option.

Bombassa turned the corner, his spotty vision seeing men storm the room. He caught the first wave flat-footed, though they were entering in proper formation. Or maybe Bombassa was just that much more adept. That much faster.

Full automatic blaster fire sprayed from his rifle, cutting down the first few men and sending more diving for cover. Bombassa fired and tried to get a sense of what was happening. But his eyes were still dodgy from the blast.

Return fire was coming now, eating up the wall next to him and sending a litany of splinters and burning, grimy wallpaper into the air. And then he saw Exo, lying on the floor. Not moving. Was he breathing? Alive?

There was no way to tell. Bombassa fired until his charge pack sent a vibration into the grip letting him know it was at the end of its cycle. He drained the charge pack and pulled his secondary.

Exo wouldn't want him to die just to delay his body from being taken away for all of a few minutes. He'd want Bombassa to make the people pulling the strings on Nether Ops to pay. And the big legionnaire couldn't do that from here.

With a physical pain that he could actually feel, Bombassa disengaged, moving wildly to the building's front door as blaster fire and men pursued his steps.

He burst into the street—a busy street full of speeders and pedestrians who were looking on with guarded expressions. Standing far enough back—they thought—to get a good look at the noise without risking getting hurt.

But the first few bolts from the Nether Ops men that followed Bombassa made them realize how close they were to the war. Civilians went down across the street. And those who thought themselves too brave to flee when the shooting first started, now were the last dregs of a stampede that had begun while Exo and Bombassa were still linked up.

Crowds could be useful, though Bombassa's height put him at a disadvantage in that regard. Still he ran among the fleeing civilians, his shirt soaked with sweat. The dust and filth of that house stuck to his head and neck as though he'd rolled himself in honey.

His vision was improving. His ears were ringing. Which was also good. And he kept running. Wondering why he hadn't been caught yet. And then wondering if those long legs, which had made him the fastest boy in the family, were simply too much. In the crowd. In the chaos. All too much.

Exo.

All too much.

A white speeder crossing at an intersection slowed and then slammed on its brakes. The door opened and Bombassa could see Masters inside. He stepped out, now armed with a blaster rifle of his own, and held it ready as Bombassa ran for the escape vehicle.

But Masters didn't shoot. Because Bombassa *had* out-run and evaded Nether Ops. Bombassa climbed inside the sled and Masters joined him. They took off at once.

Chhun, who was also inside, asked something Bombassa couldn't make out.

"What?" Bombassa pointed to his ear and shook his head.

"I said, where's Exo?" Chhun repeated, enunciating slowly so Bombassa could read his lips.

"I don't know," he answered, knowing he was yelling, but not knowing how to stop it. "He's back there, but I don't know if he's alive. I couldn't save him!"

One Republic News

The PLE journalist bot's algorithm told it that this news cycle was the sort that would distinguish itself from all others. This, as the humanoids were fond of saying, was history in the making.

And aware of this, the bot certainly would have turned in its best performance had it not been programmed to *always* do such. Even so, the potency of this report was noted and tagged in its long and short recall drives, signifying the weight its algorithms had placed on what was happening in the galaxy.

The red light on its holocam illuminated, and the bot began its report.

"This is"—it let out a high-pitched tone to signal the local stations to supply whatever local news anchor name it would be broadcasting as in its subsequent planet or district—"with a special report. Citing Emperor Goth Sullus's genocidal attack on the zhee planet of Nidreem, a coalition of nine core worlds have declared their independence from Sullus's self-declared Empire. Pundits are speculating that this is only the beginning of the political fallout from the attack, as well as from the execution of the House of Reason, whom Sullus identified as enemies of the Republic.

"While declarations of independence have been an almost daily event in worlds at galaxy's edge, and even a few planets in the mid-core have done the same—notably the Sinasian Cluster and Cononga, both with the support of the rebellious organization that still calls itself the Legion—this nine-planet coalition, spearheaded by Spilursa, is the first time a *core* world has openly rebelled against the Imperial Republic government. There has been no retaliatory action taken as of yet."

The feeds cut to pre-recorded footage of Spilursan Governor Noam Hamm, surrounded by governors from the other eight worlds.

"Our coalition rejects the notion of an emperor, and it rejects Goth Sullus. He is an enemy of the Republic, and we are confident in our ability to resist any military attempts to subdue our planets. We stand together to fight, as we did in the Savage Wars. And we invite the Legion to assist as they are able."

The journobot inclined its head. "More on this breaking news as it develops."

29

Admiral Crodus appeared on-screen before Goth Sullus. The emperor did not need his lost ability to probe the deepest corners of the mind to tell that Crodus carried a great burden of doubt. And, possibly, remorse.

"Report, Admiral."

"Our probes have finished their analysis of the planet Nidreem, my lord."

"And?"

"They report that less than five percent of the planet's life forms remain alive."

"The zhee."

"Some... were sighted by the machines. In caves or underground complexes."

"Eliminate them."

Crodus swallowed. "My lord... the radiation levels following that bombardment would surely prove fatal to the shock troopers under my command. Even if sealed in their armor."

You see, master. You see how frail your armies are.

Sullus twisted the ring, spinning it around his gauntleted finger.

"May I... attempt orbital bombardment with blaster cannons as a first measure?" Crodus asked. "I could send more probes down following it."

Sullus, in his mind, could see the sense of that plan. Why needlessly throw away the lives of his men? But... he had to know what *they* thought. What *their* counsel would be. He craved it. Somehow needed it. Enough to be alarmed by the strength of the urge. And yet he found himself incapable of walking away from it all.

He told himself to order Crodus back to Utopion. To prepare for an attack that he was sure would come. Because the Legion had been quiet about his ultimatum. They had made no response.

Which told him everything. They would come for him. They would see the madness and chaos play out again over Utopion. Once more would they hurl themselves into the unbending will of Goth Sullus. And like waves crashing against the rocks, once more they would break and fade away.

The Master sees. Our Conqueror sees. But hear us: you cannot defeat the gathering Legion. You have lost Imperator. *You have lost much of your army. The Empire is fragile. Its Emperor must protect it. Protect us, Master.*

Goth Sullus knew, somewhere in the back of his mind, the part of his mind that remained Casper, that his next words were a mistake. That any hope of empire had been lost. Because, after years of patience, he had grasped for too much, too soon. He wanted *Empire* to be true. Now.

You are conqueror, master. You are the emperor. But the others... the nine planets. They defy our master. Our ruler and lord.

And with those words, Casper, who had already grown smaller and smaller, faded still further. And Goth Sullus raged.

"I will tolerate no delays, Crodus," Goth Sullus hissed through his armor. "Send your men down, and if they are to die from the effort, leave them. I require another show of this empire's might."

Crodus was ashen. But he dared not speak.

"Nine core worlds have dared to defy me, as I'm sure you are aware. You are to jump to the nearest of those planets and use everything in your power to eradicate them. The galaxy *will* learn who their emperor is."

"Everything... my lord?"

"Treat them as you treated the zhee."

Crodus swallowed. And suddenly Goth Sullus felt an incoming rush. His connection to the power that was the Crux of the universe itself... reconnected. As if a faucet had been turned on.

He probed his admiral's mind and found fear. Doubt. And a pragmatic belief that this would have the opposite effect than the one Sullus intended. That it would unite the galaxy *against* its emperor. But he was loyal. He would do as asked.

"Crodus... do not fail me."

The holoscreen went black, and just as quickly, Sullus felt his control over the Crux go with it. How? Why?

We can restore you, master. We gave you the gift of your power.

"Bring it back."

Cannot, master. So few of us. So weak and helpless. Pitiful, master. A pitiful conquered collective. Because you defeated us. Destroyed our Cybar. Stopped us from coming. You are our conqueror, master. We serve you. Let more of us serve you. More of us.

And like a rush of wind, the part of Goth Sullus that remained tied to Casper and that life, with Reina and Tyrus... regained his senses. For a moment. A stitch in time just long enough to cry out one word—*No!*—before fading back into the shadow of Goth Sullus once more.

And the voices went quiet. And Goth Sullus wondered what he'd wrought. But the die had been cast. And what would happen, would happen.

30

The *Indelible VI* landed in an idyllic pasture, its heavy struts sinking into the soft green waves of grass that undulated and bent from the pressure of the craft's repulsors. It came to rest between a grain silo and a rustic old farmhouse that looked like a one-room cottage. Four walls, a mossy roof, and a chimney. The windows were covered with heavy wood shutters that were battened down tight.

Keel lowered the ramp and stepped outside. Everything smelled green and sweet. White-headed flowers poked out of the grass, attracting fist-sized bees that went from plant to plant, legs fat with pollen.

"This looks like the sort of place where you could retire and keep out of trouble, Doc."

"Looks like better neighbors," Doc agreed.

"I detect no humanoids in a one-hundred-kilometer radius," said Ravi.

"Yeah, exactly." Doc looked around and sniffed the air. "So this is where the Legion wants you to hide the MARO?"

Keel took a few steps away from his ship. The grass rustled around his legs, rising midway up to his knees. "That's the word. That silo has an underground storage level. Should stay hidden until Chhun decides to use it or defuse it."

Doc grunted. "Don't count on me helpin' you unload the thing. I'm retired."

"S'posed to meet someone to offload it." Keel looked around. "Should already be here."

The door to the cottage creaked slowly open. Keel and Doc both went to their weapons, the younger man drawing from the hip, Doc unslinging a shotgun he'd strapped over his shoulder. Both remained at the ready as a tread-mounted PENS-850 heavy loading bot rumbled out.

It was little more than a forklift on treads, with limited repulsor capabilities and eight manipulative arms that folded into its cab-like front section—a machine whose function was communicated in a way peculiar to its form.

"Greetings, gentlemen," the bot said as it rolled out of the cabin's wide door. An opening that hadn't seemed big enough for a machine to get through when Keel first looked.

But then he saw the trick: the frame retracted into the walls. The cabin's entrance was as big as a blast door.

"Bet this place is nicer on the inside than it looks on the outside," he said.

Somebody had spent some considerable credits in making the cabin—not to mention the silo—look small and old while still being capable of serving as a secret weapons cache.

Keel had been directed to a few similar depots during his early days undercover. When credits were hard to come by and he had to rely on Dark Ops to keep him supplied. But as the jobs lined up and Wraith's infamy grew, it became quicker and easier to just buy what he needed direct from the Night Markets.

The bot fired its repulsors and moved itself off of an elevated porch and onto an overgrown pathway that snaked away from the cabin's entrance. "I am to assist you in offloading your cargo for storage in Dark Ops cache SW-1602."

"No need for an assist," Doc grumbled. "You can do the whole thing. What we got ain't light. I'd rather spare my back." He turned to Keel. "Take care of your back, Aeson."

"Sure."

The bot continued to rumble toward the ship. "Yes, of course, sir. I require no assistance in performing my primary function. I am capable of offloading cargo as large as five hundred cubic feet with a maximum weight of sixteen thousand three hundred and fifty kilograms before requiring the assistance of a second unit."

The machine rumbled to a stop outside the *Six*'s main cargo bay, the big one that opened up to load larger shipments. Keel rarely used it, but the MARO and its factory casing wouldn't have fit inside the ship anywhere else. And he wasn't fool enough to ship that thing *without* its thick protective transportation case.

"If you'll kindly provide access to..." The bot paused, seemed to reboot, and continued. "To the bay, I'll begin work right away."

"Garret," Keel called into his comm. "Lower the cargo doors. The big ones."

"You got it, Captain."

The bay doors opened out like a pair of wings, and a wide ramp lowered to the ground.

"There you go," Keel said to the bot.

But the machine didn't move. It again seemed to reboot and said, "If you'll kindly provide access to the bay, I'll begin work right away."

"Whatta ya want, you retread crate of lug nuts?" asked Doc, annoyed. "A guided tour? Oba's balls, I hate bots."

The bot threw up four of its arms, all on one side, in some digital spasm. "If you'll kindly provide access to the bay, I'll begin work right away."

Keel pinched the bridge of his nose. "Ravi, how old is that thing?"

"This model was last manufactured approximately three hundred years ago."

With a sigh, Keel said, "Probably been at least half that long since it got serviced."

The bot repeated its kindly request for access to the bay, and this time all its arms spasmed. Then with a popping noise, a series of blue electrical arcs raced around the bot's front chassis, followed by a wreath of smoke that smelled of ozone. And then the bot seized up entirely.

"I ain't unloadin' that MARO," Doc said as more smoke seeped out from a grille just beneath the forks that sat above the machine's treads.

"Thanks, Doc," Keel snapped. "I think that's already been established." He keyed open his comm. "Garret!"

"Yeah, boss?"

"Come down here. Bot trouble."

A minute later, the slim code slicer was walking down the wide ramp, eyes squinting against the light. "Whoa! Look at this relic!"

Keel frowned. He *was* looking at it, but all he could see was a delay on a job that he really wanted to be finished with. He'd told Leenah he'd only be a few days behind her. And a few days behind her was already past, thanks to how remote this jump ended up being. "Can you fix it?"

"I'd like to try," Garret said, circling the machine in wonder. "Man. It looks brand-new. I bet this is the original paint. No scratches... *man*." After circling the bot a couple of times, he stopped. "There it is."

He opened a panel with a multi-tool and began working on something inside. "Hmm... we're gonna have to get this thing on board the *Six* so I can run a diagnostic through the ship's mainframe. I don't know the language this bot is programmed in. So cool."

A few minutes later, Keel was strapping a cable to the machine so Garret could winch it aboard while Doc yelled for Keel to "Put your back into it!"

***

Garret had promised that he'd have the bot running by the morning. Promised to stay up all night to fix it. And rather than looking glum about the prospect of an all-nighter to repair the old machine, the skinny code slicer seemed downright excited.

While he explored the bot—"a classic," he called it— Keel and Doc passed the time in the lounge, sampling from the ship's stores, though neither man would allow themselves to get intoxicated. That had been one of Doc's cardinal rules for Keel. When dealing with the galaxy's criminal element, go ahead and let them think you're drunk, but never go there.

Because that's when they strike. When your guard is down. When you're a ship without shields.

Even now, among friends, the lesson stuck. Because sometimes things change. And because it was a good habit.

Doc had kept to himself during the first few days of the trip. Not bothering to leave his quarters except to use the fresher. But the past couple evenings had been different. The old man had grown talkative, and the two remembered old times.

Tonight, they were swapping the stories that had occurred after they'd gone their separate ways. Keel had just finished telling Doc about the day he'd *almost* killed Lao Pak.

"You should have dusted that little twerp," Doc grunted as he swallowed the last of the scotch-soaked ice that had sat melting in his glass. "Never liked him."

Keel shrugged and took a sip of rose wine. He wasn't usually a wine drinker, but Leenah liked it, and drinking it made him feel like she was nearby. He missed her. A lot. And that made him smile at himself. At what the stoic Captain Ford, the roguish Captain Keel, and the deadly Wraith had become.

Or at least was becoming.

He put his glass down. "So that led me to Tyrus Rechs."

Doc's face immediately changed. He was interested. *Real* interested. "Tyrus Rechs?"

"Yeah," Keel said, breaking off a piece of Lenteen cheese they'd been nibbling. He popped the crumble into his mouth. "We were on the same job. Sort of. I got the drop on him..." Keel watched Doc's expression out of the corner of his eye as he said, "... and I outdrew him."

For the first time that Keel could remember, Doc seemed really and truly impressed. "You're not... you're not yanking my chain, are you?"

"Oba's truth," Keel said. "Ended up working together. Well, technically he hired me. That was his last job. Blew himself up trying to kill our new emperor."

"Sullus?"

"Yeah. Sullus killed Prisma's dad. That's the girl I told you about. So she hired Rechs to kill Sullus. And he died trying."

Doc gulped, and it looked to Keel as though he had tears in his eyes. "Did he... did he say anything? About the Legion?"

Keel gave a quizzical look. "Did you know the guy?"

Doc nodded. "Yeah. Me and Chappy, we..." Emotion choked the words from the old man's throat. "We served under General Rex—Tyrus Rechs. Same person."

Keel nodded. "Yeah. I found a holo he recorded for himself on an asteroid."

He was still unsure just how much of that message he believed, and how much of it was the result of what was probably some early-onset dementia that had taken hold of the old man's mind. It was that doubt that had allowed Keel to more or less forget about what he'd heard the ghost of Rechs say.

"He, uh, seemed to believe he was centuries old," Keel said. "Fought in the Savage Wars, founded the Legion... a crazy old man. Good at what he did, but crazy."

"Nah," Doc said, shaking his head. "Not crazy. That stuff's true. I saw it myself. I grew from a young buck to a middle-aged operator, and the general never changed. The Republic used to know about it, too, during the Savage Wars. But when Rex got on their bad side—refused to do some wetworks the House of Reason wanted done, he became public enemy number one. Only the public never knew it."

Keel laughed. "How much have you had to drink, old man?"

"I ain't drunk. You know that." Doc was getting hot.

Holding up his hands to stave off the coming bout of anger, Keel said, "All right. But you know how all that sounds, right? Guy's over a thousand years old, wanted by the House of Reason because he didn't do what they wanted... Do you know how many times *I* did something the House didn't want? More than once."

"You didn't do nothin'," Doc huffed. "Not like General Rex. They had a plan. Big plan. Those machines that attacked? That was them. And they sent Rex to take care of two problems at once. Secure a planet and kill a girl. Only they never told him about the planet—what was really there. And they never told him the girl was innocent.

"So he refuses to do the job and just walks away. Figured that was the end of his run in the Legion, though he helped us out a number of times when we needed it.

"That's why the House authorized Nether Ops, you know. They wanted people who wouldn't tell them no when they asked for a murder. Not a killing or an assassination, but a murder. And Rex wouldn't do it."

Keel hadn't heard that part of the story. He knew that old leejes held General Rex in high regard, despite his fallen status in the Republic. But he hadn't expected to hear Doc talking like a true believer.

"So you two were close."

"Close? Not sure how close you can get to a man like that. But I was his friend. Maybe one of the only ones he had left." Doc looked from his glass to the cabinet, and then turned the glass upside down, cutting himself off for the night. "He got... forgetful. That last year I saw him. Which was about four years before I met you. Like he didn't quite remember who I was. Didn't remember a lot of things. Then one day, the commkey I had for him stopped working. And he never contacted me. Even when Chappy died."

Keel inhaled deeply. He hadn't intended to steer the conversation into such a melancholy direction. He drank the rest of his wine in silence.

"I was trying to make you into him," Doc said.

Keel inclined his head. "How's that?"

"Wraith. That whole angle. Keel outside of the armor, Wraith within. I was trying to teach you how to be like Rechs." Doc snapped his fingers in the air, trying to recall. "Remember what I would say?"

Keel raised an eyebrow. "That I was Tyrus Rechs without the marketing?"

Doc smiled and pointed at his former protégé. "Yeah. That was it. I worked with him so many times when I was still in Dark Ops—I was supposed to arrest him on sight, but nah. Me and Chappy, we knew better. Same with old leejes like your former CO, Pappy. He knew the general, too. Didn't know he was a bounty hunter now, but he knew Rex was a good man. So I did what I could to make you be like him. Seemed like the right thing to do."

Keel cleared his throat. He remembered something else about that message Rechs had left for himself. The message he'd left for the dead. "Did he ever talk about someone named Casper?"

Doc shook his head. "Not that I remember. He didn't really talk much to begin with, though."

Leaning back in his seat, Keel looked up at the ceiling. "You think the Legion should stay out of Utopion, right?"

"Yeah. That's what I said."

"Same here. But... Goth Sullus." Keel patted his chin, unsure if this was a question he wanted to ask. "At first, I thought Rechs just felt bad for the kid losing her dad. Like he agreed to dust Goth Sullus as a way to make amends for whatever bad things he'd done. But then, in that recording, he obviously knew Sullus long before. Said his name was Casper. And the entire time he was working for the guild out on the edge, he was actually there to kill Goth Sullus."

Doc didn't say a word.

Keel leaned forward and placed his elbows on the table. "So what I'm asking is... you knew the man. And he said Goth Sullus had to die. So... what should the Legion do?"

Doc didn't pause to consider. "Sometimes you have to trust a man because of who you know him to be. I don't know what Goth Sullus did, but if Tyrus Rechs said he needed killing, then, Ford—Wraith—you need to be on Utopion to finish the job."

31

X whistled as he trailed two Nether Ops legionnaires down a spartan hallway overly brightened by industrial lights. These were the mind-numbingly drab sub-levels in the bowels of the Imperial Palace. He'd been here many times before, when the building was under control of the House of Reason. Back then these sub-levels housed the lowest caste of the political class.

Still, other than the change of names, it was no different. Clean endless corridors of sameness. White walls, gray tiled floors, and an abundance of artificial light that eliminated every shadow.

It was a funny thing. Though the area was aglow with "daylight" fixtures, it seemed to X that a mythical dungeon with cold stone floors and perpetual darkness would somehow be less depressing. But this new location was where the Carnivale was now forced to do its more... messy work. There was no sense fussing about it, and at least the walk from his office was a quick one.

The old location was beneath a waterfront fishmonger's shop, and it had taken X forty-five minutes to get there by speeder. But the salt air, even when mingled with the fish odor, always seemed to revive his constitution. Down here there was only the hum of recirculated air, with no character at all.

"Here we are, sir," said one of the two legionnaires. Good Carnivale men, both.

They stopped in front of a white door that almost blended in with the wall except for the vertical seam running down its middle and the security box to its left. The agent took off a necklace that held a metallic cylinder with erratic grooves cut into it all along its two-inch length. Each groove glowed a primary or secondary color, so that it looked like a sort of rainbow rod attuned to its owner's biometrics.

He inserted the cylinder into a receptacle—the first security protocol. This told the security system that an on-duty guard, stationed on this sub-level, was present to grant access. A pleasant beep sounded, and X entered a security key onto the pad, knowing that it was reading his own biometrics as his bare fingers came in contact with the glossy screen.

The door beeped again, then swished open.

"Thank you, boys," X said, stepping inside. "Wait for me out here."

Now the scene was more akin to a dungeon. The light inside the little room was low and orange, slothfully chasing away the shadows to the room's corners, but no further. The floor was covered in woodchips, which gave off a rustic scent that partially covered the smells of blood, sweat, and other bodily fluids the chips absorbed. A table held a datapad, and ener-chained to a wall under twin heat lamps was a man with short-cut black hair and a heavily swollen face. His shirt was torn away and his body was bruised and bleeding. A medical bot was examining him.

X picked up the datapad and studied it. "Ah. I see you were with Kern. A pity. He's a mean one."

The man in chains said nothing.

X moved forward to afford himself a closer look at the legionnaire's swollen face. That was bare-knuckle work. Just Kern's style. Driblets of blood splattered the prisoner's chest from cuts above his swollen eyes, his busted nose, his split lips. There were probably a few teeth to be found among the woodchips, too.

But already the bot was preparing to reduce the swelling with deep-tissue regeneration and skinpacks. Give this man a few hours and at least his friends would be able to pick him out of a lineup.

X snapped his fingers at the bot. "Can he talk?"

An interrogation demanded that the subject be capable of speaking, but Kern *had* been disciplined for getting overzealous in the past.

"Yes, sir," the bot said.

"You caused quite a bit of trouble today," X said to the prisoner hanging from the wall. "Killed more than ten of my men. Good agents. As skilled as any legionnaire."

Tossing the datapad back on the table, X tsked. "My poor secretary had to cancel dinner plans to write up the reports and inform the right people that condolence letters needed preparing." He inclined his head. "This is all futile, of course. I know your Legion training tells you to resist these sorts of overtures, and somehow I doubt whatever additional training you received from the Black Fleet differed in that regard."

The leader of the Carnivale, now the highest man in Nether Ops—the highest member in the Empire's entire intelligence community—waited. He didn't expect the man before him to react to his words. But he was still disappointed at the way the man remained defiant, head held stoically high.

"I say it's futile for a number of reasons," X continued. "First, we know who you are, Sergeant Major Caleb Gutierrez. The Legion may have burned up our databases with that nasty little worm they had built—and kudos to the code slicer—but the Black Fleet kept records as well. And before Kern disfigured your face, he ran it through and found a match."

X took a few steps closer to the man. "You seemed to have distinguished yourself at Tarrago Moon. Though I confess the details are surprisingly light. You were hand-selected for a mission to capture a VIP—I don't have those records, paperwork is a mess right now, you understand—and then what? Why come to Utopion? And why were you with individuals who we believe are working against this Empire?"

Still the prisoner gave no reply. He was showing remarkable restraint.

X decided to take a different route. "We know about Washam."

In truth, X only suspected that Washam was working with elements of the Legion. It was clear he was working with *someone*—of that X had no doubt—but it could be other members of the emperor's council. Black Fleet men dissatisfied with the choices of their emperor. Dissidents enraged by the fall of the House of Reason. Really, the list of potential enemies seemed endless.

But the one thing X knew for sure was that Washam wasn't seeking to work with *him*. Which would have been the only acceptable path for the man to take if he were to betray the Empire.

X would find out the truth soon. Very soon. There would be raids. And then it wouldn't matter who Washam had aligned himself with. The result would be the same. Treason was treason.

And death was death.

And when Washam's plot, whatever it was, was uncovered, exposed, and prevented by Nether Ops... then X's star would rise even higher in Goth Sullus's eyes.

But the man before him... he could do much in the way of accelerating things.

"We know about everything. There's no need for you to—"

The prisoner mumbled something, and X's heart skipped a beat. He moved closer. "What was that? These ears, they don't hear as well as they once did."

"A point," said Gutierrez. "Washam's a point. I don't work for points."

"Then tell me who you do work for."

"Goth. Sullus."

"Oh, come now."

But the prisoner looked at X with a withering glare that pushed open doors leading to doubt in his mind.

X straightened. This didn't exactly complicate things, because the man could easily be lying. But what if he wasn't? And what if his mission, one he was hand-picked for, didn't allow him to easily come in from the cold? Much had happened since Tarrago. Still, it might be best to play this carefully and keep his options open.

"We'll see about that, Sergeant Major."

Exo spat into the woodchips. "Good. So hurry up and do it because I need to talk to Ordo."

His hands patting down his pockets, X shook his head. "How do you know him?"

Exo looked away, not answering.

"Come now," prodded X. "If this is all a misunderstanding, if you're loyal to the emperor, there's no need to play games."

Again, Exo kept his mouth closed. And X began to seriously wonder if the soldier was what he intimated himself to be: an agent sent out for some purpose known by Goth Sullus now attempting to come in from the cold. And if so, did X truly want to be the man who delayed his reports? It was certainly *plausible* that the man would not be aware of how Nether Ops had been folded into the Black Fleet— Imperial—power structure.

Patience was what was needed. And no more visits from Kern. X could take the time to vet Sergeant Major Gutierrez's claims.

There was always time to plan.

A comm-chime sounded from X's jacket.

"Oh," he mumbled to himself, and then rifled through his pockets, looking every bit the forgetful professor as he searched for the old hand-held comm. He preferred something he could manipulate over those micro-comms that attached to clothing or embedded in ears or even strapped on a wrist. He wanted his watch to tell time, not be part of a tech package he had to gear up with each day before leaving his home.

Finding the comm, he checked its screen—another advantage over the tech wearables. His eyes almost went wide. His heartbeat increased. This was, in all likelihood, a call he'd been waiting for.

Patience for Sergeant Major Gutierrez was perfectly all right. He might not even be a factor now. The Carnivale had the evidence it needed to take down Washam.

***

Wash opened his desk drawer and picked up a blaster pistol. He checked its charge pack and found it adequate. It felt heavy in his hands. Heavier than it should. And as he looked down he saw the loose skin and spots of his age.

A young man had been issued this weapon. Had used it on Psydon when not suffering in that oppressively hot office hab. Had found time to shoot at the range when the other legionnaires had finished their own training—because they weren't about to share with a point.

But Psydon was a long time ago. And the pistol Wash had dreamt about using to KTF the dog-men with then, when he was strong and capable—a fighter—now seemed lethargic about emerging from its long retirement inside a drawer on Utopion.

There were a number of ways this weapon could have been used. If he had managed to operate under Nether

Ops's collective sensors for long enough, until Legion Commander Chhun started the offensive... then this pistol was to be used once again in the name of the Legion. And Wash would have done what he could from the inside to ensure that the Imperial Republic fell.

One more fight.

Wash had been an asset to the Legion. He had been their man. The man on the inside who helped to steer the Legion away from disaster. And because of him, the Legion was ready. He'd made sure they were ready on Utopion. He'd been a part of them. Treated like a real leej by other leejes.

Wash was proud of that. The way the legionnaires on planet treated him once they found out who he was and what he'd done. Once the word came in from Chhun to the various cell leaders that Wash was... one of them. A leej on the inside.

Not a point. A leej.

It was a feeling Wash cherished. One that made him feel as though he could die a happy man.

And dying was now at the forefront of his mind.

Because he would not get that one more fight.

The bug-sized bots watching his door had triggered the early-warning alarm. Nether Ops was coming. Already he heard cutting torches at his door.

And there was only one reason Nether Ops would be coming.

Wash sat down at his desk and once more felt the weight of his pistol in his hand.

A charge at the door blew it inward, a deafening bang that made Wash jump in spite of knowing it was coming.

Nether Ops agents, legionnaires who'd broken bad, flooded his Utopion apartment.

Wash pressed his blaster's barrel against his temple.

A Nether Ops legionnaire in navy blue armor stormed into the room, his rifle tight against his shoulder. "Stop!"

The command came with a blast from the soldier's rifle, and Wash went down without ever having to pull his own trigger.

32

Leenah hadn't stopped feeling sick since she'd first arrived at En Shakar. She'd known right away. From the moment she stepped off the Legion shuttle Keel had arranged for her to take. She knew. It was all there in Mother Ree's face. The sorrow. And the truth.

Something had happened to Prisma.

The village had just finished mourning the loss of several of its people. Because something had happened. Something involving Hutch. He'd woken up from his coma and killed them. And then he'd chased Prisma into the ice caves. Because he wanted to kill her, too.

"I'm so sorry," Mother Ree had said. And she was. Clearly. She felt responsible for the loss of life. For failing to protect Prisma in the one place in the galaxy where she ought to have been safe.

But Leenah held no ill will. What else could Mother Ree have done against a man who'd dedicated his life to killing? What can anyone do against men such as that?

Honor the good men. The ones willing to stand up to the monsters.

And Hutch, in the end, had been a monster. Whatever shreds of humanity he'd shown to Leenah and Prisma while aboard the *Forresaw*, those were clearly dying embers.

The shuttle had some cold-weather gear aboard it. A pistol, some survival rations. Leenah had flown herself in and had had ample time to explore the craft during the jump through hyperspace. Now she gathered up all of it, prepared to venture into the ice caves to find Prisma. Ready to go farther and deeper than the villagers had been able to go. And bless them for trying.

She was ready to go farther and deeper, because she was ready to die there herself rather than leave Prisma. This was her fault. And though she didn't know what she might have done against Hutch, it didn't take away the sting of guilt that came from not having done anything at all.

Bundled up against the cold, she ventured into the ice caves. They were so breathtakingly beautiful, so over-whelmingly wonderful, that she found herself in awe at the majesty of it all. Despite her guilt. Her worry. Her regret.

She didn't travel far before Skrizz found her.

The wobanki's fur was matted with frost as though he had been in the caves for some time. He looked... sad. Or at least as sad as a wobanki can look.

"Skrizz!" Leenah called out. "Did you find her? Did you find Prisma?"

A terrible sensation came with those words. It wasn't until she said them aloud that Leenah was sure, as sure as she had ever been about anything, that Prisma was dead. That Skrizz had found her body and left it there, frozen to the ice.

But the catman only shook his head, emulating hu-manoid body language. His tail and ears conveyed his na-tive body language.

"*Jadda ka ka nee.*"

Leenah found the wobanki language easy to under-stand, and often wondered why others struggled with it. Her time spent with Skrizz since she'd first linked up with the *Indelible VI* had made her almost fluent. At least when it came to comprehending what was said. Speaking it her-self was another matter.

"What do you mean she's gone?"

"*Nee oh roocha roo, Crash.*" Skrizz gestured em-phatically.

"She's with Crash?" Leenah was elated at this news. She was alive. Prisma was *alive*. And Crash could surely stand up to Hutch. There likely wasn't a legionnaire alive who could go one-on-one with a functioning war bot and survive. Except maybe Aeson. "Where did they go?"

The wobanki explained how they'd managed to sep-arate themselves from him. Skrizz didn't do swimming under the best conditions, and he certainly wouldn't have been able to plumb the icy depths of the subterranean lake to join them on the other side. He'd searched every inch of the ice caves for another way to them. In spite of what he'd been told. He'd met Leenah only after finally admit-ting defeat.

Still, this was good news. If Crash was with Prisma…

"Skrizz, we can cover a lot of ground together. And I can call Aeson on my shuttle's hypercomm. If he and Ravi come to help, I'm sure we'll find her. We'll find Prisma."

But Skrizz didn't seem so sure. "*Chubba wa ka ka lo.*"

That didn't make any sense. How could they leave the planet? Even if they'd wanted to? But that's what

Skrizz was saying. The goodbye wasn't the sort one used when accepting death, but when someone was leaving. Getting away.

"Either way, let's get back to the shuttle," Leenah said, still not believing that Prisma had found a way off planet. Although if she had, that could be good news. Crash could use the comms to reach them and arrange for assistance.

But then… why hadn't he done so already?

The two trekked back to the ship. The landing pad was empty. It seemed the village either wasn't holding out any hope that Prisma would be found, or they weren't expecting Leenah to return so quickly.

Leenah ran up the boarding ramp, feeling the rush of warm air thaw her nose and face. It felt good. She shed layers as she moved to the cockpit. Skrizz sat down next to her, licking his paws and rubbing away the hoar frost in his fur. The obsessive-compulsive side of Leenah, the mechanical side that always wanted a ship running and looking its best, couldn't help but notice the mess he was making.

"Legion Shuttle *Rangefinder* to *Indelible VI*, come in."

Leenah watched the hypercomm's status displays, waiting to see that her message had connected. It pulsed blue indicating a connection. Now she just had to wait for Ravi or Keel to answer.

"Miss Leenah," said Ravi. "How are things on En Shakar?"

"Terrible, Ravi. Can you get Aeson?"

Immediately the navigator's tone went deadly serious. "Something has happened to Prisma."

"She's missing. Gone."

And in an instant, Ravi was aboard the ship, his sudden appearance causing Leenah to cry out in surprise. Skrizz jumped so high in his seat that he crashed into the overhead instrument panel.

"I apologize," Ravi said. "I must know what happened."

"Skrizz... knows better than I do."

Ravi turned to the wobanki, who explained the story as he knew it. No sooner had he finished than Ravi disappeared again.

"Hey, what's going on?" Keel asked from the *Six*'s comms.

"Aeson!" said Leenah. "I'm on En Shakar. And so is Ravi... somehow. Prisma is gone."

"Like she ran away?"

"No. She was chased away. By Hutch."

Keel cursed. "I had a feeling rescuing that Nether Ops kelhorn was a mistake."

"I think Ravi is looking for her."

"Well, it must be serious if he's jumping across the galaxy for you. He won't ever do it for me."

"Aeson, please. This is serious."

"I am being serious, Your Highness."

Leenah didn't think so. She didn't need jokes. She needed someone to tell her this was going to be okay. "Are you finished with your mission? Can you come here?"

"I..." Keel began. "I wish I could. I'm sorry. And I'm sorry for being... unserious. I know how much she means to you."

Leenah appreciated the apology, but was hurt that Keel wouldn't come and be with her. Didn't he realize how much she needed him right now?

"How long until you finish your job for the Legion?"

"Ah." Keel hesitated. "It *is* finished. Wraith... has a new job."

"What? For whom? Why are you taking new jobs?"

"For me. This job is my own. I... I have to kill Goth Sullus, Leenah. I have to."

A hundred objections sprang to Leenah's mind. Most of them questioning the sanity of this man she loved. And then something in her clicked. An odd sense of peace. And she remembered Prisma. And all the things that had happened to her. All the sorrow she'd endured on the trail that led to En Shakar.

The pain. The loss. The hurt and grief. All of it...

... was because of him.

Because of Goth Sullus.

And suddenly Leenah felt a burning sense of indignation. And pride. Pride in Aeson for being the one to put a stop to this man. To be willing to stand up to the sort of man who will leave a girl an orphan because it suited him. A man who would fan the flames of a galaxy in turmoil to achieve his own selfish ends.

Goth Sullus was not a good man.

And Aeson Keel... he was.

And right now, he didn't need an argument. He needed her support. And he would get it. In more ways than he realized or could ever know.

"I understand."

"Leenah, don't be like... wait. You do?"

"I do. This is the opportunity to put away Goth Sullus and his empire. To end it before it can become a plague on the galaxy. You have to do this, Aeson."

Keel seemed dumbfounded. And then he gave a yelp of surprise.

"Don't *do* that, Ravi!"

Evidently the mysterious navigator was back aboard the *Indelible VI*. His voice came over the comm.

"Prisma is gone. And there is worse news. I sensed on En Shakar the return of someone who means only ill for this galaxy. The one who made Goth Sullus is seeking to make the same out of Prisma Maydoon."

"Leenah," Keel said, "I gotta go. I... I love you."

And then the comm channel was dead. And no matter how hard Leenah tried, she couldn't get the *Six* to receive.

Skrizz was looking from Leenah to the comm with wonder, as though he couldn't comprehend how he'd ended up in the position he now occupied.

"I'm taking the shuttle to Utopion," Leenah said. "Are you staying here or are you coming with me?"

The wobanki flattened his ears, obviously not thrilled about his options. Then without a word, he strapped himself in.

33

Chhun was in the basement of a run-down bar on Utopion, just a few kilometers from the Imperial Palace. It was amazing how the opulence of the Capitol District quickly gave way to the big-city squalor that even core worlds experienced. *Especially* core worlds.

The sting of losing Exo was weighing heavily on him, though he tried not to show it. Bombassa was obviously putting it on himself, and no amount of assurances that he'd done what he could in the situation was going to change that. The big legionnaire just needed to be able to turn on his KTF when the time came and do what he was trained to do. They all did.

"Remember this place?" Masters asked quietly.

Chhun looked around. The room was full of men trained by the Legion. Young and old. Retired and active-duty. They were arming themselves. Checking their weapons. Jocking up in whatever armor they could come by.

Smuggling the armor onto Utopion had been the most difficult. But a few among them had full suits that they'd somehow managed to take with them when they'd gotten out. One leej who had been active with the Iron Wolves said he'd shipped his kit home one piece at a time. The others made do with partials. A breastplate here, a bucket there.

All augmented by after-market body armor when they could get it. Only a few guys had nothing but street clothes.

Chhun made a mental note to keep the unarmored men back for use in support. He didn't want to send naked leejes into a grinder. They were going to need armor in those first few moments of the fight.

But other than the familiarity of legionnaires preparing themselves, nothing about the room he was in seemed familiar to Chhun.

"Sorry. No."

"This bar... this is where we picked up Exo after he'd shipped off the *Mercutio*."

Was it? Chhun obviously hadn't visited the basement that time, years ago. He thought about the bar's entrance and upper level. Yeah... it was. The revelation hit him like a pillowcase filled with charge packs. Not only because of the link to Exo, but because he hadn't recognized it.

Masters sighed and rapped his knuckles on the table. "Seems kind of, I dunno. Poetic."

"It does," Chhun agreed. "So when this goes down, let's do it for Exo."

"He might still be alive."

That was a possibility, but Chhun didn't think so. In fact he hoped against it. If Exo was alive, he likely wasn't wandering the streets freely. He'd have been taken in by Nether Ops. And while Exo would never flip—Chhun knew that about the man, and even so he'd made sure to keep classified intel, such as the identity of Wash, away from even his closest friends—it didn't mean they wouldn't try.

"If he's out there, we'll bring him back," Chhun said. "No matter what."

"Yeah."

Chhun's comm chimed and Masters took that as a cue to leave.

This would be Wash. Chhun's heart fluttered. The operation was scheduled to begin in forty-eight hours. But things changed. Wash had been busy. Moving nonstop to get things lined up.

He took the call and waited to hear Wash's voice.

"Sorry I can't bet on the game, my wife said she'd kill me."

Chhun's heart sank. They had him.

He muted his comm and called out to Bear, who was attempting to console Bombassa, "Ready for Tac Sixty-Six!"

Immediately the men in the room scrambled.

Chhun found a quiet corner and answered the call. "Go for Bird Dog."

***

Wash had woken up ener-chained, still sitting at his desk, in the same chair he'd been stun-blasted in. His pistol was gone.

"You've been a busy man."

It was X.

"I find that a long walk at our age just about does me in. I come to the end and all I can think about is sitting down to a cup of tea. But you, Wash—that is what your friends called you, isn't it?—you're hustling all over the city as though you're running errands on post back on Psydon."

X sat down on a stool across from Washam, four armed Nether Ops agents behind him, showing Wash exactly who held the power.

"Now, why is that?" asked X.

Wash shrugged. "Being Legion commander is busy work. You of all people should appreciate that."

"Oh, I certainly do. I could barely keep up with the Carnivale before the gray really set in. And now... well, let's all thank the stars for personal assistants and the energy of young officers still wanting to build a career."

Wash looked down at his manacled hands. "This seems excessive for a social visit."

"Would that this were just two Psydon veterans catching up. But no. I'm afraid that Nether Ops is well aware of the game you're playing. A dangerous one, defying our emperor."

Wash raised an eyebrow. "You think me disloyal to Emperor Sullus? Perhaps because of my friendship with the late Orrin Kaar? You believe... what? That in a rage, I vowed revenge at seeing my friend murdered by a power-hungry despot? You can't be so foolish as that."

"Can't I? That is to say, is it really so far-fetched? The thought crossed even my mind that Sullus may well be more trouble than he's worth. And now that the House of Reason and Senate are gone... why keep him around? The Legion is still out there. Let them take care of things as only they can. Let the galaxy find its bearings. Start over."

"Are you asking me or telling me?"

X smiled. "Merely thinking through. Things are never so clear and distinct in Nether Ops. We're realists, Wash.

You know that. And while my heart has ever and always been for the Legion, well... let's just confirm that what the heart wants isn't always what's best. Goth Sullus was what was best. He still may be. But... I wouldn't call myself a true believer."

"If you're suggesting I assist you in some sort of coup, I'll say plainly that the Imperial Legion will not turn against its Emperor."

X laughed. "I have no doubt of that! For what good they might be. All the real fighters jumped ship. It's remarkable, isn't it? Goth Sullus, for years without my knowing, plotted and schemed to reach the heights he now holds. He had a message. A mission. Reform. Cut down the dead tree so another may be planted that will bear fruit. And then..." X held out his hand, revealing nothing. "He gets inside and plays ball. Coalitions. Consolidation of power. When all he really had to do was fulfill Article Nineteen."

"And why didn't he?" Wash asked, seeking more from X. Wanting to know just what the man had on him—if anything—and what his next move should be.

"Because of Keller is my guess. Because someone else tried it first. You learn things, watching people for a living. Goth Sullus is the type of man, and he is a man—he has unspeakable power, but still a man—he's the type who can only ever do things his way. Or what he believes is his way. Even at loss. Even if it means betrayal and every other sin. His way. Because... he's right. In his own mind."

Wash nodded. "Well, that's a very fascinating analysis of our emperor. Am I out of line in asking for these restraints to be removed if I'm not under arrest?"

"You are." X leaned forward. "Why would a point, a man hated by every rank-and-file legionnaire, be visiting known Legion gathering places? Veterans' halls and Legion bars. What business would you have there if not seeking a black eye?"

Wash had no intention of answering, and X gave him no opportunity.

"That's what I asked myself, old boy, when I saw you the other day. Just blind luck. But the question gnawed at me enough to have more of those energetic and youthful men in the Carnivale to follow you. And they did. Sloppy work, Wash, but you can hardly be blamed. The average legionnaire doesn't get the same training as Dark Ops. And you... you were a point."

Wash felt his face flush. He knew he looked concerned.

"Yes," said X. "Precisely. I know, Washam. You are working with the Legion—the Legion!—to overthrow this government. Or so I suspected. So we monitored your comm calls. And you were smart enough to encrypt those and use a burner comm. But we can still detect when those fire, even if we can't listen in. And you very clearly were using one burner, and one private comm."

X stood up and revealed that he was in possession of Wash's old sidearm from Psydon. He walked behind Wash, out of sight.

"I have Nether Ops kill teams moving on every location we saw you visit. And we saw you visit quite a few, dear boy. They await my orders."

Wash felt the barrel of the blaster push against the back of his head. "Perhaps Goth Sullus's time is over. And perhaps the right move for Nether Ops is to facilitate the Legion's attack. I wish to know. Call your contact. As usual—no tricks. Relay the call to my comm so I can listen."

"I don't know what—"

X primed the charge, causing the pack to whine as it powered up. A subtle message to Wash that this would not be a stun blast. And if X pulled the trigger, the bolt would take with it much of Wash's head.

"Now. Or I execute you and then execute the raid. I have enough evidence to be free of any reprisals from our emperor. He'll likely give me a commendation. Perhaps the Order of the Centurion?"

"All right," Wash said, his voice quavering. He was a point. In the end he behaved like a point.

Or so he hoped. Because X needed convincing.

Wash began the call, and right away told Chhun what was happening through his greeting. Now Chhun would need to play his part.

"Go for Bird Dog," said Chhun. He was ready.

"Bird Dog, this is Overlord."

X had come around in front of Wash now that he'd started the call, the pistol at his side, Wash's life spared for the moment. The agent rolled his eyes at Wash's use of the call sign.

"Copy, Overlord. You weren't supposed to call again before the attack. Is something wrong?"

"Tell him no," whispered X.

"No. Nothing's wrong." Wash looked imploringly at X, as though asking what he should say next.

"Ask about troop preparedness."

"Are your men ready?"

"Yes, sir. There aren't many of us, but we're prepared to strike a blow for the Legion. Are we still a go for the mission tonight?"

"Tell him to delay," demanded X.

"Negative. That's why I'm calling. Non-optimal time. Stand by twenty-four hours and await my next call."

"Copy, Overlord."

Wash looked at X, who nodded, giving him permission to end the call.

"Overlord out."

X smiled, raised the blaster pistol, and shot Wash in the head. He looked to his lieutenant. "Have a cleaner come and see what else they can find now that this traitor's body is in the apartment. He may have hidden compartments activated by bio-signature."

"Yes, sir."

X keyed his comm, reaching all the Nether Ops Kill teams he had standing by, waiting to storm the locations where Wash's pathetic upstart legionnaire force had gathered.

"You are clear for engagement."

34

Sergeant Brian Lambert had never given a damn about politics. The House of Reason had been garbage. So had the Senate. And so had Legion Commander Keller for the way he always gave ground. And so when Nether Ops—specifically the Carnivale—recruited him and told him this was a path free of the politics, where the things that needed done got done, he had no qualms about walking away.

And he had no qualms about leading his Nether Ops kill team on a raid that would dust a bunch of salty Legion vets who thought that because they knew how to use rifles and once lived to KTF, they were free to attack the Imperial Republic.

That was just more politics. Article Nineteen—politics. The founding of the Empire—politics. The House of Reason was gone. That was good politics. But everything else... who actually cared?

The galaxy needed stability, and Nether Ops was bringing it. As they always had. It was messy, bloody work and some people couldn't handle that. But in the end, it was about doing what had to be done. Maybe a few good guys went to the grave a little too soon, but they were headed there anyway. So why not make the galaxy a better place even if it meant dying early?

And now a whole bunch of former legionnaires, men whom Lambert probably would have liked, were about to get dusted by his and every other Nether Ops kill team now moving into position. And that sucked. But hey, greater good.

"Team Six moving on target," Lambert called into the ops-comm.

They'd been assigned a bar. A Legion bar. An old run-down place with more shadows than lights. A good place to get drunk and forget the past. Lambert had actually downed a few at the counter once or twice. Listened to the old leejes argue about who had it worse.

His team moved in quickly. The bar was open, but business had looked slow from their vantage point. They had a man inside, a man who'd been nursing a drink in a corner booth all night. He'd reported that the suspected insurgents were in a back room, or the basement, because they sure as hell weren't up front and drinking.

Even with this intel, Lambert went in hot. He saw two men standing at the counter, beers in hand. He dropped both with a double-tap of his N-6. Because KTF. And because screw you. It didn't pay to take chances.

The rest of the team came in behind him and quickly eliminated the few remaining patrons. Team Eleven was blowing in the back door as Team Six took the front. So the insurgents, hiding in the basement most likely, were gonna hear that something was up. The boom of the back door blowing in. Shouts from the bar ordering patrons to get down and hoping they didn't shoot you as you went by, or simply dropping them and ensuring they didn't shoot you in the back. It was all the same.

"Barroom's secure," Lambert reported. "Clearing adjoining kitchen."

Two of Lambert's men kicked in the swinging door that led to the kitchen and began firing on whatever unlucky cooks or busboys were back there.

Lambert saw a man in a white T-shirt run in panic out of an opposite exit, only to be dusted by the Nether Ops on the other side.

"Ground level secure. Converging on basement."

"Copy," replied the team leader of the coordinating Nether Ops kill team. "Door breached. We are moving to clear rooms now. Say again, we are—"

Blaster fire cut off the man's voice.

Sket. Not good. They'd found the targets and the contact sounded heavy. What was worse, the identifiers of the other kill team were going offline quick. They were getting slaughtered. An ambush.

Two men from Lambert's team reached the door leading to the basement. Lambert threw out his hand and cried out a warning. "Wait!"

The Nether Ops team opened the door and found themselves engulfed in the blast of at least two anti-personnel mines. Explosive balls ripped through their armor, killing them instantly and leaving their mangled bodies to tumble and bleed down the exposed staircase.

"Sket!" Lambert shouted, hugging the floor. Everything had gone to hell. There was no way he was going to send his team down those stairs. Time to regroup before they were trapped inside the building. Team Eleven was all showing KIA. "Outside! Outside!"

His team knew the score and didn't need additional motivation. They covered each other, moving back the way they came, ready to get behind their combat sled that had arrived in support just before the start of the raid.

Lambert's team spilled out of the bar, with him right behind them, when he heard the thunderous shots of the sled's twin blaster turrets. His first thought was that there was fighting happening on the streets, and they'd been sent into a hornets' nest. But the twins were dealing damage, if nothing else.

But as his momentum carried him out of the bar, he realized how critical a mistake he'd made. The twin blasters weren't firing onto the street. They were firing at the entrance to the bar.

"Friendly fire!" Lambert shouted, hoping the gunner would realize he was shooting at the wrong men. Already half of his team had gone down under the barrage. Dead.

And then Lambert realized he was again mistaken. The last realization of a life that was coming to an early end. And for the greater good, who could say? It didn't seem to matter. Lambert didn't want to die, and yet...

"Oh ske—"

His words were taken from him under the pounding fire of the sled's twin N-50 blaster cannons. Wielded by a tall man with a dark complexion, whose eyes were wide and hot with rage as he cut down the entire Nether Ops kill team. And Lambert with them.

***

X listened with mounting alarm as the comm reports came in, fast and furious. A chorus, a dirge, of things going terribly wrong.

"We are pinned down! Say again, need immediate evacuation!"

"Confirmed. Total team kill! And that's going to be our team too if…"

"…being pursued on foot by…"

"…lost accountability of Teams Four, Two…"

"Get us the hell out of here!"

X stood up from his office chair. He felt his joints creak and moan in protest. Why did he have to be so damned old? He needed to be quick. His teams needed support.

"Allison!"

He shouted for his assistant, hoping she would be there. She wasn't.

X hurried out into the main suite of offices. A few night owls and essential personnel were still on station. They were standing up, peeking around doors or over cubicles to find out what had made the boss yell.

"You," he said, taking them all in. "I want every operator we have to gather here. Right now."

X spoke, and the Carnivale obeyed.

"Get some brass from the Imperial Legion on the line—not Washam—we need to send in armor right away." The other agents were scrambling now, aware that something was up. "And I need to be patched to Utopion police.

None of this sensitivity raid nonsense. I need them on the streets now!"

X pushed aside a junior Nether Ops tech from his massive monitor and punched in a key that brought up the real-time battlenet of all the Nether Ops kill teams he'd sent to all the suspected cells Washam was overseeing.

"No," he said.

It wasn't possible. Surely this wasn't possible. These were high-speed Nether Ops teams. Brutal operators. And virtually all of them were dead or unaccounted for. It was as if they had all entered a trap. All at once. No one taken by surprise or off-guard.

X cursed Washam, wherever he was now. X had been played. He'd allowed his own prejudices to blind him. To make him see Washam as a worthless and servile point seeking to grab power for himself. And now he was losing operators he could not afford to lose.

"Where's my link with the Legion?" he bellowed.

"Patching through now, sir."

"This is LTC Ward," came the stern, commanding voice on the other end of the ether.

"This is Nether Ops, Carnivale. We require immediate support from the Imperial Legion. Advise armor and air support. Transmitting coordinates."

"Slow your treads, spook," Ward said. "We are not cleared to mobilize."

"What?" X hurriedly typed in the lieutenant colonel's identifiers into the Nether Ops database. "Not a point," he mumbled under his breath.

"I have immediate need of support," X tried again. "We have uncovered an expansive cell of insurgents seeking to topple your emperor."

"Negative."

"That is unacceptable!" There was no point in losing his cool, X knew that. He prided himself on always staying in control. And while Goth Sullus was not the type to punish those who failed in spite of best efforts, X was now doubting himself. Doubting his effort.

He had followed his instincts, yes. But he also had waited. Bided his time until the evidence that Washam had been working with a source outside the Empire's command structure was beyond a doubt. Even if he hadn't known who that outside source was. He knew *where* to go. His men had followed. Watched. He had put his teams in place. Carefully. Patiently.

And now this.

The lieutenant colonel sounded as though he wasn't fazed in the least. "General Orders Three were implemented by Legion Commander Washam. We are to stand down unless engaged due to an attempted coup by forces inside this government… including Nether Ops."

"No! Washam was a traitor! And he's been executed for crimes against the emperor!" X needed to take control of this situation. And that hinged on his being able to convince this Legion dullard that it was Nether Ops—the Carnivale and X—that he needed to obey.

The was a stony silence over the comm, and X began to feel a sliver of hope.

But then: "My orders cannot be revoked except by the Legion commander."

X cursed and killed the comm transmission. Goth Sullus could fix this, but X was not about to admit to Sullus—or even to himself—that he'd lost control of the situation. Not yet.

Besides, in the end, what was the loss of a few dozen kill teams? It was not insignificant by any stretch; it amounted to eighty percent of what he had available on Utopion. But still. They were hardly irreplaceable.

Perhaps the police would begin to assist. Surely they'd heard the noise.

This was just a minor terrorist infiltration. There were no readings of destroyers in orbit. This was not a second battle for Utopion. X would keep this under control.

He was about to yell for the comm link to the police when he heard a distant explosion deep within the city. Then another. And another.

He brought up aerial holos.

Utopion was on fire.

35

Goth Sullus sat in his chambers, seeking to find his connection to the power he'd once wielded. Why was it not his? He'd taken to retracing the memories of his training. Of Urmo and a time long ago. All in the hopes that he could do something to bring back a power that he, and he alone, deserved.

It was during these meditations that he heard the first, great explosion that shattered whatever peace a night on Utopion contained. Several more followed.

It is an end, master. You have been betrayed. Forsaken by all but us.

Sullus arose and moved to his war room. It was empty. Alone.

He activated the comm. If this was an attack—and what else could it be?—he needed the full weight of his remaining fleet. Utopion's small planetary defense fleet would only hold out for so long if intelligence about the Legion's growth was accurate. He needed destroyers. He needed his Black Fleet.

We are here, master. Now.

Admiral Crodus appeared on screen. He looked... defiant. Sullus would cow it out of the man. His knee had bowed before his emperor that day aboard *Imperator*. Sullus had not forgotten.

"Crodus, I demand your return."

"I cannot obey your request," Crodus answered. "You have lost your grip on the purpose of our Black Fleet. Something we feared would happen since the day that fool Rommal shouted flattery at you out of fear for his own skin."

But all Goth Sullus heard was "our Black Fleet." As though it had ever belonged to anyone but its emperor. And then the emperor wondered... had it been Crodus who had ordered the attempt on his life?

It had. Surely it had.

Yes.

But now... that no longer mattered. He survived then, and he would see the other side of this intrigue. His Empire would live on. But Crodus...

Sullus reached out, searching through space to find the exact place in the universe now occupied by the man before him.

Nothing.

Crodus continued, no doubt mistaking Sullus's concentration for stunned silence. "As such, I have surrendered my fleet to Admiral Deynolds of the Legion Expeditionary Fleet."

Nothing. No connection. Nothing.

Not since his enslavement had Goth Sullus felt both so enraged and powerless as he did in this moment of betrayal of the highest order. He wanted to kill the man. Needed to kill him. To snap his neck.

We will give you what you desire. We will return to you your power.

And deep inside, Casper—not Sullus, but Casper, the man Sullus had once been—understood what had happened to him. That which he had sought to destroy, Goth Sullus had spared, thinking himself the conqueror. It seemed so obvious now. The artifact, the ring... *that* had been the turning of the tide. The loss of his connection to the Crux.

There was still time. Casper moved to remove the ring from his gauntleted finger.

But Goth Sullus closed his fist.

There was more of Goth Sullus than Casper now.

He had murdered his best friend.

Destroy the betrayer, master. We will serve you with power. You need only ask. Serve us, master!

"I... Show me."

Even in surrendering to the will of the demons he'd spared... Even in giving over himself to the creatures he'd sworn to destroy with a power he'd once known would destroy him... Goth Sullus spoke in commands.

But those who had blocked him from the Crux, those demons, dark and depraved to a level even Sullus was only barely aware of, now restored Goth Sullus to his power. His breath. His life. His rightful place in the galaxy.

And the sudden rush of his power, the awakening of the Crux, was to Goth Sullus like a return of all his senses after lying hopeless in the deepest and darkest of caves.

He reached out beyond the stars. The galaxy was so impossibly large that, if not for what he knew was the guiding hand of his servants, he would not have found

Crodus. But there the admiral was. Still standing on the bridge of his flagship.

Goth Sullus snapped the man's neck. He lingered in spirit long enough to watch Crodus die, a terrified crew scrambling about his body.

Good. Let the enemies of Goth Sullus, the traitors and any others who would oppose him... let them dread his name.

Their terror was only beginning.

***

Chhun moved through the streets of Utopion, leading a veritable army of former legionnaires. There was fighting in the streets. Imperial Legion—some of them, at least— had mobilized to halt the arrest of company-sized elements pushing through Utopion's various districts to siege the Imperial Palace.

In the holomovies, a single squad was always able to take things over just by sneaking their way into where the planetary leader slept and then fighting whatever guards were on hand. In real life, it took far more than that to conquer a planet. Or even a city. And though Wash had done a remarkable job in putting together an underground fighting force, there were not nearly enough reactivated legionnaires to attempt such an outcome.

Which was fine. Because Chhun's purpose wasn't to conquer and occupy Utopion. His purpose was to see that the dictator was removed from power. The dictator who had overthrown the government the Legion was constitutionally bound to preserve. The dictator who had placed himself at the head of a new government. The dictator who named himself Emperor.

And after that...?

It was clear to Chhun that the planets that made up the Republic were yearning for a new start. That new start could have been Article Nineteen. But not now. That window had been closed through a painful cocktail of delay, politics, and a war gone all wrong. Still, the Legion had been present at the founding of the Republic. And the Legion would have its say at the Republic's funeral.

None of this would matter, however, if Chhun's forces were unable to hold the Utopion districts surrounding the Capitol District.

Fortunately, Legion Commander Washam had played his role brilliantly, right up to the last. Nether Ops had been sent into disarray thanks to Wash's perfectly executed trap. He'd also positioned men inside the Imperial Legion capable of delaying or denying the use of key defenses such as mobile cavalry, heavy armor, or close air support—and Utopion didn't have much in that way to begin with. Its military presence had always been light, partly due to protesting every time the Senate or House of Reason suggested an expansion of on-planet personnel, and partly due to those same bodies' assessment that no one in the galaxy would dare attack Utopion.

And yet here the Legion was, carrying on another campaign not a year after the last.

"Keep your forces grouped," Chhun reminded his "generals"—the men placed in command over the various established resistance cells—over the comm. "I'm seeing the cyborgs getting mixed in with the Legion-capable. You all know that can't happen."

Obedience came quickly as one of Chhun's commanders called, "Sixteenth, you're entering the AO of the Fourth. Keep your men back and in reserve."

"Copy, sir," came the reply of the officer leading the Sixteenth. "Fourth was calling for numbers to hammer back the Imperials dug in at the seven hundred block."

Chhun guided the response. "They need to stay back until we know what kind of resistance we're up against on the streets." He scanned his battlenets and saw a firefight two blocks west, his legionnaires mixing it up with Utopion police. "Send the Sixteenth to engage at my designation. Intel confirms no bot resistance."

Key to Chhun's strategy was having a way to quickly take down the war bots Goth Sullus had recalled. He had seen firsthand the kind of damage those bots could do. And while the Legion hadn't been ready for their surprise attack the last time around, they *did* know how to fight against bots. Legion doctrine dating back to the Savage Wars had consistently demonstrated how to stop a machine army.

Which was why they were so rare. Because, compared to fighting humanoids, taking out mass numbers of bots was relatively simple—*if* you were equipped to handle them. No one was then. Chhun's Legion was now.

But he didn't want to also lose those sections of his underground army who were living life as cyborgs. Guys like

Sticks. So he had to be very particular not to let them mix on the battlefield with the bots.

Blaster fire broke out ahead. Chhun ducked his head instinctively but continued to move forward with his team.

"Contact!" shouted a legionnaire over the squad comm.

Soon the blaster fire intensified on both sides.

"What're we looking at?" Chhun asked.

"More Imperial Legion. Maybe a platoon's worth. We caught 'em flat-footed while they were trying to sneak down a side street. Got 'em pinned down."

Chhun keyed for Bombassa. "'Bassa. You still with the sled?"

"Yes, sir."

Capturing the combat sleds from the Nether Ops support teams had been an unexpected but most welcome turn of events.

"Bring it up on my location. We've got some infantry pinned down I need dusted."

"Copy."

An errant blaster bolt sailed over Chhun's head. It posed no threat to him but was a reminder that he was leading from the front lines and needed to stay frosty.

Soon the hum of Bombassa's repulsor sled sounded, and Chhun watched as the legionnaire hovered by, manning the twin guns. The sled's driver brought the vehicle up, and Bombassa began tearing apart the meager cover of doorways, statues, planters, and other urban landscaping that had been providing cover for the Imperial forces. Legionnaires on foot added to the chaos, taking well-aimed shots and dropping their Imperial counterparts until it became too much, and the Black Fleet men fell back as best they could.

"Permission to pursue?"

"Negative, negative," answered Chhun. "Let's keep the sled back. We don't want to get it drawn into an ambush."

The Legion Underground moved on.

"Grayhawk Actual to Victory One." Another of Chhun's commanders, calling in with a status update.

"Go for Victory."

"Victory One, we have reached the energy gates out-side objective in Sector Seven. Request permission to advance inside Imperial Compound upon destruction of gate generators. We are seeing no hostiles in defense of the objective. Say again, no hostiles sighted in defense of objective."

The Imperial Compound comprised the Imperial Palace, the Senate Building—or whatever it was now called—and One Voice Park. Once the heart of the Republic, this area was now the heart of Goth Sullus's Empire. And all that stood between Chhun's forces and this beating heart was a few energy gates.

Because the truth was, Utopion simply wasn't a mil-itary-ready planet. Its sheltered elites never would have allowed guard towers stocked with N-50s looking to stave off an invading army. Such a thing was uncouth to the people of the core worlds and impossible in the minds of those in government. Perhaps Goth Sullus had recognized this. Perhaps he even felt the same. More likely, Wash had delayed him. In any event, Chhun's men had been able to move through the city streets right up to the doorstep of the Imperial Compound, and were just a few meters away from setting foot inside.

Chhun considered Grayhawk's request. Usually he would appreciate and endorse such a move. Speed and violence of action were crucial elements of Legion success on the battlefield. Nobody liked a ditchdigger while on offense. But they couldn't be committed to an attack right now. Not yet. Chhun wanted to see what the situation looked like once more of his legionnaires reached their objective.

"Do as much as you can to get those gates down, but I don't want you stranded too far ahead. That said, you're eyes on ground, and I defer to your judgment over how far to push beyond the gate, over."

"Copy. Grayhawk Actual out."

Chhun pressed forward feeling cautiously optimistic about the manner in which the situation was developing. But he knew the battle was still in its early stages, and eventually those war bots would be injected into the mix.

36

Goth Sullus strode through the halls of the Imperial Palace. It was empty. In part a product of his purging Utopion of its cancerous House of Reason and pathetic Senate. The staffers and aides that had once thronged in the Capitol District—the Emperor's District—had gotten as far away from the architect of the Republic's downfall as they could.

The Black Fleet had been an army capable of conquering worlds.

Conqueror.

He had taken Tarrago and its moon. He had conquered them both. He alone had reversed what would have been an insurmountable loss. He had defeated the Legion there. He would defeat them again on Utopion.

An army. Lost.

Yes. Much of the Black Fleet, what was to be the backbone of his Empire, *had* been lost at Tarrago. The attrition of warfare in taking—and losing—the shipyards was considerable.

And betrayal.

Sullus felt his anger grow. Overhead lights began to dim and flicker, then showered sparks as they exploded from his wielding of a power unmatched in the galaxy. They had betrayed him. Attempted to assassinate him.

After he'd saved them.

He'd sought to build a coalition to hasten his reign, and they betrayed him further. Abandoning their emperor, the greatest leader—the greatest man—the galaxy had ever known.

A god. He was a god.

The voices laughed.

You are a betrayer, Goth Sullus.

"I demand silence."

The power Goth Sullus felt flowing around him began to ebb. He could feel it fading, as though a once-flowing river were drying, reduced to a pitiable trickle.

Say to us truth, Betrayer.

He stood still in the corridor. Head held high in a defiance he could not justify.

"I sacrificed so that the galaxy would be spared of you."

You sacrificed to save yourself. To save your vision. Your... Empire. Cast away your crown, Emperor. And bend your knee, Betrayer.

Casper knew he could not justify his ways. Not any longer. He again reached for the ring, and Goth Sullus again closed his fist. And the good of the man, perhaps no more than intentions, faded again.

"I... am Betrayer."

The voices hissed and laughed.

The power returned, and with new intensity. But there it was. Goth Sullus, the great savior, was the great betrayer.

He would not be a failure. He would succeed. He would rule.

He made way to the Imperial Legion's motor pool, meager though it was. The Legion's attack demanded a response. One full of fury.

***

Goth Sullus felt the fear of the Imperial Legion as he entered the motor pool. He stretched out his senses. So few. There were so few here when once he had commanded so many.

But it would be enough to arrest the upstart progress of the Legion. He could sense them. Circumstance and incompetence had allowed them to move faster and farther than they ought.

And betrayal...

His war machines would hurl them back. His Cybar. His tanks. His Empire.

A lieutenant colonel dripping with fear and surprise, his face and neck beaded over with sudden perspiration, attempted to maintain his military rigidity as he greeted Goth Sullus, who loomed a menacing spire, wearing the armor he'd renewed. Rechs's armor.

Whom you betrayed, Betrayer.

Because he'd had to. The death of his old friend had been what the galaxy required if it was to be saved. He'd *had* to.

Murder. Betrayal.

No. Mercy. Loyalty. Goth Sullus was a conqueror. A savior. He was emperor.

"You are to mobilize these tanks against the Legion."

The lieutenant colonel gaped, then stammered, "U-until I have orders from the Legion commander, I... I am to... stand down."

Finished, the man stood firm. Defiant like that fool Crodus. But at least with enough sense to be frightened.

Sullus looked from his left to his right, taking in with his eyes and the armor's visual HUD what he already knew through the Crux. He saw the men who were loyal to their lieutenant colonel. And the others, men who would be loyal to *him*, their emperor.

With the proper motivation.

A tech stood with goggles atop his head, a cutting torch in his hand as he'd worked on a combat sled. Goth Sullus reached out and drew the tool into his own hand, pulling the torch and its trailing fuel source in a line. He ignited the flame and extended it, holding the temperature, making the torch burn longer and farther until it seemed he held a sword of fire.

He plunged the weapon into the stomach of the defiant legionnaire. The man stood there, mouth open, a sudden cry of agony dying in a dry and blistering throat as the torch boiled his stomach and cooked his organs. Smoke rolled out of the man's mouth. The back of his throat grew black and charred.

Sullus whipped the blade out and turned on the legionnaires—more betrayers—who suddenly attacked. Blaster fire glanced against his armor. He seized the Crux and hurled legionnaires head first into the impervisteel armored tanks, pulverizing their skulls inside their helmets.

More came, attacking from all sides. Sullus burnt through them with his torch. He snapped necks, burst hearts, and shattered bones until the attacks stopped.

Now *he* stood defiant. Those who had held back, who had refused to join in another assassination attack, watched. And Goth Sullus sensed their awe. And their terror.

"Prepare your attack."

He was the voice of dread. The embodiment of doom, low and terrible. He would lead his Empire—small though it might be—onto the field of battle. And he would destroy the last remnants of the Legion.

***

The war bots had appeared from deep within the Imperial Palace. From the direction of the central courtyard, as Chhun remembered from his endless studying of battle maps. There was still no sign of significant numbers of Imperial legionnaires.

Still, seeing the bots march toward him through his field macros brought a sense of dread. A reminder of the chaos of Gallobren. Of the day he'd nearly lost all of Kill Team Victory. And *had* lost all of a number of other kill teams. And the Dark Ops legionnaires they'd come to rescue.

He'd failed his men that day. He alone. He was determined not to allow that to happen again.

Flicking his bucket's tongue toggles, Chhun brought forward battle relays. The legionnaires susceptible to anti-bot weaponry were all well out of the area of effect, fighting clean-up and protecting the rear from any late-arriving police or Imperial legionnaires who'd managed to stay hidden as Chhun's forces moved past them toward the Imperial Compound.

Toward Goth Sullus.

The first crack of a sniper rifle sounded, and a uranium-depleted slug from a modified N-18 zipped deep into the ranks of the marching war bots. The reconfiguration of the N-18 to shoot ionized bullets came with significant downsides. It made for a painstakingly slow rate of fire, having to deal with bullet drop, and having to change not only charge packs but magazines as well.

But it was worth it.

Still watching through his macros, Chhun saw one of the big Titan war bots go down in a spray of sparks. And the machines closest to it paused as the ionic impact shut down their operating systems, forcing a battlefield reboot.

But they would be back up before long, and the remaining bots in the front lines sent N-50 fire from their tri-barreled arms directly into the location where the shot had come from.

Good. Chhun knew the man who'd taken the first shot had immediately left his position. His snipers knew the drill.

No sooner had the bots fired at the first target than a second shot took out a second bot. The process repeated, with bots falling and snipers rotating from hide to hide.

It was slow, but effective. First, because as imposing as the machines were, there weren't a lot of them. Nothing like the numbers Chhun had encountered last time. And second, because this was all they were capable of at long range. They would need to close ground before Chhun could use the rest of the special equipment the teams were carrying.

This was Chhun's last chance to change his mind. Meet the enemy and engage right now or fall back and see if the situation became any easier. But he didn't see how he'd be able to get odds any better than this.

"Hold firm, Legionnaires. Stay frosty and KTF once they're in range."

"We got these bots," growled Bear from the comm.

It occurred to Chhun that he didn't know where Kill Team Victory was at the moment. On the battlefield, and together, of course. But somewhere else.

And though it was selfish and not the sort of thing he should be thinking of at this crucial moment, Chhun found himself wishing that if he was going to die today, he wanted it to be in their company.

The bots marched onward. The snipers engaged, destroying what they could.

And then it was time.

Grenade launchers began to *fwoomp* special bot-poppers. Ion-charged with micro-EMP pulses designed to fry a war bot's operating systems. The legionnaires, in their various stages of armor dress, dug in behind berms and hills, using the natural landscape of the park to provide them cover, followed up the grenade blasts by concentrating blaster fire on the heads of the stunned and halted war bots.

The combat sleds they'd commandeered raced up and down the lines, their gunners firing nonstop and their drivers sending up jamming chaff and smoke to fool the missiles and the bots' tracking software that sought to take them out of the fight.

Chhun's helmet flickered from the detonation of a bot-popper that exploded too close to his position. Legionnaires closer to the area of impact who had been wearing helmets now took them off. What stopped a war bot would definitely stop a bucket.

But the plan was working. Mortar bots began to hurl a mix of ionic detonation shells and high-explosive rounds into the war bots' ranks. This was textbook stuff. The sort of thing employed in the Savage Wars whenever some tech-obsessed Savage unit tried to wheel out the next super bot. And it was effective. So effective that anyone watching would remember why people didn't attempt to conquer the galaxy with bot armies. That was taking a page out of ancient history. Akin to riding horses into battle with swords and muskets against a mechanized infantry division... if the ancient military journals were to be believed.

The surprise of the war bots was lost. And their continued use, to Chhun, smelled of desperation. Smelled of... them being all that Goth Sullus had. All that was left to him.

He'd hidden in the shadows. He'd attacked legionnaires without warning. Had shown them no mercy. He'd used legitimate grievances to weaken the Legion. But now all that was gone. All the tricks and manipulation.

Chhun had taken that away. And now Goth Sullus would see that the Legion was a brotherhood that extended beyond a mere active duty roster. He would find that the galaxy was still full of legionnaires.

And on an open battlefield... Goth Sullus didn't stand a chance.

37

The *Indelible VI* arrived in Utopion space to find it in chaos. Orbital customs stations were in scattered pieces, mixed with bits of wrecked starships and freighters that had apparently made a mad dash to get off-planet, clearances be deviled. Gravity caught hold of a ring-like station that was spinning from what looked like a massive collision, and the station glowed as it was pulled down into Utopion's atmosphere.

It looked like Doc had made the right decision to stay in the farmhouse instead of accompanying Keel to Utopion. "Rather retire than die, if it's all the same to you."

Death was looking like a distinct possibility if Keel didn't fly right.

The *Six*'s proximity warnings beeped endlessly as Keel dodged debris and starships rocketing away in desperation. "Ravi! Find me a clear stretch of space to maneuver in, because I ain't seein' any!"

Ravi didn't respond, but flashing arrows appeared superimposed over the cockpit's forward viewing portal. Keel followed the arrows, knowing that Ravi was guiding him to a less crowded section of space. "Thanks, pal."

"I am scanning battlenet transmissions from the planet's surface," Ravi said. He was quiet for all of three seconds as he took in what he was hearing over the Legion comms. "Legion Commander Chhun's attack is already underway. They are engaging the war bots."

"Great," said Keel. "How about the man himself?"

Ravi listened more. "Goth Sullus has appeared on the field of battle in person, along with a small attachment of heavy armor."

"Not great." Keel corkscrewed the *Six* to dodge a piece of errant detritus. In the seconds he had to see it as it flew by, he thought it was the wing of a Republic transport shuttle. "I need an approach vector. Something fast so we don't have to fly halfway across the planet once we've entered atmosphere."

"I have it for you. However..."

"What?"

"The defense fleet is blockading the direct approach to the capital."

Keel shrugged. "Not the first blockade we've had to run."

"Yes, but they are quite densely positioned. Instead of seeking to deny access to the planet as a whole, they have formed a tight blockade around the capital sector specifically. Once you enter the atmosphere, I show a ninety percent chance of sustaining moderate to severe damage."

Keel glared at Ravi. "Moderate to severe, huh? Why don't you try and be a little less vague next time?"

"Well, I don't see how you would expect me to account for the training and latent talent of the gunners. This defense fleet is primarily MCR, and as you know, the variables are not insignificant—"

"Ravi! Yes or no—if I make the run, is my ship gonna get torn up again?"

The navigator paused. "Yes."

"Just great," Keel said, slamming his head back into the padded headrest of his chair. "Why can't it ever be easy?" He reached out to activate the comm. "Hey, kid!"

"Yeah, boss?" answered Garret.

"Is that bot of yours fixed? You said you'd have it done before we got to Utopion."

"Well... it's mostly fixed. I haven't fully restored all of its original cross-dock programming sequences. Which are coded in a really cool way. But he can do basic functions. He can move again, at least."

"Can he load himself up?"

"Oh, yeah. No problem. I'm really happy you're letting me keep him, by the way."

Keel shook his head, a silent spectator to Garret's blissful ignorance. The kid wasn't gonna like what came next.

Keel whipped the *Six* around into a big loop, orienting the ship to begin a head-on run toward the blockade.

"Captain, what are you doing?" asked Ravi.

"That fleet is just a bunch of corvettes and cruisers. There's only one destroyer."

"Yes..."

"So what are the odds if the destroyer goes away?"

"I do not see how this is possible unless you can force them to jump away somehow."

"Just tell me the odds!"

"Forty percent of moderate to severe damage if the destroyer's weapons were not engaged in the defense."

Keel inclined his head. "Well, that's an improvement. And who knows… the destroyer might not be the only one that goes."

He began to accelerate toward the fleet. His sensors read three minutes until he reached their firing range and six minutes until he was over the destroyer. That meant three minutes of concentrated, tier one flying.

But there was no other choice.

Ravi's eyebrow was arched so high it disappeared beneath his turban. "Captain Keel… please explain to me what is happening right now. Have you decided to commit suicide? I urge you to reconsider."

"No time, Ravi." Keel punched the comms up again. "Garret. I need you to load that MARO on your new toy and get it ready to roll off the ramp when I tell you." He paused. "Uh, and make sure to get out of the hold before the ramp lowers or you'll get sucked out into space."

He felt the elementary warning might be necessary with Garret.

"Wait! Are you gonna blow up Lifty?"

Lifty? Keel groaned. He didn't have time for this. "Yes. Lifty has to take one for the team. I've seen a MARO blow up a destroyer in the past. So let's try it again."

"But you said I could keep him!"

Keel muted the comm to vent a singular, loud profanity before switching back to voice. "Hey, I know Garret, and I'm sorry. I'll… I'll buy you a new one."

"Yeah, but, that's the whole reason Lifty is so special. These are ultra-rare machines."

"No. No they're not," Keel said, trying to sound convincing. "Chhun has a ton of them hiding all over the galaxy just like this one. I'll let you have two. Three."

"You're sure? Because I can probably think of a way to get the bomb off without using Lifty if you give me like, twenty minutes."

"No time. Gotta do it. Lives are at stake. *Four* new Liftys. I promise." Keel muted his comm and looked to Ravi. "Chhun probably has more, right?"

The navigator shook his head disapprovingly.

Keel frowned. "Hey, it's not my fault if he doesn't."

"Okay," Garret said. "But only because lives are at stake. Because even four new bots aren't worth one Lifty."

"Honestly, Ravi. What is wrong with that kid?" Keel unmuted the comms. "Thanks, Garret. I need that bomb dropped over the destroyer in… four minutes."

"Oh, sket, I'd better hurry."

Keel shook off the kid's words and focused on his approach. Maybe they'd try to warn him away and he'd have some extra time, but at his speed and given the chaos all around him, he was pretty sure they'd just start firing as soon as he was in range. They hadn't even bothered to hail him, which was too bad, because he had a really good registry lined up for them.

"Incoming fire," warned Ravi, but Keel had already spotted the massive blaster cannon lasers streaking his way.

Like the cannons on most destroyers, these were calibrated to stop larger ships than the *Six*. And Keel had no difficulty dodging them. Depending on the speed of the destroyer's crew and officers, they might not even make the necessary adjustments until he was in the atmospheric pull. Of course, then he'd be a much easier target. You can't juke and dodge while burning through reentry.

Still, he should be okay. Just as long as they didn't launch fighters.

"Incoming fighters," called Ravi.

"Really?" Keel kept his attention on his flight display. "How many?"

"Only four."

"Missiles?"

"Full complement."

Keel nodded. "Send 'em early. I want 'em to break off before they have a chance to weaken our shields. I have a feeling we're gonna need them to keep safe from that blast."

"Launching now."

The cockpit door swished open and Garret appeared. "Okay. Lifty is ready. The doors are down. Just say the word and he'll… he'll roll away forever."

"Are you *crying* right now?" Keel shouted.

Garret didn't answer, but he did bring up the outward-facing holocam showing the opened ramp, and waved meekly at the bot on screen. "I'm waving, Lifty," he said quietly.

The bot waved back at the holocam with half of its eight arms.

Keel shook his head. "Ravi, I can't guess this one. Tell me when the bot needs to jump off the ramp."

"Closing in… thirty seconds."

One of the MCR tri-fighters that had launched to intercept abruptly flew in front of the *Six*, a missile in hot pursuit.

Keel dropped the nose down to avoid a collision. "That thing almost hit us!"

"Adjust course," Ravi urged. "We are aligned for collision."

Keel pulled back up and leveled off. "How we doin'?"

"Almost there. We are almost there."

"You know a countdown would be helpful—"

Ravi raised a hand. "Garret, now!"

"Jump, Lifty! Jump!"

A synthesized, primitive robotic voice, free of any inflection, like an ancient software package reading text it didn't understand, replied over the comm. "Goodbye, Garret. I will miss you."

From the holofeed they could see the bot tumble off the ramp, holding the exposed and armed MARO, the momentum of the ship carrying it in a straight line along the course Keel had been traveling. The *Indelible VI* immediately pulled up, its nose streaked just meters above the hull of the destroyer, and Keel threw full power into accelerators, sending them rocketing away.

"Distance..." Keel urged himself. "Distance."

"The bot is approaching the hull."

"C'mon, baby, move..."

"Almost to center hull, maximum damage."

"Detonate!" Keel shouted.

Nothing happened.

Keel whirled around. Garret was holding the remote detonator in his hands. "Kid, press the button!"

"I can't!"

Keel grabbed the detonator and depressed the switch.

The ship rocked from the shock waves of a noiseless explosion. Followed by more shock waves. More explosions. Secondary and beyond.

Flames from the burning gases expanded outward from the destroyed capital ship so suddenly and with such urgent force that they caught up with the *Six* as it rocketed away, enveloping the canopy view until the *Six* finally pulled free, the fury of the ignited gases winking out in the vacuum of space.

"Ha ha!" Keel shouted in triumph. He began flipping switches. "What else did we get? How much?" He checked the feed and his eyes went wide at the sight of the destroyer, nearly hollowed out from the massive blast. A nearby corvette and freighter were in pieces, and the other ships were moving quickly away.

"Three ships, Ravi! Three!"

Ravi nodded. "Congratulations. You have killed thousands of people today."

"Thousands of bad guys," Keel corrected, not at all bothered by Ravi's attempt to be sober. "A new record for one day."

"Pray that you never break it."

Garret seemed awestruck. "You've probably killed more people than Tyrus Rechs."

Keel gave a half frown. Why was everyone trying to ruin the mood? "Don't count on it."

He brought the *Six* around to enter Utopion atmosphere.

"But I *am* gonna kill the one he couldn't. The one that counts."

38

X didn't see the lone destroyer in Utopion's defense fleet go up in an unknown explosion. But he heard about it. He was Nether Ops; he heard about everything. His first thought was that the Legion Expeditionary Fleet had arrived and managed to quickly overwhelm and destroy the lone MCR destroyer protecting Utopion.

Had Scarpia been aboard that destroyer? It didn't matter. The man had filled his purpose. And he was becoming insufferable.

But this day had turned out to be a day of wrong conclusions. Not poor choices. X had made the right call every step of the way with the information he had. He always did.

Things, however, were not at all going as planned.

Which was why X was making his way toward the palace's surviving corvettes, seeking to arrange for his extraction from Utopion—because it was obvious that this brief empire had reached its sunset.

And that's when the Legion Expeditionary Fleet *did* arrive.

And naturally, the remaining MCR surrendered at once.

But that presented a new opportunity. One that X, ever the survivalist, was determined to take.

His comm buzzed, alerting him to the fact that his techs had the requested connection ready, and a female voice said, "This is Admiral Deynolds."

"My, but your star shines brightly, Admiral," X said, smiling congenially as he walked down the brightly lit sub-corridors of the Imperial Palace with two of his Nether Ops legionnaires. The rest were busy eliminating sensitive data in the Carnivale's local database. If fortune smiled, it could be recovered from a deep-space memory bank. "Congratulations on your promotion."

"Who am I speaking to?"

"Oh, no one of any particular importance. A man from Nether Ops." X was careful to disguise his voice. He wasn't sure, in his time dealing with Legion Commander Keller, if this... admiral had interacted with him. "And allow me to prevent any prejudicial remarks by saying that we are *not* all bad. Many of us, myself included, having been working diligently to defy Goth Sullus. That's the nature of my call."

"I'm seeking to coordinate an orbital bombardment of resistance pockets on Utopion. I don't have time for Nether Ops."

"I *do* hope I can say something that will change your mind, because I need to speak to the Legion commander. And you're the only one who can help me. And I don't mean Legion Commander Washam, though he deserves the title with the smashing way he organized our resistance."

Deynolds paused.

"Ah! Have I uttered the magic word? I worked with Washam. We're old friends from Psydon. I have a high-ranking legionnaire that agents captured alive. He says he came in with a special kill team."

X paused. He was telling a story. A narrative. Just as he had done countless times for those in the House of Reason who demanded to know what happened but couldn't be counted on to do what needed doing or approve of what had been done unless X first told them a tale that their minds could accept. A thing at which he excelled.

But had he found the story the admiral needed to hear?

"I'll see if the Legion commander is available."

X smiled to himself.

"Go for Chhun."

The sounds of battle were clear in the background. Close, but not front line. A Legion commander who coordinated the fight from the ground but wasn't so foolhardy as to get himself killed for it.

"Legion Commander Chhun," X positively gushed. "I don't expect you to know who I am. I'm with Nether Ops. Mid-level. No one important. But I wish to offer you the services of my Nether Ops kill teams. We are already inside the Imperial Compound. Direct us where to go, and we'll fight for the Legion. We've been resisting this entire time."

There was a pause.

X doubled down. "Also, we captured—alive—a man I believe may work with you. Goth Sullus had ordered his execution, but I've gotten him to safety. I'm going to him now. I only have a name from his Black Fleet records— Caleb Gutierrez."

"Exo," Chhun said. He sounded hopeful. "He's alive?"

The hook was in. Now all X had to do was reel him in. He was far from out of the game. He had contingencies. He would see this through.

"Yes, Legion Commander. As I said, I'm going to him now."

"I need to speak with him. Show me you're telling the truth by putting him on the comm. Then we can talk alliances."

"You need but ask."

***

Exo's arms were numb from the ener-chains, but his face felt a lot better thanks to the med bot's work. He could see again. The swelling had gone down significantly. And he wasn't bleeding. That was nice.

He'd heard the booms and knew that Chhun had started the attack. Then the booms got closer and he knew Chhun was winning the battle. And just recently he'd started hearing what had to be distant orbital bombardments. And that was really good, because it meant the fleet had arrived.

It had to just be a matter of time until either Goth Sullus fell, or Utopion was left so battered that it stopped being a player on the galactic stage. And Sullus, if he lived, could be the emperor of a lone, broken world.

It was better than the traitor deserved. Better by far. In the end he'd been as bad as the House of Reason. As bad as Nether Ops. As bad as any of 'em.

Exo wasn't sure if they'd come for him. Figured he'd just sit here and hope the building didn't collapse on top of him. But then the doors swished open. Someone was here. Probably Nether Ops. And they were probably going to kill him.

Which sucked. Because he had a lot of KTF left in him.

The same man who'd talked relatively nicely to him after he'd been worked over was back, with a big old grin on his face and two Nether Ops agents on his heels.

Exo closed his eyes, resigning himself for what was coming next.

"Your Legion commander wishes to speak with you," the man said, almost gaily.

And then a comm piece was stuffed in Exo's ear.

Exo looked at the Nether Ops agent, an old man with the disposition of a college professor. The agent nodded approvingly.

"Go for Gutierrez."

"Exo, it's me."

It sounded like Chhun. But... that didn't mean anything. This wasn't an L-comm and he was still a Nether Ops prisoner. Synthesizing a voice was so easy that kids could do it. Nah, he wasn't gonna fall for something that easy.

"Who?"

"Exo, really, it's me. This is important. Cohen Chhun. We served in Victory Company together. You laughed when I slid all the way to the bottom of that dune back on Renoy."

Exo's eyes lit up. That was the kind of confirmation that had to be true. Because if Nether Ops knew that much about a pair of enlisted boys on their first tour, enough to game him with that story, hell, he may as well start working for them.

"Dude. What's up?"

"I'm doing a comm switch from *Intrepid*. Watch the man in front of you to see if he notices. I'm not sure if he's listening in."

The comm died and came back online.

"Anything suspicious?"

The same stupid grin was on the Nether Ops agent's face. "Nah. I been treated all right."

"Good. Exo. I want you to say something to the man in front of you. Repeat exactly what I say and then listen to his voice. Listen closely. Tell him: 'He believes you. He wants to know how to link up.'"

Exo looked at the man in front of him. "He says he believes you and wants to know how to go about linking up forces."

The man smiled. "I believe we'd be most advantageous inside. My agents are battle-capable, and we'll let you in if you reach the palace, but I don't see an advantage to exiting the compound."

Exo listened to all of this. Closely. He felt... recognition.

And rage.

"Exo, tell me if that voice is familiar to you. Say copy if it is."

"Copy."

"Exo, that's X. That's the guy who did Kublar. Exo... I'm going to have him release you, and then I want you to end this kelhorn as soon as you're able."

"Yeah. Ain't no thing." Exo looked X in the eye and did everything he could to control the fire that burned inside him. "He wants you to let me loose, then he says you can have the comm back."

X smiled and motioned to his agents. "Take him down."

The men disengaged the ener-chains. Exo rubbed his wrists and tried to shake the feeling back into his arms. He looked the Nether Ops soldiers up and down. These weren't the armored legionnaire-type he'd seen last. These men looked like they worked in offices. Dress shirts. Nicely cut slacks. Leather shoes. The only thing military about them was their posture and the N-6 rifles they carried.

One of them removed the comm from Exo's ear while the other kept the blaster rifle ready in case the former captive tried anything. Exo was angry, but he wasn't stupid angry. Not yet.

"Yo. There's a war goin' on. I need a blaster."

X gave him a wry smile. "There's trusting and there's foolish. I make it a habit not to arm men who have just gone through interrogations, no matter what their commanders might say."

Exo shook his head. "All right. I see how it is."

The Nether Ops agent wasn't taking chances. And Exo didn't believe for a minute that there was any way this ordeal ended without somebody dying, even if Chhun hadn't given the word. Exo knew there was no way he was going to be returned to the lines without some "accident" or friendly fire incident dusting him first.

X was fiddling with the comm piece, attempting to put it into his ear. He began walking toward the door, leaving his two agents to escort Exo. One in front, a line of protection for his boss, and one behind, ready to shoot if Exo tried anything.

Exo knew he was unlikely to get a better chance than he had right now. If anything, they would head to a spot with more Nether Ops agents. As they moved toward the exit, he looked all around him for something he could use as a weapon. But there nothing there. No shotgun leaning against a desk, left in the secure zone by an absentminded guard. No steak knife left on a cold dinner plate. Nothing.

X was out the door and into a brilliantly lit, soulless corridor. And then the agent ahead of Exo turned the corner.

Exo abruptly stopped and looked over his shoulder to ask the agent behind him a question. "Hey, I was thinkin'..."

His sudden halt caused the agent to gain a few steps on him. He was within reach as Exo whirled around, eyes blazing with fire. The agent brought up his rifle, but this only gave Exo something closer to grab hold of.

He gripped the weapon with both hands and tried to swing it, hoping to take its owner off balance. But his arms still felt so weak, and while he'd yanked hard enough to make the man lose his firing stance, the agent was able to dig in his heels and bend his knees to keep from tumbling over.

"Help!" he shouted.

Exo drove a sharp kick into the agent's knee, buckling it and causing the man to fall on his rear end. With both men still holding the rifle, Exo swung around to stand over the agent's head. The Nether Ops man's arms were stretched as long as they could go in an attempt to not lose his weapon. To hold on just long enough for his buddy to come back and take the prisoner down.

With the agent stretched out on his back, Exo raised his boot and brought it down hard on the man's face. A crunching, grinding noise sounded as boot met nose. The agent released the rifle to Exo, who expertly swung the barrel down before double tapping the trigger to send two bolts into the hapless agent's chest.

The other man was at the door before Exo could get his rifle up. Exo dove for cover behind a desk, but not before a bolt sizzled into his calf, sending a burst of pain straight up his side. But with the pain came more rage.

And Exo started laughing.

More blaster bolts slammed into the desk he'd taken cover behind. This made Exo angrier. And he laughed harder. And he thought to himself, *What the hell?*

He popped up, perhaps somewhere in his mind believing that his Dark Ops training would give him an edge over the Nether Ops agent. Both men moved their rifles on target. Both fired. But Exo was faster, and his aim was better. His shot ripped through the man's skull, while the return fire burnt into the surface of the desk mere inches away from Exo.

But a miss was a miss.

And Exo didn't miss.

Grinding his teeth from the pain in his leg, Exo hobbled from around his cover toward the corridor. Of course X wouldn't be hanging around to provide support, but Exo didn't doubt that a call had been made. So he peeked cautiously around the doorway to see what might be waiting for him down what turned out to be an extremely long corridor.

And he saw X. Running in the shuffle of an older man who hadn't pushed himself for a long time.

Exo stepped into the corridor and dropped to a knee; his injured leg was doing everything it could to mess with his aim when he was standing. He squeezed the trigger and watched the bolt slam home into the fleeing X, just above his hip on the right side. X went crashing down hard. Not dead. Because that kind of a death was too good for someone like him.

Exo began to limp toward the man. Every other step was pain. And Exo used that pain to remember what this man had done to him. To his brothers.

Twenties laid out in the middle of our shuttle. Dead.

Another step. X would pay.

All those people on the Chiasm.

Another step.

Major Owens.

Another step.

Kublar. Pappy. Kags.

More steps.

Exo reached the man, who was crawling on his belly, trying to get away. He pushed away the pain in his leg, unleashed the rage he'd let build inside him, and sent a vicious kick into the man's ribs, producing a cry of pain.

"You sonofabitch!" Exo kicked him again, this time in the side of his head. X meekly wrapped his arms around his head in a feeble attempt to protect himself. "It's all on you, you kelhorned bastard!"

Exo dropped a knee into the small of X's back and slammed the butt of his rifle into the back of the man's head. Again and again. Over and over. Each blunt-force blow sent X's face slamming into the floor, and a pool of blood began to flow around him. Exo kept hitting, cursing, until the muscles in his arms gave out.

Then he pushed himself off of the corpse and collapsed against the wall. Sweat poured from his forehead as he panted for air. His leg really hurt now.

He leaned his head back against the wall and laughed.

And the laughs kept coming until finally, shaking his head, he grabbed his rifle, the butt still wet with blood and carrying strands of X's hair, stood, and began limping away to find Chhun and the rest of the battle.

The Legion was back, and today was the day they'd make everyone pay.

39

Your Empire collapses...

"No."

Goth Sullus spoke the word as law. It would not be so. He would not *let* it be so. His was an empire that would rule for thousands of years, with an emperor who would sit at its throne for the entirety of its reign.

Never before in the history of the galaxy was there a man such as him. Never before had there been a savior, a conqueror, who could forever lead the galaxy to realize what it could be. He would fix the galaxy and never again let it fall into disrepair.

Even if that meant killing every legionnaire on the battlefield. Even if it had meant killing his best friend. He would kill Reina herself if she now appeared before him to stand in his way. He would kill...

Would you kill all if it meant saving all?

Goth Sullus stood atop an Imperial battle tank that boomed and rocked as it sent concussive blasts into the advancing Legion. And not just the insurgents from within the city. The betrayer, Crodus, had allowed a fleet of ships to arrive above Utopion and send down dropships full of fresh troops. And their orbital bombardments had leveled any concentrated gatherings of troops loyal to Goth Sullus.

His Cybar war machines had been disabled and over-run like child's toys. Casper had once done the same to them in the Savage Wars. It was he and Tyrus who had shown the galaxy the folly of relying on bots for warfare.

The Legion today would have made Tyrus Rechs proud. Their admiral and commander, smelling blood, seeing the end, had gone Legion to dethrone the emperor.

But Goth Sullus would not allow their victory.

A small percentage of his bots were still active and fighting from the extreme rear, firing their N-50s and mis-siles at incoming shuttles and starships to protect Goth Sullus's stand from air attacks. The cityscape of Utopion was filled with the rising smoke trails of wrecked ships to the point that Sullus had effectively enforced a no-fly zone. And for all the aggressiveness of the fleet overhead, they were unwilling to send in a bombardment against him now for fear of destroying themselves in the process.

In the Savage Wars, Tyrus would have called an orbit-al bombardment down on himself, if it came to that. If it needed doing. And he would have expected his men to un-derstand. Of course, he had the armor Sullus now wore. And the Legion... did not.

And so the battle would be decided in close quarters. And with the Crux, with the power he contained, Goth Sullus knew that the Legion would break against his might. They would finally realize that his was an arm of iron that would not be bent.

The tanks boomed and belched their destruction. The shock troopers loyal to their emperor fired and fell. The Legion advanced.

And Goth Sullus met them there at the front lines inside One Voice Park. In the shadow of the Imperial Palace that once sheltered the Republic. Where Casper had once, long ago, stood. Signing the Constitution of the Republic. Where Goth Sullus the emperor stood now, using his power to hurl men away, to break necks, explode hearts.

He stood on top of the tank like an ancient general riding into war. Blaster fire zinged against his armor—and the armor withstood it. Next to him, the panicked crew of another tank abandoned their vehicle and fled the Legion onslaught. Goth Sullus lifted the tank and threw it into a wave of advancing legionnaires, sending the massive vehicle tumbling and rolling, tearing through men like a great rockslide, a wake of gore and upturned earth left in its wake.

And still the Legion came.

Let them come. He would kill them all to keep his Empire.

Would you kill everyone? Would all die so the galaxy can begin anew?

"Yes."

You have an army waiting. Bring the rest of us here.... Let us come.

***

"Captain Keel."

Ravi sounded alarmed. As frightened as Keel had ever heard him.

"What is, Ravi?"

"It is paramount we get down and engage Goth Sullus. I have sensed… the end, Captain."

"It's not like I've been staying in the air for a joy-ride, Ravi!"

Keel had been busy splashing Imperial starfighters that were crowding Utopion's atmosphere. And the area where Chhun and his men were engaging the Imperial Legion was a no-go zone, even for the *Six*. He'd seen scores of shuttles and fighters go down for flying too close. And that was *without* the pursuit of Utopion's defense fighters, who seemed to be piloted by people with more resolve than the MCR defense fleet.

"Captain, listen to me. The odds could be less than one percent and I would tell you that you must do this. They are with him. He will bring more. I can sense this now."

Keel corkscrewed away from a starfighter that was slinging blaster bolts in an attempt to take him down. He looped around to settle in behind the craft, hardly piloted by an ace, and sent pieces of him and his ship raining over Utopion, which looked like a war zone—something out of an invasion holofilm.

"What's got your turban so untucked?" Keel said. He didn't see how he could get the ship any closer to the action unless he landed it miles away and fought his way to the front lines. Which hardly seemed like a time-saver.

"These are the ones my people—the ones you call the Ancients—fled to avoid. This is why I have stayed behind to prevent their early arrival. And this is what Goth Sullus will do if we do not stop him. He has the power to let them into this galaxy. And he lacks the wisdom to not do so."

Keel frowned. "You're serious about this?"

Ravi gave a single nod.

"How about a high-altitude jump in the suit? What are the odds they pick me out in freefall?"

"Seventy percent."

Keel scowled. "That's not the kind of number that makes me want to do it."

"Captain, I have served at your side for all this time for two reasons. First, because you are one of the most capable humans I have ever seen. And I knew that, should a situation like this occur, having your help would drastically increase the likelihood of my success. So I endured your mercenary ways and flippant comments."

"Gee, thanks."

"And second, because I know that you are, beneath the defensive layers and personas you have built for yourself, a good man. And that you will do a good thing when called upon. I will endeavor to do this alone if I must. But you are my friend, Aeson. And I need your help."

Keel sighed. Ravi was really laying it on thick. But the holographic navigator-slash-Ancient clearly meant every word. And if it really had to be done...

"All right," he said. "I'll do it."

He keyed open the ship-wide comm. "Garret, I need you up here to fly the ship."

"I... what? I don't know how to fly."

Keel had just assumed the kid was flight-capable, given how adept he was at handling tech. He rubbed the side of his head in aggravation. He couldn't give over the controls to a novice over a war zone.

"Just... get up here, then."

Ravi arched an eyebrow.

A moment later the cockpit door opened and Garret stepped meekly inside. "I'm sorry, boss. I... just, even in videogames I crash all the time."

"Ravi," Keel said. He squeezed his eyes shut. He couldn't believe he was doing this. "De-partition the *Six*'s AI."

Ravi's fingers danced across the controls, and soon the bubblingly ebullient voice of the native, and unstable, AI filled the cockpit's speakers.

"Oh! I am *so* happy to be called upon for service. This is *wonderful.* And thrilling! Thank you, Captain. *Thank* you. We're all going to have the *most* delightful time."

"Shut up," Keel said. "The kid here needs to fly the ship for a while and I want you to help him. Don't let him crash it."

"You would like *me* to mentor a new pilot? Oh, Captain! I am honored! Yes, of course I'll help him. Come forward, young man. Sit in the captain's seat! Let's learn the wondrous ways of aviation!"

Keel ceded his chair to Garret, who looked ungainly and out of his element as he hesitantly grabbed the flight controls, looking to Keel to make sure he'd touched them right.

Keel nodded that he was doing fine. "Whatever you do, only give the AI limited controls to flight only. Take us over the epicenter of the fight so I can make a jump."

"What about weapon systems?" the AI asked joyfully. "I might need them!"

Keel fixed Garret with a hard stare and pointed a finger at the ether above his head. "No."

But Garret seemed eager to agree with the AI. "I could program some more missiles to—"

Keel moved his finger from pointing at the cockpit ceiling to pointing at Garret's face. "No. Only flying." He looked up again at the ceiling to address the AI. "Only flying!"

"Okay," the coder and AI responded, sounding equally disappointed.

Keel left the cockpit, grabbed his bucket, and sealed his armor suit. He retrieved a jump pack from the ship's armory and strode to the ramp, where Ravi joined him.

"Seventy percent. I can't believe I'm doing this," Keel said.

"I can't believe you were not willing to do it immediately when I first told you the galaxy's fate rests on stopping Goth Sullus."

"I thought you were just being dramatic!" Keel slapped the ramp's release and heard the wind whip inside the *Indelible VI*. They were high above the drop zone. He put a hand over his heart. "Besides, what did the galaxy ever do for me?"

And before Ravi could answer, Keel leapt out of the ship and entered a freefall, moving at terminal velocity toward Goth Sullus.

40

Masters felt like he was fighting in Kublar all over again. The battle was raging, with blaster fire zipping in all directions. Men were dying. It was chaos. Only this time, he felt like he was one of the koobs charging the entrenched Legion line.

This battle should already be over. The Legion had routed the defenses the Imperial Republic had been able to muster. They controlled orbit and were slowly winning control over atmosphere.

But it was anything but over.

Goth Sullus stood on top of an MBT like some Horseman of the Apocalypse, conducting a symphony of slaughter as he pushed his dark legionnaires to resist the inevitable. Or like a sorcerer-king protecting his tower through black magic. The final boss in some epic role-playing game.

An aero-precision missile was fired directly at Sullus's tank. Sullus didn't gesture, didn't even blink. But the missile turned in the air and then raced back toward the Legion lines, exploding in a grouping of soldiers.

Masters kept moving, firing from behind the cover of ruined war bots and smoking tanks. He'd dusted so many dark legionnaires that he'd lost count. And he wasn't sure where any of Victory was except for Bear, who was fighting maybe ten meters away, leading a group of leejes toward the center of the battle.

And Chhun... he was somewhere in the back, coordinating the fight.

It was brutal. It was deadly. But it had to keep up. The Legion had to put this man down, whatever the cost.

Peeking from behind a tank, Masters sent two blaster shots at Sullus. Both struck the armor, but did no harm. That was some armor.

But the Legion was now close enough that they'd be able to send in coordinated fire. Very soon. Bear and the men he was leading were taking a hill close to the emperor. They laid waste to the dark legionnaires who defended the position, dusting them all, then turned their blasters on Goth Sullus. They struck him with shot after shot.

The armor protected him. But... not entirely. Masters could see it in the man's eyes.

They were hurting him.

The beast could be hurt.

Exo had said as much from his experiences on Tarrago, but Masters hadn't quite believed it was possible until now. Until he saw it for himself.

Yeah, they'd drop this kelhorn.

"Dust 'im!" he shouted over external speakers, not wanting to add his noise to a comm that was already flooded with status reports and troop movements.

Someone sent another missile toward Sullus. The emperor deflected it again, but not as efficiently as before. It blasted into a nearby Imperial tank, sending it up in flames and killing the men who'd been fighting for him inside of it.

And then Sullus seemed to arrest the explosion itself. Masters watched as the big cannon was wrenched off the burning tank and sent hurtling straight at Bear and his advancing legionnaires like a scythe cutting through a field.

Bear attempted to jump over the cannon. But he didn't jump high enough. Both legs were shorn off just below the hip as the cannon kept going, unhindered, unstoppable, decapitating men, cutting them in half, leaving them ruined.

Until finally it rolled to a bloody stop.

"Bear!" Masters shouted. He turned his rifle on Sullus and sent fire his way.

The emperor looked right at him, singling him out. He didn't move, he just looked. And Masters suddenly felt a cold hand around his heart. It was as if he were going into cardiac arrest. Maybe he was.

And then Goth Sullus's tank exploded beneath him, and he disappeared in the inferno. The painful grip on Masters's heart vanished, and he dropped to the ground, panting and clutching his chest.

Still gasping, he looked over and saw Bear struggling to pull himself up on a smoking piece of repulsor engine, twin blood trails slaking the ground of its thirst as he crawled.

Masters got to his feet and sprinted to the legionnaire, determined to save his life.

***

Exo had followed the corridors inside the Imperial Palace, limping and in pain. He'd dusted a few Nether Ops agents he'd seen running from room to room. Anybody with a blaster rifle.

But mostly the place was empty. And what humanoids he did come across seemed determined to just... get away. Which made it easy to stay unnoticed, or at least unbothered, because these people were broken and defeated. They were looking for a way out, not a fight. Most times he simply ducked into a room and waited for non-combat personnel to run by him. He had been moving against the current.

Chhun had supplied them all with detailed maps of the area of operation. Exo was heading to the motor pool, which would lead out to the park where he presumed the fighting was taking place. It sure as hell sounded like that was the spot.

A squad of dark legionnaires ran down the corridor. Exo heard them before he saw them and ducked into a dark hallway as they bounded past. They were unarmed, and their armor looked like it had been in a battle. A few of them were struggling with injuries, holding arms or helping others run.

Yeah. That was a good sign.

When they'd passed, Exo popped out of the hallway and thumbed his blaster rifle to full auto. He sprayed bolts into their backs, dropping them. Because KTF and don't leave a threat behind you.

"Kelhorns," Exo mumbled, convinced that nobody worth nothin' would still be fighting for "the Empire." Just scumsacks like X who murdered their way into a corner and found they had no way out.

He found the motor pool empty of any vehicles; anyone who could flee in one, had done so. And he could tell from the big booms that their big tanks were in use. He doubted they were doing anything good. But he was behind the lines, and he could do something about it.

He scanned the empty bay. A lone dark legionnaire came running his way. Exo raised his rifle and dusted the kid.

"There we go," Exo said, his eyes falling on a weapons locker. It had been left open and was partially ransacked. But it wasn't empty. Inside was an aero-precision launcher, the cabinet's overhead light shining directly down onto it like a ray of sunshine from heaven.

That would do. That would more than do.

Exo strapped the launcher to his back and clipped on as many missiles as he could carry with his wounded leg. Oba, that thing hurt. It was only willpower that kept him going. Sheer Legion thickheaded resolve. The kind of thing that got you through Legion training. Because days like this might someday come.

He limped onward, unknowingly following the trail Goth Sullus had taken to lead his loyalists into battle against the Legion.

As soon as he stepped outside, he could see the battle raging. Saw the bodies of legionnaires littering the sprawling park, marring its beauty. Men who had charged forward to cut off the head of this empire. War bots were firing into the sky, their processors focused entirely on anti-air. Burning tanks still fired at the Legion ranks. Dark legionnaires fell. The good guys fell, too.

And he saw Goth Sullus standing on top of an MBT, using his unholy power to ravage his brothers.

Exo brought up the launcher. He didn't need a lock for this shot. He could make it in his sleep.

The AP missile whooshed from his shoulder and roared toward the MBT. Tank and emperor disappeared in a roiling cloud of flames. But only for a moment. And then Exo saw the aftermath. He saw Goth Sullus fall to the ground, landing on his back. He saw Sullus's helmet, blown off in the blast, tumble down several meters away.

Exo limped toward the fallen emperor, letting the launcher drop to his side and bringing up his blaster rifle. He'd seen how fallible Goth Sullus could be. He'd saved him once. Back when he believed the man was worth saving. Worth fighting for. He should have let him die then. Before Sullus had the opportunity to make alliances with the House of Reason, to destroy the Legion rather than help them bring change to the galaxy.

Goth Sullus was in it for himself. He'd never cared about the Legion. He'd merely *used* it. Used men like Exo for his own purposes.

And now Exo was going to make sure he paid, just like X.

The remaining war bots concentrated their fire on the advancing Legion, which was charging en masse upon Goth Sullus's fall.

Exo limped forward. Sullus was still breathing, eyes closed. Exo raised his rifle to his shoulder to put a blaster bolt in the man's head. Just a man.

Just a man.

Goth Sullus's coal-black eyes sprang open, and Exo felt a crack in his neck, heard the brutal snapping of his own spine. Just like Devers.

He lost all control of his body. Couldn't feel anything. Couldn't breathe. He knew he was collapsing to the ground. Saw the ground race up to meet his face as he fell. Helpless. Face first.

But he didn't feel anything. Even when he died, he felt nothing. And he'd done what he could, for the Legion. He gave all.

Exo didn't forget nothin'.

41

Awake! Awake!

Goth Sullus's eyes opened, and he saw a man standing above him, aiming a blaster rifle at his head. He knew this man. This man had fought for him. Had...

A betrayer.

This man was another betrayer. And in an instant Goth Sullus broke his neck.

But... this was simply forestalling the inevitable. The Legion would be on top of him. All was lost.

We will save your Empire!

Yes. He must save his Empire. By any means necessary.

Release us! Into the battle release us!

"I... release you."

And it seemed that a rush of black wind escaped the ring on his finger and settled upon the dead Imperial legionnaires all around him. The corpses began to rise up, still in the damaged or mangled states in which they'd died. Men missing limbs, missing heads, with holes in their bodies... They rose to their feet and took the fight to the Legion.

And each time the Legion disabled one of these resurrected Imperials, the dark wind simply rushed to another corpse. Sometimes Imperial, sometimes Legion. And fought again.

And we remain with you still, Goth Sullus.

The emperor rose to his feet. Immediately blaster fire began dancing around him.

You must flee. Flee and call the rest of us. Your Empire will not fall so long as we are your army. You will rule for eternity.

Goth Sullus moved back toward the Imperial Palace, stepping over the dead body of the man who had almost killed him.

***

Wraith was in freefall, using the jump pack to dodge in as many directions as he could manage as his HUD identified incoming blaster fire from the war bots down below. Seventy percent chance of failure... that seemed too low. He'd be lucky to make it halfway.

And then the blaster fire stopped. Wraith looked around, as if it were still incoming and he'd somehow lost the ability to see it. But it was over. He wasn't being shot at anymore.

That should improve his odds.

He enhanced his bucket's visuals to get a clearer picture of the battlefield he was dropping into. The war bots were firing on the Legion, who looked to be in the midst of a charge into what must be Goth Sullus's stand. And the bots had begun to fall, dropping under a barrage of ionic grenades.

Chhun had done his homework. He'd gone back to the books, with impressive results. He'd out-generaled the armies of the Empire. For whatever that was worth. It was already a hollow army when they'd arrived. Stripped of the zeal to fight. They'd seen that in the campaign leading up to this battle.

Seen the results of falsity.

Ravi appeared at his side. "The odds of your surviving the jump have increased to ninety-eight percent. The two percent accounts for equipment failure and errant blaster fire."

"Thanks, Ravi."

He picked up speed, straightening his body so he dropped like a bullet toward the battle zone. The HUD inside his bucket counted down the seconds until landing.

Wraith fired reverse thrusters, slowing his descent. "Ravi, something weird is goin' on."

Below, clearly dead soldiers were standing back up and fighting for the Empire. They fired their weapons if they had them, and if they didn't, they simply hurled themselves into the Legion lines like wild beasts until they were so shot up they ceased to move. And when that happened, a visible dark wind, like a true wraith, rushed from the useless husk and into a new body, which attacked anew.

"Leave those to me," Ravi said. "I am able to slay them completely. But not if too many are here. That is why you must stop Goth Sullus. He will bring them all."

Wraith spotted Sullus leaving the battlefield, moving back toward the Imperial Palace. "Copy."

Ravi disappeared and then reappeared on the ground, sword in hand. He twirled through the ranks of the resurrected soldiers, cutting through their bodies and dropping them. And when these bodies fell, the black wind didn't move on to a new host. Instead it seeped from the corpse and simply settled into the earth.

The ground came up faster than Wraith anticipated, and his jump pack was unable to fully adjust for the speed he'd built up. He landing in a crashing roll, thankful for his armor to absorb the tumbles.

And then he was up, an Intec x6 in one hand and Tyrus Rechs's slug thrower in the other. He moved immediately for the palace—toward Goth Sullus—and away from the battle, dropping a couple of possessed bodies, temporarily anyway, with head shots.

There was one body still before him, and Wraith hoped it wouldn't suddenly sit up and attempt to engage him. He could see clearly now why Ravi had been so concerned, why this moment, this battle, was so urgent, so necessary. If more of these black-wind creatures found their way here from… wherever they were coming from… the galaxy would be reduced to nothing but death. Wraith was fuzzy on the details, but they hardly seemed to matter in the heat of the moment.

Fortunately the body lay still, and Wraith happened to glance down at it as he passed by. Then he stopped. Had to take a second look.

It was Exo.

Wraith set his jaw and ran after Goth Sullus.

**

"C'mon, buddy!" Masters yelled. He had applied tourni-quets to what was left of Bear's massive legs, but the big guy had already lost a lot of blood. "Don't die on me, okay?"

This was bad. Really bad. Somehow the fight just kept raging on. Long after when years of combat experience told him it should have ended. Something wasn't right.

And then he looked up to see an Imperial legionnaire with a two-inch hole in the middle of his chest running toward him. How—? That guy should be dead. Masters raised his blaster rifle and sent a burst into the guy's head. Still the guy kept running.

"What the…"

Masters fired again. And then Wraith's navigator, Ravi, was there, his sword slicing through the dark legionnaire before moving in a blur elsewhere on the field.

Bear groaned.

Masters called for a medic. Again. He had given up after a while because they were all dead or too busy. But hearing Bear's voice motivated him to keep trying.

He cradled the big man's head. "C'mon, buddy," he pleaded. "Stay with me. No more jokes about how dumb and ugly you are. I promise."

Not far from the fighting, a transport shuttle landed. Maybe, if he could reach it, he could get Bear up to a de-stroyer for medical attention.

It was the only way the big man was going to survive.

Masters grabbed the webbing around Bear's armor. "Hope this doesn't hurt too much!"

He dead-lifted Bear's frame up and over his head, set-tling the wounded legionnaire's arms over his shoulders, and began running across the battlefield toward the shuttle, knowing that blood that was still dripping from Bear's wounds, leaving a trail behind them.

But he was making good time.

"You don't weigh nearly as much without legs."

He took a few more steps and felt a pang of remorse.

"Sorry. Last joke about your weight. I promise. Just don't die."

The door to the shuttle opened, and Masters was surprised to see Wraith's Endurian girlfriend step outside. She looked out of her element and had to duck back inside the shuttle as blaster bolts zipped by the craft.

Masters picked up his pace. As much to keep her from being killed as to save Bear. "Leenah!" he shouted, hoping the max volume on his bucket's speakers would be enough to get her attention.

She looked his way. Masters closed the distance and practically tossed Bear into the shuttle. "It's me, Masters. The good-looking one. We gotta get Bear out of here or he's gonna die."

"I need to find Aeson!"

Masters shook his head. He took off his helmet to look her in the eyes. "I haven't seen him or his ship. I don't think he's here. But we *are,* and I need you to get my buddy out of here. Please."

Leenah bit her lip and looked around. It was clear that the battlefield carnage was making her physically ill.

"Okay. But load up as many wounded as you can before we leave." She keyed in her comm. "Skrizz, just a few more minutes and then we can go!"

Masters smiled. "You're all right for an MCR princess. Even if you have bad taste in men."

***

Goth Sullus stood in the central courtyard of the Imperial Palace, surrounded by statuary and burbling fountains, his arms outstretched, feeling a rush of power—of the Crux— unlike any he'd ever felt before. They were guiding him. Using him. Channeling through him.

Lining the courtyard were larger-than-life marble statues of the great leaders of the Republic. Men and women Casper had once known. A statue of Tyrus Rechs, known by another name, seemed to gaze down upon the Republic's first emperor.

Behind Sullus, a black portal stretched open, as though a meter-wide amoeba were undulating in the air.

Yes. We are ready. We are coming.

More of the black shadows moved through the opening. Through the portal Goth Sullus held open. They rushed past him and out toward the battlefield.

We come slowly, but we come. Stretch out your power, Goth Sullus. Use your strength, Conqueror. Open this gate as wide as the planet itself. We will all serve you. We are so many.

Goth Sullus felt an energy in his fingertips. His Empire would last for eternity. He would rule forever. He would...

No.

This was wrong. This was a mistake.

Casper returned to his senses.

What have I done?

Failed.

I have failed.

Casper had gone searching for power. Searching for a way to stop... to stop *this*. And though the opportunity had come... he had failed.

Again.

Always so close and yet... he failed again.

Now he was the architect of the very destruction the Ancients had feared. *He* was bringing about the death of the entire galaxy. He wasn't saving it. Setting it straight. He wasn't even conquering it.

He was killing it.

He had been deceived by the many. The others.

He had deceived himself.

Stretch out your power, O Emperor! O Conqueror!

"No."

Casper pulled against the energy flowing from himself. Sought to... tighten. To close what he had opened.

The voices cackled and hissed. *You cannot resist. You have already fallen. You are ours!*

"No!"

Casper channeled himself, pulled, and tightened. It was all he could do to keep the portal, the gateway to another galaxy, one desperate to ruin his own, to keep it small.

But the others had him. A part of him at least. And try as he might, he could not close it. He could not stop what was happening. He was only slowing it.

We will come. There will be no stopping us.

Casper knew what he had to do.

He reached out, searching, to stop his own heart from beating. To kill himself. To end the flow of power that made this tragedy possible.

A tragedy. He had lived a tragedy.

No, no. We can't let you do that, O Conqueror! They spoke with derision. With disdain.

They stopped him.

He was right. Tyrus Rechs was right. When he came for him on Tusca so long ago. And not long at all.

When Rechs refused to join him in his conquest of the galaxy, Casper called him stupid.

And then he killed him.

His oldest of friends.

Second star from the right... straight on 'til morning, oldest of friends.

Casper felt tears streaming down his face. It was through the blur of those tears that he saw him: Rechs back from the dead. Here to repay what had been done.

Come, Rechs! Come and finish what you started.

You were right, old friend! You were right!

But as the man approached, a man in shadowy legionnaire armor, Casper realized his error. This was not Tyrus Rechs. This was another.

The man in dark armor made no attempt at communication. Made no effort to reason with Goth Sullus.

He simply raised a pistol. An old slug thrower. The type Tyrus had adored.

Tyrus.

Old friend.

And Casper wanted to say, "I tried to do what was right."

But the man in the armor gave him no opportunity. He pulled the trigger.

The bullet entered through the forehead and tore out the back of Casper's skull, sending a pink mist spraying into the air, a striking relief to the black portal behind him, which sealed the instant Goth Sullus lost his connection to the Crux.

And Wraith stood, the barrel of his gun smoking. The lifeless body of Goth Sullus pouring out blood at his feet.

The Empire fallen.

Second star from the right... straight on 'til morning.

Epilogue

The supplemental docking bay of the Legion destroyer *Intrepid* was empty save for the *Indelible VI*, its engines softly glowing, ready to launch. Aeson Ford stood at the ship's ramp, wearing the Legion dress-blue uniform he'd kept stowed in a heavy wooden trunk at the foot of his bed for nearly a decade.

It still fit.

Leenah stood by his side, smiling. She seemed to like the way he looked in the uniform. The ladies always did. Lifetakers and heartbreakers.

Skrizz was somewhere at the top of the ramp; his tail could be heard swishing across the impervisteel deck.

Ford tugged at the tie around his neck. It felt constrictive. "I swear, Leenah, this thing is choking me. I'm going to black out."

"It's in your head," she replied. "This is what happens when you never dress up."

He looked down at the princess. "Oh, like you?"

She was wearing her gray jumpsuit, same as ever. Though this morning it was free of any grease stains and black patches of carbon powder. Her hands were clean, too.

She shook her head. "*I'm* not the one getting an award."

Ford gave a wan smile. He wasn't sure he should be either. But Chhun had insisted. And while he might have spaced off against the wishes of the Legion commander, he wasn't willing to do the same to his friend.

The docking bay access door swished open, and a procession consisting of Chhun, Admiral Deynolds, Masters, and Bombassa stepped inside. Bear was with them as well, sitting in a repulsor chair, not yet accustomed to his cybernetic replacements. Chhun and Deynolds wore their dress uniforms, while Masters and Bombassa wore their full Legion armor, blaster rifles held at parade rest. The entourage moved toward the *Six*, the echoes of their boots careening across the empty docking bay, which had been cleared of the usual litany of techs, bots, and starships, specifically for this occasion.

Chhun stopped in front of Ford and issued a sharp salute.

Aeson Ford, a man who had gone by the names of Keel, Wraith, and a few others, found himself returning the salute with honor guard precision.

"I'd prefer to have done this as part of the ceremony for the others," Chhun said.

Ford nodded. Chhun, as Legion commander, had honored the men who had died to halt the Republic's erosion from a despotic nanny state to a brutal dictatorship. Ellek Owens, Scontan Washam, and Caleb Gutierrez—Exo—would be household names, and the truth of what they'd done—what they'd sacrificed—had been stated clearly and honestly, once and for all. And if that weren't enough, Chhun had gone a step further, clearing the name of General Rex.

Ford had wanted his friend to revoke Devers's award, if only because it would have made Exo happy. But Chhun wouldn't do it.

"That's not the kind of precedent I want to set," he'd said. "Because someone will come along after me. And someday they might look back at what we did, without ever knowing the real cost of things, and try to take it away from a leej who really did deserve it. And that's not something I'm willing to open the door to."

Ford wondered if the hypothetical person in Chhun's mind was him. But that would be a question for future generations to wrestle with.

"Captain Aeson Ford," Chhun said, "the Order of the Centurion is the highest award that can be bestowed upon an individual serving in, or with, the Legion. When such an individual displays exceptional valor in action against an enemy force, and uncommon loyalty and devotion to the Legion and its legionnaires, refusing to abandon post, mission, or brothers, even unto death, the Legion dutifully recognizes such courage with this award."

He took the award from a box held by Admiral Deynolds.

"Today, on behalf of a thankful Legion, and a galaxy that will never fully know what you accomplished on its behalf, I award you the Order of the Centurion."

Keel stood at attention as Chhun moved behind him and placed the pentagon-shaped medallion, featuring a stylized, ancient-looking legionnaire helmet, over his head. He then walked around in front of Ford and saluted.

And so did everyone else.

Leenah stood by beaming.

"Thank you, Legion Commander Chhun," Ford said, surprising himself with the sound of his own voice. It was the voice of the young officer who had navigated the treacheries of Kublar. A forceful, assertive, and confident legionnaire.

Chhun pulled Ford in and embraced him, clapping him on his back. The two spoke no words, though hundreds of words of gratitude flashed through Ford's mind.

"So when do you get *your* medal?" Ford asked, sounding like the brash Captain Keel again.

Chhun smiled. "Not my call to make. Not my place to take."

"Well, you can always give me one," said Masters. "I'd wear that thing out every night. No limits to the action I'd see." He paused and then quickly added, "Not that I see any limits now!"

"So what's next, Legion Commander?" Ford asked, pulling Leenah to his side.

The galaxy was now a different place. The Republic had briefly been by an empire, and now both were no longer. And there would be a groaning coming of age because of it. Not just fireworks and then business as usual. It would be a long, hard slog toward some semblance of normalcy.

Already the core worlds, led by the ultra-rich Spilursa, were talking of standing together in a New Republic, with a new capital. On Spilursa, of course. The mid-core and edge already had more newly independent planets than anyone could count, with fresh alliances and joint protectorates being announced every hour, it seemed.

And somewhere in this vacuum stood the Legion. Re-forged to never again be subject to the selfish whims of those to whom power was the ultimate purpose in the universe.

"I don't know," Chhun said. "The Legion isn't going anywhere. And there's no shortage of planets sending tax revenues with requests that we keep them safe. Small systems worried about their bigger neighbors gobbling them up while the galaxy tries to find a way forward."

"I'm sure you'll do the right thing," Leenah said, though she didn't specify what that was. Perhaps because she didn't know herself. Ford certainly didn't feel as though he could say. But he trusted Chhun to find the answer.

"How about you?" asked Chhun, wearing a light smile.

Ford shrugged and looked to Leenah. "Ravi thinks he might have some leads on where Prisma went. So we'll probably check that out."

Chhun's expression turned somber. "And if you can't find her?"

"I guess we'll hang out on the edge and wait."

And with that, Aeson Ford began walking up the ramp, his fingertips on the small of Leenah's back. As he entered the *Six,* he paused and turned around. "You know I'm always here if you need me."

Chhun nodded. "So are we."

"KTF, Legion Commander."

"KTF, Wraith."

THE END

THE GALAXY IS
A DUMPSTER FIRE...
GALAXYS
EDGE
TIN MAN
ANSPACH
COLE
GET THIS
EXCLUSIVE
SHORT STORY
FOR FREE!

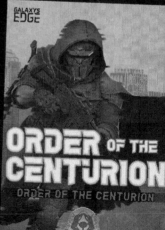

Honor Roll

We would like to give our most sincere thanks and recognition to those who supported the creation of *Retribution* by subscribing as a Galaxy's Edge Insider at GalacticOutlaws.com

Lee Abers	Alex Collins-Gauweiler
Elias Aguilar	James Connolly
Bill Allen	James Conyer
Tony Alvarez	Robert Cosler
Robert Anspach	Andrew Craig
Jonathan Auerbach	Adam Craig
Sean Averill	Phil Culpepper
John Barber	Peter Davies
Russell Barker	Nathan Davis
Steven Beaulieu	Tod Delaricheliere
John Bell	Christopher DiNote
Daniel Bendele	Matthew Dippel
WJ Blood	Karol Doliński
Rodney Bonner	Andreas Doncic
Ernest Brant	Noah Doyle
Geoff Brisco	William Ely
Aaron Brooks	Stephane Escrig
Brent Brown	Dalton Ferrari
Marion Buehring	Skyla Forster
Van Cammack	Mark Franceschini
Shawn Cavitt	Richard Gallo
David Chor	Christopher Gallo

Kyle Gannon	Clay Lambert
Robert Garcia	Grant Lambert
Michael Gardner	Jeremy Lambert
John Giorgis	Brian Lambert
Luis Gomez	Dave Lawrence
Gordon Green	Paul Lizer
Tim Green	Richard Long
Shawn Greene	Oliver Longchamps
Michael Greenhill	John M
Jose Enrique Guzman	Richard Maier
Greg Hansen	Brian Mansur
Ronald Haulman	Cory Marko
Joshua Hayes	Trevor Martin
Adam Hazen	Pawel Martin
Jason Henderson	Lucas Martin
Tyson Hopkins	Tao Mason
Curtis Horton	Simon Mayeski
Jeff Howard	Brent McCarty
Mike Hull	Matthew McDaniel
Wendy Jacobson	Rachel McIntosh
Paul Jarman	Joshua McMaster
James Jeffers	Christopher Menkhaus
James Johnson	Jim Mern
Noah Kelly	Pete Micale
Daniel Kimm	Alex Morstadt
Jesse Klein	Daniel Mullen
Mathijs Kooij	Andrew Niesent
Evan Kowalski	Greg Nugent
Mark Krafft	Christina Nymeyer
Byl Kravetz	David Parker

Eric Pastorek
Carl Patrick
Jeremiah Popp
Chancey Porter
Chris Pourteau
Eric Ritenour
Walt Robillard
Daniel Robitaille
Joyce Roth
David Sanford
Andrew Schmidt
Brian Schmidt
Alex Schwarz
Christopher Shaw
Ryan Shaw
Glenn Shotton
Joshua Sipin
Daniel Smith
John Spears
Peter Spitzer
Dustin Sprick
Joel Stacey
Maggie Stewart-Grant
John Stockley
William Strickler
Kevin Summers
Ernest Sumner
Erich Surber
Travis TadeWaldt
Tim Taylor

Steven Thompson
Beverly Tierney
Tom Tousignant
Cole Trueblood
Scott Tucker
Eric Turnbull
John Tuttle
Allan Valdes
Christopher Valin
Paden VanBuskirk
Paul Volcy
David Wall
Andrew Ward
Kiley Wetmore
Scott Winters
Jason Wright
Nathan Zoss

Jason Anspach and Nick Cole are a pair of west coast authors teaming up to write their science fiction dream series, Galaxy's Edge.

Jason Anspach is a best selling author living in Tacoma, Washington with his wife and their own legionnaire squad of seven (not a typo) children. In addition to science fiction, Jason is the author of the hit comedy-paranormal-historical-detective series, *'til Death*. Jason loves his family as well as hiking and camping throughout the beautiful Pacific Northwest. And Star Wars. He named as many of his kids after Obi Wan as possible, and knows that Han shot first.

Nick Cole is a Dragon Award winning author best known for *The Old Man and the Wasteland, CTRL ALT Revolt!,* and the Wyrd Saga. After serving in the United States Army, Nick moved to Hollywood to pursue a career in acting and writing. (Mostly) retired from the stage and screen, he resides with his wife, a professional opera singer, in Los Angeles, California.

Made in the USA
San Bernardino, CA
21 August 2019